The Peninsula

by

Amy Craig

The Peninsula

COPYRIGHT © 2022 by Amy Craig

Cover Art by *Diana Carlile*

The Wild Rose Press, Inc.
PO Box 708
Adams Basin, NY 14410-0708
Visit us at www.thewildrosepress.com

Publishing History
First Edition, 2022
Trade Paperback ISBN 978-1-5092-4253-5
Digital ISBN 978-1-5092-4254-2

Published in the United States of America

"Tomorrow, I'll show you what I found."

"I have a better idea." Gesturing toward the glowing, red exit sign, he waited for her to fall into step. "Come to dinner with me and meet a potential investor."

She stopped and shook her head. "It's too soon. I can defend the hybridization, but not what I produce from them."

"Your call." Shaking his head, he passed her and made his way toward the hall's end.

Security lighting along the floor cast his shadow on the wall. *The man won a Nobel prize. Who am I to doubt his leadership?* Following in his wake, she scrambled for a reason to postpone dinner until she felt sure about the results. "I should replicate my findings before I discuss them outside our workgroup."

Waving a hand over his shoulder, he continued walking. "This investor does not need a final report. May is a beautiful month. You should come to dinner."

Duty and defiance warred, stealing objections from her lips.

Dr. Stefan opened the door and turned. "The investor is my nephew"—a slight smile cracked his wrinkled face—"the good one."

Praise for Amy Craig

"Amy Craig gives readers a cinematic joy with A WINTER ROSE. Be transported to Washington and fall in love among dormant fields full of hope and promise. It's the perfect read to escape reality and dream of living on a flower farm in the Pacific Northwest."

~*Lucy Hudson*

~*~

"I promise you'll get swept up in the love story of Julien and Eliza. I could hardly turn the pages fast enough! A perfect escape for lovers of romance and sexy scenes."

~*Lauren G. Lyon*

~*~

"Amy Craig blends a perfect combination of emotionally rich characters and strong chemistry in *A WINTER ROSE*. But will Julien's and Eliza's attraction survive the winter and bloom into something as beautiful as the flowers she grows? This small town romance weaves a wonderful story about navigating the past while risking a second chance at love."

~*Brooke Taylor*

~*~

"I like that Luke was playing matchmaker for Eliza and Julian. They make a great couple. Eliza wasn't sure that she could let go of the pain of her previous marriage to Erik, who completely took over her business/farm. Julien, on the other hand, was also having problems committing to Eliza due to the fact that he lost his leg in an accident. I'm glad that it worked out for the both of them."

~*Mary B.*

Dedication

To Buffy, who sometimes lets me win.

Chapter One

Assay chemicals and plastic sheeting gave the laboratory an antiseptic, industrial smell. Hadley and her fellow graduate students worked to keep the space tidy, but long after her peers left, flyers, notebooks, and pencils littered the worktables and humanized the space. At fifteen minutes past midnight, she scratched the paper cap covering her long hair, sat back from the microscope, and exhaled into the deserted room. *Many gaps about the biosynthesis of cannabinoids exist, especially for the minor components, but the scientific community knows even less about what the compounds can do. I dosed these nerve assays with T-83, and they don't signal pain.*

Rubbing her hands over her face, she wondered if she spent too many hours over the microscope. In February, she finished her Ph.D. dissertation on synthetic production of cannabidiol, but May graduation loomed, and analyzing CBD derivatives kept her from enjoying Palo Alto's cool, spring nights. *Maybe the assays are bunk.*

"Hadley?"

A scream ripped from her throat, and she covered her mouth. Turning on her stool, she met her Ph.D. advisor's clouded, blue gaze. Beneath the LED lights, his meticulous, white hair and crisp, buttoned shirt shone against the shadows. "Oh, Dr. Stefan. It's you."

The man cocked his head. "Who else would I be?"

His question, posed in German, calmed her nerves. For more than a decade, he taught her his native language and everything he knew about synthetic biology. "The hour's late." Standing, she closed the lid on the assay tray and pulled off her cap. "Nobody should be here."

"And yet, here you are." He held open the door to the hallway. "Take a break, Hadley. Give your mind time to reset."

Nodding, she walked past him and frowned. The lab's bright, white lights distorted the passage of time, but the hallway's quiet shadows confirmed the hours she spent toiling over her experiments. "My results are excellent."

He clasped his hands behind his back and kept pace.

Hearing his soft, noncommittal hum, she cleared her throat. "Tomorrow, I'll show you what I found."

"I have a better idea." Gesturing toward the glowing, red exit sign, he waited for her to fall into step. "Come to dinner with me and meet a potential investor."

She stopped and shook her head. "It's too soon. I can defend the hybridization, but not what I produce from them."

"Your call." Shaking his head, he passed her and made his way toward the hall's end.

Security lighting along the floor cast his shadow on the wall. *The man won a Nobel prize. Who am I to doubt his leadership?* Following in his wake, she scrambled for a reason to postpone dinner until she felt sure about the results. "I should replicate my findings before I discuss them outside our workgroup."

Waving a hand over his shoulder, he continued walking. "This investor does not need a final report. May is a beautiful month. You should come to dinner."

Duty and defiance warred, stealing objections from her lips.

Dr. Stefan opened the door and turned. "The investor is my nephew"—a slight smile cracked his wrinkled face—"the good one."

"The good one?" she asked.

He winked and stepped into the stairwell.

Left standing in the hallway, she thought of her research objectives. The humble little plant that graced album covers and stealthy, undergraduate text messages might lead to advances in pain relief. Who was she to decide whether something or someone was good? Grinning, she jogged down the steps to tell Dr. Stefan she would come to dinner. She stepped into the foggy night air, surveyed the brightly lit sidewalks, and realized she waited too long.

Riding her bike through downtown's quiet streets, the damp, chilly air suppressed her thoughts and promised sleep's escape. She locked her bike in front of her townhouse, let the metal lock clang into place, and approached her rented townhouse. The building's brown, wood siding helped it disappear behind a screen of trees and modern design, but yellow light and painted wood left plenty of room for shadows.

Reaching for her cross-body purse, she realized she left it in the lab and cursed. Upstairs, her childhood friend, Gary, slept in a dark bedroom. *I hate to wake him, but…* She tried the knob and found it unlocked. *What the fuck, Gary?*

Shaking her head, she let herself into the townhouse, armed the alarm, and shelved her outrage for another day. Settled in bed, she clutched a pillow and waited for sleep, but excitement kept her awake. Dr. Stefan taught her a new language, but he ignored questions about his family and personal life. *What does he mean by the good nephew?*

Tossing and turning, she debated how to describe her work to a stranger. *If I'm right, the derivatives are effective pain relievers, but they carry none of opioid's addictive qualities.* Memories of her mother's addiction haunted her, but she disciplined herself to think of the future. Pulling the blanket over her head, she tried counting sheep.

The animals mocked her. Their quiet bleats asked, "Who do you think you are?"

I'm doing the best I can to make the world a better place. Near sunrise, her adrenaline subsided, and she surrendered her insecurities. Closing her eyes, she let her mind wander to green valleys and shifting sunlight. Memories of her mother's addiction pulled her back to her research. *Am I up to the task?*

****

The next day, caffeine revived Hadley's abilities, and she returned to campus. *What if I made a mistake in my analysis? I have to repeat the procedures before the experimental design makes sense.* She spent the day behind her locked office door, reviewing data and ignoring her phone. Hearing her inbox chime, she blinked and focused on the computer screen. A campus organization promoted a meditation event on the Great Lawn. Rolling her eyes, she closed the program and checked her computer's menu bar for the time. *I don't*

4

have time for deep-breathing exercises.

Her back ached from hours of analysis, but she stood and straightened her shoulders. *Dr. Stefan's my advisor, but the results are mine. Dinner means nothing but a free meal.* She swallowed and hoped bravado would carry her through the evening.

Stepping from the building, she zipped her jacket and merged with the students and families strolling Palo Alto's shaded streets. A cool, evening breeze invigorated her step and lightened her mood. The city harbored a world-renowned university and ranks of aggressive entrepreneurs, but she appreciated the city's character and tree-lined streets. Residents favored simple pleasures like corn ice cream and handcrafted, single-source tequilas…

A scooter zipped down the sidewalk.

A woman yelled at the driver.

…and traffic ordinances. Smiling, Hadley detoured around the outraged citizen and knew the evening fog would muffle emotions and noise. *This place feels like no other place I've ever lived.* Her phone rang, and she pulled it from her jacket pocket. "Yep?"

"I have your purse," Buffy said. "I tried to reach you all day, but Gary told me not to disturb you when you're working in the office."

She wondered if she worked too hard. Buffy's freckled cheeks and hazel eyes often danced with mischief. *We should grab more beers and fewer pipettes.* "I'm surprised I'm still alive."

Buffy laughed. "Don Quixote lived too."

Pausing on the sidewalk, she swallowed. Buffy compared their CBD research to the famous dreamer's quest, but she wondered if the master's student knew the whole story. *I'm not interested in chivalric romances. I'm interested in keeping families together and avoiding the pain of watching loved ones rot.* She cleared her throat. "Don Quixote dies at the end of Part Two, Buffy. He falls ill, renounces chivalry, and dies."

"Damn," Buffy said. "I never finished the book."

She frowned. Torn between her dinner reservation and her desire to retrieve her purse, her lab notebook, and her dignity, she made a decision. "That lab's secure. Put my purse in my filing cabinet, okay?"

"Dr. Stefan mentioned your dinner plans. Don't you need your card?"

"I have ScanCharge. I'll use the card stored on my phone." Ending the call, she rounded the corner and saw Dr. Stefan standing outside a Greek restaurant. The building's plaster exterior and stained wood reflected the whitewashed buildings dotting the Aegean Sea.

He leaned on a wooden bench, but he nodded at every woman who passed him.

How does a man with such old-fashioned mannerisms know so much about neurotransmitters? "I'm glad you picked the restaurant. Business deals make me think of dark booths, steak, and potatoes."

He opened the restaurant door. "If you want steak, we can go somewhere else."

"No, this restaurant looks great."

He gestured for her to precede him. "Ladies first."

She rolled her eyes. For such an accomplished and respected scientist, his formality and nostalgia amused her. She switched to German. "One day, your old school manners will get you in trouble."

Laughing, he cupped her elbow and urged her forward. "I doubt I'll live that long. I'm starving, aren't you?"

Her rumbling stomach betrayed her, and she walked through the door. Hanging copper pots and a roaring, wood-burning fireplace evoked the nostalgia of a sprawling farm kitchen. Round tables sat beneath rustic, wooden beams and warm, yellow paint graced the walls. The rich aroma of savory, roasted meats and pungent, charred herbs captured her attention. She eyed a pizza exiting the restaurant's wood-fired grill and moistened her lips.

"Hi, Miss Heron! Can I help you?" The hostess tilted her head.

Blinking, Hadley struggled to place the woman. After teaching so many undergraduate classes, she lived in fear of forgetting her former students' faces and names. *I think she took my class on engineering ethics.* "Hi, Cynthia."

"Oh, my gosh! You remember me?" Cynthia's blonde ponytail bobbed, and she clasped her hands against her chest.

"Barely." Hadley swallowed. "Dr. Stefan reserved the table."

A server in a white apron stopped and jerked his head toward an unmarked door.

His pockmarked, ebony skin shone against the staff uniform, and his muscles strained the restaurant jacket's seams. Hadley wondered if she should recognize him, too.

"Take them to the courtyard," he said.

Cynthia's gaze widened.

Dr. Stefan offered Hadley an arm and walked through the crowded restaurant. "Ah, I love the courtyard. Don't you?"

She scanned the dining room. Families traded news and gossip over hot bread and olive oil. "What courtyard?"

Cynthia opened an unmarked door and stepped back.

The dining room's rustic wooden beams gave way to patio lights swaying in the soft breeze. Candles flickered on a table set with three place settings. "Oh, that courtyard." Her stomach rumbled, and she wondered if nerves or hunger would embarrass her first. Walking into the intimate setting, she placed a hand on the back of a chair, smiled, and hoped she looked blasé. "The restaurant hardly advertises this space."

"Why should they?" Dr. Stefan pulled out a chair. "The beauty lies in its discretion."

She took the seat and surreptitiously helped him slide in the chair. In old press photographs, his muscles and broad shoulders looked like hallmarks of a leading man, but cataracts dimmed his blue eyes, and white hair replaced his black style. *What will I look like when I'm old? What will I have accomplished?*

"Georgios doesn't advertise the courtyard for a reason." Dr. Stefan sat and put his napkin in his lap. "Local technology entrepreneurs and venture capitalists love their food, but they pay a premium to dine alone."

"What did you mean by the good nephew?" She unfurled her napkin and placed the cloth in her lap. "How many nephews do you have?"

He swirled the ice in his water and smiled. "Two to be exact."

"And the bad one?"

"He won't trouble you." His expression tightened. "To succeed with your research, you need Johann's discipline and his deep pockets. He's the right choice."

His proclamation unnerved her. Dr. Stefan's guidance usually came with hints of old-world aftershave, not ultimatums. Uncertainty raised gooseflesh on her skin, and she wondered if a family investor would be too close to home. She refused to start the meeting at a disadvantage. "What happened to peace, love, and horizontal organizational structures?"

Rubbing the condensation off his glass, he shook his head. "That's not how life works in Germany." He looked up. "Trust me, my dear, the view is much better from the top."

His bittersweet smile struck a chord in her heart, but his hidden vulnerability intrigued her. Adjusting her seat, she acknowledged her impending graduation signaled the end of his guidance but hoped their relationship would mature to friendship. *What tradeoffs have you made, Dr. Stefan?*

The server walked into the courtyard and presented a bottle of cabernet.

Turning, Dr. Stefan scanned the label and nodded. "Very good."

Wordlessly, the server filled their glasses and accepted two dishes from a busser. "Smoke-tinged artichokes and roasted eggplant skewers." He placed the dishes on the table and backed away.

She caught his appraising stare, but she looked away and focused on the garlicky yogurt sauce and delicate olives edging the plate. The eggplant glistened with olive oil. Licking her lips, she raised her wine and wondered when to begin. "Your nephew is late."

"By design, I'm sure," Dr. Stefan said. "Johann doesn't make mistakes."

She choked on the rich liquid. "Everyone makes mistakes."

He glanced up. "Not this man. He runs an international holding company. He has no room for mistakes."

She sipped her wine and wondered if anyone could be that perfect. "How convenient."

"Nothing in business is convenient, my dear. Winning takes luck and strategy. To succeed with your harebrained schemes for a foundation, you'll need both tactics."

She sat straight. *Harebrained? I've always been upfront about my desire to give away my research.* She mustered her talking points, but hearing someone approach, she covered the top of her wineglass. "No, thank you. I've had plenty."

"That's a pity. I thought we had just begun."

The speaker's warm, guttural voice came from the back of his throat. She recognized the lingering consonants of Dr. Stefan's accent, but her stomach clenched at the reverberations. *Damn, I must be hungrier than I thought.* Turning, she saw a tall man standing behind her chair. His cropped black hair put military commanders to shame, his wool suit fit like a dream, and a gold watch peeked from his shirt cuff. Realizing she stared, she blinked and focused on the ground. *I should have finished my wine.* Gathering her courage, she peeked at his ring finger and ignored the visceral pleasure of finding it bare. *This isn't a date.*

Squaring her shoulders, she focused on his face. A pale, two-inch long, vertical scar marred his right cheek. Curiosity flooded her mind with questions. *He's a decade older than me, and his attractiveness doesn't matter. He's here to talk about research and nothing else.* She met his bright-blue gaze and offered him a polite smile.

"I'm not the server," he said.

His clipped response eroded her confidence. "I gathered that fact."

Dr. Stefan rose. "Good evening, Johann."

Affection softened the sounds of his German salutation. After her sister died, her parents' affection shriveled into perfunctory pats. Her friend Gary's lazy, heavy-armed hugs reminded her to accept life's simple pleasures. Watching the men exchange greetings, she warmed toward their connection.

"Uncle." Johann kissed his uncle's cheek. "How are you?"

Remembering her manners, she stood and pushed back her chair.

"Please, don't stand on my account." Johann spoke in English and offered a hand. "I am Johann zur Hausen."

"I gathered." She cleared her throat. *I can't do business with this man. He's handsome to the point of distraction, and the minute he plays hardball, I'll melt.* "I've made a mistake. I'm not ready to discuss my research findings."

Dr. Stefan stepped closer. "My dear…"

Johann met his uncle's gaze, held up a hand, and nodded. "Enjoy your dinner."

Dr. Stefan rushed around the table and stood between them. "Wait, wait, wait." He shook a finger at her and at Johann. "Don't be hasty. Hadley needs a champion for her groundbreaking research."

She raised her chin. "I do not."

"You have the means to commercialize Hadley's findings." Dr. Stefan bridged the space between them. "You have something worth protecting."

He made eye contact with each of them but settled on her. She crossed her arms.

"Johann's holding company owns stock in pharmaceutical corporations with more resources than our lab. In eighty years, I've learned one thing"—he cupped both their elbows—"egos impede progress."

Johann raised an eyebrow.

Dr. Stefan dropped his hands. "If nothing else, share a meal with an old man. You never know how much time I have left."

She rolled her eyes, dropped into her chair, and reached for her wine. "Really, Dr. Stefan?"

He grinned and reclaimed his seat. "Really, Hadley."

Johann draped his suit jacket over the unoccupied chair's back and unfurled his napkin. "Very well."

His movements were as crisp and precise as the snap of a flag. She averted her gaze and examined the bougainvillea climbing a trellis. *I have to stop looking at this man.*

"I see my uncle can still manipulate his students," Johann said.

She laughed, raised her glass to him, and grinned.

His expression softened.

Big mistake. Heat flooded her stomach. Sitting straighter, she focused on her advisor.

"Hadley is my best student," Dr. Stefan said. "I wouldn't call you two together on a whim. Her work on strain hybridization deserves your attention."

Johann nodded and jerked his chin toward the door

to the restaurant.

The server appeared with a glass of iced tea and set it in front of Johann.

Johann smiled. "Thank you, Damon."

"The chef's menu?" Damon asked.

Johann nodded.

She frowned. *How does Johann know the server?* "You don't drink?"

"Sobriety is an advantage."

His mouth smiled, but his gaze never softened with shared laughter. She questioned his motivations and put down her wine glass. "I am more than capable of taking care of myself and my research. I don't need a parasitic venture capitalist to build me up, saddle me with a leveraged buyout, and drain my research for profits." She lowered her voice. "I want drugs to help people, not deplete their bank accounts."

"How does she know so much about business?" Johann asked his uncle in German.

Dr. Stefan shrugged. "Kids these days. Also, I taught her German."

Both men stared.

She smiled. "I know many things." *Like your language and how to avoid giving away my life's work.* She grabbed an olive, popped it in her mouth, and vowed to conduct the meeting in English.

"You might know many things, but do you know how to use them?" Johann lifted his fork and separated the delicate portions of an artichoke. "Tell me where you grew up, Hadley Heron."

"In Marin." She reached for her fork and wondered how much he already knew about her life. Dr. Stefan's loyalty hovered at the edge of her consciousness like an unanswered question. "The Bradson School. East Bay for undergraduate." She speared a bite. "Palo Alto for the research you want."

"What kept you so close to home?"

His direct question caught her attention. She imagined him reading her background report and searching for her motivations. "My sister was very sick until she passed."

He inclined his head. "I'm sorry for your loss."

Nodding, she thought of Jecca, her freckle-faced sister who never grew up. Jecca's personality had shimmered with happiness and fixed the wobbling dynamics of their nuclear family. After Jecca died, their mother descended into a spiral of grief. Opioids leveled her pain, but she floated near life's surface and refused to wet her feet. Hadley cleared her throat. "Where do you call home?"

"*Hannover*. My family lives near the city forest, *Eilenriede*. I grew up roaming the expanse of parks, forests, and gardens while my nanny chatted with her friends near the lake. For a space in the middle of a city, the forest offers adventure and solitude for a boy."

"Lovely." She grabbed a skewer of eggplant and used her fork to remove the savory tidbits. Stabbing her finger with a fork tine, she swore.

"Problem?" Johann asked.

Looking up, she smiled. "Great park for after-school adventures."

"I spent my terms at boarding school." He frowned. "My family does not condone adventures."

Dr. Stefan coughed.

"Sorry, but I missed that part." She raised the skewer. "Something distracted me."

Reaching across the table, he took the skewer, used the side of his fork to remove the eggplant, and handed back the naked skewer. "Use your hands."

On you? She swallowed and met his gaze. "Like a crass American?"

He looked at Dr. Stefan. "Nobody can blame you for your heritage."

Dr. Stefan raised his wine glass.

"What's the name of your holding company?" she asked. "I thought Dr. Stefan's family built things. Like bridges."

Johann leaned back in his chair. "They do, and they did, but Germany's industrialists shun the limelight. My grandfather started a mechanical engineering firm to fabricate precision products. The profits went to diversification. He guarded his family's privacy and raised my father, Rudolf, and Uncle Stefan in relative austerity."

Dr. Stefan coughed. "Relative austerity? We peeled potatoes in the kitchen garden until our hands bled."

Johann cleared his throat.

"Charming story," Dr. Stefan said, "but our father was quite rich."

Hadley squinted and replayed every vague description Dr. Stefan had previously offered. This sudden detail into her mentor's history eroded her reserves. "Since when? How rich? Why don't you drive a nicer car?"

"The 1975 hatchback is a classic!" Dr. Stefan slapped the table.

The dishes rattled.

Johann's laughter filled the intimate space and bounced off the plaster walls.

Looking at him, she wondered what else cracked his façade.

He smiled. "You are an American."

The wellness industry pushes four trillion dollars, and the legal cannabis industry rakes in tens of billions of dollars. Holding companies with lots of zeros on their balance sheet don't intimidate me. She returned his smile. "I assume Grandpa zur Hausen isn't counting his Marks by hand."

Johann shrugged. "I don't know the exact value of my grandfather's wealth."

"I hope you have a better handle on yours." The quip pleased her, and she waited for laughter.

He raised an eyebrow. "I do."

Wrinkling her nose, she used her hands to separate an artichoke. *Arrogant, German asshole.* The buttery, lemon sauce coating the vegetable melted in her mouth, and she swallowed.

"After the war," Johann said, "my grandfather invested in a pharmaceutical corporation and several other ventures. The pharmaceutical corporation manufactures human and veterinary medicines, consumer healthcare products, and biotechnology products. Layers of interconnected holding companies manage our family interests. Do you need a balance sheet before we continue discussing your research?"

She pondered the question. *Would it matter? When I'm pricing bulk grains at the co-op, every big number feels beyond my reach.* Gathering her courage, she shook her head. "No, I'm more interested in your vision." Turning to Dr. Stefan, she frowned. "If your family's rich, why can't you launch my"—she tapped her lip—"harebrained foundation?"

Setting down his fork and knife, Dr. Stefan smiled. "I am no longer part of the family."

Rubbing her forehead, she struggled to understand Dr. Stefan's statement, but the act smeared melted butter on her temples. She reached for her napkin before anyone else noticed. "Why?"

"I refused to sign the family code of conduct."

She blinked and wondered if she fell down the rabbit hole.

Johann cleared his throat. "The story's point is simple. Our family eschews notoriety."

Shifting in her chair, she faced him. "My research will lead to public attention."

He tightened and released his fist. "The forty-five richest Germans have the same wealth as the country's poorer half. I understand the difference between notoriety and attention."

"But you don't understand what I've found." Her statement came out as a whisper.

He leaned forward. "Tell me."

His voice, deep and low, curled her toes. "No." She cleared her throat. "Explain the code of conduct."

He nodded. "In my family, wealth comes with responsibilities and expectations. When children turn sixteen, they agree to eschew the day-to-day workings of the family businesses, avoid public photographs, and decline interviews."

Dr. Stefan laughed. "I was such a disappointment."

She stared. *Why would a brilliant man refuse to sign the code? He won a Nobel Prize, for goodness's sake. What kind of code could hold him to a higher standard than the scientific method?* "So, no vacation selfies?"

Johann sipped his tea. "Social media is out of the question."

"And the bad nephew?" She wondered what kind of rebellion earned that notoriety. *Maybe he lit the code on fire.*

Dr. Stefan and Johann looked at each other.

"Never mind Günter." Dr. Stefan cleared his throat. "He refused to sign the code of conduct, obliterated his trust, and filled the social pages with his exploits. He's a *Bananenbieger*."

She picked apart and translated the compound word. *Banana-bender? Is he gay?*

Johann adjusted his seat. "The code covers shares in the family firms, succession, and guidelines for social conduct."

She sipped her wine and wondered when the server would return to refill the velvety liquid. The whole bottle might be in order. "Which section covers predatory business practice?"

Johann toyed with the empty skewer on his plate and dropped it.

The quiet ping echoed in the courtyard.

He looked up. "Section seventeen. Ms. Heron, I will never lie to you."

Did he consider lying? Pushing back her chair, she deliberated bolting for the door but hesitated. Johann looked like old pictures of Dr. Stefan, but his intensity came from more than color film.

Damon approached and gathered dishes. Leaning down, he spoke to Johann.

Unable to hear, she tapped her nails against a glass.

Johann raised a hand and interrupted Damon. "Excuse me. My friend often runs odd jobs on my behalf."

Does Germany have a mafia? She looked toward the restaurant. The open door and wood-fired pizza waiting in the main dining room tempted her to flee the patio's old world charm. Before she could bolt, Damon left the patio, and she turned in her chair to meet two steady, blue gazes.

Johann lifted his fork. "The code's sections on religious tolerance, modesty, and respect for others might impress you."

His salvo soothed her suspicions. "Who wouldn't be impressed?"

"Günter."

His name settled in the silence like a heavy weight in a still lake.

Damon returned and set down three identical plates. "Lamb *souvlaki* with roasted potatoes and a salad made from tomatoes, cucumbers, and red onions."

Did anyone ask me what I wanted to eat? She shifted in her seat, pushed her food around her plate, and digested Johann's story.

"You're not hungry?" Dr. Stefan asked.

She stopped playing with her fork. "Why do I feel like I'm the next course?"

Dr. Stefan laughed and speared a bite of lamb. "My dear, Johann is your ally. I wanted nothing to do with my father's restrictions, but Johann learned to navigate life's complexities. He has the experience to guide you through the next steps of your development. Who am I but an old man who likes to dither in the laboratory?"

Putting down her utensil, she folded her hands and placed them in her lap. "The university's Office of Technology Licensing sent me a checklist." Feeling her fingers dig into the backs of her hands, she loosened her grip. "I'll follow the checklist."

"And non-profit foundation was an option?" Dr. Stefan took the lamb from his fork.

She swallowed. "Dr. Stefan, I understand most discoveries move to biotech or big pharma, but I want my research to help people."

He nodded.

"Let me tell you of my ideals," Johann said. "Perhaps we are not so far apart."

She took her first bite of lamb. The fresh herbs and savory juices matched the courtyard's decadence, and she considered setting aside her research for the indulgence. *I live on farro, beans, and kale. My life couldn't be farther from the black-tie butlers and silent women he knows.* She wondered how many plates of lamb and bottles of wine she would need before she could mimic jaded indulgence.

"My country suffers from *Sozialneid* and *Schadenfreude*," Johann said. "The journalists lean left, and the public lobbies against policies that benefit plutocratic families. My family learned to shun ostentatious displays of wealth."

She chewed the meat. *Class envy and the pleasure derived from another person's misfortune won't win friends in Silicon Valley.* Swallowing, she met his gaze. "That's practical, but I don't need an angel investor." She looked at Dr. Stefan. "Or a high-handed nephew. What's really going on?"

Dr. Stefan set down his fork. "Günter knows about your research. He knows you found something. Perhaps he knows more than me."

She scanned the courtyard and gripped the chair's

armrests. "How? When?"

"I don't know, but you must stay ahead of him."

Shaking her head, she looked back and forth between the two men. Years of scribbled notes and benign whitepapers covered her tracks. As far as the public knew, Dr. Stefan's Therapeutic Cannabis Program screened CBD products for melatonin and heavy metals. "I don't understand how Günter could know my name much less what I discovered. I don't sell CBD gummies on the street corner."

Johann choked on his tea and set down the glass. "I doubt Günter's in the market for gummies. Why buy what you can steal?"

She imagined a person lifting a decade of work from her resume. "Impossible."

"Is it?" Dr. Stefan asked. "Günter called me and asked too many pointed questions."

She studied her mentor's face. "And you're not close?"

"Not close enough."

His counseling expression faltered, and she glimpsed unspoken regrets.

Setting aside her fork, she leaned back in her chair.

"Part of the family code rewards innovation," Johann said. "Günter might intend to leverage his way back into the fold."

"And you want to block him?"

He shook his head. "My uncle praised your work. I welcome new technologies, but not on Günter's terms. His influence humiliated our family in the past. Nothing has changed."

"You do want to block him." She shook her head. "Well, my research isn't worth his time. The results won't generate significant profit. After I recoup the initial investment, the findings will enter the public domain. Someone might use the strain as an anti-inflammatory treatment for multiple sclerosis or find an off-label use I never considered, but the meat belongs to me."

Johann nodded. "Günter is desperate."

She narrowed her gaze. "How desperate?"

"Desperate to steal the thing you value the most," Dr. Stefan said.

In the fading light, his blue eyes seemed cloudier. She felt the soft tap of his palm against her forearm and knew he meant well, but Johann's arrogance seemed less threatening than Günter's desperation.

Dr. Stefan lifted his hand. "Partnering with Johann is the best course of action."

She nodded and rested her chin on her palm. Looking at Johann, she considered the implications of his involvement. "If you die, who inherits the family business?"

"A public trust, but I assume Günter would contest the will."

"You might champion my research and die tomorrow." The thought saddened her more than it should. *I barely know the man. Who am I to care if he and his brother want to play tug-of-war with their lives?*

Leaning back, Johann crossed his arms over his chest. "I have no plans to die."

She rubbed her chin. The comforting gesture would lead to blackheads, but she had bigger concerns. "Distracted people make foolish decisions. I am not distracted."

He nodded. "I haven't spoken to Günter in years."

"Why not?"

"Pride," he said.

"His or yours?"

He inclined his head. "What a difficult question. Neither of us placed a call."

She wondered how he could be so cavalier. *I would do anything to talk to Jecca one more time.* "Perhaps you should pick up the phone." Dropping her hand, she placed her napkin on the table and stood. "I assume you're paying for dinner."

Johann raised an eyebrow. "This is not a date."

"It's not a business meal either. It's a setup. You ordered. You pay." She looked at Dr. Stefan. "In the wrong circumstances, intimacy feels a lot like intimidation. I'm not assigning my research discoveries to your nephew's holding company."

Dr. Stefan smiled. "Then let Johann help and protect you as a favor to me."

Oh, brother. "I don't need protection. I'm a Ph.D. student with a green thumb for weed. The only people I fear are the freshmen who want to raid my lab." She looked at Johann.

His lip twitched.

Noting the achievement, she walked away from the table.

Damon opened the door and readmitted her to the restaurant.

"Which way to the restroom?" she asked.

He pointed toward two wooden doors with carved panels.

"Thank you."

Nodding, he returned to his post by the door.

She smiled her thanks and considered her meal. "The restaurant lets you come and go?"

Glancing at the dining room, he cracked a smile. "Cocky Black servers are always a hit in this town. When Mr. zur Hausen isn't in the country, I enjoy collecting tips."

She gasped. "He doesn't pay you a living wage?"

"I meant investment tips."

Catching a smart watch peeking from the sleeve of his jacket, she swallowed. *In this town, technology doesn't separate social circles, but attitude does.* She considered his face and wondered if a dermatologist could have salvaged his teenage skin. "Are the tips paying out?"

He shrugged. "I've considered giving up my side gig."

"Isn't this your side gig?"

"Mama Clarke taught me to keep my options open." He winked.

Smiling, she turned to walk away. *Having a mother who cared must have felt nice.* The thought brought her up short, and she looked over her shoulder. "What was her job?"

He took a deep breath. "For a long time? Welfare recipient."

"There's no shame in that fact."

"That's the same thing she said!" He smiled. "When I started asking for more than fruity cereal, she scraped together her money and took a risk. Now, nobody messes with Mama Clarke."

Or Hadley Heron. "Is he a good man?"

"Who?"

She looked at Johann and Dr. Stefan in the

courtyard. Beneath the lights, their convivial meal could have taken place in any German café, but the topic could alter her life. "Johann." His name felt familiar, like a word she heard but never placed.

"He is."

She nodded and met Damon's gaze. "Thank you."

The restroom reserved for women smelled like lavender and rosemary soap. Water dappled the countertop, and a crumpled hand towel littered the floor. *Don't tell the VCs.* Sitting in the stall, she watched another woman's soft flats glide across the glazed, tile floor. Walking to the vanity, Hadley left room for the other woman, washed her hands, and checked her hair.

The woman emerged from the stall and met her gaze in the mirror.

Bloodshot, her eyes looked like she had been up all night. *Her allergies are probably acting up.* Hadley edged closer to the wall and checked her reflection. The whites around her honey-colored eyes remained clear, but she wondered if too many late nights in the lab degraded her intuition. *I wish Gary were here to give me a second opinion on whether to trust Johann.* She drew a deep breath. *I trust Dr. Stefan. Can't I trust his nephew?*

The woman reached for a linen towel.

Hadley recoiled against a brush of contact, closed her eyes, and cleared her throat. *The bad nephew is a specter. Nobody knows or cares about my work. Günter probably wanted to make small talk with his estranged uncle.*

The woman crumpled the towel and gestured toward the door. "Please, you go first."

"Thank you." Hadley reached for the door's brass handle and congratulated herself on staying calm. Stepping past the threshold, she looked for Damon but found the hallway empty.

The woman brushed past.

Hadley paused. The dining room's chatter sounded like a picnic gone awry. Ceramic plates clattered on the tables and chairs scraped on the tiled floor. She peered into the dining room. The wood-fired grill flared and emitted a hellish red flame. Smoke gathered near the ceiling.

Diners gestured to jacketed servers. Men and women rushed to control the flames, waving their arms and dueling with competing fire extinguishers.

She stepped toward the open-air patio, but realized she needed an exit. *What is going on?*

A swarthy man opened the front door. Sweat matted the silver hair at his temples. He dabbed the moisture with a handkerchief and shoved the linen in his pocket. "The fire department is on the way!"

Turning toward the door, diners grabbed belongings and upset chairs. Glasses spilled, and overhead sprinklers kicked into gear, drowning the room.

"Everybody out!"

A fire truck roared up the tree-lined street, its sirens wailing.

She looked over her shoulder toward the courtyard.

Johann offered his uncle an arm, led the man to the hallway, and jerked his head. "Follow me."

She pulled back her chin. "I know how to exit a building."

He raised an eyebrow. "Then why are you still

here?"

Late nights and a dream can only get me so far. Her response lodged in her throat. Straightening her shoulders, she marched through the chaos.

Damon rushed to her side and took her arm. "Out you go."

Shaking free, she met his gaze. "I'm good."

He looked at Johann and nodded.

Stepping into the night air, she swallowed. Dr. Stefan stood amid the exiled diners, his face as white as his hair.

Johann barked orders to Damon, his jaw as set as stone.

Shivering, she stood alone in the crowd. She should have known dinner with an investor would be too simple, but a glimmer of hope kept her going. *What if someone believed in my research and let me go back to dreaming the impossible dreams? What else could I achieve?*

Someone grabbed her arm and tugged her into the crowd. "Damon, I'm good!" Bracing her feet, she swore, and the pull vanished. She looked for Damon's pockmarked face and found a multitude of anxious diners snapping pictures and tittering into their cell phones. *Damon?*

Near the restaurant, Johann and the owner escorted diners to the sidewalk.

She rubbed her arms in the heavy evening fog. Smoke lingered near the building. A shower would wash away the smell, but she needed to leave.

Damon followed the pair carrying a painting of two ancient Greeks playing a strategic board game.

She moved toward the familiarity of her advisor.

"Are you okay?"

Dr. Stefan nodded and leaned on his nephew. "I'm too old for these shenanigans."

Johann advanced on Damon. "You left your post."

Sweat dripped from Damon's forehead. "A fire erupted in the kitchen."

"I don't pay you to put out fires." He lowered his voice. "I pay you to watch out for my interests."

She sympathized with Damon, but his alert, unblinking stare looked ready for another challenge.

"It won't happen again," Damon said.

I thought Dr. Stefan's exams were tough. Good for you.

Johann nodded then opened the passenger door of a matte gray luxury SUV. "After you, Hadley."

She lifted her chin. "No."

He frowned. "No?"

Dr. Stefan cleared his throat.

"I have options." She rubbed her face and felt the exhaustion weighting her eyes. Grit rubbed against her skin, and she wondered if she smelled of smoke. "I don't need your help."

The crowd shifted and cleared a path for the first responders.

Jostled by the movement, she realized she had thirty seconds to say her piece. "I'm not content to play rag doll while two impetuous boys engage in a tug of war over my research." She focused on Dr. Stefan. "Make that three boys."

Johann frowned. "Come to my office. We can work out your concerns."

Dropping her arms, she raised her palm and hoped the lamb imbued her with enough zing to end the evening on a high note. "What do you know of my concerns?"

"You fear losing control." He frowned. "I won't let you fall."

Lowering her hand, she allowed his solemn affirmation to sink in. How much time had passed since anyone offered to support her? She considered the tension in his jaw and the way he squared his shoulders like a shield against the world. *How many times have you thrown yourself into the fray for your family?* Swallowing, she nodded. "Maybe." She cleared her throat and looked at the stretch of fabric covering his chest. "You forgot your jacket."

He rubbed his jaw, but a brief smile replaced his solemnity. "I don't need it."

She raised her chin. "I don't do stoic."

He glanced at his uncle.

Dr. Stefan shrugged.

A firefighter stopped beside her. "Miss, you and your friends need to clear the area."

Recognizing the firefighter's authority and need underpinning his command, she moved to comply but turned and surveyed Johann, his uncle, and his helper. "I don't want to get involved in your family feud."

Damon tugged at his ear.

Dr. Stefan wiped his brow.

Johann stepped forward.

Meeting his gaze, she took a deep breath. "And I don't need a ride home." Head held high, she walked through the crowd, but she wanted to turn and catch a final glimpse of Johann's steely blue eyes. *Why do all the hot men have to be assholes?*

Chapter Two

"Dr. Stefan wants to see you," Gary said.

Hadley looked up from the computer and blinked in the small, shared office. "What?"

He spun a ballpoint pen between his fingers and lounged on his side of the office.

Hours of work left his dirty-blond hair tousled, but she saw the same pink-cheeked boy she knew as a kid. Now longtime roommate and pseudo-brother, he knew almost everything about her, like not to interrupt her while she worked.

Gary pulled the pen from his teeth. "Your. Advisor. He wants to see you."

"When?" She tucked her hair behind her ears and filed her research results. She and Gary held court in one of the dim rooms reserved for Ph.D. students. Their scribbles filled a whiteboard with colorful formulas and chemical structures, but she kept her notebook in German, and password protected her files. *Who knows who cleans the offices?* Standing, she shook out her patterned sundress.

"Now?" Gary stretched. "He came by thirty minutes ago. You nodded."

She loosened the button on her sweater and frowned. "Impossible."

Shrugging, he put his feet on the desk. "Maybe you inhaled more smoke than you let on. You should rest and let Buffy handle the analysis."

"I'm fine." She rubbed her eyes, stretched her arms over her head, and replayed the speech she rehearsed. *Thanks for setting up the dinner, Dr. Stefan. I appreciate your intent. Johann's investment isn't the right fit. I'm going in a different direction. Your family needs group therapy.* She smiled. *I'll save the last bit for graduation.*

Walking down the long hallway, she headed toward Dr. Stefan's spacious office. On either side of the hallway, students toiled behind wide glass panels, moved carts of samples, and tested CBD products for potency and contaminants. Revenue from the Therapeutic Cannabis Program funded and legitimized the lab space, but an anonymous grant bankrolled Dr. Stefan's more esoteric research efforts. *Dr. Stefan promised to reveal the funding source after graduation. Johann might be rich, but his pockets can't be this deep.*

"The meal could have gone better."

Recognizing Johann's voice, she paused in the hallway outside Dr. Stefan's door.

"You said you could handle her," Dr. Stefan said.

"I can."

She rolled her eyes at Johann's quick, guttural response and peered into the room to find her bearings. Dr. Stefan and Johann stood side by side behind the professor's desk. Sunlight streamed through the office windows and backlit their features. A large, brown package sat on Dr. Stefan's desk. He turned the box from side to side like a kid savoring wrapping paper.

She glanced at a framed photograph of two boys lounging in an inner tube. She thought the photograph looked like a stock image, cocky boy on the right looked suspiciously like Johann. She rapped on the doorframe. "What's in the box?"

Both men looked up.

Their identical furrowed brows made her smile. *I recognize that look.* Stepping inside the room, she caught the faint scent of witch hazel and bergamot. She looked for the source of the fresh citrus, but her gaze landed on Johann.

He nodded.

Dr. Stefan walked forward, palms open. "Hadley! I'm so glad to see you. How are you feeling?"

"Well enough." She risked a glance at Johann.

He held her gaze.

Folding, she looked away and approached the desk. The emblem of the German Institute for Biophysical Chemistry shone on the package's top left corner.

"Look at these *Briefmarken*." Dr. Stefan caressed the German postage stamps. "So much prettier than industrial bar codes. We all need beauty in our lives, don't we, Johann?"

His nephew grunted.

She kept her gaze on the package. In the antiseptic, industrial research environment, it looked entirely out of place.

"The botanical images and beautiful colors remind me of childhood summers in *Hannover*."

The memory softened her approach toward the encounter, and she looked up.

Dr. Stefan rubbed his hands and smiled. "I'll never forget the quiet stillness of willow trees swaying in the breeze." He sighed. "The park was so much more peaceful than the competitive *Scheisse* I've dealt with for the last five decades*."*

Yesterday, she would have laughed, but Johann's presence made her feel like a child defending her turf. Keeping her mouth shut, she glanced at the package's cellophane envelope. The raised seal of the prestigious *Göttingen* institution shone through the travel-stained envelope. *The sender applied old-school postage stamps but typed the address label? How weird is that?* She cleared her throat. "About last night…"

"An error," Johann said. "You need not concern yourself with Günter. I will handle him."

She frowned. "I'm more concerned about my research than your family feud."

"The fire was suspicious."

Wondering if she should have mentioned the quick grab amid the crowd, she rubbed her arm. *Johann doesn't need to know I left on the television and the lights while I slept.* "I hardly noticed." She considered an exposition on gender equality, but Dr. Stefan's milky, blue gaze remained fixed on the package. *Let the professor have his fun.* "What's in the box?"

Dr. Stefan reached for a silver letter opener. "A student worker delivered a gift. As soon as I signed for the package, he left."

"That's weird." *If the mailroom sensors detected something amiss, the university's shipping and receiving protocols would hold the package.* She questioned whether a package could arrive on campus without passing through the mailroom. "What could be in it?"

"A present," Dr. Stefan said.

She sat on the edge of his desk. Dr. Stefan graduated from *Göttingen* and gave last year's commencement speech. "While you were a student, maybe you forgot to pay your library fines."

Shaking his head, he opened the envelope. "The Director and Head of the Department of Neurochemistry do not care about library fines." He removed a letter from the box and read it. His hands shook, but he smiled.

She leaned over his shoulder and struggled to decipher the German prose.

Dr. Stefan handed the typed letter to his nephew. "Flattery will get you anywhere."

"I doubt it." Johann read the letter. "The institute hopes the small, historical trifle within the box will help Uncle Stefan commemorate fifty years of scientific research. It recalls the idealism of his first letter of motivation and asks him to consider the romanticism of his younger days."

"I could have figured that out." She wiggled her butt against the desk. When applying for graduate programs in Germany, applicants submitted a letter of motivation. Her letter would have been brief. Who could argue with eliminating pain? "You didn't give me time to finish reading."

"Spoiled brat," he said in German.

Dr. Stefan snorted. "Who wants to be young anymore?"

Hadley straightened before his speech turned into a soliloquy. "Dr. Stefan, I want to talk about the derivatives research. Should I make an appointment"— she raised her eyebrows—"with you?"

He gestured toward a chair.

She crossed her arms and stared down Johann.

"I am leaving," Johann said, "but come to my

office to discuss your research."

Dr. Stefan hefted the box in his hands. "Phew. I'm eighty years old."

Johann rubbed his temple. "I meant Hadley."

She watched him leave. *Spoiled brat? How about arrogant asshole?* Frowning, she replayed the previous night and buried her attraction to the man. "Dr. Stefan, Buffy and I are ready to repeat the assays, but I don't think we should re-run all the compounds." She hoped a firm stance would help her avoid hours of lecture and debate. "I think we have a winner."

His posture shifted, but he continued reading the heaps of praise and philosophical questions in the letter. Finally, he looked up. "Repetition is the heart of research. Eventually, you get lucky."

She frowned. *Or you put in the hours required for diligence.* "Lucky isn't the goal."

He waved off her argument. "The faculty already accepted your dissertation. Tell Johann what you found with your assays."

Straightening, she surveyed the orderly precision of his office. Accolades filled the shelves, and framed photographs commemorated his prizes. *I'm not ready.* "The letter's a gracious gesture. Where will you put the gift?"

Smiling, he folded the letter and placed it in his desk drawer. "That depends on what is inside the box!" He sliced the packing tape. Dulled from a voyage around the world, the polypropylene split, and the box popped open. "I wonder what relic of history waits within this corrugated treasure box."

"Are you sure it's not a whoopee cushion?"

He looked up. "A what?"

"Just a joke, Dr. Stefan. I hope you enjoy your present." She walked toward the doorway and paused. "Are you sure you should open that box? The letter lacks a signature. Anybody could have sent it."

He squinted. "Are you here to steal my pig?"

The colloquial expression elicited a smile, but she remained focused on the strange package. "Maybe you should save the gift for your retirement party and open the box with the rest of the gifts?"

He waved a hand across his chest. "Did I ask for a party?"

"No."

"Then let me celebrate my accomplishments."

Exhaling, she tried not to feel dismissed and wondered how much influence Dr. Stefan retained. His achievements advanced science, but with his focus on retirement, she would have to make her way in the world. "I guess we'll talk about my research later."

He nodded.

Leaving the man to savor his reward, she considered the hunch that had kept her awake at night. *The polymer activates MOR proteins without spiking dopamine, but the neural assays behave strangely. Absolutely no evidence for tolerance exists.* She pivoted to return to Dr. Stefan's office, too proud to let him brush off her achievement.

Light flashed, and a wave of deafening sound raced down the hallway. As the detonation's intense heat and pressure ripped through corridor, pain followed, and she collapsed and fought the urge to heave. Around her, walls of tempered glass shattered and fell to the floor, lab occupants screamed, and the pulses of heat and cries of her peers pinned her to the floor.

Please, let everyone live.

Squeezing shut her eyes, she felt the building shake and roll as seismic features absorbed the blast. The swaying amplified her nausea, and her stomach roiled. She clasped a hand over her mouth and heaved. Time slowed as smoke and pain slowed her sense. Fighting for purchase, she dropped her head and pressed her ear against her shoulder to block alarms and anguished cries. *I have to get up. I have to move.* Her vision wavered, and she squeezed shut her eyes. *I have to evacuate.* Scrambling to all fours, she coughed and peered through acrid smoke and falling debris. A fire burned in the lab on her left.

Researchers yanked fire extinguishers off the walls, struggled with the pins, and dropped the heavy cylinders to the floor.

The loud, echoing thuds made her wince, and she squeezed shut her eyes. *I swear, undergraduates are more trouble than children.*

The researchers stumbled past. Their international cries of alarm created confusion as thick and heady as the smoke pouring from the hall's end.

Realization dawned, and she widened her gaze. Scrambling to her feet, she pushed through the crowd, ignored the alarms, and raced toward the man who felt as close as a father. "Dr. Stefan!"

She skidded to a halt in his doorway. Daylight poured through a hole in the exterior wall, and water streamed from the fire suppression system. Looking down, she saw a crowd of people standing on the lawn. Johann stood in the middle of them, his expression firm amid a crowd of gaping countenances.

Heart pounding in her chest, she fought the instinct

to lean toward the smoking hole and verify Dr. Stefan's absence. He had plucked her from the obscurity of freshman biology and guided her for close to a decade. *He talked me through the intricacies of his language, strain hybridization, and academic politics. How can someone live one minute and perish the next?* She sank to her haunches and covered her face. *With Jecca, I had time!*

Campus police cars skidded to a halt in front of the building, their sirens screaming.

She opened her eyes and leaned toward the promise of authority.

A squadron of trained officers navigated the disorder and rushed toward the building with their guns drawn. Authoritative shouts permeated the chatter and the hysteria of displaced international students.

Johann stood resolute on the lawn. Looking up, he cocked his head.

What if he's the bad nephew?

A second wave of emergency response vehicles filled the great lawn with firefighters and paramedics.

Overwhelmed, she shook off her confusion and sighed.

Turning, Johann disappeared amid the commotion.

Wiping the sweat from her brow, she found blood staining her fingertips. The glimpse of mortality broke her stunned acceptance, and fear pushed her back to the hallway's safety. Amid the remnants of the building, she felt security and peril pulling her in two directions. *How close did I come to joining Dr. Stefan?*

Buffy rushed to her side.

Her freckles and sandy-blonde hair disappeared beneath a fine coat of dust. Water streaked the dust and painted her features with theatrical absurdity. She felt the woman pull her toward the exit sign.

"What happened?" Buffy asked.

"I don't know." Amid the dust-choked debris, an ignorant mistake no longer seemed likely. She recalled the corrugated box and felt grief welling in her throat, threatening to spill from her lips like a heaving admission of defeat. She clamped shut her mouth and gripped Buffy's hand. *The explosion claimed one research collaborator. I can't afford to lose another one.*

Buffy coughed. "Dr. Stefan was such a kind man. A gas explosion must have caused the accident."

"A gas explosion." Hadley frowned. The explanation sounded hollow.

Nodding, Buffy moved toward the staircase.

A squad of security officers ran past, but a trailing officer stopped and caught his breath. "If you are able, please exit the building." He directed them toward the stairwell. "We need to secure the crime scene's perimeter."

His clipped command confirmed her fears. *Dr. Stefan's office is a crime scene.* In an instant, she rearranged her life into acts that made sense and acts that warranted further investigation. Fears about the security of her research felt overblown, but she scrolled her memories for strangers. Had she passed someone lingering near her office? Was everything in the same place she left it?

"The police will find a faulty connection and a spark of friction." Buffy opened the door to the stairwell. "Accidents happen."

She repeated the mantra like a prayer. Hadley

leaned against a cold cinderblock wall. The painted surface supported her weight, and she closed her eyes to acknowledge her grief. "I hope you found your willow trees, Dr. Stefan."

****

Forensics crews erected white tents and portable security lights. Working through the afternoon, they collected information and pieced together clues to identify the violence's source.

Huddled beneath a disposable blanket, Hadley answered the investigators' redundant questions. Left alone for short spells, she scrolled through social media accounts circulating incendiary comments, security footage, and pictures of officers digging through innocuous backpacks. Bystanders jabbered about what they saw. She closed her eyes. *When will it end?*

Two hours before the evening news, she stood at the crowd's edge and watched a press conference.

The police chief stood next to the university president and swore the explosion had nothing to do with domestic terrorists or known criminals.

There's no way you could know that right now. She looked for a familiar face in the crowd. Onlookers raised smartphones and live-streamed the event, but nobody watched her. *I'm going home.*

She retraced her steps through Palo Alto's streets. The shops and restaurants looked decades out of date. Trash pooled near an overflowing receptacle, and a collarless cat darted between iron fence posts. At her front door, she unlocked the door, opened it, and paused. "Gary?" Stillness greeted her question. Slipping inside the townhouse, she checked the locks, lowered herself to the ratty futon, and flipped on the evening news.

The anchor led with the president's message and cut to the sweat-stained police officer who directed her and Buffy to exit the building.

"Explosions do not destroy evidence; they blast it into thousands of tiny bits and pieces. We'll find the evidence. We'll find the scraps of DNA and the shattered switches, relays, and circuit boards that survived the blast. If a pipe housed the bomb's components, fragments of metal carrying residue landed nearby." He puffed out his chest. "We'll find the explosion's cause."

"So you're saying it could have been a pipe bomb?" a reporter asked.

The officer shook his head. "I can't say much about the details of the case. Bomb experts and federal agents began an international investigation to determine the root cause."

He looks intense. She closed her eyes. *And clueless.* Shutting off the television, she pulled an afghan around her shoulders and closed her eyes. Dr. Stefan's milky-blue eyes refused to fade. His infectious enthusiasm carried her through her lowest moments. After learning her thesis committee had signed off on her dissertation, he broke formality and hugged her in the hallway. *The police have nothing, but Dr. Stefan had a hunch.* She closed her eyes. *Where's the evidence?*

****

The ensuing police investigation felt more disordered than an undergraduate career fair. Sitting in a room at the police station, Hadley replayed her dinner with Dr. Stefan and Johann. A yellow light fixture dominated the tiled ceiling, and a small camera blinked in the corner.

"After the fire, who grabbed you?" Lieutenant Anthony Jayne asked.

His black hair shone beneath the overhead light. She respected his position, but a quick Internet search revealed police lieutenants were like middle managers in the world of law enforcement. *He probably spends his days doing paperwork. When Dr. Stefan died, a superior undoubtedly gave him broad directions and a small army of jaded sergeants and eager detectives.* "That's the thing," she said. "I don't know."

"Have you seen Johann zur Hausen since that night?"

She considered her answer. If she mentioned seeing Johann in Dr. Stefan's office, the police would narrow in on Johann's proximity to the package. She witnessed the men's shared affection and knew Johann had nothing to with the blast. Last night, she considered calling him, but she second-guessed what to say. *Hey, so about the brother? By the way, want to bone?* She squeezed shut her eyes and smothered a laugh. *How sophomoric.*

Lieutenant Jayne narrowed his gaze. "Is there a problem?"

Yawning, she shook her head. "Exhausted. Sleep eludes me."

He nodded. "I know how that goes. Tell me again what you're studying?"

She recited the abstract for her upcoming paper on the synthetic production of CBD.

"Erogenous system?" He scratched his head. "Are you sure you're studying weed?"

Ignoring his joke, she exhaled. "I said 'endocannabinoid'." She stretched out the syllables as if a room of undergraduates held their fingers over their laptops, poised to take notes.

He blinked.

Fearing further misunderstandings, she weighed the risk of a drawn-out interview. "I study weed."

He grinned. "Right. Your roommate, Gary, said you're about to be rich."

Thinking of Gary, she rubbed her temples. *I'll wring his scrawny neck. I don't need Palo Alto's finest chasing a rabbit's trail.* She looked at the earnest lieutenant and offered him a placid smile.

He thrust out his chest.

The camera in the corner blinked.

She leaned forward. "You know what, Lieutenant Jayne? Gary is mistaken. Any adult can walk into a recreational marijuana dispensary and buy sufficient weed to obliterate his or her weekend. My research merely streamlines CBD production."

"That's not what Gary thinks. He thinks your procedures will lower the cost of commercial productions. He said someone left a threat in the comments on your last journal article." The lieutenant held up a computer printout. "I have a copy of the comment."

She shrugged off the anonymous comment. "The world is full of people with a terrible sense of humor. Unless they can use spellcheck, I don't take them seriously enough to care."

He frowned and scrutinized the printout.

Rounding the table, she pointed to the melodramatic threat. "The commenter put an extra 'g' in 'strangle'."

Squinting, Lieutenant Jayne traced a finger beneath the letters. "The spelling hardly matters. The commenter specifically mentions your research."

She read the text again and sighed. *I can't be responsible for every misogynistic couch surfer with a Wi-Fi connection. Analysts estimate the market will swell to twenty-five billion dollars. An intellectual property gold rush looms, and I don't have time to twiddle my thumbs and worry about couch jockeys. The sooner I stake my IP claim, the sooner I can defend it.* "Look, Tony. May I call you Tony?"

Lieutenant Jayne smiled. "Oh, sure."

"Right. So, Tony,"—she slowed the tempo of her words and held back her impatience—"I told you my lab studies cannabidiol. My team thinks CBD has massive untapped potential, but a certain segment of the population thinks it's no better than snake oil."

He scratched his hair. "Isn't it all a marketing ploy?"

She rubbed her temples. "CBD's popularity continues to grow, but laborious production limits the market. I work on cannabis strain hybridization." She swallowed. *And cannabis pharmacology.* "Synthetic CBD is the future, but it's not sexy enough to end a life."

He frowned.

"Think about what the agriculture industry did with corn."

Stretching his jaw, he stared. "Come again?"

"Big Ag spent billions of dollars perfecting crops. Do you think their scientists worried about death threats?"

"So, capitalism rules the market," he said.

"I'm attempting to get ahead of capitalism!" Impatience raised her voice, and she took a deep breath.

He cocked his head.

She took a calming breath. "I don't know who left the comments. I don't know why Gary mentioned my research. To most people, it's boring."

Nodding, he jerked his head toward the door. "Let me walk you out."

Leaving the police department, she glanced over her shoulder at the building's tall, narrow windows and art deco columns. Beneath the word *police*, a flight of red steps descended to the sidewalk. The clean, capital typeface looked professional, but she wondered about the force's efficacy. Passing under the header, she marched down the red steps and shook out her hair. *As if anyone would find their presence here confusing.*

She scanned the people waiting at the bus stop, loitering on the corner, and exchanging small talk beside a car.

A black man holding a newspaper glanced up.

Is that Damon? She shook her head and blamed exhaustion. *No, it couldn't be.*

In the week after the explosion, different agencies asked her to repeat her story. She buried the event's subtleties and stopped thinking about her answers. Unable to resurrect Dr. Stefan, she fast-forwarded through the scene like an old movie she watched too many times.

Other students had different reactions. The student worker who delivered the package fired up a printing press and sold twenty-dollar T-shirts. *University: It's a Blast.*

The next day, Hadley sat in her office and tried to concentrate.

Buffy walked by her office's open door wearing one of the entrepreneurial student's creations. She made eye contact, but she waltzed into her interview with local police.

"Is that outfit in good taste?" an officer asked.

Buffy raised a coffee mug, opened her hand, and let the mug drop to the floor. "I didn't sign up for the Spanish Inquisition!"

At the sound of shattering ceramic, Hadley winced. She put down her copy of the university daily and looked at Gary. He plied her with ice cream, soulful looks, and open-ended questions, but exhaustion kept her from recounting the tension between Dr. Stefan's nephews. "This whole thing seems surreal."

He grunted.

"What if another bomb exists?"

Looking up from his computer screen, he exhaled. "You always overreact. Who sleeps at their desk?"

She looked at the half-dead plants lining the bookshelf. *Who can't commit to a plant?* Remembering the university advertisement for meditation, she practiced calming breaths and looked at Gary's desk. Papers and coffee-stained printouts littered the surface. *I told him to buy cactuses. He wouldn't let an animal starve. Why can't he bother to water his plants?*

She considered the sleek laptop occupying the center of her desk and the orderly, spiral-bound notebook containing her thoughts and hypotheses. *I have room to dream, and I have room to water plants.* She released her breath. *I have everything I need to succeed.*

Gary leaned back in his desk chair. "Another bomb won't go off. You're a graduate student. If you sold your product, you'd be a rich graduate student. Who would want to kill you?"

She and Gary fantasized about alternative lives, but she chose the path that helped the most people. "That's the problem. I don't know who killed Dr. Stefan either." Opening her laptop, she pulled up the security and encryption program running behind her other applications. *No threats detected. What if Günter is a threat?* She considered laying out her concerns and looked at Gary.

He tapped his keyboard. "We shouldn't be in this mess."

I shouldn't burden him. She opened a feed to the lab. "What does that mean?"

"Grad school should have delayed adulthood and filled my bed with undergrads. Instead, you and Dr. Stefan are always chattering in German. It's annoying." He cleared his throat. "Was annoying."

"Gar-Bear."

He shook his head. "Whoever planted that bomb should stop playing fantasy role-playing games and live in the actual world where people work for a living. I hope the police catch the fuckers."

"Me, too." She slumped in her chair. "I miss Dr. Stefan." Looking at Gary, she considered leaning against his shoulder.

He nodded. "The man seemed pretty decent."

Frowning, she thought about the few times she saw the men together. "If you spent more time together, you would have liked him."

"My advisor's okay." He picked something from

the edge of his nose.

She closed her eyes. "I need someone else to deal with my paperwork."

"Why? Graduation is in a week. Start applying to post-docs and milk the end of your funding."

"I think I have post-dissertation stress disorder." She rubbed her head.

"What does that mean?"

Smiling, she opened her eyes and met his gaze. "I struggle without productivity."

He looked at her notebook. "What's going on with your other experiments?"

Pulling closed the notebook, she frowned. In the world of pharmacological research, one round of assays meant nothing, but two rounds established a trend. *Gary has a propensity to skip corners. He's been riding my coattails since we left Marin. I can't risk muddying the results just to get him involved in this work.* She picked at her cuticles and considered a faded motivational poster from the 1990s. "Hmm. I'm not sure. Since the explosion, my research has been a mess."

He frowned. "You're here seven days a week, and you're not sure what's going on with your experiments?"

"Buffy helps me." Dodging the question bought her time to plan her next steps.

"Buffy is your lab rat."

Bristling at the insult, she straightened her shoulders. She might be the expert in cannabidiol derivatives, but Buffy measured the neural cells' health and monitored the effects of different compounds. Their collaboration stemmed from an agreement between the School of Medicine and Dr. Stefan's lab to unlock the potential of strain hybridization. "You shouldn't call her that name."

He lifted a pencil and twirled it between his fingers. "Haddie, the undergraduates call her 'Speed bump' for a reason."

"That's just mean. She does outstanding work."

Dropping the pencil on the desk, he rubbed his neck. "Sometimes outstanding work isn't enough."

She drummed her fingers next to her keyboard. "I saw you flirting with her last week."

His cheeks blushed. "I thought we might work together sometime." He cleared his throat.

At the thought of Buffy running Gary like a well-oiled machine, she laughed. "Let's get out of here, Gar-Bear. The only thing that can shake my depression is a bout of physical activity. Your choice. Running or tennis?"

"I vote for a smoke," he said.

"I hoped you'd say tennis."

Laughing, he stood. "Is there any reason we can't do both?"

Twenty minutes later, at the sports center, she swiped her student ID and leaned over the receptionist's desk. "Which tennis courts are free?"

The student worker kept his gaze on his phone. "Uh, maybe two and three over on the south side."

Gary sighed. "I hate those courts. What else have do you have?"

"Nothing, man." The worker looked up and adjusted his visor. Shaggy, black hair protruded from the band. "Tennis practices and camps have priority over your lazy ass. We only hold a few courts for university members. If you're so particular, reserve online."

Gary braced his arms on the desk and leaned over the pimpled undergraduate. "You should change the system so I can make a recurring reservation."

"Hmm. Student worker or IT genius? Which am I?"

Gary sneered. "You're lucky you make ten dollars an hour."

"And you're lucky your daddy pays your tuition."

She grabbed a bright white towel. "We'll take the second one."

Both men looked at her.

Interrupting the testosterone match made her feel older than her years. Shaking her head, she led Gary to the courts. *He's always the one to lay blame or take shortcuts, but he's the only person I can call in the middle of the night.* Stepping onto court two, she smiled and lowered her sunglasses. The hard court amplified the sunlight. Bright-white regulation lines glistened in the heat. *Screw the investigation. I need this release.*

Her serve battled Gary's dominant forehand, and the first set went to a tie-break. At six-six, she finished the contents of her scratched water bottle and grinned. "Seven points?"

He nodded and served from the deuce side. His ball skipped across the service line.

Swinging, she missed the ball. After they switched sides, she called the score. Her serve nicked the tape. *Yes!*

Gary called a fault.

"Gar-Bear, I saw it bounce!"

He crouched and readied his racket. "It's my call, Haddie."

Shaking her head, she tossed the ball in the air. Her arm ached, but she raised the racket, brushed the ball, and slammed it with all her might. Her forward motion sent the ball spinning over the net, and she watched the ball hit the same spot.

Gary watched the ball bounce and stood. "Double fault. Zero-Two."

She switched to the deuce side and focused on spin.

Gary returned her serve.

Running in for a drop shot, she sent the ball over the net, but Gary hardly moved. She made a fist. "Get the ball!"

He stopped playing and laughed. "You're trying too hard. If I were mean, I'd call a voice fault."

Breathing hard, she wondered if she should have swapped deep breathing exercises for a stint on the debate team. "Why didn't you return my shot?"

"You need a win, Haddie. You don't look good."

She adjusted her visor. "I don't need a chauvinistic concession. I need a legitimate win!" Dropping the extra ball onto the court, she stomped toward her bag. "My serves both went in."

He threw an arm around her shoulder. "What's wrong? You're tense. Enjoy the win."

Shrugging off his embrace, she shoved her racket in her tennis bag. "What's wrong? My advisor won an early cremation, police officers contaminated my lab space, and I spent three days cleaning up forensic powder. I needed you to fight, not to forfeit the tie-break as a chauvinistic gesture."

"You sound like my mother."

I feel like one! She chucked her water bottle at his

head.

He caught the bottle.

Rolling her eyes, she planted her hands on her hips. "Grow up, Gar-Bear."

He raised his chin. "I'm trying."

She swung her bag over her shoulder and held out a hand for her water bottle. "Then grow some balls."

He offered the water bottle, and his hand shook. "That's a low blow. How long have we been friends?"

"Forever." She took the bottle and downed the contents. *That's the problem with family. You can't fire them.*

"I'll make dinner," he said. "Stir fry?"

Wiping clean her mouth, she nodded. "Sure. I have a few more things to do at the lab."

"Will you ever stop?"

She thought of her mother, wide-eyed in front of the television, and knew she would do anything to keep another person from lingering in shadows and questioning his or her worth. "Not until I've accomplished what I set out to do."

He swiped his hair off his face. "But your weed's so good."

Rolling her eyes, she set off across campus, ventured into the empty quad, and wondered who lurked in the shadows. Nobody played in the fountains or loitered between the interconnected buildings. She sighed. *This university is more than a collection of classroom spaces and department offices. Gary is more than a lousy tennis player. I don't know if I would have survived without his constant encouragement and offbeat humor. He might ride my coattails, but I'll make sure we both survive the ride.*

Two people waited at the designated stop for the university's free shuttle system.

Content to be close to other humans, she took her place beside the couple. The university's zero-emission bus arrived on schedule. Climbing the shuttle's steps, she looked over her shoulder and wondered why she still felt so alone.

Chapter Three

Lieutenant Jayne's earnest phone call garnered Hadley's respect, but his floundering investigation undermined her confidence in the local police force. Two days after her last visit, she faked a smile for the police station receptionist. "Hadley Heron."

The woman looked up, nodded, and slid an adhesive visitor's badge across the desk. "By now, you probably know your way."

She perked up. "Does that mean I can skip the escort?"

The receptionist's smile widened, but she shook her head. "Absolutely not."

Sitting in a 1950s chair, Hadley waited for the lieutenant to appear and escort her to an interview room. The chair's wool cushion scratched her legs. She straightened her sundress beneath her thighs, gripped the wooden frame, and drummed her fingers. Lieutenant Jayne wore too much hair gel and stumbled over four-syllable words, but he wore the badge.

Strolling past the receptionist's desk, he nodded and held out a hand. "Thank you for coming back, Miss Heron. I hope this meeting will be our last."

She stood, drew back her shoulders, shook his hand, and stopped herself from waltzing past the receptionist. "After you, Lieutenant."

He led the way through security. "Do you want

anything to drink? We have water and a vending machine."

She wrinkled her nose. "I'm good."

"The City Council approved a new public safety building on Sherman Avenue, right across from the courthouse. In the meantime, we're stuck here."

Acoustic tiles and terrazzo floors proved the City Council's conservative approach toward physical upgrades. "The building reminds me of old sitcoms. Paper cups and smoldering cigarettes."

He laughed. "The new communications tower will be 135 feet tall and very high tech." He dropped his voice. "The shooting range will have automated targets. Did you know I'm a High Master shooter?"

Meeting his gaze, she decided not to mention the robotic instruments in her lab. "Cool."

Clearing his throat, he pointed to a staircase. "This building called for a downstairs range, but I guess the city ran out of money. Now the basement hosts the Emergency Operations Center."

"That's a pity." Feigning interest in the old building's subtleties, she peered through windows and nodded, but her mind drifted to her research. *How much will clinical trials cost? What's the timeline for production?*

"I could take you to the commercial range sometime. Knowing how to handle a gun can be helpful."

She tripped on her feet. The sharp squeak of rubber on linoleum echoed in the hallway. Reaching for the nearest wall, she caught her balance. "What?"

Lieutenant Jayne offered her a hand.

Shaking her head, she raised her chin and hoped

she looked competent and worldly. "I'm not interested in learning to fire a deadly weapon." She watched him shrug and avert his eyes like a toddler with an unpleasant taste in his mouth. *I make drugs, not war.*

Opening a solid wooden door, he stood back and revealed an interview room.

Another drab room and another unobtrusive camera. This room smelled of stale urine and spilled coffee. She wondered if the department used the space for a drunk tank. *Couldn't we settle for sweat and fear?* Holding her breath, she dug a peppermint out of her purse and chose a chair at the scarred table.

He lifted a sheath of papers from the table and examined them. "We spoke to Dr. zur Hausen's nephews. Neither man raised red flags. Did your advisor say anything else that seemed odd?"

In her mind, she replayed her meal at the Greek restaurant. Viewed in hindsight, every comment held unexplored nuances. "He spoke about retirement like the end of an era. I kept wondering if he was sick and didn't want to tell me. Could you mine his accounts?"

"Not yet." The lieutenant put down the papers. "What about your accounts?"

She guarded her research like a honey badger, but her purse held her notebook. As long as the low tech, innocuous pages stayed in her possession, nobody could hack her research. Standing, she sent her chair skidding across the terrazzo floor. "My research has nothing to do with Dr. Stefan's death."

He cocked his head. "You were the last one to see Dr. zur Hausen alive."

She turned her back. "I could have died beside him." Mortality felt like a lump in her throat.

Swallowing, she faced him.

"Please sit down, Miss Heron." He slid a box of tissues across the table. "The department has no qualms with your research, but I believe you undersold your discovery's commercial potential. If a connection exists between your work and the death of your advisor, I suggest halting your research or seeking protection."

From whom? She crossed her arms. "If you have no further questions, I'll stop wasting your time."

The officer blinked. "Your mentor is dead."

She dropped her arms and pushed down the grief threatening to choke off her words. "I don't know who killed Dr. Stefan. Do you have reason to believe I need an armed escort?" Part of her hoped Lieutenant Jayne would assign a rookie to her lab. *At least a police presence would scare away curious students.*

He shook his head. "Without a credible threat, I can't assign a safety officer to ordinary citizens. Decide, Miss Heron. Are you in danger or not? I'm offering you protection."

The stalled investigation undermined her confidence in the offer. Shaking her head, she grabbed her purse and considered her response's ramifications. Admitting danger would halt her research and mark her as an oddity on campus. She forced a smile. "Let's conclude this little tête-à-tête so I can return to my research."

He lifted a pen and made a note. "So you don't feel threatened?"

"Not at all." She toyed with her hair. "At first, I thought a gas explosion occurred." The explanation sounded as stupid as her act. Dropping the strands, she straightened her shoulders. "I'm going back to my lab."

He nodded and looked up from his note. "You have my card. Keep your eyes open."

She paused in front of the door. *We're not playing cops and robbers anymore, Lieutenant.* Faint lines fanned from his eyes, and she wondered if he and she were the same age. In another life, she might have bumped into him at a bar and thought him handsome. "Thanks, Tony."

"What are you doing tonight, Miss Heron?" He cleared his throat. "Will there be crowds of people? Unfamiliar situations?"

Her bravado faltered, and tears sprang to her eyes. "I'm attending a funeral."

He put down his pen. "Be careful."

The numbness following the explosion had worn off, and the funeral would trigger her grief, but she met Lieutenant Jayne's gaze. "Solve the case."

"Your life is important."

Is it?

He reached across the table, palm up.

Clutching her purse, she wondered if the police academy made recruits practice empathetic gestures. "I'm fine."

He withdrew his hand. "You don't believe the department can protect you."

Look what happened to Dr. Stefan. She smiled, hoping he saw a woman cloistered by academia. "I'm not important enough for protection."

"Your academic credentials say otherwise."

She bit her lip.

Straightening the buttons on his uniform, he stood and crossed his arms. "You're hiding something. Tell me what you're really researching."

"Nothing of consequence." The memory of Johann striding from the smoking restaurant brought a smile to her face. *Heroes don't look back*. The tongue-in-cheek 1990s skit seemed as ridiculous as her predicament. *I don't need a hero. I need a few weeks of uninterrupted work and a grant.*

The lieutenant cocked his head.

She cleared her throat. "When you solve the case, the whole campus will rest easier."

He nodded. "Happy to be of help."

Before she said anything she regretted, she left Lieutenant Jayne, peeled the visitor badge from her shirt, and tossed the sticker in the trashcan.

The receptionist looked up.

Hadley ignored the woman. Free of the building, she jogged down the red steps and inhaled. Sunlight streamed through the redwood trees, but memories of the dust-choked hallway surfaced and stole her breath. Where was the fast-forward button when she needed it?

"Hadley, are you okay?" a man's voice asked. "Do you need help?"

Turning, she slammed a hand against her chest. Damon stood in the conifers' shadows. "Have you been following me?"

"All week," he said.

"Tell your boss to mind his own damn business." Shaking her head, she unlocked her bicycle and cut through the Palo Alto traffic. *The scientific method didn't prepare me to fear for my life. If I wanted to watch my back, I would have joined the mafia.* She blinked, squeezing the tears from her eyes.

The streetlight changed, and she passed under the state highway, escaping to the tree-lined freedom of

University Avenue.

Coeds sunbathed on the lawns and rang their bicycle bells. Tourists clogged the footpaths.

She shook her head. *How quickly they forget death.* Making her way through the maze of buildings, she stopped at the edge of the police tape bordering the lab. The taped perimeter separated debris and spectators, but it did nothing for the hole in her heart. Climbing off her bicycle, she secured it to a bike rack and looked at the void. *Whether my research bears the responsibility for your death or not, Dr. Stefan, I'll finish what I started.* She exhaled. *Nobody doubts your legacy, but I'm so close to making a difference in the world. I wish you were still here to see me do it.*

****

The wide oak trees of Baja Mesa Memorial Park shaded a columbarium. Inside the stone structure, the recovered remains of Dr. Stefan rested in peace. Hadley stood next to Gary and wished the shade extended to the lawn.

A crowd of faculty, students, and press wore jeans and semi-formal attire.

She bore the midday heat in a formal, black dress. *Dr. Stefan's at peace; that should be enough.* Searching for a spot of brightness, she looked at the multinational students. Dr. Stefan's mourners wore wrinkled polos and poorly ironed dress shirts, but he would have worn a formal suit and a pocket square. She sighed. *Wrappings don't matter. Compared to Chinese funeral customs, this gathering looks downright pedantic.* She held a hand against her chest and took comfort in her heartbeat. *He went out with a bang, but we're still here. The least we can do is to memorialize him with solemnity and praise.* She scanned the crowd, searching for Johann and his infamous brother.

Hands clasped behind his dark suit jacket, Johann stood to the side of the podium. He shook hands with a distinguished man, stepped back, and offered the man the podium.

Why do men look so good in suits? Focusing on the event, she bit her lip and swallowed.

The white-haired speaker adjusted the microphone. "My words are inadequate to convey my grief, but I will do my best to deliver my remarks." Pushing his way through his prepared remarks, the German settled into a cadence. "Dr. zur Hausen's Nobel Prize laid the foundation for the generations of students who will follow in his footsteps."

Waiting for the eulogy to end, she focused on the columbarium. *That's what I'm afraid will happen.* Designed to hold cremated remains, the building looked like a piece of modern art. Wreaths of lilies framed the entrance.

"We begged Dr. zur Hausen to return to his homeland and serve as the Director and Head of the Department of Neurochemistry." The speaker cleared his throat and continued. "Friedrich Dürrenmatt said, 'Dealing with death is the root of culture,' but we were not ready to surrender Dr. Stefan."

Her throat constricted, and she swallowed.

"Today, we bear witness to Dr. Stefan's life. Before leaving this lawn, permit yourself the luxury of a tear. Before turning the next page of your notebook, pause for a moment of grief. Remember this man who touched your lives. At some point, a small, marble shrine will mark Dr. zur Hausen's life, but your memories of the man are fresh. Strive to preserve the spirit of innovation that led Dr. Stefan to sign his letters, '*Lindere den Schmerz deiner Freunde und Feinde.*' "

Gary leaned toward her. "What the hell does that mean?"

She glanced at him. "Mitigate the pain of your friends and enemies."

He scratched his scalp and twisted his face.

"Empathy was the driver behind his life." She pitched her voice to avoid disturbing the other guests. "He felt taking away the pain of his friends and enemies was his job."

"Your advisor was weird." Gary swatted a fly from his nose.

She gaped. "Seriously? The man's dead."

A mourner shushed her.

Gary shrugged. "I thought the German was bad enough. Did you guys have to coin taglines, too?"

She thought of her mentor's milky-blue eyes and smiled. "Yes."

The speaker concluded to a smattering of applause.

A park attendant closed the door of the columbarium, signaling the end of the service.

A woman wearing a black lace veil wailed.

Hadley struggled to identify the woman, but her shaded profile revealed few details. *Could she be a lover? Dr. Stefan revealed nothing about his personal life, but I can't ignore the presence of his nephews. Who else stands in this crowd, ready to mourn or vilify him?*

Gary straightened his blazer. "Are you coming to dinner?"

She shook her head and stood. "I want a few minutes to say goodbye. When I'm done, I'll grab my bike and head home."

"In that dress?"

She nodded and fingered the loose, black skirt.

He looked over his shoulder. "If you change your mind, I'll come get you."

Biting her lip, she managed a smile. "Thanks, Gar-Bear."

One-by-one, a series of black town cars carried dignitaries and relatives to a funeral meal at a local restaurant. She watched Johann accept condolences and direct the crowd. Nobody matched his resolute, blue-eyed countenance. *Setting aside pride and making amends is the easiest thing in the world. Where is his brother?*

An hour passed, and the honorifics drifted away.

She remained, staring at the columbarium and listening to the quiet songs of the birds. *What would my peers say about me? Did I get lucky with my research? Am I the speed bump, and the credit all belongs to Dr. Stefan?* Closing her eyes, she rubbed her temples. *What if the shadows are real? I can't lose my life before I prove my worth.*

A cloud passed in front of the sun. Registering the shadows, she glanced around the lawn and realized two other people remained. The attendant from the memorial park wore a navy suit with an embroidered crest over his left breast pocket. He toyed with something in his pocket, and the sunglasses shading his eyes suggested an endless capacity for patience. *At least one of us understands the certainty of death.*

Johann stood to her right.

Lifting her chin, she searched for the citrus hints she caught in Dr. Stefan's office. *A long time has passed since I've thought of anything but my research. Instead of living inside the cloistered walls of academia, I need to socialize. I need to stretch my limbs, act like a tourist, and find a friendly audience.*

Turning, he made eye contact.

All thoughts of performing vanished. His bright-blue eyes reminded her of a younger version of Dr. Stefan. Widening her eyes, she felt her heart clench, and she gasped.

He closed the distance, drew her close, and wrapped her in his arms.

Laying her head on his chest, she sobbed. The upwelling of grief shook her body like a dam losing control. Mourners streamed past them, but she hid her face until the sobbing subsided. Pulling away, she wiped her eyes. "I'm sorry."

He cupped her elbow. "Are you sure?"

Dragging two hands across her face, she nodded. After Jecca's death, she thought her tears had run dry. "I'm o-okay. You should leave for the funeral meal."

Shaking his head, he pulled a handkerchief from his breast pocket and offered her the fine cloth. "That is unnecessary. I dislike attention."

She dabbed her eyes. "The code of conduct."

A smile cracked his façade. Dropping his grasp, he straightened his tie. "Claustrophobia."

The quiet precision of his words soothed her raw emotions. Swallowing, she looked at the abandoned lawn and wondered what could be more inappropriate than hitting on a man at her advisor's funeral. "I don't want Damon to follow me around town."

Johann raised an eyebrow. "You shouldn't have seen him."

She shoved his handkerchief into her purse. "I have enough shadows."

"I assume the lieutenant offered you protection. Take it."

She sniffled. "I don't want it."

He sighed. "Then you'll have me."

Shaking her head, she cleared her throat. "Dr. Stefan's death has nothing to do with me. I'm insignificant."

"You're not." He stared. "Dr. Stefan loved you."

Tears filled her eyes.

"He loved you like a child. Don't push me away, Hadley. Let me protect you."

She swallowed. "And my research?"

He nodded.

She looked at the pale, two-inch, thin vertical scar marring his right cheek and wondered what kind of violence marked him. The hot, summer breeze teased her senses, blending his earthy citrus scent with the sharp tang of cut grass. Shaking her head, she focused on the turf and the reminder of why she stood on the lawn. *Get over it, Hadley. He's here to mourn and monitor you, not help you scratch an itch.* Shifting her attention to the park attendant, she nodded her thanks for the employee's continued presence. *Well, at least I have a chaperone or a witness to my naïveté.*

The guard nodded.

She turned to leave.

A gunshot silenced the birds.

For a heartbeat, she felt nothing but pressure. Memories ricocheted through her system, the lines blurring reality and creating a rippling confusion. *Not the lab!*

The birds took flight.

Pain seared her forearm's tender flesh. Screaming, she grabbed the gunshot wound. Blood seeped between her fingers.

"Hit the ground!"

At the command, she turned. The guard ran toward her, his hefty weight straining the confines of his suit.

A second shot rang out.

The lawn absorbed the impact of the bullet, and dirt at the guard's feet flew into the air. He dropped to the ground and covered his head.

Pivoting, she searched for the shooter and expected the cold, blue-eyed precision.

Johann dropped to his knee and yanked her to the ground. "Stay down."

Breathing hard, she followed his gaze to the oaks. A figure in the shadows shifted in and out of focus. She realized the solemn grounds offered little protection. Amid the trees and tombs, grief turned her into a sitting duck, but outrage overpowered her desire to run.

The security guard crawled toward her. "Stay low."

His hiss sounded desperate.

Johann remained on his knee. Withdrawing a gun from his suit jacket, he braced his arms and assumed a steady stance. "Come out, Brother."

The gunman shifted with the shadows.

She inhaled and imagined Lieutenant Jayne's reproach during their next question-and-answer session. *How many people will die before you finish your research? Are the results worth the mounting debt?*

A third shot whizzed past Johann's head.

"Don't kill him!"

The security guard whimpered.

Johann ignored her plea and fired his gun.

The figure in the shadows jerked. A moment later, he stumbled and fled.

"Did you just shoot your brother?" Cradling her bleeding arm, she struggled to her feet. "I told you not to shoot him!"

Standing, Johann brushed the grass from his pants. "He shot you first."

She looked at her limb and estimated her blood loss. The thick liquid dripped on the grass, but she could have done worse with a box cutter. "The bullet only grazed my arm."

"I'm a better shot." Grabbing her uninjured arm, he pulled her away from the guard. "Let's go."

She planted her feet. *I am a strong, independent woman. Years of academia dulled my social skills, but I understand the difference between self-preservation and reckless abandon.* She strained her ear, hoping for sirens. *At least Lieutenant Jayne comes with a shield.* "No."

He tugged her into motion.

Pain and confusion permitted her to move her feet.

Nodding, Johann loosened his grip.

"Wait!" She spun to locate the park attendant, but she found him flat on the grass. His hands covered his head, and his sunglasses lay in the grass. "Radio for help!"

The guard looked up.

"Let's go," Johann said.

"I said 'No'." His stone-faced expression gave her second thoughts about her decision, and she stepped back.

"You wish to die on this lawn."

His guttural, hard statement shattered her resistance. *I should have taken his warning seriously. Chaining myself to the police station seems reasonable, but coming here does not.* Swallowing, she looked at the blood seeping from her arm. *Am I next?* "We need to report this incident to the police. Facing the consequences of what we've done is the only solution."

He looked past her shoulder. "You've done nothing."

"Then why are you kidnapping me?"

Exhaling, he shook his head.

The wail of sirens approached.

He looked at her injured arm and met her gaze. "Come with me, please."

The hint of formality comforted her. "We should wait for the police."

"Why?" he asked.

Blood welled through her fingers, and she struggled to ignore the pain "Do people often shoot at you?" His lips hardened into the cynical line of an experienced soldier, and she feared the answer.

"This time won't be the last." He looked at the blood trailing down her arm. "Use the handkerchief to stop the blood. You're ruining your frock."

She eyed the gun in his other hand. He held it with quiet confidence, barrel pointed to the ground. *Fuck the dress.* Looking up, she narrowed her gaze.

"I won't hurt you, Hadley."

Believing him, she exhaled, pulled the linen from her purse, and pressed the fabric against her arm. Her nerves screamed, and she cursed. "I should have stayed in the lab."

He put a hand on her back and applied pressure.

The latent strength of the gesture felt different from his commanding grip. Accepting the pressure and warmth, she followed his lead.

"My uncle spoke fondly of you," he said.

She glanced over her shoulder. "He didn't ask you to shoot a man on my behalf."

Johann nodded. "No, his generation wouldn't have done that. His only warning would have been a quiet word. He knew how to change his ways or bear the consequences."

She stumbled. "Civil discourse."

He caught her elbow. "Backed by brutality."

Looking around, watched the security guard raise his head. "Maybe I should wait for the police."

Johann urged her forward. "Most people would say 'thank you for saving my life.' "

She thought about the figure in the shadows. *Had Johann's bullet found its mark?* "I don't think the shooter wanted to kill me. All three times, he missed."

"My brother is a terrible shot."

She rolled her eyes. Years of northern California politics buttressed her sense of right and wrong, but Johann's shooting stance looked polished and resolute. "Is that why you didn't kill him?"

He stared straight ahead. "I grazed his leg. He gets one warning."

Hearing the menace behind his vow, she shuddered and wondered what history they shared. "What happened to learning-curves?"

A smile cracked his stiff façade. "Günter has fallen off the curve more times than I can count."

She shifted the blood-stained handkerchief. "This type of shit doesn't happen to me." She flexed her arm and watched the blood well. "To skip the ache of messy relationships, I buried myself in research."

"Life doesn't spare cowards."

Jerking her gaze away from the wound, she exhaled. "Now you tell me." Taking a deep breath, she struggled to compartmentalize the fear and uncertainty crowding out her life's work. *Every hour spent worrying about my safety erodes the time I have available for research. Coincidences don't form patterns. Dr. Stefan drilled that fact into my head, but why would Günter care if I created a non-addictive alternative to opioids?*

Looking over her shoulder for answers, she saw a cowering security guard and a swarm of first responders occupying the lawn. She sighed, knowing she needed time to untangle the events of the last week. "Um, thank you for saving my life."

Nodding, he dropped his hand.

The subtle pressure at the base of her spine disappeared, and she regretted the absence. *Would he have let me run?*

"You're welcome."

His softened voice sounded like the gentle abrasion of a favorite sweater, the kind she turned to when winter's damp chill overwhelmed the heaters. No matter how many times she washed the sweater, pulling the woolen fabric over her head felt like coming home. *Why does Johann's touch make me want to arch my back and purr?*

"Wait!"

Stumbling, she looked over her shoulder.

Johann gripped her good arm.

The guard rose to his feet and took several steps toward them. "You can't go!"

The confusion on his face implored her to stay, but she moved closer to Johann. "I'll give you an hour to explain how you plan to deal with your brother."

He nodded and replaced his hand at the small of her back. "That will be enough."

I hope so.

Chapter Four

Hadley considered the matte-gray luxury sedan parked on the side of the street. *Does the company make other colors?* "What happened to the SUV?"

Johann opened the passenger door. "Get in."

Hesitating, she held her injured arm close to her body. His chivalrous gesture brought her back to the Greek restaurant. "I'll get blood on your seat."

After staring at the leather, he looked up. "My housekeeper will remove it."

She blinked and considered her options. *What would I do if the man led me to a dented van? I'd probably run like hell and wave down a stranger.* She looked at his brilliant blue eyes and thought of the hours she spent reviewing source materials and techniques with Dr. Stefan.

"Decide, Hadley."

Swallowing, she lowered her body to the warm, leather seat and tucked her legs into the dark footwell. Bits of grass clung to her heels, and she wondered if she should blaze a trail of DNA across the door panel.

Johann rounded the hood.

His glacial blue eyes matched his heritage, but still waters ran deep. *They're just as capable of obscuring hidden dangers.*

Sliding into the driver's seat, he checked the rearview mirror.

A police cruiser passed the car and pulled into the parking lot.

"Here's your first lesson, Hadley: Never leave your escape vehicle in a parking lot."

She gaped. "I don't want lessons. Tell me why your brother hates you and take me to the emergency room. Your clock is ticking. I have no problem calling the police."

He put the car in gear. "Second lesson: Don't make threats unless you intend to follow through with them."

She shifted away from his censure and looked out the window. "I'm not threatening you."

"Aren't you? I can almost hear you cataloging my features. I'll save you the trouble. Six feet, two inches, two-hundred pounds." He revved the engine.

She looked at his chiseled profile. "Shouldn't you use metric?"

He smiled. "Aren't you a good, little scientist?"

Bristling from his condescending tone, she pulled his handkerchief from her wound. A thin rivulet of blood ran down her arm and dripped on his upholstery. She waited for a reaction and considered doing it again to rile him. "If someone shoots you, that information will be handy."

"Lesson number three: People don't shoot me; I shoot them."

She slumped in the seat and leaned her head against the headrest. "I don't want any part of this game. Why didn't your parents come to the funeral? Let them referee their overgrown man-children."

He slowed for a stoplight. "Uncle Stefan and my father, Rudolf, had a falling out."

"At least it didn't end in a shootout."

A curt nod, and he checked the rearview mirror. "Children grow up and mediate their family drama. Life goes on."

She thought of the years since Jecca's death and her mother's spiraling addiction to prescription opioids. *I wasn't ready to grow up.* Looking in the side mirror, she saw the distinctive light array of a police cruiser and wondered what plan Johann would reveal.

The light changed, and he eased off the brake.

The purring restraint of the car's massive engine barely made a sound. "If you drove a compact car, you'd be more inconspicuous."

"Compacts can be good cars." He shifted. "This sedan is the company's best-selling model. It has six hundred horsepower and over six hundred foot-pounds of torque. Should I tell you how fast it goes in sixty seconds?"

"No."

He smiled. "Let's just say a compact cannot keep up."

Can I? Leaning back, she focused on the panorama roof and the lull of rippling shadows. Her arm ached, but shock buffered the pain, and the blood no longer flowed. *I should call Gary.*

The car climbed the foothill roads toward the rustic, residential enclave of *Las Colinas*. The neighborhood's large, custom-built homes and stunning San Francisco vistas made the enclave one of the most desired spots on the Peninsula. She leaned her head against the car's soft leather interior. "I figured you would stay at a hotel like The Dalbergia."

"I doubt I could bring you through the lobby dripping blood."

"Then where are we going?" she asked.

"My home."

He made decisions without asking her, but the alternatives paled in comparison. One look at her townhouse, and he would laugh. She looked out the window and considered the tree-lined hillside. The homes sat back from the road, surrounded by enough acreage to create privacy amid the very wealthy. *Like this man would live anywhere else.* She turned her head and stared. "I thought you were visiting."

"Did you?" He glanced to his right. "You know I have local investments."

She snorted. "Everybody on this planet is an investor."

He smiled. "The holding company doesn't run itself. I oversee our subsidiary's policies and management decisions, but I don't run day-to-day operations."

"So you let other people do the work?"

He kept his gaze on the road. "That's one way of looking at it."

She crossed her arms. "What's another?"

"Companies need my money to accomplish their work."

The truth hit too close to home. She pulled out her cell phone, and the strength of the signal amid the golden, oak-covered hills surprised her. "I have to make a call."

"The car has a repeater."

She rolled her eyes. "Of course it does." Her response sounded bratty, but she looked at him and saw his wide smile. Feeling her cheeks warm, she considered the way his smile transformed his face. The subtle web of laugh lines softened his granite features and hinted at hidden warmth.

He glanced away from the road.

She focused on his eyes, wondering if the color changed with his mood. *What would have happened if I'd met you on a sunny beach? I'd have been too shy to utter a single word.* She stared out the windshield.

Johann rounded a curve, and a thick, metal gate appeared at the end of the road. He slowed the sedan.

She watched his movements, looking for signs of impatience while he fumbled with a gate controller or entered a code. *What happens when he can't control the world?*

The gate swung open without a discernible command.

Dammit. She looked out the window.

Winding the car through a tunnel of Italian Cypress trees, he kept both hands on the wheel.

The foliage gave way to a sleek, gray estate. Floor-to-ceiling panoramic, glass walls mirrored acres of vineyard grapes. Shutting her mouth, she faced him. "How many companies are in your portfolio?"

"Enough." Skirting her gaze, he parked the car on stone pavers and walked around the vehicle.

Asshole. She gripped the handkerchief and struggled to climb out of the low-slung car.

"Allow me to assist you," he said.

Looking up, she met his gaze. *What choice do I have?* Accepting his hand, she felt the strength in his grip as he pulled her to a stand. As soon as she found her footing, the contact vanished. *My choices don't matter. I'm a means to an end.*

Turning, he strode toward the front door.

Instead of blooming containers, she found two, abstract steel statues. *I doubt he does a lot of entertaining.* Resolved, she followed him through the front door and recognized the pattern of preferences linking his possessions. Walnut cabinetry and stainless-steel appliances anchored an open floor plan. In the middle of the room, white leather furniture and cold, expensive tchotchkes suggested a decorator's touch.

Beyond the floor-to-ceiling windows, expansive concrete decking gave way to the oaks and vineyard rows. Distant views of the city captured her attention, and the luxurious house receded from her thoughts. "It's beautiful."

He walked up. "I agree."

Turning, she considered him. "Did you build this house?"

He nodded. "The view sold me."

The intensity of his gaze felt too personal. Frowning, she considered the oak-covered hills dipping toward the bay. *He probably scouted the land with satellite imagery and made the owner an offer they couldn't refuse.*

Heels clicked on the floor.

Turning, Hadley saw a woman wearing a gray sheath dress. Her severe, black hairstyle and heavy, foundation-based makeup added a decade to her looks. *The housekeeper.*

The woman frowned.

Hadley exposed her wounded arm.

Widening her eyes, the housekeeper opened a cabinet and withdrew a box of supplies and a thick, white towel. She placed the medical gear on the polished concrete countertop and busied herself in the kitchen.

"Thank you," Hadley said.

The woman nodded.

Johann gestured toward a barstool. "Have a seat."

Complying, she peeled the handkerchief from her arm. The action tore the clot, and the blood flowed. Wincing, she blinked back tears of frustration and looked up.

His gaze softened. "Would you like a drink?"

She swallowed the pain and gripped the counter. "Yes."

He removed his suit jacket and draped it across the back of a white leather couch.

Beneath his shoulder, a leather holster held his gun like an extension of his skin. Standing, she walked to the kitchen sink, turned on the water, and let the cooling liquid wash away her blood.

The housekeeper placed a clean dishtowel near her elbow.

Nodding her thanks, she dabbed at the wound and watched Johann.

He poured a measure of whiskey into a crystal glass, walked to a wall devoted to wine storage, and selected a bottle of red wine.

His muscles shifted beneath his shirt, and she looked away. *He's completely at home with violence. With or without the gun, he could injure me, but what a way to go.* The joke felt too close to home, and she bit her lip to remember her circumstances.

He placed a glass of wine on the counter.

She glanced at the splashes of blood filling his kitchen sink. The colors looked too similar. "In a minute."

He nodded and sipped his whiskey.

"I thought sobriety was an advantage."

Raising his eyebrows, he saluted her. "Dulled senses can be an advantage. *Prost.*"

Lifting her glass, she raised it to her lips. "I should maintain my guard."

"You should." Setting aside his drink, he opened the box of supplies.

The housekeeper rushed to his side.

"I have it," he said.

She backed into the kitchen's work triangle and wiped the immaculate counters.

Extending her arm, Hadley steeled herself for pain. "Your plan."

He dabbed the damp towel against her wound. "In time."

She winced. "Just do it."

Nodding, his approach shifted.

His sure, deliberate strokes cleaned the wound, but her nerves screamed in protest. She retracted her arm, but he held it fast. The show of strength gave her something on which to focus, but the anchor summoned an unexpected response. Thick veins rose across his tanned skin, and dark hair brushed the crisp edge of his shirt. *The man works out.*

He looked up. "Most people would have fainted by now."

She clenched her teeth. "Fainting would have been smarter." Glancing at her glass of red wine, she wondered how fast she could finish the bottle. *So much for dulled senses.*

"If you had fainted, I would have left you at the cemetery."

"Perhaps that would have been smarter."

The housekeeper laughed.

Johann frowned. Extruding clear gel from a tube, he cupped Hadley's forearm and swabbed the ointment along the wound.

His hand warmed her skin, the gel lessened the pain, and she exhaled. Small droplets of blood escaped the protective shield. She encountered hemostatic treatments in her research, but most of those drugs stung or were noticeably exothermic. "What is it?"

He wrapped gauze around her arm. "Proprietary."

She frowned and avoided making eye contact to hide her frustration. Reaching for the cabernet, she held the wine in her mouth long enough to wonder if she imagined the clove and licorice flavors. "Your wine and your ointment are excellent."

A half-smile tugged at his lips, but he turned and walked toward the windows. "I have a cooperating arrangement with a local winery. The pretentious owner cashes my checks and claims my grapes go into the wine."

The thought of him rolling up his suit pants and stomping the grapes almost made her forget the wound. "Do you believe him?"

Shrugging, he shook the ice in his glass.

She watched his Adam's apple move.

"The grapes disappear, and the concept amuses me." He cleared his throat. "The gel is effective?"

She raised her arm and examined the bandage. The gel would buy military combatants time to flee, first responders time to evacuate, and athletes time to shatter records. Endless commercial possibilities swirled in her mind, and she searched for a flaw. "How long will the numbing effects last?"

"Twenty-four hours."

She met his gaze. "We agreed on one."

Nodding, he pushed the medical supplies to the side of the counter. "So we did."

The housekeeper whisked away the goods.

Johann cleared his throat. "Hadley, you are a smart woman. Nobody accidentally fires three shots."

She swallowed the heavy implications and focused on the man standing in the room. "Why did you fire back?"

"He presented a threat."

"That's not enough," she said.

"I've never shot a person unless I feared for my life or for those under my protection." His jaw tensed. "You are under my protection."

He moved so effortlessly with his gun, she wondered if it felt like an extension of his body. Her entire life, she relegated the machines to backwoods hunters, criminals, and civil enforcement, but none of those characters poured her wine. "I didn't ask you to protect me."

He nodded and looked toward the distant views. "My uncle did."

"Well, he's dead." She winced and felt the heavy silence in the room. "I'm sorry. That comment was careless. I'm on edge."

"Understandable." He paced the cold, formal room and sipped his whiskey. "May I tell you a story?"

She looked at the housekeeper.

The woman nodded.

"Please." Hadley adjusted her seat.

Johann cleared his throat. "When I was eighteen

years old, a university student kidnapped and murdered Jonas von Becker. He was an eleven-year-old boy from a banking dynasty. I was an idealistic youth with an overbearing patriarch."

She refused to let tragedies fall like a line of dominoes. Swirling her wine, she lifted the glass and sipped. "I'm sorry. Watching the news feels like a downward spiral."

Johann set down his glass and crossed his arms. "That child ran around our family picnics."

Hearing the pain behind his admission, she tilted her head and wondered if he mourned Jonas or the vestiges of his youth. "I'm sorry, Johann." His name sounded formal and mature. "I appreciate your loss."

He cleared his throat. "Discretion does not ensure success."

The moment of vulnerability vanished, and she imagined his voice commanding a boardroom.

"Jonas' death affected my brother and me in different ways. Günter withdrew. He spent weeks watching the trial and questioning the coverage. I learned to protect myself. Uncle Stefan knew I could protect you."

"How?" She frowned.

His hands encompassed the living room. "You are here."

"How did you learn to protect yourself?" Her question felt more substantial than she expected. Isolated in a near-stranger's luxurious home, she felt vulnerable to his whims, but she sensed his story's gravity.

"I joined the *Bundeskriminalamt*. The Federal Criminal Police Office provides twenty-four-hour protection for Germany's highest-ranking politicians. Even though the *Kanzleramt* is ten times larger than the White House, all German state leaders maintain private homes and preserve the right to go about their business." He cleared his throat. "My uncle knew I traded years of service with the BKA for the peace of mind of understanding my limits."

"The bomb obliterated my limits." She sighed. "A rich kid bodyguard. Did the instructors let you skip the class on manners?"

He rolled up his sleeves. "I assure you, few elected officials mind their manners."

"But how did you do your job? Wasn't your presence a distraction?"

"My father walks down the street without notice because the family code of conduct guards our businesses and our lives. Discretion removes publicity and threats."

"You radiate threats."

He cocked his head. "Do I?"

Exhaling, she looked away and marveled at the lack of pain in her arm. Flexing her fingers, she watched her tendons move without the systemic effects of oral pain relievers. *If I never felt pain, what would happen to my life? The body's reaction is an evolutionary development. Run, hide, and lick your wounds.* She reached for her phone. "I'm calling a lift."

The sun sank beneath the western horizon. Far from industrial development, it left behind soft, pink skies and clear, evening air.

He straightened a stack of books. "You can stay in the guest house."

Shaking her head, she focused on her phone. "No,

thank you."

Walking over, he removed the device from her hand. "Your research makes you vulnerable. Uncle Stefan told me you're onto something big."

She stilled. *How did Dr. Stefan know?* Staring at Johann, she questioned her assumptions about family loyalty and the shades of black and white governing the world. *When the other person holds a gun, deviations and percentage points leave room for permanent error.* "If you know what I discovered, why didn't you protect your uncle?"

Without glancing at the screen, he put her phone on the counter and leaned close and jabbed the counter. "Don't let Uncle Stefan's eccentric knowledge base fool you."

This close, she tried to focus on his words and ignore the heat of his skin.

"Uncle Stefan knew the risks of your research, and he knew the implications of Günter's call. My brother refused to sign the code of conduct, burnt through his trust, and filled the social pages with exploits, but he is intentional and absolute." Johann straightened. "Searching the family for weaknesses to exploit sounds just like Günter."

She wanted to pull him closer and figure out why he smelled so good. Instead, she leaned back and braced her arms on the counter. "Killing Dr. Stefan was a bit of overkill."

Johann nodded. "I concur. Perhaps he held a grudge."

She cocked her head. "I'm glad I'm not part of your family."

He crossed his arms. "In my experience, people

choose life over uncomfortable circumstances."

She tilted her head. "I'm still here, aren't I?"

Clearing his throat, he stared at the twilight-tinged vineyard grapes. "You are."

"So, whatever is going on with you and your brother"—she gestured toward the room and the unfathomable experiences of her afternoon—"I don't want any part of it. Get him under control, and get me out of this mess."

Issuing a verbal command, he activated the panoramic, floor-to-ceiling glass walls.

The walls retracted and admitted the evening breeze.

Unable to resist, she gravitated toward the open space. The freedom of the seamless indoor-outdoor layout gave her room to breathe and inhale the cooling air. Crickets chirped in the oak trees, and an owl hooted in the distance.

Johann walked to her side. "You want to release your findings into the public domain."

She nodded. "Public access."

"I believe Günter pressured Uncle Stefan to grant a sole license for your research. When that failed, he eliminated Stefan and came after you." Johann shook his head. "Such a child."

She replayed the chaotic days following the explosion. "Why did he wait for a public gathering?" Carrying her wine glass toward the open air, she let the night's soft vibrations soothe her uncertainties. "Why don't you share your suspicions with the police?"

He snorted. "You've met them."

Thinking of Lieutenant Jayne's eager bravado, she knew he would pale against someone of Johann's size and intent. "The FBI might be more appropriate."

"I have similar resources," he said. "Trust me. I can deal with my brother."

Turning, she put down her wine glass on the firepit's edge and considered him. *He uses verbal commands to activate an integrated home automation system, wears a holster with the ease of a leather belt, and drives an ostentatious sedan with the aggressive precision of someone who enjoys testing the* Autobahn's *limits.* Despite the freedom of the evening breeze, she bit her lip and brainstormed other ways to secure her safety. "People don't look to pampered execs for their investigative abilities."

"Uncle Stefan knew I could protect you." He gripped her elbow and turned her to face him. "Take advantage of what I'm offering."

She pushed against his chest. *The only thing I want to take advantage of is you.* No longer fighting tears, she felt the tension in his embrace and the allure of succumbing to his protection. Spreading her fingers, she inhaled and smelled warmth where she expected coolness. Looking up, she focused on the two-inch scar marring his face and knew he would never give her a second glance to be this close. "I'd like to leave now."

He lifted her chin. "Would you?"

Pressing her lips against his, she stole the kiss he withheld. His lips softened, and she broke contact, sighing for what she could not have. "I don't need a protector."

Lifting her hand, he ghosted her fingertips along the scar. "When Günter and I were children, he hurt me. He is cold and manipulative."

She brushed the late-day stubble on his skin but

pulled back her hand. "He struck you?"

"While I slept, he cut me with a knife. He meant to blind me."

Clutching a hand against her chest, she wondered whether Johann chose California for its climate or for its distance from his brother. "Why would he do that?"

Johann released his hold. "He wanted something of mine."

"Did you retaliate?"

He shook his head. "I was fast enough to escape."

She analyzed the echoes of vulnerability and hope flashing across his features.

His gaze focused. "And then I became faster."

Considering her position and the pristine bandage on her arm, she stepped back. "I don't want any part of this family reunion."

His jaw ticked, and he grabbed her uninjured arm. "Günter is desperate. He will come after you until you relinquish your research or die saving it."

The bullet's pain was too fresh to forget. Instead of fearing death, she considered the hand wrapped around her skin. A stranger's touch should alarm her, but his relationship with Dr. Stefan lent Johann familiarity and security. *Nephew or not, I've met enough jerks to understand the value of space.* "Release me."

Flexing his hand, he complied. "I'm sorry."

She believed him. "If Günter wants the research, why would he kill me?"

"He blew most of his inheritance." Johann exhaled. "Why buy what you can steal?"

She rolled her eyes. "I'll publish what I found and sic the university on him."

Johann snorted. "I'm sure that strategy would be

effective."

His condescending tone spoke volumes, but she hated the thought of admitting her vulnerabilities.

He stared at her lips. "Until I can flush him out, stay in the guesthouse."

She scanned the vineyards. "The guesthouse?"

"It's very comfortable, and you'll have everything you need." He cleared his throat. "I prefer to keep this battle out of the press."

Cradling her arm, she shook her head and stepped back. "I have to finish my research."

"The anesthetic will wear off in twenty-four hours. You won't want to touch anything, much less type or operate delicate machinery."

Scrambling to find a solution to his observation, she focused on the things she could control. "I'll stay at my apartment. Nobody will see me hunt and peck."

He scoffed, stepped away, and faced the city view. "For an intelligent woman, you have zero common sense. Silicon Valley's wealthiest residents live in these hills. Spend a day doing nothing and borrow a school horse from the Community Barn."

"I can't ride a horse with one hand."

"Go hiking in the Preserve." He shrugged. "Poke around the open space. What do you Americans call it? A staycation?"

"You would let me do that?" she asked. "Just loaf around and pretend to be idly rich?"

He nodded. "With an armed escort."

She stretched her jaw and considered the hillside. "Most staycations don't come with armed escorts."

"Women trip over themselves to stay here."

She snorted and looked at him.

He raised an eyebrow.

"Do you let them?" she asked.

"I'm letting you." He frowned. "Though you don't seem to want the privilege."

Under any other circumstances, she wanted the privilege naked and playing on repeat until she figured out why the man intrigued her. "Why?"

"I feel responsible for you," he said.

She sighed. *So much for the kiss.* "That's ridiculous."

He cocked his head. "Is it?"

"Yes, it is." She looked at her sleek surroundings and wondered whether the side tables held arsenals and the guesthouse came with a panic room. "I've always been particular about my accommodations. You want to play bodyguard? Guard me at my home."

He advanced toward her but stopped short of making contact. "Do you understand the threat, Hadley? He killed his uncle. He lashed out. There's no reason he'll stop before he gets what he wants."

Looking at the bandage on her slack arm, she thought of the security guard cowering beneath the memorial oak trees. *Three shots, but two of them missed. What if the fourth had found its home?* She swallowed. "I understand the threat."

He stared.

Standing straight, she camouflaged her weakness and fatigue. *I won't give ground. He owns so much of it already.* "My house or the lab."

"Fine. We will stay at your house."

She thought he would balk. Looking at the living room's white leather furniture and the busy housekeeper, she reconsidered her ultimatum. "My house doesn't have the same amenities."

"I will sleep on your couch."

He walked into the house with the precision of a general preparing for war. *We'll see how long you last in my world, rich man.* "Johann?" Clearing her throat, she raised her voice to span the distance.

He turned. "Yes?"

"Your hour is up."

He nodded.

"I have one condition." She held up her finger.

"Tell me about your condition."

In any war, strategy can best strength. "Give me the formula for the pain-relieving gel."

He started. "That's what you want?"

A slow smile warmed the precision of his features. The glimpse of approachability softened her approach. Surrounded by luxury and sun-drenched Californians, his loneliness had verged on bitterness. *I want you to reunite with your brother. I want you to have the chance I never had.* Shrugging, she rubbed her arm. "The formulation intrigues me."

Walking into the kitchen, he retrieved the gel and tossed her the container. "You'll figure it out."

She slipped the container into her skirt pocket.

He walked close. "You'll heed my warnings for a week and give me time to lure my brother into an intervention."

His voice, barely above a whisper, sent chills racing across her skin. She swallowed. "That's all you'll get. After the week passes, I don't care how many assassins creep through the bushes." She walked her fingers up his shirt. "If I need protection, I'll let domestic security forces protect my ass."

He smiled. "Lucky officers."

She laughed and dropped her hand. Surprising him felt almost as good as kissing him, but she doubted she would have the chance to do either very often.

"I'm sure Palo Alto's finest would do you proud."

The statement grounded her thoughts, and she replayed Lieutenant Jayne's boast. *Would the officer shoot to kill?*

Johann cleared his throat. "The mission of the BKA is Protect, Salvage, and Evacuate."

She swallowed and looked at him. "What stage is this?"

"Salvage."

Thinking of Dr. Stefan, she touched her arm. "I thought you would say 'protect'."

He looked past her.

A ghost of regret softened his features, and she wondered what mistakes he made in the past.

"You don't understand the threat." Shaking his head, he walked off the patio.

He misses his brother. The glimmer of vulnerability cemented her resolve. Afraid of what she might find in the darkness, she entered the house.

"Is there anything I can do to help you, Mr. zur Hausen?" the housekeeper asked.

Her accent marked her as a nonnative English speaker, but her bright lipstick and narrowed gaze conveyed a no-nonsense dedication to Johann, his house, and her determination to manage Hadley like an unwanted insect. She swallowed. *I won't attempt to charm her with my Spanish.*

Johann withdrew his phone and tapped the screen. "Silvia, please make Miss Hadley Heron comfortable.

In the coming week, you'll see a lot of her."

Silvia raised an eyebrow defined by a black brow pencil. "Comfortable?"

Hadley swallowed and cleared her throat. "Thank you. I am quite comfortable."

"*Puta codicia.*"

She gasped. "Did you just call me a whore?"

The housekeeper cocked her head. "Excuse me, Miss Heron?"

"I must have misunderstood what you said."

The housekeeper smiled and turned to Johann. "Will the two of you eat here tonight?"

Johann fired off a string of text messages. "I don't think so. It's been an interesting day. Miss Heron would probably prefer to spend her time in neutral territory. Is Damon on staff tonight?"

Is he joking? She thought about their first meeting at the Greek restaurant and wondered how her life could have changed in so little time. *Dr. Stefan should still be with us.* "Maybe we can pick up burgers on our way to my apartment."

The housekeeper put her hands on her hips. "I have steaks."

"I like steak." She held up her hands. "Really, I don't want to be any trouble."

Johann looked up and cracked a smile. "Hadley, you define trouble."

She returned his smile and glanced at Silvia, hoping for a merry trio.

The woman raised her lined eyebrows. "*¿Creerse la última cerveza en el desierto?*"

She blinked. *I have no idea what she said. Beer?*

Johann put down his phone. "Silvia, stop insulting

Miss Heron in Spanish. If you want to go head-to-head with the woman, do it in English."

The housekeeper smiled and blinked her eyes. "Yes, Mr. zur Hausen."

Unsure if she would win the next battle, Hadley swallowed.

Chapter Five

Hadley watched Johann retreat down a hallway lined with solid bedroom doors. Lights followed his progress and extinguished in his wake. Left alone with Silvia, she swallowed, poured another glass of wine, and fished out her cell phone. *Until this wound heals, life will be awkward.* She juggled the device, set it on the concrete countertop, and turned on the speakerphone. "Call Gar-Bear."

"Calling Gar-Bear," the digital assistant confirmed.

Gary answered on the first ring. "Where are you?"

She scanned the hillside and chose geography over details. "In Los Altos."

"I thought you were going home. Why didn't you come to Dr. zur Hausen's dinner?"

Working with the brilliant man fed her intellectual curiosity, but facing scores of curious mourners terrified her. At any moment, a well-meaning faculty member would ask her about Dr. Stefan, and she would break into tears. Closing her eyes, she released a deep breath. "Lately everything's been a bit too much."

"I hear that, but I'm…"

The line went quiet. She wondered if they had a poor connection.

"…surprised you're out on the town."

Not exactly. "Gar-Bear, we have a problem." Cutting through her complication reaction to Johann, she opened her eyes and focused on facts. "Someone fired a gun at the cemetery, and the bullet grazed my arm."

Silvia looked up.

Gary stayed quiet.

Hadley checked her reception. The screen displayed a full flight of bars, and the call timer ticked higher and higher. "Did you hear me?"

"What?" he asked.

His question sounded too impatient for a long story. She reached for her wine and strolled the room. "In the park, someone shot me and wounded me." She cleared her throat. "In the aftermath, I also acquired a very precise, autocratic guardian angel."

"Does this have anything to do with Dr. zur Hausen's death?" Gary asked.

She reached toward an abstract canvas on the wall and stopped herself. "What else could it be?"

He cleared his throat. "I'm glad the shooter missed you."

Are you? Looking up, she found Johann standing at the room's edge holding a weekender and a garment bag.

He cocked his head.

She swallowed. "So considering the threat, said guardian angel is staying with us for the time being."

"What? We don't have a lot of space," Gary said.

Thinking of the Scandinavian futon occupying their living room, she smiled. Multiple university students had passed out or thrown up on the exalted piece of furniture. "He said he'd sleep on the couch."

"Whatever, Haddie. You always do what you want to do."

The concession soothed her, and she picked up the phone to end the call. "Thanks, Gar-Bear, I'll catch you later."

"Actually, I'm going out. The animal shelter organized a fundraiser, and I promised to help run the raffle. After we close the doors, the other volunteers and I will probably get drinks."

"You're going out?" She looked at Johann and took the phone off speaker. "Is that safe?" Hoping her whispered question remained in the hilltop mansion, she shifted the phone to her ear.

Johann shrugged. "His choice."

Thanks for having my back, you German asshole. She smiled and hoped the expression sweetened her tone. "Gar-Bear, why don't you stay home?" Based on the experiences over the last decade, redirection had a fifty-fifty chance of success with Gary. "You can meet Johann and join us for takeout."

He snorted. "No thanks. We'll all be there in the morning,"

She sighed. "Fair enough." Ending the call, she stared at the phone.

Johann stood at the edge of the counter. "Do you trust your roommate?"

She retracted her chin and looked up. "Of course I trust Gary. Our parents played tennis together for forty years. We grew up side by side in the juniors program, clutching our first rackets. He's like my brother." Defending her childhood friend felt as natural as drawing a breath.

Handing his luggage to Silvia, Johann lifted his suit jacket. "Childhood intimacies can crumble."

She looked at the distant glow of the city and

thought about Marin County's residents sleeping on the other side of the Golden Gate Bridge. Three hundred thousand people called the county home, but to every child, parental figures mattered the most. "Or the people you trust can stabilize the rest of your life."

Johann opened the front door, waited for her to exit, and opened the passenger door.

"I can operate a car door." She slid past him and claimed her seat.

"Are you always this much trouble?"

She shrugged and reached for the passenger door.

He relinquished his hold. "Of course you are."

The door's muffled close gave her room to breathe. She noticed the wilting blades of grass she left in the footwell. Without his anesthetic gel, she might feel just as limp, but she remained alert.

Walking around the vehicle, he dropped into the driver's seat and pressed the ignition button,

The vehicle lit up.

She shifted in her seat.

He glanced over. "Are you hungry?"

"I could eat." She fiddled with the touch screen and searched for contemporary folk music.

He traced the steering wheel's audio control buttons, but he drove down the hill listening to the college radio station.

Traffic on Sand Hill Road stalled their progress. Peering down the road, she saw a line of cars waiting for a guest to turn left into The Dalbergia Hotel. *I'm surprised he doesn't want to sit at the indoor-outdoor bar and gossip with venture capitalists. The terrace has magnificent views of the surrounding mountains, and he could stake out his claim for Cougar Night.* The car turned, and traffic eased. She risked a glance. *How old is he?*

Near downtown, she watched a man waiting at a red light puff on a cigar. *Maybe Johann prefers Hemmingway chic.* La Bodeguita Norte *isn't too far away.* She stroked the car's soft leather interior. *Hand-rolled cigars wouldn't impress him.* Her stomach rumbled, and hunger undermined her cheerful, defiant resolve. She turned down the radio. "Curbside has car service. I can order two burgers from the app."

"Do it."

Before she could place the order, a notification from Gary lit up her phone. The message contained an image of her roommate crouched next to a long-haired Labrador mix with a lolling tongue. The pup's bow tie and party hat suggested someone at the shelter had a sweet spot for the mutt. "He is so frickin' cute."

Johann shifted in his seat. "Cute?"

She turned the phone toward him. "Look at this heartbreaker."

"I'm driving."

The car probably has autopilot. Respecting his statement, she zoomed in on the picture. "You're missing out. I could spend all night cuddling with him."

"Are you talking about the dog or your roommate?"

At the thought of spending a night tangled up with Gary, she snorted. *We tried that once as undergrads and agreed never to discuss the awkwardness, so long as we both shall live.* "I'm definitely talking about the dog."

"Dogs are messy."

She smiled. "And loyal."

He put on the turn signal. "Most women don't gush over a picture of their friend hamming it up with a dog. Gary means a lot to you."

More than you know. She completed the dinner order and dropped her phone in her purse. "A puppy is a better chick magnet than a sports car."

"I don't need a chick."

"And Gary's not my boyfriend. He's like a floppy, big-eared brother." She smiled. "He loves animals and sports, but not me. At least, not in the way you describe."

Nodding, he made the turn onto the street leading to Curbside. "If you sent him a similar picture, would he gush?"

"Gush? He would probably sketch a blunt on the picture and send it right back." She stared out the window. "I trust him with my life."

"That's what I needed to know."

Turning, she met his gaze. "For Curbside, turn left at the next light."

"Silvia's steak is delicious."

She smiled. *Does it come with a side of arsenic?*

At the local hamburger bistro, she and Johann ate on metal picnic tables. He was as fastidious with french fries as he was at the Greek restaurant. *I shouldn't have kissed him.* "Tell me something about Dr. Stefan."

Johann wiped his mouth. "He kept a bottle of digestif bitters in his desk drawer."

"No!"

Nodding, he looked toward the glowing entrance to a corporate campus.

She popped another fry in her mouth. *This land used to belong to cattle ranchers. Is Johann's office nearby?* After the hamburger, she opened the passenger door and let her food coma and her trust in Johann erase her worries. Feeling the seat warmers kick in, she smiled.

"Your color's back," he said.

She smiled. "I could sleep."

"Do it."

I'd rather do you. Yawning, she leaned back her head and closed her eyes. Built to impress, the car's rumbling engine soothed her. Feeling the car slow, she blinked and recognized her complex. After the events of the last week, the townhouse's carpeted beige rooms and fenced wooden decking should comfort her, but she acknowledged the overgrown landscaping and rotten wood lent the building an air of general disrepair. When she moved into the unit, she and Gary came to an agreement with the landlord. They funneled their stipends into exorbitant rent, and he ignored mounting code violations. *The townhouse isn't much, but it's ours.*

She directed Johann to a visitor's spot and yawned. Climbing from the vehicle, she approached the flickering, yellow porch light and struggled with the front door lock. Standing beside her, he had the decency to feign ignorance. She jiggled the key and shook the painted, metal door.

The doorknob rattled in response but failed to yield.

Swearing, she kicked a pile of flyers. *Why can't they use our mailbox like the rest of the advertisers?*

Johann broke off a piece of the doorframe, examined the moisture damage, and tossed the scrap in the overgrown bushes.

She watched the exposed wood disappear into the foliage and frowned. *What other discarded scraps and treasures are buried in this ground?*

He took the key from her hand. "Please, let me help you."

Feeling the warmth of his touch, she acquiesced, leaned against the painted exterior, and watched him wrestle with the knob beneath the light. Moths buzzed the exposed bulb. She brushed away the bugs and tightened the bulb.

"You'd be more secure at my house," he said.

"I have a security system." Her defense sounded as weak as the plastic alarm panel waiting inside the townhouse.

Shaking his head, he held the knob and threw his shoulder against the door.

It popped open and the telltale "beep" of the alarm panel waited for a code.

"Is anyone monitoring the system?" he asked.

She shrugged. "The landlord has the complex under contract or something."

He toed a forgotten yellowed newspaper and entered the townhouse. "Unlikely."

She bobbled her head from side to side and mimicked his certainty. *We can't all be millionaires. Wait. Billionaires.* The alarm's beep punctuated her mockery, and she turned to silence it.

A car drove past and slowed.

Cradling her arm, she felt the absence of Johann's solid presence. She stepped inside and moved to enter the alarm code.

Cutting off her progress, he punched in four digits. "I hate those things."

She rolled her eyes. If he thought she left the factory code in place, he had another thing coming.

The panel light glowed red, and a warning alarm beeped.

She smiled and leaned against the wall.

He entered two-two-four-eight.

The light turned green.

Apprehension flamed her exhausted stress hormones. She straightened and felt chills race along her arms. "How do you know my security code?"

Flipping on the lights, he scanned the first floor living room and the kitchen. "The wear pattern shows on the keypad."

Confirming his statement, she wet her lips. "But you shouldn't know the order."

"People often use letter mapping to remember codes. 'A-C-G-T' was a lucky guess." He peered into the kitchen.

Gary's comforting presence would go a long way toward easing the building's menace. She swallowed.

Johann stopped in the middle of the living room and crossed his arms. "You realize you're not the only person in town who understands a nucleic acid sequence?"

She scratched her scalp and struggled to mount a defense.

"Anyone who knows your background could have figured out the code and disarmed your system. Hell, Damon's probably done it while you were out. Predictable."

She looked up. "What other series of letters did you consider?"

Jiggling the lock on an aluminum window, he

shook his head. "Those numbers also spell 'bait'."

"Well, good thing we're not going fishing." She plopped onto the worn futon and leaned her head against the wooden frame. "I don't want more gunfights. My research should alleviate pain, not inflict it. I'll give you and Günter a bag of seeds, instructions for synthesis, and let you two duke out the production methods." She met his gaze. "Back in Germany."

Dropping the blinds over the window, he turned. "I told you I live here."

I've seen your house. I'm sure it's one of many. "For how long?"

"Until my father passes." Pulling over a chair, he turned it and straddled the back. "Scientists at Berkeley announced the reproduction of major cannabinoids using yeast and biosynthesis. Your dissertation is impressive, but it's not what Günter wants."

"Exactly!" Taking a moment to digest his understanding of his uncle's research, she reminded herself she was one of many scientists striving to make the world a better place. "I've tweaked the process. When my article on the advanced synthesis of CBD comes out, you won't even need me."

Folding his arms across the back of the chair, he exhaled. "I don't need you, but you need me."

She lifted her chin. "I don't need a trained killer." Watching his expression, she waited for the barb to hit home, but he remained steadfast, and the words bounced off his disciplined reserve. "Johann…"

He held up a hand. "Americans are so righteous. Where do your politicians stand on abortion and the death penalty? Gun ownership extends the same question. Do desperate situations warrant taking a life?"

He tapped his lip and held out his palm. "In my book, the question is all or nothing."

"I don't keep a gun in the house," she said. "I made my decision."

"So have I." Removing his jacket, he revealed his holster and laid his jacket over his lap. "That doesn't mean I made it lightly."

Feeling the pressure of the ensuing silence, she thought of the brief tug she felt outside the Greek restaurant. Wondering whether the action belonged to Günter or a crowd member, she swallowed and acknowledged the comfort of Johann's presence. "I'm not expendable."

"No, you're not." He stood. "But you are idealistic and ignorant."

She struggled to her feet. "I'm not the person who blew up the damn lab. I'm not the person who yanks women around outside restaurants or fires guns at a funeral."

Johann narrowed his gaze. "Who touched you?"

"I don't know! Someone outside the Greek restaurant."

He swore and turned. "Protecting you in this ratty apartment is ten times more difficult. Why do you live like this?"

His question filled the room and raised her hackles. "On a graduate student's budget, this townhouse is luxury!"

"Your family has money."

"That doesn't mean I use it!" Her heart raced, and she wished the man had another reason to glower in her living room. Looking at the swell of his thighs, she wondered what else he packed. *Twenty minutes and we could both feel better.*

He raised an eyebrow.

She shook her head and walked to the under-stairs closet. Pulling blankets and pillows from the shelf, she tossed them on the futon. "Enjoy playing guard dog. Say hi to Günter. Kibble's in the fridge."

He rubbed the back of his neck. "You're ridiculous."

"And you're overbearing."

"Come back to my house. Silvia will spoil you."

"Yeah, right." She climbed the carpeted stairs and paused halfway up to look over her shoulder. "I don't need a staycation. I need to return to my research."

He remained at the foot of the stairs.

I should have gone to the shelter and adopted a real dog. As soon as Johann gets what he wants, he will abandon me.

Johann tested the railing's strength.

Fine. Maybe he'll spring for lattes. Looking at the mass-marketed furniture, she imagined him tossing and turning. *When insomnia hits, at least I'll have company.*

Following her gaze, he moved aside the bedding and tested the foam padding.

She reached the top of the stairs and turned to stare. "Don't shoot Gary."

He straightened. "Goodnight, Hadley."

"Goodnight, Johann." She shook her head. "Sleep well, if you can." Dismissing the weak spray of the fiberglass shower stall, she collapsed on her bed. Her mattress and the downstairs couch tied for lousy credentials, but the mattress belonged to her. Reaching for a pillow, she bumped her arm and winced. Before she could second-guess her impulse, she dialed

Lieutenant Jayne's number.

"Hadley, what's wrong?"

She sighed and lost her nerve. "I called you on accident. I didn't want to end the call in case you saw the missed call."

"Are you sure you're okay?"

"Yeah. Why are you working this late?" she asked.

"Why did a shooting happen at the funeral?"

She swallowed and remembered Johann driving his expensive car down the beautiful, tree-lined street leading from the cemetery. Despite the beauty, blood still dripped from her arm. *I live on the most expensive spit of land in the country, but life on the peninsula can be deadly.* "I don't know."

Her bedroom door opened.

Looking up, she saw Johann's silhouette.

He leaned against the frame and cracked his knuckles.

Each pop made her flinch. She rose to shut the door in his face. "This is a private conversation."

The lieutenant coughed. "Hadley, if you need help, tell me."

Irritated by Johann's constant presence, she put the phone against her shoulder and pushed him back toward the hallway.

He remained in the same spot and pushed up his sleeves.

Dropping her hand, she turned her back and focused on her phone call. "I'm absolutely fine. Everything is under control."

"If you need us, we're here," Lieutenant Jayne said.

She ended the call and frowned at Johann. He had

no problem invading her meager privacy, but before she raged, she recognized he stopped at the threshold. A less exhausted woman would have slammed the door in his face.

"How's the good lieutenant?" he asked.

She stuck out her chin. "Courteous and deferential."

He shrugged.

The man exuded calm and focus. She wanted to strip naked and watch him cave, but tears of frustration threatened to spill down her cheeks. Sniffing, she bit her lip. "You have one week, Johann."

"That's all I need."

She nodded. "What makes you believe he'll come to you?"

"He's running out of options." Straightening, he filled the doorway. "Will you uphold your end of the deal, Hadley?"

"What's in it for me?"

"Answers." He formed his hands into a steeple and flexed out his palms. "The gel. Freedom to continue your research. Life."

Life. She stared at the carpet and thought of her mother's glazed, primetime addiction, her sister's horrible, recurrent pain, and her single-minded, stubborn determination to make the world a better place. Johann offered her protection on his terms, but she was so afraid to bend she rebuffed him at every turn. Remembering the kiss she stole, she felt her cheeks warm and cupped her injured arm. The bandage looked pristine, but the skin beneath tingled with sensation. Pain might be twelve hours away, but no matter how she felt about Johann's wry humor and casual dominance, reality beckoned. She pulled the antiseptic gel from her purse and unwrapped the gauze. "Go to bed, Johann." Hearing silence, she looked up and found him gone. She stopped unwinding the bandage and listened for movement in the townhouse. The door remained closed. Confident he would claim the futon, she sat on the bed and let exhaustion claim her resolve. Tomorrow, she would figure out how to accommodate Johann and his immutable will without acting like a spoiled brat. She yawned. Maybe less of a spoiled brat.

****

Sunlight streamed through the mini blinds in Hadley's room. She rubbed her eyes and marveled at sleeping through the night's restorative effects. Bumping her wounded forearm against the side table, she swore, thought of Johann, and swung her feet over the side of the bed. *I promised myself I would play nice.*

Padding down the stairs in a T-shirt and a pair of drawstring pants, she found Gary and Johann glaring at each other over granola yogurt. Johann's biceps strained the sleeves of an undershirt. *When he wore a suit, ignoring his body was a lot easier.* She opened a cabinet. "Did anyone make coffee?"

"No." Gary ground out his response.

She considered her friend's bedhead and the dark purple shadows beneath his eyes. "Rough night at the club, Gar-Bear?"

He sat straighter and brushed his hair from his eyes. "If we brought home company, I thought we agree to text."

She dumped grounds in the coffee pot, pushed the brew button, and dropped into a chair between the two men "I told you about him."

Gary scanned the man. "He doesn't look like a guardian angel."

She glanced at the scar on Johann's cheek and the shadow of stubble darkening his chin. Pulling the granola closer, she opened the box. "He does not."

Johann cleared his throat. "I'm right here."

She stole Gary's empty bowl and filled it with granola for herself. "However, he has a stake in a pharmaceutical company."

Gary slid the yogurt across the table. "Really?"

"Right here," Johann said.

She grinned.

Gary leaned back, grabbed another spoon from the drying rack, and dropped it next to his donated bowl. "Haddie, what went down last night? Was it road rage? Did you call the cops?"

She dumped granola in a bowl and exposed her bandaged arm.

Johann turned her forearm and inspected the wound. Nodding, he adjusted the loose bandage and released his grip. "It looks better."

Indulging in the moment of contact, she turned her head and found Gary staring. Pinned beneath his scrutiny, she frowned. "I don't know why someone shot at me. The bullet grazed my forearm. I can't chalk up the bombing and the gunfire to coincidences. Johann thinks his brother, Günter, might be behind the shooting."

Gary blinked. "Maybe the shooter was out hunting squirrels."

Johann choked on his orange juice.

Shrugging, Gary swallowed his bite. "Someone

should look at that wound."

She shook her head. "I don't have time. After a good night of sleep, the wound feels better."

He glanced at the bandage. "The shooter didn't want you to get better."

Self-conscious, she tucked her arm in her lap. "It will probably scar."

Johann stood and dumped his bowl in the sink. "You'll barely notice it."

"Johann?" she asked.

"*Ja?*"

She smiled and watched for his reaction. "Silvia's not here, and I'm not doing your dishes."

He winced.

Gary slapped his knee. "Welcome to my world."

Johann reached for a sponge.

While she ate, she watched the two men dodge each other in the small kitchen. Gary's tousled hair and lean frame made him look pre-pubescent next to Johann's streamlined bulk. *I can't imagine a situation where they would be friends.*

A knock on the front door interrupted her thoughts. She exchanged looks with Gary. Neither of them expected guests. Figuring Johann could fend for himself, she rose and opened the door. Anyone who knocked before lunch could ignore her pajamas.

Lieutenant Jayne and a sallow, bleach-blonde officer stood in the morning light. The lieutenant kept his thumbs tucked in his pants pockets.

His confident smile looked full of swaggering bravado. She cleared her throat and smiled.

"Good morning, Hadley," he said.

"Good morning, Lieutenant Jayne."

"You can call me Tony."

She nodded and looked at the blonde officer. Fine lines spanned her forehead, but her expression remained neutral.

"My name is Captain Sarah Wilson. We have a few questions for you, Ms. Heron."

Doubting she had the right answers, she repeated her smile. "I thought I'd met the entire squad."

The blonde smiled. "Special times call for special measures."

And more experienced agents.

"Who is it?"

Gary's voice echoed from the tiny kitchen. She made room for the two officers to enter the townhouse. "It's the police."

Gary and Johann attempted to pass through the kitchen doorframe at the same time. The restricted space immobilized them.

At the noise, Captain Wilson turned.

Johann shifted his shoulders and pushed ahead, clipping Gary's shoulder.

Gary rubbed his arm. "C'mon, man, that hurt."

Lieutenant Jayne stepped closer and peered at her arm. "Why are you wearing a bandage?"

She cocked her head. "Someone shot me."

Lieutenant Jayne dropped open his mouth. "Is that why you called me last night?"

The captain stepped forward. "When did this incident happen?"

She blinked. "At Dr. Stefan's funeral. I thought you knew."

The officers looked at each other.

"You're too close." Captain Wilson turned to her.

"Why didn't you report the injury?"

She dropped into a plaid easy chair. "The bullet grazed my arm. I didn't want to stick around to give the shooter another chance."

Captain Wilson folded her arms. "Innocent victims usually stay at the crime scene."

Agreeing with the woman, she swallowed her guilt for letting Dr. Stefan open the package, but she remembered her bargain with Johann and widened her eyes. "The shot terrified me. I can't remember a thing. I ran."

Captain Wilson peered at her arm. "Did you seek medical attention?"

She shook her head, peeled back the bandage, and exposed the wound. It no longer bled. The townhouse's dingy windows dimmed the sunlight and diminished the mark. "I have terrible medical insurance. The wound will barely scar."

Lieutenant Jayne squinted at Gary and Johann. "Mr. Bezelle, where were you during this incident?"

"I was at the funeral meal." Gary looked at Johann and sneered. "And you?"

Hadley held her breath.

Johann stepped forward and extended a hand. "Captain Wilson, I am Johann zur Hausen." He nodded toward Lieutenant Jayne. "The lieutenant and I have met. You bring us alarming news. Should I worry about the possibility of further incidents?"

Lieutenant Jayne crossed his arms. "You keep showing up, don't you?"

Her protector took his time answering the good lieutenant, but the longer he waited, the more Lieutenant Jayne shifted and worked his jaw. Hadley wondered if she could learn Johann's trick and apply it to entitled undergraduates asking for a grade boost.

The shorter man blinked first.

"Hadley is a good friend of the family," Johann said. "She needed time to grieve, and I stayed by her side."

Lieutenant Jayne loosened his collar. "Most people send flowers."

Johann smiled. "I prefer a more personal approach."

Captain Wilson checked her notes. "Will the other funeral attendees confirm your attendance?"

Turning his attention to the officer, Johann nodded. "Of course. How could they miss me?" He offered her a smile. "I stood right by the podium."

Narrowing her gaze, Captain Wilson scanned the room. "The things people can miss would surprise you." She opened her notebook. "Let's go back to the facts. The cemetery attendant reported an exchange of gunfire between two men and a brunette woman." She looked at Hadley. "I assume that was you."

Standing, she walked to the front door before the officers dug up issues she barely understood. If she let Captain Wilson and Lieutenant Jayne run unchecked, she might spend the day replaying events without achieving a resolution. The bombing that killed Dr. Stefan remained under police investigation, but Johann's hypothesis about the shooter offered hope. "I really appreciate the courtesy call, officers, but this tragedy isn't *Death at a Funeral*. Perhaps all three of us now need police protection?"

The captain sized-up Johann. "I doubt it."

Lieutenant Jayne cleared his throat. "We'll speak

to our Chief of Police. For the time being, stay close to home. If you see anything suspicious, call the department."

Gary mumbled a response.

"Excuse me?" Captain Wilson asked.

Looking up, Gary looked at two police officers focused entirely on him. "I said, 'What a great idea.'"

Johann came to the door. "If you identify the shooter or need further assistance, please contact me. After my uncle's death, you have my number. I do not want my family to worry about additional incidents."

Distributing their business cards, the officers left the townhouse.

She shut the door, leaned against it, and stared at the two men.

Gary tossed the business cards in the junk bowl and crossed his arms. "I am not staying in this townhouse all day."

"You don't have to stay here." She straightened. "We'll be safe enough at the lab."

"I'm not so sure about that." Gary shook his head and climbed the stairs. "Stay away from foreign packages, Hadley"—he paused and looked at Johann—"and foreign men."

"We need to go shopping," Johann said.

"I bet your girlfriend loves it when you say that phrase."

He exhaled. "Shopping for things to cut down those ridiculous bushes, install a better deadbolt, secure the windows, and add cameras."

She gripped her fists by her head and squeezed close her eyes. "Please don't make me go to the big box hardware store." Opening her eyes, she checked for effect.

Johann frowned.

"I can't stand how many screws and fixtures need reorganizing."

Johann shook his head. "Idealistic and ignorant."

"What does that mean?"

"It means we won't find what we need at a big box store."

Plodding down the stairs, Gary carried his laptop case. "I can come along and help you."

Johann crossed his arms. "That won't be necessary."

"I pay half the rent."

"Good. Hopefully, you'll also get a good night's sleep."

Gary sneered. "Before you showed up, I had no problems sleeping."

She cradled her arm and remained quiet. Looking at the two of them, she wondered if circumstances would ever make them friends.

Johann muttered something about the responsibilities of having children. Claiming his overnight bag, he retreated to the upstairs bathroom.

She imagined him fumbling around the tiny room and towering over the particleboard cabinets. *We'll see how long he lasts in my world.* Remembering how quickly her social constructs collapsed on the cemetery lawn, she gripped her arm and swallowed. *He's not here for a date. Without him, how long will I last?*

Chapter Six

Hadley spent the twenty-minute ride to East Palo Alto looking out the window and longing for the greenery of University Avenue. Downtown's charming stores and well-kept houses gave way to overgrown yards and pockets of trash. Wary pedestrians eyed Johann's sleek sedan but never made eye contact. "Maybe the depot would have been a better option."

Johann shifted, his gaze narrowing. "You don't feel safe with me?"

She swallowed. "I don't feel safe with your brother."

He parked the car in front of a convenience store. "This is Damon's neighborhood, and Günter knows his loyalty. Günter's won't risk another embarrassment."

I hope you're right.

He paused, one hand on the door. "I appreciate what you did at the apartment. Deflecting Lieutenant Jayne's questions must have been difficult."

She sighed. "I didn't fool Captain Wilson."

"We stalled their investigation. You honored our agreement, and that means a lot."

Shrugging off the moment's intimacy, she looked out the window at the nondescript store. Faded advertisements plastered the windows, and thick security bars added a layer of protection. Taking a deep breath, she climbed out of the car. "I'm not sure I had a better option."

"You always have an option." He pushed open the store's glass door and held it.

A bell chimed.

Walking past him, she scanned the interior. The place smelled like cinnamon, stale grease, and tobacco. Leaning bags of corn chips warred with Mexican snack foods, their wrappers a rainbow of foreign joy. Advertisements for wire transfers and lottery tickets hung from the ceiling.

The woman behind the counter stared.

Arms crossed, she presided over her goods like a school principal on a field trip. Her sleek, gray-tinged hair and gold jewelry looked out of place in front of rows of cigarette cartons. Hadley swallowed.

Shaking her head, the woman yelled for Damon.

He came through a pair of swinging double doors wearing jeans and a long T-shirt.

Hadley grinned at his jovial expression.

Johann received a handshake.

Cocking his head, Damon pursed his lips. "I didn't expect to see you so soon."

"Nice store," she said.

He jerked his head toward the woman behind the counter. "The one and only Mama Clarke."

She whipped her head and took a second glance at the woman. *She scraped together her money and took a risk.* Swallowing, she offered the woman a tentative smile.

Mama Clarke pursed her lips and shook her head.

Hadley turned back to Damon. *If I'd seen him on the street, I wouldn't have given him another thought, but I met him wearing a pristine, white jacket.* "Thanks for looking out for me."

"I'm less conspicuous than Johann."

Swallowing, she nodded. "Thank you."

Johann cleared his throat. "We need to fortify Hadley's apartment. She declined my housing invitation."

Grinning, Damon rubbed his hands. "I have everything you need. People don't need an excuse to come in and out of a convenience store at all hours of the night, but I promise you, they get what they need."

She looked at the colorful stacks of candy. "I doubt you're talking about gum."

He laughed. "I'm talking about gadgets for home security and protection. Spike strips? Knockoff video doorbells? I have them."

Recalling Johann's quip about messy pets, she tried to keep a straight face. "Trained guard dogs?"

Damon wrinkled his nose. "Too messy."

Johann laughed.

She rolled her eyes. *When my coworkers stuck to the scientific method, my life was much easier.* She re-oriented her expectations of life in the twenty-first century. "Guns?"

Damon widened his gaze. "Mama Clarke sells snacks in the front, and I sell goods in the back. The police might classify those goods as stolen property, but my shop's a bootstrap hardware store. Guns?" He shook his head. "That's dirty business."

She rubbed her arms. *Some people don't share your convictions.* "I liked you better when you eavesdropped on entrepreneurs for investment tips."

Rubbing the sides of his mouth, he shrugged.

"What does that say about you?"

She raised her chin. "I'm a cloistered academic who prefers skipping illicit markets?"

He laughed. "Well, this illicit market's safeguarding your ass. Until you've lived in my world, don't judge it."

"Amen," Mama Clarke said.

Turning, Damon held open the double doors.

Johann placed a hand at the small of her back.

She leaned into the touch for a moment, then straightened and walked past Damon. Cardboard boxes lined a riveted steel hallway, and a walk-in freezer waited at the end of the hall. *I draw the line at going inside that room.*

Damon shifted a stack of boxes and revealed a door.

She swallowed. *Compared to the ice vault, that door looks relatively palatable.*

Unlocking the door, he revealed a windowless room lined with locked cabinets. Shelves held bits of technology marked with tags. Bins of cell phones grouped by make and model sat on the floor. *The last time I cracked my screen, I wish I knew about this place. Instead of replacing the glass, I would have upgraded.*

Johann strode into the room.

Swallowing, she crossed her arms and followed him. Stale air made the space feel smaller than it looked. Afraid to touch anything and unsure of what would happen next, she hovered near the back wall. "What do people do with all these phones?"

Damon glanced at the bins. "The NSA can't accurately track burner phones. People…"

He stretched the word like he swallowed an unsavory pill. The federal government funded fifty percent of basic research projects. Dr. Stefan had a private funder, but without big government, scientific research would retreat to corporate labs. Deflecting the government never entered her mind. If they scoffed at her research, she needed to make a better case for what she found. Damon, on the other hand, sold illicit goods. Maybe she should have chosen the big box hardware store.

"…want to be off the grid, or they want anonymity to conduct their affairs." He shrugged. "I don't really care why people buy the phones. I unlock them, and Mama sells prepaid SIM cards."

Johann held up his phone and handed the device to Damon. "I made a list of what we need."

Scanning the list, Damon unlocked a metal cabinet.

On gray felt, knives and pepper spray cans rested next to unidentifiable electronics. She frowned. "You don't need all this stuff."

He kept his back turned. "Why not? Somebody has to sell it."

"What happened to tech investment?"

Gesturing to a metal chair, he shrugged. "Sit while you wait."

She perched on the cold aluminum and sought Johann's reassurance in the small room.

He smiled. "Ask him where the money goes."

Damon stilled. "Don't make it such a big deal, Boss."

"He sends neighborhood kids to colleges," Johann said.

She looked up. His restaurant eavesdropping

teetered on civility's edge, and the bootleg hardware store looked suspiciously like a gang stock room, but she lacked a concrete reason to view him as a criminal. "Really?"

Damon cleared his throat. "Everyone deserves a chance."

She gripped the edge of the metal chair and swung her legs. "Where did you go to school?"

He turned. "Hadley, if I'd gone to school, the goods I'm selling wouldn't have fallen off a truck."

She frowned. "Is that a euphemism?"

Laughing, he shook his head. "Rebuilding a neighborhood takes more than money. East Palo Alto doesn't have Fruitvale or the International Corridor. The EPA's working-class business district failed, and the Victorian houses never made it this far south." Turning, he opened his hands and gestured toward the contents of the small room. "All the profits from my enterprise go into building my neighborhood's future, one kid at a time."

"But what message are you sending those kids?"

He shook his head and returned to the list. "This neighborhood isn't your home, Hadley. You shouldn't care about the message."

Leaning forward in the chair, she braced her elbows on her keens and tapped her foot. "You have a world-class research institution just up the road. Billionaire tech investors." She glanced at Johann. "Use them."

Damon whistled and scrolled through the list. "Johann does his share. Those academics up the road? They'd reject my money faster than an actress greasing entry for her kids."

"Run for city council," she said.

He laughed.

"At least get a tax ID."

"Now you sound like Vivian." He turned back to the cabinet. "She cornered the market on cool and aloof."

Who's Vivian? Taking his hint, she settled into the chair. "I'm sure the kids are grateful, but you're missing more than Lake Merritt."

"If my scheme needs a lake, I'll dig it."

You and what army? Twenty minutes later, she followed Johann out of the convenience store. He carried enough sensors and electronics to elicit squeals from a high school robotics team.

Damon threw in a pink can of pepper spray. "It's on the house."

"Thanks." She wondered if she should refuse the girly gift.

He winked. "I hope you won't have to use it."

She sighed. "Me neither."

On the drive back to the townhouse, Johann took business calls.

She listened to the quick exchanges of information and wondered how long Damon would need to swap his street smarts for Johann's executive polish. *They're living parallel lives, but they're not equal, are they?* She wondered if Damon would feel comfortable accepting a donation when her research matured. Staring out the window, she exhaled. *Don't count your chickens before they're hatched.* At the townhouse, she opened her laptop and frowned. "Do I need to be here?"

"You need to be within my sight."

Flopping onto the plaid easy chair, she messaged

Buffy.

—*Small delay*—

Buffy responded.

—*Don't worry. I can follow a procedure.*—

Johann dismantled the security system and installed smart locks. Screws anchored cameras on the apartment's popcorn ceilings and textured walls.

As he held a tool above his head, she watched his muscles flex. "The BKA taught you to use a screwdriver?"

Looking over his shoulder, he sighed. "Brat."

Retreating to her bedroom, she played down the sound of a cordless drill, but a large object thudded to the carpeted floor. *There goes our rental deposit*. Using one hand, she summarized her research results. The slow pecking left her feeling inept, but Buffy's updates soothed her nerves. She considered undertaking article revisions, but she heard the front door slam. *Johann must have gone outside. Since he's improving my home, I should probably offer to help*. She grinned. *Or suggest he take off his shirt.*

A gas-powered hedge trimmer roared to life.

She plugged her ears. *Maybe not*. Eying the bathroom door, she rose to shower before twenty-first-century feminism guilted her into yard work. Steam filled the small bathroom, and she used a plastic grocery bag and a roll of tape to protect her wound. Submitting to the warmth of the shower, she smiled. The water pressure was crap, but the restriction helped her water bill and the needs of the drought-prone area. She thought of Johann's compound. *Altruism aside, I could still go for a jet-lined soaking tub.*

She turned off the shower and reached for the

towel but found an empty rod. "Shit." Cracking the bathroom door, she listened for movement. The heavy-handed *clack-clack* of metal shears assured her the hedges kept Johann busy. Taking a deep breath, she made a run for her room. The dash felt silly and exhilarating until she passed the staircase.

Johann froze with a hand on the railing. Amusement pulled at the corners of his mouth.

She kept running. "You didn't see that."

"See what?"

Slamming her bedroom door, she belted her robe and took a deep breath. *I'm just a body. Flesh and blood. Except this body belongs to me.* Opening the door, she faced him.

Laugh lines crinkled the corners of his eyes. He handed her a towel, turned, and walked down the narrow hallway.

"Who's trimming the bushes?" *Oh, damn, did I have to say that?*

He paused and cleared his throat. "Your roommate offered to help. I believe he reconsidered his priorities."

She exhaled. "How convenient."

He scanned her towel-clad body. "Indeed."

Her cheeks warmed, and she eased close the door. If she reversed the situation, she would have looked, too. If she had the situation under control, she would have invited him into her room.

Twenty minutes later, she came downstairs wearing a pair of jeans, a tank top, and her favorite blue, long-sleeved shirt. Fraying embroidery covered the shirt. She purchased it at the Telluride Bluegrass Festival, and she refused to part with the worn fabric.

At the kitchen table, Johann and Gary stared at an

online news article profiling her research.

Despite the long-sleeved shirt, a chill raced across her skin.

Johann looked up. "Did you explain your research to the police?"

"Gary did."

Gary pointed to a chart on the screen. "Her results are promising."

You don't know the half of it. Determined to hold on to her findings until she could defend them, she ignored the praise. "That poster was about procedures. It's nothing."

"It caught a reporter's attention." Johann scrolled through the article on Gary's laptop. "Who else knows what you're doing?"

"Except your uncle, no one had access to my results."

Gary leaned back and crossed his arms. "Not even Buffy?"

Brushing hair off her face, she shook her head.

He rubbed his jaw. "What if something happens to you?"

She shrugged. "The university will access my accounts."

Johann rose. "I won't let that happen."

"The access?"

He raised an eyebrow. "The threat."

His promise warmed her, but Gary hovered nearby, and she cleared her throat. "You belong to the Dark Ages."

He shook his head. "Physical combat can satisfy me, but violence is my last resort."

What else satisfies you? She walked to the sink and

squeezed drops of water from her hair. She should have let them fall to the floor. The carpet could use a good wash. "You know what I find satisfying?"

He scanned her outfit.

She withstood the inspection. *This is who I am, Johann. Take it or leave it.* She felt as naked as her hallway dash, but she held back her shoulders.

He made eye contact.

"Research." She put her hands on her hips. "I find research more satisfying than anything in this house." Turning, she walked straight through the kitchen, grabbed her purse from the floor, and walked out the door. *Have fun, boys, I have work.* Taking a deep breath, she waited for Johann to run after her. When he abstained, she scanned the late afternoon street, looking for threats. *Whatever. I can't live my life in a bubble.*

The thought of analyzing the results of the polymer experiments put a spring in her step, and she made a beeline to her lab.

Buffy looked up from the microscope. "The neurons in the assay respond exceptionally well to the T-83 compound. What's in it?"

She took charge of the microscope and hedged her response. "CBD derivatives."

Buffy rearranged her sandy-blonde ponytail. "But which ones?"

"I'll check my notes." Wanting to keep Buffy from second-guessing the research until she could determine what to do with the results, she adjusted the resolution on the microscope and checked cell signals. *The results speak for themselves. I knew I was right! Dr. Stefan must have known it too. But how did Günter know?* Exhaling, she looked up to find Johann standing in the doorway sporting a pair of reading glasses and an old-fashioned wool hat.

"Can I help you?" Buffy asked.

"Hallo."

A deep accent stretched the ending of the word, and his hat's shadow hid his features. Turning to examine the lab name and shifting his feet, he looked both cuddly and confused. Pleasure was her first impulse, but she assumed he designed his getup to teach her a lesson, and she had no time for his schooling.

"I am Frank zur Hausen. Could I see my late uncle's lab?" he asked.

Buffy cocked her head. "How did you get in here without a badge?"

Hadley smiled. *Thank goodness someone has some sense around here.*

Fuddling Frank shrugged and pushed his glasses back up his nose. "I followed *die* someone in?"

Hadley rolled her eyes. *Oh, brother.* She stood to intervene.

Buffy walked toward Johann and patted his arm. "Let me show you the lab. I'm so sorry for your loss. Dr. zur Hausen was such a kind man."

Nodding, Johann wiped at his eye.

He followed Buffy like an obedient puppy. *Well, that takes care of both of them.* She changed the controls on the assay and gave thanks the lab's bright, white lights kept darkness at bay. The lab equipment monitored the assays, but her observations picked up the performance details data overlooked. When reached a stopping point, she stood and stretched her back, looking outside to gauge the time. *It must be late.* In the adjacent room, empty lab desks confirmed the time. "I've found it."

"Found what?"

Gasping, she turned and found Johann sitting in Buffy's chair. The thin, vertical scar on his cheek paled against the tight precision of his facial muscles.

He unclenched his arms and rose, bracing his weight on the black lab table. "You're not chasing anti-inflammatory drugs to treat multiple sclerosis."

She stepped away from the table. "No, I'm not."

"Rheumatoid arthritis and inflammatory diseases?"

She shook her head.

He rounded the table. "I know about your mother's addiction. You're chasing an opioid replacement, aren't you?"

How fast can I run?

He narrowed his gaze. "You need layers of protection, Hadley. Every drug company in the world will challenge your claims, not to mention the threat from illicit markets."

She checked the hallway and found it empty. "That sounds sinister."

"It should." He straightened.

The stillness of the lab permeated her fear. "Where's Buffy?"

"I tied her up and threw her in the closet."

She scanned the room, searching for a closet. "You did what?"

Shaking his head, he exhaled. "When she left, you were so absorbed in your work you said you would take responsibility for me. That was two hours ago."

She stopped looking for a closet and frowned. *Did I do that?* "Wait! Why did you call yourself Frank?"

He shrugged. "It's my coffee shop name."

"How pedantic."

Walking around the table, he cupped a shoulder. "I'm here to protect you."

In the lab's antiseptic frigidity, his touch burned her skin. She shifted out of his grasp. "I don't need your protection."

"I walked into your lab and took a tour. These idiots you call friends can't protect you."

She raised her chin. "Buffy is very caring."

He scowled. "Hadley, do you understand the threat to your life?"

Swallowing, she wondered when he learned to imbue his voice with such severity. "Yes."

"Do you? I've bid millions of dollars to control this type of intellectual property. Competitors in San Francisco want to tweak oxycodone to produce sustained pain relief with less euphoria. Nerds in Mountain View think they can cut off the triggering circuit that leads to addiction."

She kept abreast of competitor research, but nobody had published results to make redundant her mission. "Have any of them been successful?"

"I can't tell you that fact."

Smiling, she looked at her research. "I'll take that as a 'no'."

His fingers turned her chin. "Hadley, you have a problem."

She inhaled his unique scent and tried to stay focused on her research. Despite finding herself isolated in the lab with him, her racing pulse and throbbing core echoed her curiosity. Under different conditions…she wet her lips but reached for her pencil.

Swearing, he hoisted her to the lab table and

pinned her hips. "This is what you want from me? A quick release?"

She grinned.

"Fuck." He yanked her to the edge of the table and pulled her mouth to his.

The heat and precision of his kiss destroyed her defenses. Gasping, she threw her arms around his neck and pressed closer to his chest, tightening her legs around his waist as he laid waste to her lips. Her pulse skyrocketed, and she tore away her lips, scanning the table for expendable equipment.

"You're worth more than a quick fuck."

She felt him release her hips and turned, seeing his shoulders heave. "Let's not be hasty. Researchers, they're a dime a dozen."

He laughed and hung his head. "No"—he swallowed—"they're not." Raising his head, he exhaled. "I don't mix business and pleasure."

Rejection plowed through her cheeky defenses. "No, I'm sure you don't." Jumping off the table, she turned and tidied the surface.

"Your research," he said.

She shrugged. "Before it can hit market, my discoveries have to move to animal testing and phased clinical trials. I try to avoid excitement, but I think I'm onto something." She looked over her shoulder. "I only have one life to live, Johann. *Lindere den Schmerz deiner Freunde und Feinde*."

He ran a hand through his hair. "I forget your German is more than a show."

I forget you're an asshole. She cleared her throat. "The grammar is complex, but the compound words make sense. Learning Dr. Stefan's native language helped us talk about research at conferences and trade shows. It's a crowded field."

He rubbed his chin. "You're not the only researcher with language skills."

"You think that's how your brother learned about my work?"

"I doubt Uncle Stefan rang him and had a little heart to heart, but anything is possible. The explosion might have had nothing to do with my brother."

"And the gunfight?"

He sighed.

Exhaustion weighed down her limbs and muddled her thoughts. "I want to go home now."

"Come back to my house," he said. "It's still safer than the particleboard shack where you live."

She shook her head and cleared her workspace. "I want to sleep in my bed. I'm pretty sure your brother knows where you live."

"My home is secure."

"So is my apartment, thanks to you."

He pulled his phone from his pocket, tapped the screen, and showed her Gary smoking a bowl on the fenced patio. The front door of the townhouse stood wide open and admitted the evening breeze. "You call this secure?"

Grabbing the phone, she squinted at an array of miniature screens. The one featuring the door to her bedroom caused her to gasp and drop the device. "You can see everything on your phone?"

He picked up the device and brushed off the screen. "I've already seen you naked."

The memory of her hallway dash flooded her cheeks with color. "I'm going home and dismantling the cameras. I thought the surveillance was all downstairs."

Shrugging, he slipped the phone in his pocket. "I monitored the common spaces. If you choose to strut around naked, I'll enjoy the show. Let me take you to my house. Walking down the streets exposed isn't safe."

She crossed her arms. "I've walked down these streets for close to a decade."

"But someone killed your advisor." He rubbed his lip. "Yesterday, they took a shot at you."

"Has it only been a day? I thought Günter was to blame." Looking out the window at the verdant lawn, she pushed the grief from her voice. "You were in the office when the package arrived. You could have killed that man at the funeral. The only common denominator I see is you."

He laughed. "If I wanted to kill you, Hadley, you'd already be dead."

The absurdity of his statement freed her from the banal tasks required for modern science. Verifying the security of her equipment, she grabbed her purse and walked out of the lab. He followed her through the maze of the building, two steps behind her lead, but she felt no fear.

His sleek sedan waited at the curb. A parking ticket fluttered beneath the windshield wiper. Crumpling the fine, he stashed the paper in his pocket. "I'll drive you."

She shook her head and turned toward downtown. Beneath campus lights, palm trees swayed in the onshore breeze.

"Where are you going?" he asked.

"I feel like walking. People pay good money for

cool summer weather."

He looked at the sky. "The forecast calls for rain."

"Not soon." She walked away.

"You can't keep walking out on me, Hadley." He raised his voice. "We have an agreement. Your safety depends on my protection."

Lengthening her stride, she followed the sidewalk downtown. "Watch me."

His sedan followed at a glacial speed, blocking traffic and causing multiple pedestrians to stop and stare.

Ignoring the attention, she kept her gaze forward and covered the blocks. Hunger and defiance compelled her to stop at her favorite restaurant for Chow Mein.

Johann engaged his car's caution lights and blocked the right-hand lane.

She swallowed a laugh and watched the cashier package enough food to feed a small army. Students loved this place; every meal resulted in leftovers.

"Somebody ought to arrest that fool," the woman said.

Hadley reached for her carryout bag. "He'd probably buy his way out of the jail cell."

The woman laughed and turned the register screen for her signature. "Ain't that the truth?"

Signing her name, Hadley wondered if discovering who shot her would free her or leave her feeling abandoned.

****

In front of the townhouse, Johann climbed out of the sedan and faced Hadley. "You think you're funny. The next time you want to pull a slow-moving stunt, tell Lieutenant Jayne to follow you."

"Great idea." She waltzed toward the door. "Find a visitor's parking spot, or management will tow your car."

"They will not," he said.

She waved off his claim. "Suit yourself." Reaching for the doorknob, she saw a crack of light and realized the door stood ajar. *Fuck me.*

Johann waited behind her.

Taking a deep breath, she shifted the Chow Mein and pushed open the door. The hinges groaned. Dropping her purse by the door, she scanned the first floor. "Gary?" Her voice wavered.

He ambled into the kitchen.

Relief released her breath. Walking into the kitchen, she unpacked the waxed cardboard takeout boxes and placed them on the table.

Gary dropped into a chair and reached for the nearest box. "Haddie, you're the best."

Scraping splinters from her chopsticks, she smiled and met Johann's gaze. "At least someone thinks so."

He turned his back to her and threw the deadbolt.

The ominous click stilled her movements, but she chose a carton, opened it, and leaned against the kitchen counter.

Eying the remaining takeout box, he opened it and used a plastic fork to lift a bite. "Are you oblivious, ignorant, or willful?" A noodle hung from his mouth. Using his thumb, he deftly slid it into his mouth.

She smiled and slurped her noodles. The trio would never be friends, but savory noodles brought out their common ground. "Based on the conferences I've attended, academic research is as cutthroat as the business world."

"Ignorant." He shook his head.

She set aside the carton and drummed her fingers on the countertop. "I'm not ignorant. The only advantage you have is your bottom line's transparency. If I could call up a private security detail, I wouldn't need your paranoia and extensive protection techniques."

He put down his fork. "You think that's how my life works?"

"How many assistants do you have stashed around the world? Is Damon a project or an asset?"

"Damon is an employee and a friend."

She picked up her carton, took a bite, and swallowed her food. "You don't talk to him like a friend."

Johann stared.

You don't talk to me like a friend either.

"My assistant's name is Vivian."

She narrowed her gaze. "I've never met her."

He frowned. "Why would you?"

"You took over my life. Why shouldn't I know everything about you?"

Gary snorted. Kicking up his feet on an unoccupied chair, he leaned back and shoveled noodles into his mouth.

Johann shook his head. "You don't understand my world. That's what makes the threat of violence so dangerous."

She laughed and claimed her seat at the table. "And you don't understand mine. That's what makes you dismiss it."

Gary's nose twitched.

He looked back and forth with the fogged

confusion of a man who could spend fifteen minutes deciding whether to brush his teeth. She made sure they never ran out of toothpaste.

"Haddie is really smart. She'll soon be Dr. Heron."

"Fantastic," Johann said. "You can refer to her as your friend, the late Dr. Heron."

Gary yawned. "That's not part of the plan."

Johann looked at the graduate student. "A Ph.D. can't protect her from a gun."

Gary opened his mouth, closed it, and frowned. Standing, he headed toward the refrigerator. "We have time. Slogging through this stupid program will take me years. I should have gone straight to work. I'd be a helluva lot farther along by now."

She empathized with his frustration. "Oh, Gar-Bear, you can do it."

He turned.

Meeting the same wide, brown eyes she saw her entire childhood, she hesitated, but his dilated pupils distorted his focus. "You just need a goal."

Frowning, Gary cocked his head. "Dr. zur Hausen exploited you, Haddie. He treated you like a slave. Go teach the undergrads, grade the papers, schedule office hours, and sort out all the drama with the office staff." Rubbing his temples, he leaned his head against the refrigerator. "I couldn't handle that shit."

"Drop out," Johann said.

Johann's disdain truncated his words. She wanted to stand and shield Gary from his cutthroat suggestion, but he had to fend for himself.

"Within ten years of starting graduate school, less than sixty percent of doctoral students get their robes. You'll have plenty of company on the other side of the divide."

Gary opened his eyes. "You're right, man. Some part-time professors earn less than secretaries. That's just fucked up." He banged his head against the appliance.

Jumping up, she pulled him away from the refrigerator and led him to a chair. "Part-time professors get paid by the classes they teach." She rubbed his shoulders. "You're improving the world, Gar-Bear. Your ideas about pain tolerance are intense."

Looking up, he squinted. "Even if I get a position, I won't get tenure. I'll spend the rest of my life scraping by for a paycheck, paying off my loans, and worrying about retirement."

She dropped her hands. "Gary, your rich hippie parents pay your rent."

He smiled and raised a finger to his lips. "Shh."

Johann cleared his throat. "Is this a game?"

Gary faced him. "Do you want to offer me a job? The pharmaceutical industry is a dumpster fire of Ph.D. graduates."

"No." Johann crossed his arms. "You failed the first interview."

Gary glared. "I could run your company."

Scanning Gary's dirty sweatshirt and unlaced shoes, Johann cleared his throat. "I doubt it."

Looking at the two men, she considered her options. Exhaustion won. Putting away the food, she slung her purse over her shoulder and bailed on the testosterone match. Giving him the bird, she headed for the bar and the oblivion of legal drugs.

Chapter Seven

Johann ran and caught up to Hadley. "Where are you going?"

"To relax." She tossed the remainder of her dinner into a trashcan. Despite the comforting takeout, her confrontation with Johann and Gary suppressed her appetite.

"Hadley, you can't keep…"

Pivoting, she looked around and threw up her hands. "Where's the threat?"

He frowned.

"Have you tried calling your brother?" she asked.

"He won't take my calls."

Of course, he tried. Shaking her head, she walked two blocks to The Gryffin. Light and music spilled from the building. Inside, a crowd of locals listened to a flatpicker's bluegrass chords. Leaning forward, eager to join the sway, she pulled her license from her purse and thrust it toward the burly doorman. "Hi, Rick."

The man smiled. "Missed you lately."

"Been busy." Averting her gaze from Johann, she hoped he took the hint and went home. *To fucking Germany.*

Johann pulled out his credentials.

Looking back and forth between them, Rick met Johann's gaze and shook his head. "I've seen better fakes."

"Don't be absurd." Johann thrust his identification toward the bouncer.

Taking advantage of the distraction, she merged with the crowd. The swell of conversation and hard-driving music soothed her nerves and downed her doubts. *Where else can you forget you're alone?* Gravitating to the stage, she watched Jackie pluck the guitar strings, her foot tapping the floor with a steady beat. A blissful smile disguised the musician's effort, but she saw the sweat on Jackie's temples and smiled, knowing how much work went into the songs.

The banjo and fiddle players stepped back, softening their notes to an ethereal melody.

Jackie dropped the rhythm chords and picked out a complex pattern.

Like the rest of the audience, Hadley leaned forward.

Johann walked up to her side and offered a glass of red wine.

His presence felt as unexpected as the otherworldly music, but his proximity centered her. Frowning, she accepted the glass.

He leaned close. "I didn't tamper with it."

The low timbre of his pledge resonated beneath the music. "I know." Taking a sip, she let the crowd press them together and caught his hint of citrus. After showering, he had smelled bright and crisp, but the smell had deepened, teasing her with hints of something herbal and masculine. She shook her head and created space. *Sweat. It's probably sweat.*

The song ended, and a fellow graduate student wandered over. The man sized-up Johann, shouldered past his hovering presence, and leaned close. "Are you singing?"

She shook her head. "Not my show."

"You're being modest." Turning, the man and waved toward Jackie. He pointed to Hadley and stuck his thumb in the air.

Hadley shook her head and planted her feet.

He looped his arm through her arm. "C'mon."

Johann unwound his grasp. "Release her."

The student sneered. "She needs to sing."

"She makes the call."

Johann's dark, guttural response no longer sounded comforting. To diffuse the situation, she considered shoving her purse into his arms and climbing up on the stage, but caving felt like the wrong call. She stepped back from the pair.

The graduate student squared off against Johann. "Who do you think you are?"

Noting his menacing overtone, adjacent audience members created space.

Then again, singing might be the very thing she needed. Fleeing the simmering tension, she turned toward the pleasure of the stage. *My parents ignored me long enough to teach me a lesson. When people lose themselves in their song, they don't see you until you belt out your lyrics. Even then, they might not care.* Climbing two steps, she leaned close to the guitar player to make her voice heard. "Hi, Jackie."

The woman smiled. "Haven't seen you in a while."

She looked at the crowd straining The Gryffin's walls.

Johann stared back.

His blue eyes reflected the stage lights.

The belligerent graduate student chose that

moment to punch his chest.

Johann barely flinched.

Bad choice. She wondered what it felt like to slam your hand into two hundred pounds of disciplined resistance. Clearing her throat, she trusted Johann to take care of himself. "I've been busy," she said to Jackie. "Something easy?"

The flatpicker nodded and led with the intro chords for "Wayfaring Stranger."

Cradling the microphone, Hadley thought of the old bluegrass records in her dad's study. She used to talk to the famous artists on the covers of Johnny Cash and Emmylou Harris, but like her mother, they stared. Blinking back tears of frustration, she sang the first verse.

Her voice wobbled, and she smiled in apology. Every time she sang about *this world of woe*, regret tore apart her heart. She held back the tears.

The crowd cheered.

She ended with the hope of seeing her sister and all the loved ones whom she lost.

Applause and wolf whistles erupted from the crowd.

Grinning, she acknowledged their honest support. *That song's for you, Jecca. I wish you were here.* Retreating from the front of the stage, she let the stage musicians soak up the crowd's praise, and she hoped their clever instrumentation covered her cold start. She stepped off the stage.

The graduate student pushed a bottle of champagne into her hands. Clutching a bag of ice to his eye, he slung an arm over her shoulder. "With that kind of voice, I don't know why you're toiling away in the labs."

Clutching the champagne, she nodded and ducked free of the man's embrace. *Well, at least Johann didn't kill him.*

Bluegrass music filled the room. The crowd shifted and jostled her into her supporter. *Dude needs a shower.* Adjusting her purse, she sought Johann in the crowd.

Someone handed him a cigarette. He took a long drag and blew the smoke above the crowd.

An audience member waved his hand in front of his face. "You can't smoke that in here."

The student jeered, took another drag, and threw an elbow at the stranger.

Freezing, she felt the booze-tipped evening teeter on the edge of violence.

Johann blocked the altercation and turned his back on the arguing men. He jerked his head toward the door. "Move. The bouncer will take care of him. Again."

Worried about her peer and what he might do next, she peered around Johann's solid frame and saw Rick holding the man by the shirt collar. Relief drained the last ounces of courage and defiance from her frame. She nodded and fit herself to Johann's side. The heat of his skin felt nice beneath his crisp, white shirt. *The heat would feel even better without the shirt.*

He tucked an arm around her and shouldered his way toward the exit.

A soft summer rain fell from the night sky. Holding the glass bottle against her chest, she lifted her face. "You were right about the rain." The cracked concrete in the parking lot caught her shoe. Stumbling, she clutched him for support.

He picked her up and carried her away from the bar.

She tensed, but the steady rhythm of his steps carried her farther from the restless tension inside the building.

"I didn't know you could sing."

She closed her eyes and relaxed. "You don't know everything, Johann."

He hesitated at the street corner.

She opened her eyes. A car passed, its lights as bright as the stage lights. "Go left."

"I know my way to your *scheisse* townhouse." He turned right.

Laughing, she closed her eyes and nestled against his chest. "Why don't you have an accent?"

"Boarding school."

Of course. Peeking through her lashes, she saw the entrance to the small park. Oak trees and LED lanterns led to dark shadows and the quiet water of a pond. A willow tree's lazy branches grazed the surface of the water.

Choosing a bench, he lowered his body to the rain-soaked slats.

She struggled against his hold. "You'll get wet."

He tightened his grip. "Be still for a moment. Do you ever rest?"

She let the rhythm of his breathing set the pace. "I'll rest when I'm dead."

"I would prefer a different answer."

"So would I." She closed her eyes. "But I chose academia. Publish or perish."

"Tell me what happened to your sister."

"She died." *But you already know that.*

He remained silent.

Sighing, she turned her face away from his chest and looked at the willow tree. "Jecca beat childhood leukemia. We thought she was in the clear. We thought the radiation and the hospital stays were behind us. Osteosarcoma struck at fourteen. She died within a year."

"What a terrible way to lose a loved one."

She closed her eyes. Instead of resenting Jecca, she had reveled in her younger sister's attention. The effort of a tickle returned riotous laughter. A trip to the zoo yielded wide-eyed amazement. "The doctors did everything they could to save her."

Extracting herself from his arms, she settled on the bench's wet slats. The bottle of champagne felt heavy and cool in her hands. She popped the cork, took a drink, and let the sweet bubbly carry her back to her childhood. Memories of a freckle-faced sister with sun-gold highlights flooded her vision. Long, tawny limbs spread over white, plastic chairs. An aquamarine pool, shared books, and a box of colored pencils.

She took a long pull of champagne. By the time Jecca doubled over and admitted her pain, those memories held no promise. "Our family felt perfunctory. She fixed the wobbling stool. She made us feel whole."

"I'm sorry for your loss. Your parents are still alive, aren't they?"

"Barely." She took another drink. "I learned not to depend on them."

Pulling her back to his lap, he gripped her hips. "You look so carefree, but you're stubborn and independent. No wonder you succeed in the lab."

She smiled and closed her eyes. His comfort felt safe, and she reveled in the freedom of losing control. "I know. It's a terrible combination."

"Not really."

Exhaling, she relaxed her shoulders. "I want to spare people the pain of losing their loved ones to drugs."

"But you won't risk love yourself."

She shook her head. "Losing people feels too painful. I don't think I could do it again."

He repositioned her on his lap. "I miss my brother, too."

Shifting, she stroked his face, watching him close his eyes for a breath. "I know you do."

"How?" he asked.

She dropped her hand. "Why else would you put up with me?" Taking another sip, she shifted her legs. *The champagne tastes like sunshine.*

He cleared his throat. "Stop wiggling."

She met his gaze and swallowed. Despite the soft drizzle and the swift bubbles, she felt the heat and pressure of his erection. "You said he burned through his trust and made a fool of himself."

"He did, but he also told me I was a *Gutmensch.*"

Picking apart the word, she squinted against the effects of the alcohol and the pressure beneath her thigh. " 'Good human' is an insult?"

He laughed. "The word sounds like a compliment, but the phrase is an insult. It's someone who tries to control disputes and calm situations without taking criticism. It's someone who thinks their cause is always ethically superior." He paused. "Günter went rogue, and

I helmed the family. You can move on, too. You can accept the pain of your childhood without shutting down your emotions. Your research won't suffer."

Strawberries and sunshine. She blinked and took another sip. "When Jecca died, I found my limit."

He pulled the bottle from her hand. "I think you loved my uncle."

"Dr. Stefan was easy to be around." Leaning her head against his chest, she closed her eyes and found the safety of common ground. "He reminded me of Jecca, full of energy and enthusiasm. I miss him."

Shifting her weight, Johann stood and pulled her to her feet. "You're missing the common denominator."

Grasping his forearms to steady her balance, she felt the latent strength in his arms but refused to look up. *He thinks I'm a child.* She released her grip, brushed the wet seat of her pants, and stepped back. Hiccup. Covering her mouth, she averted her gaze and feared his condescending expression would shatter the remnants of her dignity. Stomach acid burned her throat, and she regretted the effervescent indulgence. *Nothing tastes like strawberries and sunshine for long.*

Tucking an arm around her waist, he pulled her close and tipped up her chin. "Hadley, the brightest mirrors reflect the sun. Your determination and commitment fuel your research discoveries. They don't come from Dr. Stefan."

"He taught me everything I know." She closed her eyes, fighting the booze-soaked melancholy stealing her balance. *Life isn't a tube of fruit-flavored lip gloss. I don't care who's hiding in the shadows. Johann's here. Let them come.*

"You put in the hours."

She hiccupped. "Buffy thinks I'm idealistic."

"She's not the only one." Dropping her chin, he took her hand and left the champagne bottle near an overflowing recycle bin.

Walking beside him, she fell into a peaceful rhythm. He tucked her into the passenger seat of his sedan, and the car climbed the hills to his home. Watching the city disappear, she knew a single word would stop their ascent, but she leaned forward, wondering how to get into his pants. The windshield wipers moved from side to side, their soft rhythm calling her to sleep. Her head followed the pattern, and the muffled growl of the engine toyed with her consciousness. A champagne-laced burp slipped past her lips. "Excuse me."

"Go to sleep, Hadley."

She grinned.

The gates opened, and the trees gave way to vineyard rows. He parked the sedan and cut the engine.

Stumbling from the car, she ignored the allure of the house and staggered to a chaise lounge. A soft mist hovered in the air, refusing to fall. It beaded on her hair and created a soft haze around the security lights.

Using a voice command, he activated the gas firepit.

She leaned against the headrest. "Some people use matches."

He smiled. "Some people don't know any better."

Raising her head, she frowned. "Some people would rather not know."

"What does that mean?"

The weight of making an argument felt too heavy to bear. Yawning, she tucked her purse under her head and closed her eyes. *I'm better when I'm sober.*

"Hadley?"

She ignored the inquiry. *If dulling my senses is the best cure for pain, consider them dulled.*

"Hadley?"

She waved him off. "Goodnight, Johann."

He draped a jacket across her chest.

The jacket smelled of leather and citrus. "Thanks." She smiled, letting herself succumb to the pull of the ancient, effervescent drug. Years of research and accumulated knowledge subsided. Sighing, she tucked her head against her hand, but the articles in her purse made a lousy pillow. Pulling it free, she dangled it toward him. "Hold this for me?"

"Your purse?"

She yawned and repositioned her hands beneath her cheeks. "I'll know if you read my notebook."

"How?"

She smiled. "You won't be able to stay silent."

****

"Miss Heron," a woman said. "Miss Heron, come inside or the sun will burn your skin."

Hadley blinked and turned away from Silvia. She ran her tongue along her teeth and tasted stale cotton. Champagne and three bites of Chow Mein had left a mark. Squinting against the morning light, she wondered how long a woman wearing a gray sheath dress and overly bright lipstick could stand the heat. *Who even wears red lipstick?* Realizing Johann's housekeeper persisted, she blinked. The acres of vineyard grapes came into focus. Struggling to sit up on the chaise lounge, she turned and confirmed the sleek estate's floor-to-ceiling, glass walls. *Any manner of wild animal could have taken a bite out of me.* She scrambled to her feet.

"It's okay, Miss Heron." Silvia held up both hands and stepped backward. "Johann is at his office. You and I are the only ones out here."

Pain tenderized her arm, and she clutched the appendage *I'm not sure being alone with Silvia is a comforting thought.* Dropping back to the chaise lounge, she looked up. "How can I be stupid enough to leave myself this exposed?"

Silvia cracked a smile. "There are people who have stupid days, and there are people who are stupid every day. You do not strike me as a stupid woman."

"I spent the night out in the elements."

The housekeeper snorted. "Mr. zur Hausen has a very large fence."

"Fence?" Silvia's teasing tone caught her attention, but a headache squeezed her temples. Rising to her feet, she squinted, took a deep breath, and stumbled toward the house. "I'll call a car."

"How about an omelet before you go?"

Nodding, she fell for the mere promise of protein and cheese. Bathed in sunlight, the house's dark walnut cabinetry and stainless-steel appliances gleamed. She climbed on a barstool and wished she had a pair of sunglasses.

Silvia pulled eggs and vegetables from the refrigerator and set them on the concrete countertop. "What would you like in your omelet, Miss Heron?"

"It's just Hadley." She rubbed her eyebrows. "Do you always call him Mr. zur Hausen?"

"To his face."

She braced her elbows on the island and hung her

head between her hands. "Silvia, do you have any coffee?"

"We have everything."

Of course you do.

Silvia coated a ceramic pan with butter and left it to warm on the gas cooktop. She dialed a cup of coffee on a super-automatic machine and pushed the brew button. When the chortling subsided, she slid the steaming cup across the counter and offered her a small carton of cream. "This will help."

Hadley skipped the cream and took a deep, satisfying sip.

Singing to herself, Silvia sliced vegetables.

Her wicked-looking knife gleamed. Closing her eyes, she raised her head and accepted the consequences of her rebellion. Her head ached, and she stranded herself with a wise-cracking woman wielding an immense butcher knife. "I suppose Johann has a habit of bringing home damsels in distress?"

Silvia shook her head and kept slicing. "You would be the first."

"How long have you worked for him?"

"Fifteen years."

She almost choked on her coffee. "He hasn't brought home a woman in fifteen years?"

Stilling her knife, Silvia looked up. "I wouldn't call the other women damsels in distress."

"No, of course not." Frowning, she looked into her coffee.

"If you stay long enough, you will meet Miss Vivian Hoat. Once a week, she comes over for lunch."

Her head snapped up. "His assistant." She imagined an older woman with a strict part, red lips, and a matching gray sheath dress.

Silvia nodded and set an omelet on the countertop.

Abandoning all thoughts of other women, she took a deep breath of the steam escaping the omelet and forgot her headache.

"Do you want salsa or hot sauce to accompany your breakfast?"

Tearing off the end of the omelet, she let the buttery eggs melt in her mouth. "I'd love some salsa, if you have it."

"We have everything, Miss Heron." Silvia set down a dish of salsa and stepped away from the island.

Swallowing, she met the woman's shrewd, brown gaze.

Silvia raised her eyebrows and handed her a fork.

"Thanks." She broke off a bite and savored rich oregano fresh from an herb garden. She summoned a smile. "Thank you for breakfast. It's delicious."

The woman nodded, and a small smile loosened her red lips.

She allowed herself to take a deep breath. *I hope Vivian Hoat knows who runs this house. Sticking around to see two strong-willed woman duke it out might be worth my time, but I have work to finish.* Pulling out her phone, she opened the app to call a ride. "I'll be out of your hair in a few minutes."

"That's unnecessary, Miss Heron." Silvia pulled keys from a rack. "I will drive you home."

"Thank you."

Lowering the keys, Silvia hesitated. "Would you like to shower? The guest bath has views of the vineyard."

She held up her hand. "That's okay. I'd rather go

back to my townhouse."

Silvia crossed her arms. "It is a very nice bathroom."

Considering how she passed the night, she wondered how bad she smelled. *A view and a plush towel aren't bad choices.* She looked at the winding drive. "Will Johann be home before his lunch appointment? He has my purse. I don't want to be an imposition."

"He will not mind at all. He asked me to take care of you."

"Oh." She stood and ran a hand through her hair. "Does he always get what he wants?"

The housekeeper smiled. "If it's good for him."

Leaving the kitchen, Hadley followed Silvia's instruction toward a guest suite, started a shower, and washed away the gritty feeling of too much self-pity. Four sleek showerheads surrounded her with hot water. Cedar and lavender-scented steam filled the glass enclosure. When drought awareness kicked in, she turned off the spray and reached for a fluffy, white towel. *This bathroom is not just nice. This bathroom is Ritz Carlton nice. French Riviera nice. Promenade des Anglais nice. No wonder he found my mad, carpeted dash amusing.* Turning on a high-powered vent fan to clear the steam, she looked at her reflection in the mirror and realized her head hurt more than her arm. Opening drawers, she located a hairdryer.

A muffled voice came through the door. "Your clothes are ready, Miss Heron."

"Thank you, Silvia."

"You know he stayed outside all night."

She cleared her throat and stepped closer to the

door. "Excuse me?"

"Missing his sleep is not good for him."

Years of diminishing her presence in her parents' household made her swallow. "I'm sorry?"

"*Espero que valga la pena.*"

"What?" Hearing the woman's heels click in retreat, she added Spanish to her task list and cracked the door to the bathroom. Her clothes waited on the immaculate, white bed. Slipping on her jeans, fresh and tight from a hot dryer, she skipped the embroidered long-sleeved shirt meant to hide her wound. Rolling her shoulders in the freedom of a tank top felt good. "Silvia?" She raised her voice and headed to the kitchen. "I'm ready to go back to town."

Johann stood in front of the wall of glass.

His suit looked immaculate. She admired the sunlight shining over his shoulders, but the steel accents and white upholstery reminded her of her guest status. *The windows are probably so energy efficient that I would never feel the sun's warmth in this house.*

He opened the windows.

She felt the early summer breeze and heard leaves skittering along the ground.

"Silvia went to the fish market. Your purse is on the island."

Tucking both hands in her pockets, she rocked back on her heels and wished she could see his face. "Thanks. She said she would give me a ride home."

He turned and cocked his head. "Funny, I understood she needed fresh fish for lunch."

Walking to the island, she opened her purse, pulled out her phone, and frowned. "Lunch isn't for an hour."

He looked toward the automated gates. "I don't

control that woman."

I'm not sure anybody controls that woman. Catching his face in profile, she smiled and gave him credit for Silvia's continued presence. The man radiated precision and arrogance, but Silvia did not seem like the type of woman to tolerate inappropriate behavior.

He walked toward her. "Let me see your arm."

She held it close.

"I came home to check on you, Hadley. Put me at ease?"

I can think of several ways to put you at ease. She extended her arm. "It's fine."

He touched the pale flesh bordering the wound. "No sign of infection."

She met his gaze. "Your antiseptic gel worked."

Releasing her, he stepped back. "Good."

Reverse engineering the gel took the backseat to her CBD research, but the prize tempted her. "How long will it take me to determine the structures and concentrations of the components?"

He crossed his arms. "Chemical composition analysis has many limitations."

Waving a hand in the air, she dismissed his claim. "Buffy is a badass. She knows a variety of analytical methods."

"I'm sure she does, but unknown substances are difficult to identify."

She decided to goad him. "A week?"

He smiled and shrugged out of his jacket. "That would be impressive."

The sleek lines of his gun holster banded his shoulder. She swallowed. "And if the deformulation works, Johann? Will you threaten me with legal action?"

Laying his jacket over the back of a hair, he shrugged. "I gave you the gel, Hadley. You can do as you wish, but I doubt you will replicate it." He grinned. "Or keep it stable."

It's unstable? She sighed. "You have very little confidence in my abilities."

"On the contrary. You're brilliant, but many pathways to success exist."

She looked at the city nestled in the valley and wondered if Palo Alto would ever feel safe again. "Like the witness protection program?"

Rolling his eyes, he walked into the kitchen. "Your propensity to wander off maddens me." Filling a glass of water, he sipped it and set it on the island.

I can think of other ways to madden you. She claimed a barstool. "Working is not the same thing as running away."

"Work remotely."

She twisted on the barstool. "That seems impossible."

"Life is full of seemingly impossible tasks. As a scientist, you overcome them." He rolled up his shirt cuffs. "I have something to teach you."

She watched his forearms flex and chased the shadow of his form beneath his shirt. Left undone, the top buttons exposed his skin, and she considered the possibilities of seeing more than a shadow. Two days of proximity had smoothed the rough edges of her fear and given her heart a healthy reason to race. *I have several skill sets that I'd be willing to practice on this man. How long will he view me as a liability?* Meeting his bright, blue gaze, she imagined running her fingers through his jet-black hair. "I think I have Stockholm Syndrome."

He frowned. "Pardon?"

She cleared her throat. "Nothing."

Withdrawing his handgun, he laid it on the kitchen counter.

She looked at the sleek weapon and shook her head. "Not the skills I had in mind."

"Hadley, I can't be with you all the time. When you're stressed or upset, you bolt. How will you defend yourself when I'm not there?"

"Pepper spray?"

"Effective at close range. If someone's that close to you, you're already too late."

The cold factuality of his voice brought gooseflesh to her arms. She rubbed her skin and shook off the memory of Lieutenant Jayne trying the same move. *Why do men always want to teach women to shoot firearms? If I wanted to shoot a gun, I'd go to a range and learn how to do it myself.* Crossing her arms, she shook her head. "I'm not carrying a gun on my body."

"Keep it in your purse."

"My notebook takes up space. Did you read it?"

"No." He leaned forward. "You can trust me, Hadley. Stay close to me. No more running off. No more flights of fancy. Can you control your impulses for a week?"

Dismissing his scatterbrained insinuations, she focused on the impulses that sent her pulse racing every time he walked into the room. Time seemed to slow. "What if I kill your brother?"

"I will not blame you. Günter chose his path."

She backed away from the gun. "I can't take away

someone you love, Johann. I can't do that to anyone."

He straightened. "And I cannot leave you unprepared to face him."

She nodded.

"Let me teach you how to use the gun. If I do my job, you'll never operate it."

She watched him take a deep breath. His chest expanded, and a glimpse of vulnerability slipped through his iron reserve. "I trust you."

"People are fallible," he said.

Tilting her head, she focused on the thin, vertical scar marring his cheek. *What kind of perversion led Günter to harm his brother?* Thoughts of swimming in the Russian River with Jecca flooded her memories. Jecca often climbed on her back and pushed her below the surface of the cold water, but even as water stole her breath, she trusted her sister to back down. *We fought for attention, but we never fought for wealth and assets.* She met Johann's gaze. "People are also capable of redemption."

"You're optimistic." Withdrawing a wine bottle from the recycling drawer, he placed it next to the gun. "Don't tell me shattering glass and shattering a life have the same consequences."

She exhaled and considered the thick, green vessel. The rational part of her mind confirmed the object's inanimate status. *The gun's a machine. It's a piece of technology, and it's nothing more and nothing less.* "One bottle. That's it."

"And then?"

She dragged her teeth along her lips.

"You're insufferable."

Grabbing the bottle, she swung it and walked

toward the doors. "Fancy word."

"Brat."

Glancing over her shoulder, she grinned, but the heat of his gaze could have melted glass. She swallowed and extended the bottle.

He passed through the doorway and placed the bottle on top of a vineyard post.

Following him outside, she stood in the middle of the outdoor entertaining space like a reluctant participant waiting for her turn to dance.

"Always treat a gun like it's loaded. Until you're ready to use it, keep it pointed in a safe direction. Until you've made a conscious decision to shoot, keep your finger out of the trigger guard."

"That won't be a problem." She crossed her arms. "I don't even want to touch the gun."

He placed the gun on the firepit's edge. "Desperation will conquer your aversion."

"I doubt it." She stepped closer.

"Pick up the gun with your dominant hand and hold it high on the grip. Keep your trigger finger on the outside of the trigger guard."

At the gun's weight, she recoiled. Taking a deep breath, she tightened her grip and stretched her pointer finger so far past the trigger guard her tendons strained.

He corrected her grip. "Wrap your other hand around your dominant hand. Your hands should fit together like pieces of a puzzle."

The heat of the midday sun reflected off the hardscaping. Following his precise instructions, she felt sweat creep down her back and blamed her shaking arms on her hangover.

"Stand with your feet and your hips shoulder width

apart. Bend your knees for stability and raise the gun. You're not worried about target practice and aligning sights. The bottle's stationary. Take a deep breath, use your dominant eye, and aim."

She followed his instructions and paused. "That's it?"

"Pull the trigger."

"Right." She swallowed. Behind the bottle, bright green grape leaves shifted in the wind. She focused on the bottle's white label. Narrowing her gaze blurred the cold metal in her hands and shifted it out of focus.

Johann moved closer.

Her vision swayed, and she lost sight of the target. Shaking her head, she took a deep breath. "Now what?"

"Squeeze the trigger until you feel resistance and then keep squeezing. The discharge will surprise you. You don't want to tense up and anticipate the recoil."

She cleared her throat and looked at him. "Maybe you should demonstrate."

"You've already seen me shoot a gun, Hadley."

"I know." Biting her lip, she focused on the bottle and prepared to take a shot. The dark edge beneath his polish terrified and thrilled her, but she tightened her finger on the trigger.

Chapter Eight

Her concentration wavered, and Hadley thought of the figure hiding in the cemetery's deep shadows. *I'm not playing a carnival game. The blaze on my arm will heal, but the moment of vulnerability will remain for the rest of my life.* She exhaled. *I'm practicing the difference between life and death. My death.*

The wine bottle shifted out of focus. Blinking, she steadied her arms. Minutes passed. The gun felt heavier, and the sun shone brighter. She constructed features for Günter and assembled fragments of his life story. *He hurt people.*

Johann remained quiet.

Lowering the gun, she set it on the firepit's edge.

"I knew she wouldn't do it," a woman said.

Hadley inhaled.

A black sedan retreated down the drive.

Diva. Turning, Hadley faced a woman wearing a sleeveless, white sundress. Her curled blonde hair and immaculate lipstick made her look like a starlet from a 1950s color film. Exhaling, Hadley planted her hands on her hips. *Apparently, I'm underdressed for the occasion.*

The woman strode past her, and her heels clicked on the stone.

Wishing she stopped after the first glass of champagne, Hadley rubbed her temples.

Picking up the handgun, the woman fired it with one hand.

The green bottle shattered.

Hadley winced, and the gunshot's crack lingered in the sun-baked air.

Putting down the gun, the woman wiped clean her hands.

"Your assistant?" Hadley asked.

Johann nodded.

At once, Hadley understood the woman once shared his bed. Scanning her immaculate outfit, she felt even more than underdressed. "Nice shoes."

The woman smiled with the friendliness of a hungry lioness.

"Don't forget Ginger Rogers did everything Fred Astaire did, backwards and in high heels," the woman said.

Looking at the shards of glass scattered across the ground, Hadley shook her head at the reference to an old Frank and Ernest cartoon. She squared her shoulders and faced the manicured woman. "Don't forget the director called 'Cut,' and all the actors stood."

The woman smiled. "Touché."

Stepping off the patio, Hadley gathered the shards of glass.

Johann caught her arm. "Don't worry about the mess. Silvia will sweep up the shards."

Uncomfortable with another person picking up after her, she freed her arm. "Looking after me isn't Silvia's job."

"Removing hazards that would harm my guests *is* her job."

She looked at the glamorous woman in the sundress. *Maybe you should pay Silvia more.*

A car passed the gate and traveled up the drive.

Not another mistress.

Johann held out a hand and accepted the pieces of glass she had removed from the ground. He preceded her to the patio and gestured to the woman who upended her informal dominion over the estate. "This is Vivian Hoat, my executive assistant."

The woman held out a hand. "Hello, Hadley, it's a pleasure to meet you."

She shook the woman's hand and looked to Johann for guidance on the basis of her presence at the estate.

He nodded. "Vivian is well aware of our predicament."

"Perhaps she should be my bodyguard?"

Vivian smiled. "Günter is a formidable threat. You're much safer with Johann's protection, but I advise you to keep an eye out for his housekeeper."

"I'm sure that's excellent advice." She turned and watched Silvia climb from the car carrying a large bundle wrapped in brown butcher paper. "I'm ready to go home now."

Johann nodded.

Hesitating, she questioned her inability to shoot the gun. *If I'd given myself another chance, could I have shot the bottle?* Afraid of the answer, she walked toward Silvia.

The housekeeper shifted the bundle in her arms. "Where are you going, Miss Heron?"

"I think I've worn out my welcome. Take me home, please."

"Won't you stay for lunch?" Silvia asked.

"That's very thoughtful." She linked her fingers and stretched them toward the ground. "I have a lot of research to finish."

Silvia frowned. "You need to eat."

She unlaced her fingers, tilted her head, and chose a fact-based approach. "You fed me an omelet."

Silvia thrust the paper-wrapped fish across the counter. "I'll feed you more."

Taking the unexpected weight, Hadley forgot about the gun, her compulsion to flee Johann, and his glamorous assistant. He might lecture her about yesterday's disappearing act, but he came looking for her, and she preferred the intimacy of their misty park bench to this bright, midday lesson. In the sunshine, her inability to pull the trigger and shoot a glass bottle left her feeling juvenile. After a decade of academic research and perseverance, she should have the discipline to perform a clinical task. Meeting the challenge in Silvia's gaze, she took a deep breath. "As soon as I finish the meal, you will take me home?"

Silvia smiled. "Yes, Miss Heron."

Why does she look like the cat that caught a fish? She shifted the package to her hip. "I'm only staying for lunch because you let me take that shower."

"Wait until you see the master bath." Silvia chuckled.

Johann cleared his throat and led the party into the house.

Vivian settled on the white leather couch and crossed her legs at the ankle as if she spent her spare time studying royal etiquette blogs. Given the threat of comparison, Hadley loitered near the windows. *When was the last time Vivian made a naked mad dash to her bedroom? Can I make it outside the lab?*

Pulling dishes from the refrigerator, Silvia hummed.

We're quite the triad. She waited for Johann to set the tone.

He walked into the kitchen and cleared his throat. "Hadley may come and go from this house as she pleases. If Günter or another suspicious person approaches the property, secure the house and remain inside the building."

"Yes, Mr. zur Hausen." Silvia resumed her song.

"I'm in no mood for games."

Silvia stopped singing. "Life and death are never a game, Mr. zur Hausen. That's why you hired me." She dropped her voice. "Fifteen years ago."

He nodded. "Thank you, Silvia."

Hadley left her outpost and settled on a barstool. "Why should we remain inside the building? I've seen enough action movies to know what happens next."

Vivian covered a yawn. "The builders installed windows made from bulletproof glass."

She looked at the windows. "Of course."

Johann activated a touchscreen. Instrumental music played, and the lights dimmed.

Silvia continued the preparations.

Vivian tapped on her phone.

Looking at Johann, Hadley realized she was the principal beneficiary of the show and tell. "So, the building does tricks."

"The automation system recognizes voice commands." He rattled off a string of instructions in German and asked her to repeat his commands. "The computer will store your voice as a temporary guest profile."

She complied, hoping the computer accepted her pronunciation. *Then again, I learned everything I knew from Dr. Stefan.* She repeated the first command.

Vivian looked up. A frown marred her flawless skin. "You speak German?"

Smiling, she raised her chin and repeated the second command.

The automation touchscreen flashed green.

Johann's instructions progressed.

Each phrase roused her curiosity. Realizing the system went beyond digital assistants, smart thermostats, and efficient bulbs, she learned the house lights and ventilation system could respond to her movements and track her location. Motion sensors and receivers permeated the rooms, and passive near field communication tags fed data to the system. Glancing at the wall near the front door, she noted the absence of physical switches. "Do you face a lot of imminent threats, Johann?"

He cocked his head. "Why do you ask?"

She gestured toward the electronics. "Are you overcompensating for something?"

He crossed his arms. "My time in the BKA taught me to be ready for all outcomes. The mission of the BKA is 'Protect, Salvage, and Evacuate.' "

"I wish it was 'family counseling and conflict resolution.' "

"So do I." He set down the controller.

She swallowed. "Play "Lick the Beat." "

The pop music hit filled the room.

Vivian rolled her eyes.

I love it when she does that.

Johann turned an ear to the speakers and frowned.

She swallowed. *That song might have been too much.* Canceling the command, she picked at her nails and avoided his gaze. "I wanted to test out the system. Don't worry. I'm not addicted to the top forty."

"I like pop culture," Vivian said. "The predictability soothes me."

Hadley smiled. *You would.*

Silvia unrolled the butcher paper and exposed several sea bass. She placed a fish on a butcher-block cutting board, opened a drawer, and removed a chef's knife.

Drumming her fingers on the countertop, Hadley wondered how long manners doomed her to polite purgatory. She watched the housekeeper slam the knife into the butcher block. As a sea bass lost its head, flecks of pink-tinged juice and loose scales flew from the fish and landed on the concrete countertops.

Vivian wrinkled her nose. "Oh, Silvia, I hate when you cook sea bass. The fish make such a mess."

The housekeeper nodded. "I believe you mentioned that fact." She slapped another fish on the cutting board.

Wrinkling her pert nose, Vivian shifted on her chair. "So, Hadley. Johann tells me you're a Ph.D. student. You must be very smart."

"I try." She sounded like a flattered pupil and wrinkled her nose.

"But really, the Department of Chemical and Systems Biology?" Vivian blinked several times. "It all sounds so complex."

She narrowed her gaze. *Is she Ginger Rogers or Mata Hari?* Looking at her white dress, she thought about the impracticalities of the color. *At least Johann's suits are navy, gray, or black.* "Tell me, Vivian, what does an executive assistant do all day?"

Vivian waved a hand in the air. "Oh, this and that."

"Over lunch?"

"Johann and I are old friends." Vivian smiled.

Hadley considered a variety of responses, but she matched Vivian's smile and scanned the room. An architectural paperweight caught her eye. Picking it up, she considered throwing it at the panoramic, bulletproof smart glass. *Maybe I've underestimated my capacity for violence.*

"Did you always want to be a biologist?" Vivian asked.

Putting down the paperweight, she turned her back on the woman. *My favorite color is green, and I like puppies.* She stared at her reflection in a steel-framed mirror, but she only saw the dark shadows beneath her eyes. *Does she think I'm twelve?*

"I've always found biology particularly fascinating," Vivian said. "Aren't we all just animals at heart?"

Turning her gaze from the mirror, she focused on the woman. "Evolution produced a few interesting specimens."

Vivian raised her eyebrows. "Such as?"

Smiling, she decided to answer the woman's first question. "After I finished my master's degree, I focused on chemical and bimolecular engineering."

"And what did you study in undergrad?"

"Physiotherapy and pain management."

Vivian leaned forward. "So what is the big research secret? Günter acts like he's dying to have your research."

Looking at Johann, she waited for a signal.

He raised his eyebrows.

She considered Vivian. If she trusted Johann, she had to trust his assistant as well, but neither party deserved to know the scope of her findings. "I fine-tuned the reproduction of major cannabinoids using yeast and biosynthesis."

Vivian's polite smile faltered. "Oh, is that all it is?"

She smiled and thought of the polymers she tested. "More or less."

Johann cleared his throat and gestured toward the farthest wing of the house. "Vivian, would you mind joining me to review our upcoming events? Schedule changes triggered travel adjustments, and I'd like you to address them."

The woman uncrossed her legs and rose from the couch. "Of course." Her heels clicked on the floor, and she followed him down the hall.

Silvia put down her knife. "What is biosynthesis?"

The housekeeper's spark of interest caught Hadley's attention. She settled near Silvia, but she left enough space to keep fish juice off her clean clothes. "I'm short-cutting the production processes to conduct medical research on marijuana extracts."

Silvia nodded and sprinkled salt on the fish. "They're legalizing the drug."

"More and more states allow its use."

Silvia looked out the window. "I never thought legalization would happen. The ripple effects will be huge." She shook her head and frowned. "So what's the big secret?"

The combination of Silvia's stern countenance and

graceful integration into Johann's life inspired her to trust the woman. "CBD contains over one hundred chemicals, but the chemicals occur in tiny quantities, and they're hard to extract. Scientists don't understand their function, but biosynthesis uses yeast to make purer, less expensive sources of those chemicals. Given enough feedstock, we can play with the outcomes. I didn't come up with the idea of biosynthesizing the process, but I made it better." She shrugged. "Maybe I'll find a few novel cannabinoids."

Silvia glanced at the hallway where Johann and Vivian disappeared. "You're not telling me the complete story."

Clever woman. She tilted a vase of flowers and saw a near field communication tag. When the water in the vase evaporated, the NFC tag probably sent an alert. *I'm sure the house also has ears.* She wanted to trust Johann and his staff, but she had a hard time extending that trust to hackers with an interest in home automation systems. "It's complicated."

Silvia sliced the fins from the sea bass. "I'll tell you something valuable, Miss Heron. There was a time when Vivian Hoat didn't make appointments for lunch. She didn't sleep in the guest room, and she didn't bill her time making Johann's travel arrangements."

Biting her lip, Hadley contained her vindication and toyed with a leaf in the flower arrangement. "What happened?"

"I don't know." Silvia sprinkled pepper on the fish. "He's very loyal."

Hadley looked up. "She's very possessive."

The housekeeper smiled. "You do not strike me as a stupid woman. One day I hope you will tell me about the rest of your research."

"I hope so, too. Right now, they're preliminary results and the promise of a dream."

Silvia looked up. "Isn't that where we all start?"

The perceptive statement unsettled her balance in the house. She shifted on the barstool and pulled out her phone. Pretending to read the news, she thought of Jecca struggling while cancer attacked her body for a second time. She thought of her mother sitting in front of a bright television, unwilling to feel pain, while her father scurried to make it through the day. Then she thought of herself alone in the lab. *We all start with the promise of a dream, but where do we end up?*

Rhythmic clicks warned her of Johann's and Vivian's return.

Looking up, she realized Silvia had finished searing the fish and had set the monolithic dining room table with crisp linens. Grabbing her shirt to cover her arms, she took the seat Johann offered.

Vivian launched into a stream of questions.

Johann responded and kept pace.

Hadley felt completely out of the conversation. Ignoring the woman's tactic, she picked at her sea bass and listened to their business chatter. *Small talk is more stressful than defending a thesis. Given a choice of afternoon activities, I would settle for a solid nap in a dark room.*

Vivian speared a tomato. "*The Gast Club* invited you to speak in ten days." She popped the red orb in her mouth without disturbing her lipstick.

How does she do that? Moving medallions of roasted squash across her plate, she hoped Silvia would ignore she failed to eat her vegetables. Pushing away her plate, she placed her napkin on the table. "I hardly think Johann's the poster child for the local tourism industry."

"*The Gast Club* is the San Francisco chapter house of German Friends International. GFI is a worldwide organization dedicated to environmentally conscious tourism, protection of natural and cultural heritage, and climate protection." Vivian blinked. "You grew up in Marin. I thought you would know of the organization."

"Sounds fancy." Hadley blotted the napkin against her lips.

Johann cleared his throat. "Hardly, it's a Bavarian wooden lodge with a view of the redwoods, a dedicated membership base, and a decent selection of beers."

She shrugged. "That sounds fun. Maybe I'll visit one day."

"Come with me." He set down his utensils.

She focused on the reason she sat in his house. "A week."

He dipped his chin.

Vivian speared another tomato. The vegetable split and seed-flecked juice seeped onto the plate. "Hadley, make sure you check their website. They're only open for visitors on selected weekends." She glanced at the fraying embroidery on Hadley's long-sleeve shirt, popped the tomato in her mouth, and chewed. "Then again, you might enjoy hiking in."

Lab politics had nothing on this woman's genteel barbs. "Yes, I probably would." Taking a sip of her water, she cocked her head. "Do people ever call you Vivi?"

The woman raised her eyebrows. She turned to Johann. "You also have an invitation to dine with the governor."

Johann kept his gaze on his plate. "Decline it. The single-payer system makes sense, but I'm withholding my campaign contribution until he puts in place advanced mental health services."

"Does he know that?" Vivian asked.

Johann sipped his water. "He does."

Vivian tapped her phone.

Hadley wondered if she could accelerate the woman's departure. "So, Vivian, you're in charge of keeping Johann moving in the right direction?"

"I'm in charge of making the arrangements he needs."

Silvia set a plate of cheese on the table. "Aren't we all?"

Johann frowned and looked at the housekeeper. "I heard that."

She smiled. "Yes, Mr. zur Hausen."

Hadley laughed, but she sensed the tension radiating from Johann, and his tight-lipped frown confirmed her impression. His posture had straightened into rigid formality, and the familiar ease of their outing had vanished. *I prefer bantering without an audience.* She smiled at Vivian. "I suppose you've worked for a lot of elite customers."

"Yes, I have a diverse portfolio of projects. I used to work for a global management consulting firm."

"Do you miss the action of leading projects?" She aligned her unused utensils. "In the movies, the executive assistant always covets the boardroom. Don't you just want to take something in hand and make it your own?"

Vivian stared out the window. "I miss the action."

"I have an inquisitive roommate who always wants to know what people make. It's a crass hobby, but what's your going rate? Do you personalize your tricks and services?"

Turning from the view, Vivian tucked her hair behind her ear. "I prefer not to discuss my compensation."

She waved a hand in the air. "That's all right. I'll make up something about servicing clients on a sliding fee schedule."

Patting her napkin at the edge of her lips, Vivian placed it on the table. "If you're implying what I think you're implying, the answer is no. I don't turn tricks for wealthy men."

At being called out, Hadley swallowed.

"I'm starting a data analytics business called Hoat Analytics. In a few years, I won't lead projects, but I'll lead an entire company."

"Um-m."

Vivian raised her chin. "If you'll excuse me, I need to speak in private with Johann. He squeezed a call with the Palo Alto police department into his busy schedule. I hope your research hasn't distracted him from his work."

Turning to Johann, Hadley tilted her head. "Do I need to be there?"

He turned his glass on the tablecloth.

She watched the ring of condensation expand like a seeping shadow.

"Do you want Lieutenant Jayne to know we're spending every waking hour together?" he asked.

"Not every hour." She dropped her voice. "You left me alone last night."

He rubbed the back of his neck. "I stayed by your side."

"You didn't have to stay."

"You were vulnerable." He opened his mouth but remained silent.

"And your uncle asked you to protect me." She pushed her chair from the table, forced a smile that burned her cheeks, and stood to face Vivian. "Nice having lunch with you. I enjoyed the fish."

Vivian set down her fork and stood. "I'm sure."

Placing his napkin on the table, Johann rose. "Excuse me, Hadley. Silvia will get you anything you need."

Standing next to each other, he and Vivian looked like the perfect, polished pair. She watched him walk away and wondered if he hated the meal. She replayed his tight-lipped frown. *I think he hated it. How do I make him laugh?*

Silvia turned on the sink faucet.

Picking up plates, Hadley carried them into the kitchen.

The housekeeper shook her head. "You couldn't resist poking that woman, could you?"

Stacking the plates on the countertop, she averted her gaze. "What did I do?"

"You practically called her a hooker."

"Not exactly." She swallowed a niggle of guilt. "You gave me the idea."

The housekeeper crossed her arms and let a dishrag hang over her elbow. "I never said a word."

Biting her lip, she realized she went too far.

Silvia put down her dishrag and braced her arms. "Fine. I'll apologize."

"Good." Silvia wiped the counter. "She never made him happy."

Hadley looked at the ceiling camera and wondered if anyone watched the exchange. The call with the police could leave Johann precise and controlled or tight-lipped and frustrated. She wondered if she could redirect his emotions into something more productive than a lecture. *Joke him out of his mood?* Wandering to the refrigerator, she refilled her glass and smiled. *Irritating him would be easier.*

"I can take you home now, Miss Heron," Silvia said.

She paused, glass in hand. "That's probably for the best."

Vivian entered the kitchen in bare feet. Her shoes dangled from her left hand, one heel broken and hanging at an odd angle. Her immaculate lipstick remained intact.

"What happened to your shoe?" Hadley asked.

"I tripped."

"Are you okay?"

The woman stared.

She swallowed. "I shouldn't have asked about your compensation."

"Trust me, Hadley. I can afford new shoes." Vivian smiled.

She felt like a floundering pupil. "I'm apologizing, from one over-educated woman to another."

After a moment, Vivian nodded and turned to Silvia. "Please take me back to the office. Johann requested Hadley remain at the house."

Silvia reached for her keys. "What happened to your conference call?"

175

Johann's administrative assistant looked at the closed office door. "He said he would handle the call."

So close to fleeing to the safety of her townhouse, Hadley watched Silvia's car disappear down the cedar-lined driveway and searched for the resources she needed to handle Johann. Impatient with her padded jail cell, she prowled the house. *One bottle of champagne landed me in this mess.* Catching her clean-faced reflection in the tall mirror, she looked at her healing arm and amended her thoughts. *One bottle of champagne, several bullets, one exploding package, and a Dickensesque story about peeling potatoes.*

She opened closets and lifted objects. The guest bedroom where she showered held few secrets, but the hallway doors tempted her curiosity. The first night, Johann had entered the room at the end of the hall. Assuming the conference call would occupy him, she headed toward that room.

Silvia was right. The bed and sitting area looked like a hotel brochure, but the open concept master bathroom came with yards of cement tile, a freestanding silhouette bathtub, and a wall of glass leading to an outdoor shower. The sight mesmerized her, and she considered the decadence of a second shower in the high-end room.

"Do you like what you see?"

Johann's question sounded like a caress. *Only if you'll join me.* Keeping her gaze on the fixtures, she imagined him stripped to his skin beneath the hot spray and ached to join him. *I'm a scientist. Lust is a chemical reaction.* Her rationalization failed, and she succumbed to the image and the coiling tension in her core. A heartbeat later and she turned. "I doubt you get a lot of outdoor showers in Germany."

"Only in the summer months." He leaned against the doorframe, arms crossed.

She bit her lip and wondered if she would always link him with summer. Even now, surrounded by echoing tile and the smell of fresh linens, she caught a faint hint of his aftershave. The combination of simmering heat, aged herbs, and fresh citrus pulled her toward him. *He's steady and sure, but he's also hot as fuck.* Remembering his straightlaced mood over lunch, she considered the consequences of her trespassing and scratched her scalp. "Your assistant doesn't like me. I'm sorry for ruining the meal."

He shrugged. "Vivian can be a little territorial."

Dropping a hand, she nodded. "Why do you employ her?"

He straightened, pressed a panel, and revealed a closet stocked with rows of monochromatic suits. "She is very good at the work she does."

But not good enough to win the prize.

He stared at the suits. "She's very organized."

"But?"

Turning his back on the rows of lightweight wool, he shrugged. "Polished objects bore me."

I wouldn't bore you. Remembering she spent the last decade in a research lab, she frowned. "What put you in such a funk today?"

He placed a pair of shoes on a shelf.

"What? I can prowl around your house, but I can't ask questions?"

"Damon found Günter."

With Günter in tow, the threat to her life dissipated, and the construction binding her to Johann's side crumbled. She wanted to clap, but she struggled to complete the gesture. "That's good, right? Where is he?"

Turning, the crease between his eyes deepened. "The hospital."

"You mean, because you shot him?"

He shook his head. "Alcoholic neuropathy. He's been in hospital for a month."

She winced and cataloged what she knew of the condition. Symptoms manifested as spontaneous burning pain, enhanced sensitivity to stimulus, and aversions to everyday activities. Until patients sobered and allowed their nerves to heal, many patients remained disabled. "You don't have to worry about me anymore."

"Yes, Hadley, I do."

She crossed her arms. "You have a very unhealthy obsession with unknown threats."

Closing the distance, he wrapped an arm around her waist. "Who shot you?"

Swallowing, she searched for a pithy answer that would win her a point and give her an entry into strip off his clothes. *I'm just an obligation. Check the family code of conduct.* "I don't know."

"Exactly." His touch fell away, and he moved toward his closet.

She struggled to rub the warmth back into her arms. "Aren't you relieved?"

"I don't know yet."

His doubtful response validated her nerves. "I'm ready to go back to town."

Hand on a rack of clothing, he paused. "I had something else in mind."

She straightened. "What happened to your busy schedule?"

"I asked Vivian to clear it."

At the thought of Vivian's broken shoe, she grinned. *Was she so startled she tripped?*

Taking a step closer, his expression softened. "I realize you didn't ask for this commotion, Hadley. You didn't ask me to take over your life."

"Dr. Stefan did."

"I understand why you want to flee."

She smiled as if his statement was the first reasonable thing he had said all day. *Finally, a dose of empathy.* Then she thought of the bomb. "You didn't start the sequence."

His posture stiffened. "I will end it. Can you give me the rest of the week?"

She nodded.

After walking into his closet, he emerged wearing a pair of cargo shorts and a short-sleeved button-up shirt.

His shirt's pale blue-green color surprised her into silence. *Who is this man who looks like he came straight from the pages of a trekking catalog?*

Johann smiled. "Speechless?"

"I've only seen you wear gray or black." She ran a hand through her hair to diffuse her reaction. His clothes brought him closer to her daily interactions, but his muscled limbs and exposed, tan skin gave her a reason to wet her lips. "Maybe navy."

He laughed. "Do you want to go for a hike or not?"

She swallowed. "So the real assailant has an easy shot?"

He opened a cabinet-clad refrigerator and pulled out two refillable water bottles.

"Don't people have, like, scopes?" she asked.

"You've been watching too much television, Hadley. The shooter in the cemetery was not a trained assassin."

No, but you are. "What about your call with the police?"

Grimacing, he pocketed a bottle and tossed the second.

She caught it. "The call was that bad?"

"Lieutenant Jayne did not appreciate my suggestions." Placing a pair of sunglasses on his head, he walked into the hallway.

She scurried after him, impatient to understand how he planned to unearth an unknown assailant without interfering in the police investigation. *Won't the two forces come to a head?* Exhaling, she thought of the edits waiting on her computer and the research haunting her dreams. "Can Silvia pick up my laptop?"

"Yes."

His unequivocal answer soothed her nerves. She looked at her slim-legged jeans and figured she could cuff them or cut off the legs. "How strenuous is this hike?"

He tipped up his lips in a half-smile. "How strenuous do you want it to be?"

The hint of possibility tipped her indecisiveness. Thinking about the outdoor shower, she matched his controlled enthusiasm. "Wear me out, Johann."

Chapter Nine

Acres of golden grass rippled in the hilly preserve.
A grove of oak trees crested the nearest hill, but Hadley
moved her gaze to the horses grazing in an open
pasture. The animals wandered toward the fence, their
soft nuzzles searching for treats. With no food to share,
she held out her palm and scratched their noses.

Johann rubbed their necks and offered good-
natured pats.

She sipped from her water bottle. *Lucky horses.*
Hiding her gaze behind the rim of the container, she
wondered why the wilderness loosened his control.
Amid the hay-scented animals, his tight-lipped mood
fell away like his casual clothes freed an easy, athletic
grace held captive by the suits. *If we'd been born in
different circumstances, we would both be different
people.* Taking a deep breath, she considered the sun-
baked grass. "I didn't realize how much open space
existed back here."

He patted the last horse's flank.

The animal wandered off. She hoped they found
satisfying snacks.

"Conservationists spent years stitching together
parcels of land."

"Did you contribute?" she asked.

"I played a part." He looked at the oaks crowning
the hillside and led the way to a corridor linking the

preserve with a network of associated open spaces. "Quarry Trail crosses private property via a District easement. We can go as far as you want to go."

"To the coast?"

He looked at her cuffed jeans. "That would be quite a trek."

"Right. Let's get over the first hill."

He set a steady pace and nodded at hikers coming down Black Mountain's trail.

She struggled to keep up. Sweat dripped down her back, and she considered shucking her jeans.

At the crest of the hill, company on the trail dwindled.

Free of the blazing sun and steep ascent, the valley felt more intimate.

"Let's take a break."

She retreated to a stand of trees stippled with moss and lichens and braced her hands on her knees. "Are you carrying your gun?"

From the dirt trail, he scanned the hillside. "The biggest threat out here is a mountain lion."

She looked up. "What if Günter has friends?"

"He has no money to pay them."

"Somebody has money." She straightened and rolled her shoulders. "The third time might be a charm."

"I think you have time. When a woman has a series of accidents close together, people take notice of the trend."

Emerging from the shadows, she joined him on the bare dirt trail. "In an ideal world, a threshold wouldn't exist."

He nodded. "In an ideal world, humanity wouldn't

compete for resources."

"Have you ever been poor, Johann?"

He jerked his head toward the trail and resumed walking. "Not in the genuine sense of the word. I worked for a small salary with the BKA, but I had other resources."

"Did your coworkers know that?"

"We did the same work and ate the same food."

She jogged to his side. "But you didn't have family disasters, student loan payments, and unexpected auto repairs."

Holding back a branch, he let her advance on the trail. "Your family is hardly poor."

"I haven't touched their money." She watched a butterfly dance through the knee-high grass.

Johann moved ahead. "Why not?"

Pride? Stubbornness. In the dry, afternoon heat, the truth felt like a painful lump in her throat. The butterfly abandoned her. "My mother said her life would be easier if I'd gotten sick."

"Hmm."

She hurried to catch up. "Don't you think that's a lousy thing to say to a child?"

He glanced over. "I do."

"But it doesn't shock you?"

"You only get one mother." Stopping, he lifted his sunglasses. "You understand the concept of *Klarheit*, Hadley. Her admission was honest. Grief might have undermined her ability to lie and save face, but nobody's perfect."

"Aren't you?" She rubbed her temples, slick with perspiration, and braced a hand on her hip. "Your family code contains all the guidelines you need. When in doubt, check the code."

"It's not comprehensive."

She anchored her other hand and squared off against his dismissal. "When Jecca died, I was still a child. I needed my mother as much as Jecca had needed her."

He narrowed his gaze. "You're not a child anymore. Get over it."

Her mouth dropped open. "Finally, we agree on something!"

He raised an eyebrow.

"I'm not exhausted, intoxicated, or insufferable." Grabbing his hand, she pulled it onto her breast. A heartbeat of silence passed, and she felt his heated caress. Her core pulsed, and she kissed him, her lips crashing against his without pretense. Without the hindrance of logic and thought, their skin touched, and need raced through her system. Her gaze widened. *Shit. What have I done?*

He kissed her back.

Grabbing his shirt, she held tight and explored his lips. His skin smelled like eucalyptus swaying in the dry, summer heat. She felt his palm at the base of her spine, sweat gathering against her skin, while the other hand kneaded her breast. The pressure felt primal, the blood drained out of her head, and she swayed. "More."

He gripped her shoulder and held her steady. "You need to drink more water."

In the bright sunlight, she blinked. "That's what all the men say."

Shaking his head, he pulled her close and exhaled. "I doubt it."

She wondered if she should apologize or kiss him

again. *The CBD research can wait.*

He brushed her lips with a thumb. "Stop looking at me like a science experiment. You're distracting me, and you're supposed to be off-limits." Shaking his head, he turned and followed the trail out of the valley, his stride lengthening.

"What section of the code says I'm off-limits?"

He looked over his shoulder. "All of them."

She tabled her thoughts and hurried to catch up. As she reached the summit, she pulled in short bursts of air, but she admired the expanse of houses and commercial properties filling the valley. "I've never seen this view." Turning, she looked at him.

Sweat beaded on his temples, and his chest rose and fell beneath his aloe-colored shirt. He finished his water bottle. "Do you want to keep hiking?"

Only if it leads us both to your shower. She inhaled and remembered his admonishments. *This isn't a date.* "Silvia is probably at the house with my laptop."

"You don't sound pleased by that prospect."

Making a noncommittal sound, she followed his lead and looked at the city laid out below the sunbaked hill. Standing by his side, she felt more exposed than she did strolling the streets of Palo Alto. *How many fucking kisses does it take to get laid? I have to survive this maddening week without losing life, limb, or heart.* She exhaled. "I have too much research and not enough time to do it."

He removed his sunglasses. "But you like stress."

Why do his eyes have to match his shirt? A thermal teased her hair. Brushing the strands from her eyes, she faced the wind and reveled in the sun's warmth. "Right now, I like a lot of things. I shouldn't have kissed you.

You made your position clear. I'm sorry."

"You don't look sorry."

She turned away from the acres of preserve dotting the coastal hills. "Too many years of research and not enough life."

He dropped his sunglasses over his eyes. "You fluctuate between hard-driving scientist and flirty ingénue. I find the character trait both charming and infuriating."

She frowned. "In a few weeks, you can call me Dr. Heron."

"Is that what you would prefer?"

Tilting her head, she considered the question. "I don't know."

He sighed. "Hadley, I would like us to remain friends. Vivian and I have a productive business partnership, but I find mixing business and pleasure gets messy. Let's get back on track. Tell me more about your research. Your real research."

She narrowed her gaze. "I don't want to be your next Vivian."

"I told you, she's a friend."

"Who knows what you look like naked." She closed the space. "I'm not interested in separating business from pleasure. When I go for something, I go all in. I know you're not immune, Johann. Kiss me like you mean it or fuck off."

Hi jaw tightened. "You don't want that kiss."

She bit her lip. "I do."

He put a finger under her chin, tipped it up, and touched his lips to hers.

She felt the hesitation behind the gesture and imagined his muscles quivering with restraint. Or distaste. Pulling back, she met his gaze. "Try harder." The challenge ignited a spark in his gaze, and his wide blue eyes locked on hers.

Shifting his hand, he cupped the back of her head, lowered his mouth, and crushed his lips to hers.

The moment she opened her mouth, he claimed the rhythm, his unrelenting pressure challenging her to accept his pace. Choosing to acquiesce, she reveled in the shaky inhalations leaving her breathless. For days, they danced around each other, pushing and pulling for dominance. Now, stripped of what brought them together, his kiss felt like a cascade of water, heavy and sweet after a desperate thirst. She gloried in the feel of his sun-baked body and submitted to the hard, sharp-edged desire roiling her core.

He drew back.

"No!" She gripped his shirt and held fast. Sunlight hurt her eyes, and she blinked, heart pounding as she caught her breath. "I want more."

He smiled. "You're a clever woman, but sex doesn't simplify your problems."

Licking her lips, she wondered how long the hike down the mountain would take. "When someone wants me dead, what's one more problem?"

"I'm attempting to protect you, Hadley."

"And I'm attempting to get laid." She pressed a hand to her stomach where an aching need demanded more than protection. *I might as well go out with a bang.* Meeting his gaze, she smiled. "I thought we'd already moved onto salvage. Pick up the pieces and enjoy what you have."

"I'm reevaluating my assessment."

"Good." Turning, she made a beeline for the trail

before she lost her nerve. "Let me know when you catch up."

****

Short of laying claim to a flat rock, Hadley knew she had to get down the mountain before she found satisfaction in his arms. *I don't care if the entire police force shows up. He's mine.* Sneaking a side glance, she smiled and listened to the swaying grass and hidden insects. *First, get him naked, then deal with the consequences.*

Strolling past the gate marking his property, she admired the summer sun sitting low in the sky, stretched, and searched for something worth saying.

He strode past her and opened the door.

Fine. You can play hard to get. Following him inside, she found her laptop sitting next to a bottle of red wine, two glasses, and a charcuterie plate. Ignoring the elegant cursive of Silvia's handwritten note, she fell on the olives and salty cheese. *Sex can wait.*

"Silvia left a cold salad in the refrigerator."

"Good, I'm starving." She swallowed a bite. "I barely ate at lunch."

"I noticed."

"You didn't see the omelet Silvia made me for breakfast." Slowing her feast, she focused on chewing. "I could get used to that woman's cooking."

He narrowed his gaze. "I give you free run of my house, and you want my housekeeper's cooking?"

She swallowed. "The omelet was very good."

"Maybe we should go out to eat." He took a deep breath. "After the hike, you probably want fresh clothes."

"I know where to find the washing machine." She

pushed the plate of delicacies toward him. "Eat, Johann."

"Your roommate might worry about you."

The thought of Gary pacing the townhouse made her laugh, but if Johann cared about Gary's frame of mind, he could pull up the video feed monitoring the townhouse. "Silvia didn't sneak past the building's new systems. Gary obviously knows I'm here. What's wrong? One minute you're kissing me back, and the next minute, you're kicking me out of your house."

"I'm accustomed to people using me." He ran a hand through his hair. "I can't figure out your agenda. You know I'll protect you."

She riffled through the island drawers, found a corkscrew, and opened the bottle of cabernet. "I am trying to use you, Johann." She met his gaze. "I want sex."

The admission cracked his reserve, and he smiled. "You'd be more comfortable at your home."

"You've seen my bed."

"Hadley…"

"You insisted we stay at your house." Sipping the dry red with hints of pepper, she handed him a glass and enjoyed the tingle of skin brushing skin.

He accepted the glass.

She toyed with a button on his shirt and savored the proximity. "Isn't this what you want? Complete control of the situation?"

He stilled her hand. "Not quite."

"Turn off the cameras, Johann."

"Why?"

She smiled. "I don't like an audience."

Taking a deep breath, he sipped his wine.

"*Ausschalten der Kamera.*"

The home automation system's control panel flashed a confirmation.

She grinned. Miles of hard hiking banked memories of his kiss, but pleasure simmered beneath her skin's surface and waited for kindling. She sipped her wine, set aside the glass, and grinned.

The crease between his eyebrows deepened. "Don't look at me like that."

Ignoring his curt tone, she traced his abdomen's muscles, raised her eyebrows, and met his gaze. "Like what?"

"Like you have stars in your eyes."

"I know the person I kissed." She flattened a palm against his skin.

"Do you?" He cupped her elbow. "I'm warning you, Hadley, I don't get close to people."

She smiled. "Indulge yourself, Johann."

He stared at her lips and lifted his wineglass.

The long, seductive sip drew her closer.

"Not under these circumstances," he said.

She set aside her glass. "What are you afraid of?"

"Making a mistake." He put his wineglass next to hers. "Making enemies. Not being fast enough to protect you."

She nodded and released a button on his shirt. "You're not making a mistake. You programmed the house like Fort Knox, and I won't become an enemy." She pressed her breasts against his torso and shifted.

He caught his breath.

The reaction emboldened her. "I'm not asking for speed."

"You're taking unnecessary chances."

She smiled and licked her lips. "I don't think so."

He tightened his grip on her arm. "Listen."

His measured tone caught her attention. Blinking through her single-minded daze, she looked up.

"You don't know me. You don't know what I've done and what I'm capable of doing. I want you, but if we go down this path, I won't ask for forgiveness."

Pulling free of his grip, she pulled his shirt over his shoulders. "I'm saying yes."

"I'm not a kind person, Hadley." He shrugged free of the fabric but remained stationary. "When you understand who you picked, you might be sorry."

"Thanks for the warning." *And the mansplaining, you arrogant, sexy asshole.* She pulled off her tank top and stepped out of her jeans. Standing in her sweat-soaked underwear, her chest rising and falling with deliberate breaths, she raised her eyebrows and looked at him. "I still pick you."

He touched the sunburnt skin near her shoulder. "Why?"

Turning her head, she watched her flesh pale beneath the pressure, and she met his gaze. "I've always loved that feeling. It's a sweet reminder of a day spent too long in the sun." *Even if the pain of the following days brought tears to my eyes.*

"Are you warning yourself?"

She hooked the button on his shorts and grinned. "No. I'm making you a promise. I'm not the only one who will burn."

Dropping his head, he grazed his teeth against her neck.

The soft pain caused her to catch her breath. His erection pressed into her thigh, and she leaned into the threat.

"You will regret crossing this line," he whispered.

"I doubt it." Turning her head, she captured his lips and pushed him to respond, establishing her ability to sway and tempt him into losing control. Need together held their bodies, her tongue pushing and pulling against his dominance.

He backed her into the island and knocked the vase to the floor.

She glanced at the mess, her chest heaving. *Fuck.*

Picking up her body, he skirted the shards and pivoted to the living room.

The show of strength sent a rush of oxygen coursing through her system. Against her body, his muscles contracted and flexed. The taste of his skin lingered on her lips.

In the fading light, he lowered her to the white leather couch.

The lamps cast shadows between his muscles. Raising a hand, she traced the thin line of hair disappearing beneath the waistband of his shorts.

Bringing her hand to his lips, he kissed it and rose.

She grabbed the waistband of his shorts. "I have an IUD."

He groaned. "Thank God for science."

Laughing, she patted the couch.

Dropping one knee on the white leather, he pulled her bra straps from her shoulders and cupped her breasts. "I heard you were brilliant, but I never expected you to be beautiful. Staying away from you felt unbearable." Lowering his mouth to hers, he kissed her and pressed her into the couch.

She closed her eyes and savored his weight relaxed

against her body. Running her hands along his back, she followed the heated arch of his muscles before they disappeared beneath his waistband. Turning her head, she kissed the salt dried along his neck. "Take them off."

"That can wait."

She raised her hips and pressed her body against his frame. "I don't think I can."

Sliding his hands down the valley between her breasts, he spread a palm against her stomach.

"Johann…" She lost her train of thought and savored the touch.

Braced on one elbow, he lowered his head and pulled her nipple into his mouth.

The delicate tension and scrape of his teeth sent her back arching off the couch.

Teasing the rosy bud, he kept her hips immobilized.

The contrast of pleasure and pain escalated her frustration. She bucked him off and braced her hands on the white leather. "Take off your shorts." Each word cost her a breath.

Smiling, he rose and complied, leaving on his briefs. "So demanding."

She looked at him and raised her eyebrows. "You have no idea."

He pushed her back to the soft leather. "Neither do you."

His gaze glinted with promise. She lifted an arm and hooked it around his neck. "Show me." His touch felt like the burn of a hot bath. The room's cold, encompassing air pushed her to seek his heat. She matched his kisses. The possibility of retreat felt wicked and cruel, like the sear of ice when she wanted to burn. Wiggling out of her jeans, she faced him on her knees.

He pushed her onto the couch.

His legs tangled with hers, his strength held in check by his rigid control. As his hands molded and possessed her features, he tested her responses and chased her sighs of pleasure. She wondered if it was too late to beg.

Cupping her sex, he pulled his finger along the drenched fabric separating her skin from his touch.

The friction clenched her inner muscles, and her breath fled. She knew he felt the wetness coating her sex and hoped it removed his doubts. Asking for more, she arched against his hand and buried her face against his neck, eager to close her eyes and focus on his touch.

He pushed aside her underwear and ran his thumb along her exposed skin. Raising her ass from the couch, he slid two fingers into her body, stretching her wide as he thumbed her clit and pumped his hand.

The rhythm sent her tumbling over the edge, and the orgasm slammed through her system. She cried out as her body went rigid, then limp. Holding onto his arms, she groaned and parted her lips to taste the salt on his sweat-tinged skin.

"*Mehr?*" he asked.

Withdrawing from the shelter of his frame, she met the intensity of his shining, blue gaze. His fierce, protective expression and the tight line of his mouth should have frightened her, but she understood the man behind the disciplined mask. He gave more than he would ever take. "Yes," she whispered her response and ran her thumb along his bottom lip.

Smiling, he shed his briefs, gripped her hips, and turned her until she straddled the edge of the couch.

The air caressed her soft ass, and she felt open and vulnerable.

He ran a hand down her back and centered her hips, spreading her cheeks.

Posed before him, glistening and exposed, she wiggled her ass.

He tightened his grip.

The playful gesture soothed her nerves, but she looked over her shoulder and caught the intensity in his gaze. He bit his lip, looking at her like fine art. The playfulness fell away. *I need him.* He pushed his thumb into her heat, as patient as a summer day. The renewed friction stole her breath and her focus. As her muscles clenched and accepted the angle, she gasped. Arching her back, she pressed her body against his touch. "More, Johann."

Withdrawing his thumb, he guided his erection into her body with a slow thrust, held her hips, and stilled. "*Mehr?*"

She exhaled, feeling the size of the man stretching her core, his hips tight against her ass. She moved against him, testing his control. "More." He grunted and withdrew, sliding into her heat, the movement as smooth as silk.

"More!" Shifting the angle of her hips, she met his thrusts and absorbed every hammering impact, feeling the heat and fury of his possession. When the pressure built, she cried out, came again, and arched into the heat of his pounding possession.

Losing control, he pumped into her sex, shuddered, and held her close as the echoes of release rippled through her muscles.

She kept her eyes closed as her heartbeat slowed, content to simmer in his arms. When he withdrew, heat flushed her cheeks, and she rose to her knees.

"You're beautiful, Hadley. Beautiful and fierce."

Climbing from the couch, she faced him and smiled. "Don't forget filthy from the hike."

He rose and tucked her hair behind her ear. "I have a solution."

She wet her lips. "Pity. I hoped you wanted more."

"Trust me, I do."

The heat in his gaze could have melted steel. She reached for him, eager to claim victory.

Shaking his head, he took a hand and pulled her toward the master bedroom. The wall of glass opened to expose the outdoor shower. His command sent a spray of water cascading over cement tiles, and he pulled her under the spray.

Dirt gave way to water and friction as she reveled in the slick possession of his palms. "This is heaven." Soap-slicked calluses skimmed her curves, and his kiss sent her mind racing toward thoughts of giving and receiving pleasure. She dropped to her knees and took him into her mouth.

He braced an arm against the privacy wall. "This isn't necessary."

She tightened her lips, moving her head beneath the spray of water.

He gasped her name and pulled her to her feet.

"What happened to empowering women?"

Shaking his head, he picked her up, pushed her back against the wall, and supported her hips. "If I give you any more power, you'll kill me."

Wrapping her limbs around his slick, muscled frame, she trusted his broad hands to clutch her thighs and steady her against the wall. The water slipped between their bodies, and his first thrust felt like the return her aching body missed. Tipping back her head, she let him ravage her neck. Within the cloak of water, she felt supported and anchored to the heady combination of sweat and sinew that had haunted her dreams.

"Hadley." He captured her lips and pulled back, meeting her gaze. "You'll undo me."

"That's the point." Biting his lip, she rode his thrusts until her breath escaped in shallow pants, and her body ached, desperate for relief. The first stars shone in the night sky. She stroked the back of his neck and matched his pace, linking her hands to anchor her body against his skin.

Hitching her higher with one hand, he cradled her head.

Drops of water beaded on his eyelashes, but his gaze remained fixed on her face. Secure in his grasp, she closed her eyes against the unbearable brightness of his gaze and succumbed to the new angle, trusting him not to let go.

Satisfaction left them both panting. His head rested against hers, and he lowered her feet to the ground.

She stood beneath the shower spray, arms entwined around his neck as she caught her breath. Opening her eyes, she saw her reflection in the glass. Reality and pleasure warred for her attention. *I barely know this man. He's a trained killer.* Instead of bolting, she raised her head and confronted the truth. *He's done nothing but protect me.* The range of outcomes felt too vast to distill into a solution set. Sighing, she closed her eyes and leaned against his shoulder. *I want him.*

"Satisfied?" He stroked her back, his chest rising and falling beneath her cheek.

"No." She reached for him.

His cock twitched against her thigh.

Feeling her stomach rumble, she paused. "Johann, I'm starving."

Laughing, he turned off the water. "*Ja*, I can tell."

"You're very perceptive." She reached for a stack of thick white towels and wrapped up her hair. "Kind of slow on the uptake, but perceptive."

He secured a towel at his waist and teased a droplet hanging from her nipple. "I appreciate the details."

"And when you don't?"

He narrowed his gaze. "I'm missing something important."

She kissed the corner of his frown and grabbed another towel. "Not tonight, Johann. Let me enjoy you before reality sets in. You make me feel safe."

He rubbed the spot she kissed. "I believe you."

Letting the comment linger, she lifted a bottle of his aftershave. Amid the bathroom's polished surfaces, the stylized, old label and blue liquid looked out-of-place. Removing the top, she inhaled. The mix of bergamot, lemon, lavender, and rosemary made her smile. Undiluted liquid smelled unmistakably of him, but she searched for a calming base note. "I wouldn't have expected a high-powered investor to wear something this old-fashioned."

"When I was a child, my father wore it." He took the bottle and set it down.

He brought the calming depth missing from the

scent. Setting aside her hunger, she eyed the broad white bed.

Reaching toward her, he lowered his head.

"Not so fast." Dancing from his grasp, she sashayed toward the door, looked over her shoulder, and watched his gaze follow the sway of her hips. *How far will he let this attraction go before he reins me in?* "Food, Johann. I require food."

Standing in the center of the bathroom, he nodded and tightened the towel around his waist.

The adjustment did little to conceal his interest.

Feeling like a goddess, she strode from the room and threw their clothes in the washing machine. Rifling through a basket of clean clothes, she hoped Silvia understood the mess. Clothed and loose-limbed, she pulled the dinner salad from the refrigerator and left the dressing to warm on the counter. Knowing the charcuterie board would be a caloric disaster, she set it aside, poured a glass of water, and rifled through Silvia's pantry until she found a jar of cashews. Popping a handful in her mouth, she reached for her laptop. *I'll just take a glimpse at the results.*

Chapter Ten

As Hadley connected to the house's Wi-Fi network, the machine warmed. *One day, I'll have a tablet, a wireless keyboard, and a satellite connection.* A dozen messages waited in her inbox, but she scanned the metadata and decided not to open them. *I spent most of the day playing hooky. I won't spend the rest of it answering emails.*

Zeroing in on Buffy's message, she decoded the results from the most recent assays. *I knew it! But how did Johann's brother know?* Memories of Dr. Stefan pulled her in two directions. Afraid of the possibilities, she opened her final Ph.D. journal article and responded to editorial comments. The article outlined the process improvements from her dissertation. Unlike her assay work, she had repeatable, defendable data.

Wearing drawstring pants, Johann joined her in the kitchen and surveyed her setup. He poured two glasses of water, left one beside her, and walked toward his home office.

Turning, she zeroed in on the pants riding low on his lips. The swell of his muscles teased her memory, and she rose to follow him.

Her laptop pinged with an email notification.

Sighing, she glanced at the screen and saw another email from Buffy. Instinct told her to close the laptop and walk away, but years of labor and inquiry compelled her to move the pointer. The return key's soft click echoed in the modern house.

He stopped walking and turned. "Is something wrong?"

Swallowing, she looked out the window. *A hundred things are wrong. You rocked my world. I should be in the lab, but a lunatic threatens my life, and the only thing I can think about is your ass.* She considered lying. "More research results."

He narrowed his gaze. "Promising?"

She closed the laptop. "I hope so."

"But?"

"The hour's late." She pushed away the machine. "I don't want to rock the boat."

He reached forward but dropped his arm. "How's your arm?"

She shrugged. "Nothing another orgasm won't fix."

He gripped the counter's edge. "This conversation isn't a joke."

She wished she had a supply of warm hoodies to ward off the chill in his voice. Lacking provisions, she peeled his hand off the granite and laced her fingers through his fingers. "The research started before I knew you, Johann. My work is important to me, but you're not entitled to see it." Raising his hand to her hips, she smiled. "I see no evidence Günter is after my raw data."

He stroked her cheek "My brother's still a threat."

"Not from the hospital." She released his hand. "You said the house is secure."

He stared at the laptop and worked his jaw. "Tell me what you're doing so I can better protect you."

Sighing, she drained the glass of water. "No."

He raised his head. "You don't trust me?"

"I do, but once you know what I discovered, the knowledge complicates this thing between us."

"This thing between us is a fling. You have daddy issues."

An hour ago, she had her legs wrapped around him, but now, she had daddy issues. Protecting her life came naturally, but honoring her autonomy would require more practice. She let her jaw hang open and waited for him to self-correct.

He walked across the room. "As soon as the adrenaline subsides and you've scratched an itch, you'll grow bored and look for someone your age."

"Really? You know me so well."

"I know you can be…"

She threw up both hands. "Irresponsible? Insufferable? Petulant?"

"I would say brilliant and passionate." Coming back to her side, he stroked the back of a hand along her collarbone. "But stubborn and independent, like me."

"I'm not stubborn."

He smiled. "Call your parents."

She raised her chin. "Call your brother."

A slight smile teased his lips. "You go first."

She rubbed her face and dreaded admitting how little her parents participated in her life. "My parents aren't"—she exhaled—"resources. After Jecca died, the hospitalist wrote a prescription and walked from the room. Nobody asked my mom about her prior history of drug abuse and mental health problems. Nobody asked her if she saw a therapist. When the first bottle ran out, I waited outside her bedroom and hoped she would emerge. Instead of staggering into the light, she *lost* prescriptions and drove from pharmacy to pharmacy looking for the pills she needed to bury her pain." She made air quotes around lost because if any of the pharmacists cared about their customer, they would have done their due diligence or called the police.

"Hadley." He pulled her close.

She resisted. "Jecca screamed until palliative care wasn't enough. My mother screamed until she found medicine that numbed her pain. I understand why she gravitated toward Jecca, but I needed her, too."

"What about your father?"

She snorted. "To save his wife, he mortgaged his life and sat by her side until rehab worked. What was the point? She spends most of her days in front of a television." Biting her lip, she remembered the loneliness of her senior year. "When I needed support, nobody looked up."

"And?"

She blinked. "What do you mean, and?"

"How old were you, Hadley? How much coddling did you need?"

Swallowing, she thought of the wide-eyed undergrads arriving on their first day of class. "I knew nothing about the logistics of adult life."

"And your family lost a child." Running a hand over his face, he sighed and pulled away. "You survived."

She threw back her shoulders. "I want to do more than survive."

"Me, too."

He turned, his gait as still as the conversation. She wrapped her arms around her middle. Standing in a multi-million dollar house, she second-guessed her aloof, guarded host. "Can I sleep in the guest bedroom?"

"Sleep wherever you want, Hadley, but eat dinner first."

She looked at the meal waiting for wine-soaked laughter and long, decadent promises. "Will you join me?"

He shook his head. "I have work."

"Of course you do."

He paused and looked over his shoulder at her laptop. "Hypocritical?"

Does he care? Exhaling, the conversation's tension leeched from her body. "You scare me." The moment of honesty hung between them like an open door.

Retracing his steps, he kissed her. "Good."

The brush of lips made her sigh and want to surrender everything on her laptop.

Pulling back, he stared.

His quiet contemplation made her squirm.

"What's the difference between protection and defense?" he asked.

The question stumped her. She shook her head.

"Defense requires an attack."

Looking at the laptop, she rubbed her forearm.

"Open up, Hadley. I will defend you, whether you're in my bed or out of it." Leaning close, he pressed a kiss to the soft hollow behind her ear. "*Du gefällst mir*," he whispered. "I'd rather you sleep in my bed."

I like you. The simple endearment sent a bolt of desire coursing through her system. Flushed, she turned, but she watched him retreat to his home office.

The laptop's cooling fan emitted a quiet whir. She picked at a salad and waited for the cheese's salt and the tang to pique her interest. Nothing tasted as good as Johann's skin or mimicked his curt appreciation. Refilling her glass of water, she grabbed her laptop, retreated to his bed, and positioned herself in the middle. She might not belong in this house, but she would make a place for herself.

****

Waking before the sun came up, Hadley felt the heat of Johann's body pressed against her back. Smiling, she turned, and his affirmative response egged her on. Memories of the prior night gave her a reason to drag her teeth along her bottom lip and wonder if he had strong opinions about morning sex.

He tightened his hold on her waist. "I can hear you thinking."

Twisting free, she flopped on her back. "That's my stomach rumbling."

Leaning over her, he frowned and tucked an errant strand of hair behind her ear. "I told you to eat."

She smoothed the worried expression from his brow and wiggled until her body felt secure against his frame. "I tried. What am I thinking?"

"About taking advantage of me"—he shifted—"and I'm all about equal rights for the opposite sex."

She traced the stubble on his chin. "I don't think Title IX applies to bedroom sports."

He caressed her side. "It should."

Are you holding open tryouts? She glanced at her laptop and the empty wine glass sitting on the side table. "Johann, I have something to tell you."

He stilled his hand.

She took a deep breath. "I agreed to present at the West Coast Synthetic Biology Research Conference. The paper's a lighter version of my journal article."

"When is it?"

She closed her eyes and braced for impact. "Tomorrow."

He tensed. "How big is the conference?"

Swallowing, she risked opening one eye to gauge his reaction. His jaw muscle twitched. *I had one night. I certainly enjoyed it.* Looking higher, she dared to meet his gaze. "A few thousand participants." Rolling away, he collapsed on the bed and let loose a string of German Dr. Stefan never taught her.

"Absolutely not," he said.

His weight made a dent in the mattress. To avoid rolling into him, she sat. "I'm not asking you."

He stared at the ceiling. "Hadley, I can't protect you in that kind of situation. Every stranger with a credit card will know how to find you in the exhibit hall."

"This conference is very important." She pulled a pillow into her lap. "It focuses on advances in science, technology, applications, and investments related to my field of academic study."

"You'll present your work to a room of strangers, but you won't let me see your laptop."

She looked at the outdoor shower and figured she had seen the last of this house. "The research on opioid replacements is too rough. I'm presenting the synthetic production of CBD. To build my credibility, I have to show the world my work."

"Send a co-author."

She raised her eyebrows. "He's dead."

Johann rolled his eyes. "Send Buffy."

Drumming her fingers on the pillow, she shook her head. "That wouldn't be fair. She's only a first-year master's student. The audience would destroy her."

He snorted. "She'd have a blast." Climbing out of bed, he stood in the open room, naked and shameless.

Starting at his shoulders, she followed his abdomen's disciplined lines and his thighs' thick muscles. The entire package appealed, but she stared at his cock's proud jut. *I should have kept my mouth shut for another twenty minutes.* Raising her gaze, she met his glacial stare and chewed her lip.

"You know what else is good for credibility?"

She swallowed. "A post-graduate fellowship? Clinical trials?"

"Are you planning to live in the actual world, Hadley?"

She climbed out of bed. "Johann, I've lived there since the day Jecca died and my parents left me standing by her hospital bed."

"Such a tragedy," he said. "You rent a townhouse in one of the most expensive places in the world. You spend your days toying with assays to prove you're smarter and more valuable than your sister."

Throwing aside the pillow, she stared. "Toying?"

"I don't care if you pay your bills. You're still foolish."

She threw her arms wide. "Did you inherit all of this wealth?"

"*Ja*, Hadley. I did." He rubbed his chin. "But I'm using it to better the world."

She stripped off her shirt and borrowed pants. Pleased at the way his body responded to the challenge, she dropped the garments to the floor. "I don't need your protection."

He slapped the bedside table. "Skip the conference!"

"No." The show of violence accelerated her heartbeat, but she held her ground.

He crossed his arms. "Go get your clothes, Hadley. If you won't be rational, I might as well return you home."

She turned her back on him. "I'll ask Silvia to do it."

The bed groaned, and he walked toward his closet. "It's Sunday, Hadley. Even Silvia gets a day off."

She bit her lip. "Take me to the lab." *At least there, no one will see me cry.*

****

A badge admitted Hadley to the building, and she took the stairs to the third floor. The door to her shared office stood wide open. Peering around the frame, she exhaled. "Gary."

He looked up and cocked his head. "Haddie. Where have you been?"

"With Johann."

"Oh." Scratching his scalp, he tousled his dirty-blond hair.

"Oh?"

"He seems like a tool."

She pulled her desk chair away from the desk. "You're jealous."

He laughed and tossed a pencil into the air. "Is that any way to talk to your childhood friend?"

She moved a stack of papers and blew out her breath. *If not Günter, if not Dr. Stefan, then whom?*

"What did you tell the police about my research?"

"Not much. I only know the bare minimum."

"Then you shouldn't have said anything."

"Maybe they can help you. Before the German prick came along, you were at the lab all hours, and when you were home, you weren't sleeping. I'm worried about you."

Going to all-girls school never held so much appeal. She exhaled and spread wide her fingers. "I have everything under control."

He pecked at his keyboard. "Whatever you say, Haddie."

Gary's version of overprotective male was about as ferocious as a lab rat. Standing, she moved to rub his shoulders and reclaim the camaraderie that carried her through so many years of research. Instead, she upended a stack of books and papers. "Geeze. What is all this stuff?"

Looking up, he frowned. "What do you mean? I'm neck-deep in research. Until I finish my literature review, I can't form a thesis committee."

She scooped up his reference books and highlighted printouts. *If you spent less time playing online poker and smoking weed, you'd be farther along in your research.* Years of mutual dependency softened her frustration with her predicament. Swallowing, she placed the stack of papers near the wall where it had less chance of tipping over. Draping her arms over his shoulders in an awkward back-hug, she rested her chin on his hair. "I'm sorry, Gar-Bear, I just can't believe you still print out things."

He patted her arm draped across his chest. "I'm a visual learner."

She left a sloppy wet kiss on his cheek and straightened, thinking about the time she spent re-drawing diagrams and color-coding flashcards on his behalf. "I know. You're like a brother."

He laughed. "Is that why you always left your exams on your desk and picked at your cuticles until the bell rang?"

"Sibling rivalry has drawbacks." She tilted her head. "Competing with a person you love feels like shit."

He turned in his chair and looked up. "Hadley, I didn't need your help."

Then why did you always look at my exams? Settling on a warm smile, she needed his steady, goofy presence to ground her uncertainties. "Of course not."

Nodding, he reached for the papers stacked near the wall.

She went to the lab and hoped he caught up. Lagging behind never mattered in the early years, but she had to get ahead of whoever targeted her.

****

The West Coast Synthetic Biology Conference filled two floors of San Francisco's sprawling conference center. On Howard Street, banners flapped in the damp, summer wind, and drivers discharged a steady stream of passengers. Hadley pulled close her jacket.

In the pre-function lobby, crowds queued, jostling for personal space and waiting for the exhibit hall to open. A bevy of international students stood at the hall's exterior glass walls, snapping pictures of the city and public gardens.

Hadley and Johann slipped through the door

reserved for presenters. Buffet tables steamed with chafing dishes and waited for dishes of pasta and cuts of roast beef. She ignored the area reserved for foodservice and consulted the map of the poster session. Paper numbers in numerical order crowned the top of large, black display boards. Her booth stood near the exit door. "Weird," she said. "Why isn't my paper with the rest of the CBD research?"

He widened his stance. "This position is more defensible."

Rolling her eyes, she put up her poster in the designated space. Johann stood to the side, quiet and watchful while the growing crowd of academics and industry professionals traded greetings and exchanged notes on the morning sessions. She glared. "You'll scare away my audience."

"Good."

A man in a black neoprene jacket walked up. "Ms. Heron, I'm Richard Jenkins from Ithaca. I had a hell of a time finding you, but I've looked forward to your poster since I downloaded the proceedings."

She shook the man's hand and smiled at the introduction, but his flushed skin and whiskey-tinged breath made her wonder if he would remember the conversation. "How can I help you?"

"How will your research change the market for CBD?"

Shrugging, she fanned out stacks of synopsis and contact cards. "That's hard to say, Richard. I'm not an economist, but I hope efficient production will expand the product's reach."

"Surely you've thought about the physical logistics? No more greenhouses packed with pungent plants? The race for infrastructure could become a relic." He jabbed the table. "You need to capitalize on your development."

"I disagree." She crossed her arms and challenged Johann's steely confidence. "I'm not interested in profits."

He blinked. "Who funded your grant?"

Uniformed employees opened the exhibit hall's doors, and the first pulse of attendees flooded the room.

She focused on the man from upstate New York. "A private donor. Unfortunately, Dr. Stefan's death means the donor's identity stays private unless he or she renews the grant."

"Lucky you." The man hiccupped. Looking over his shoulder at the encroaching masses, he shook his head and wiped the back of a hand across his mouth. "Solo presenters have to stand by their presentation. I don't want to lose my credentials."

She managed a weak smile but doubted he saw it. "Good luck."

Johann moved close. "We need a code word."

Tying him to his bed and taking charge of his pleasure hovered near the top of her to-do list, but she doubted the conference put him in the mood for that kind of kink. She smiled and chose something innocent. "Cotton Candy."

He frowned. "If you feel threatened, how will you slip that phrase into the conversation?"

"If I feel threatened, I won't say anything. I'll plant my feet and scream like a wild banshee." She scanned the room. "Who would assault me in front of a thousand witnesses?"

He rubbed his jaw. "Interesting, but effective."

"I didn't ask you to come."

"Damon wasn't available."

She rolled her eyes. "Damon would have been more fun."

A pair of plaid-shirted academics approached the table. The first man's badge identified him as a researcher from a university in Jiangnan, China.

"Please tell me about your strain construction," he said.

"I constructed the strain using a Cas9-based toolkit." Noting his heavy accent, she slowed her speech and used scientific terms to convey her research. "The DNA integrating sequences…"

Next, a group of tittering high school students swarmed the booth.

Their chaperones stood back and looked at their phones.

Eyeing the shifting herd, she realized their questions could consume her evening.

A kid at the group's front leaned forward. "Why doesn't the FDA regulate CBD products?"

A classmate snickered.

She met Johann's amused gaze and turned back to the students. "It's a controlled…"

A stout student pushed through the front line. "Nicky, I told you CBD's non-psychoactive and has no side-effects."

"Shove off, Alfred."

She cleared her throat. "You're both right. CBD is a mood-altering substance, but it won't intoxicate you. We're looking for side effects. The good ones. That's why CBD might be a viable medicine." She gestured to her poster. "Do any of you want to know about synthetic production and strain construction? Strain hybridization?"

"Not really." A girl at the group's back tossed her hair. "They just wanted to show off, sneak away, and get high."

Hadley forced a smile. "I heard the conference set up a fondue fountain."

Students widened their eyes, and the swarm shifted.

Gary strolled past, hands tucked deep in the pockets of his khakis.

She stepped past the table. "You came."

He nodded and scanned the room. "Full house."

"I'm sure the attendees would be interested in your perspective. Stick around and help me field questions about emerging trends."

Looking toward the students headed for the fountain, he shrugged. "Maybe."

"Oh, come on, Gar-Bar." She linked arms with him.

"I'm fine, Haddie." He jerked his chin toward the table. "You're running out of handouts."

Turning, she saw one sheet of paper remaining on the table and pulled back her arm. "Thanks." Crouching to retrieve more handouts, she reached beneath the skirted table and sorted through her supplies.

"Good turnout," Gary said.

Johann grunted.

"You'll stand guard all night like a member of the KGB?" Gary asked.

"Wrong country," Johann said.

Stifling a laugh, she stood and returned Gary's departing wave.

Three hours later, her feet pained her, a pile of business cards filled her pocket, and conference attendees had claimed every one of her handouts. Johann remained at her side. A few attendees had misconstrued his presence and asked about the paper, but he had deflected their interest and redirected the questions.

"I'm impressed," he said.

She nodded and searched for a water bottle. "Science is my life." Coming up empty-handed on the water bottle, she turned and took down the laminated poster, pulled her purse from beneath the table skirt, and dropped the business cards into the plastic tube. The conference organizers would mail the items back to her lab. "You'd be impressive talking about your holding company."

"I doubt people would find that speech as refreshing as I find you."

Meeting his gaze, she smiled. "Thanks."

"Good evening!"

Turning, she found a middle-aged man wearing a suit. His highlights and even tan made him look Johann's age, but he leaned on a cane.

She tensed, prepared for Johann to dismiss the man toward the emptying exhibition hall.

Johann smiled and took the man's hand. "*Sakmann, wie geht es dir?*"

Their conversation tested the limits of her comprehension, but she enjoyed listening to Johann's voice rise and fall with the banter of familiarity.

He turned to her. "Hadley, excuse me. This is Horst Sakmann. We served together in the BKA. He is here as the private security coordinator for a tech

CEO."

She shook the man's hand. "*Guten Tag.* Which one?"

The man pointed to a woman wearing a cream suit and towering heels. Her loose, glossy, black curls and flawless, light-brown skin could have graced a catwalk, but locals knew her as a decisive businesswoman who founded and ran ScanCharge, the payment processing application.

During a live interview, a reporter had made the mistake of shortening Anna Claire's name. The man had endured a berating lecture on respect, but the people standing in a semi-circle around Anna Claire were unlikely to repeat his mistake. Her height and heels raised her high cheekbones above the heads of her lackeys. She pointed toward a display.

In their eagerness to respond, two lackeys bumped into each other.

"Private security coordinator?" Hadley asked. "Don't most of the local CEOs settle for five o'clock workouts and digital surveillance?"

Horst laughed. "They might keep their staff out of sight, but I promise you they're around." He glanced at his employer and shrugged. "I might not like her methods, but the money is good."

"I bet."

He cocked his head. "Tonight, Anna Claire is hosting a cocktail hour at the Zeta Hotel to meet the best and brightest conference attendees. She bought out Trance. You and Johann should come."

"I'm hardly the best and the brightest." She covered a yawn.

Horst winked. "Such a pretty thing. Who knew you

would also be modest?"

Johann cleared his throat. "I don't think so, Horst."

Stepping forward, she wondered if Johann could relax into a crowd's energy. He stayed by her side at The Gryffin, but Horst's presence might relax his stance. "That would be great."

"No, it would not," Johann said.

"Can we bring Gary?" she asked.

Johann widened his eyes. "No."

She winked. "Worried about a hangover?"

He raised an eyebrow. "Among other things."

"I will add you both to the guest list." Horst shrugged. "If it makes sense, come."

"*Vielen dank.*" She offered a hand and hoped the formal phrase's irony penetrated Johann's steady reserve.

He waited until the man was out of earshot and shook his head. "I haven't scouted the Zeta Hotel. Trance is on the mezzanine level. No reliable security exists in that kind of place."

"Enough security exists for a guest list."

He crossed his arms. "Do you enjoy flouting my ability to take care of you?"

She thought about the day she spent attending to her research while he worked. He agreed to accompany her to the conference, but the terse ride into San Francisco confirmed his opinion of the outing. "Your protection techniques are extensive."

"You're still alive," he said.

She sighed. "And exhausted. I'd do a lot for a cocktail."

He gestured to the conference room's perimeter. "Behold, a full bar."

She considered a glass of watered-down Chardonnay. "I'd prefer a whiskey."

"Come back to my house."

The intensity of his gaze sent a thrill through her system and suggested quick forgiveness for her transgressions. *How much whiskey would I need to disarm him?* Shaking her head at the prospect of finding herself in the guest room, she grabbed her purse. "Horst is your friend. Surely, you trust him. If I'm in danger, two protectors are better than one."

He shook his head and looked toward the exit doors standing wide open. "Life doesn't work like that. When a car ran over his leg, he retired. You saw the cane. He can't run."

"He looked capable enough."

Johann exhaled.

The jostling conference hall attendees muffled the deep sound. She rolled the edge of her poster. Triggering Johann's jealousy might be fun, but absorbing the blowback would devastate her. She thought of his sedan, restrained and elegant, but ready to run. Slipping the poster into a metal carrying case, she exhaled. "Remember the part where I didn't ask for a looming companion? It's just a drink, Johann. We'll be in a smaller environment, and you'll be right beside me."

He scanned the conference hall and examined two security guards bent over a trashcan.

She stepped closer. "I deserve a break."

Looking away from the staff, he exhaled. "Just one drink, Hadley."

Grinning, she looked across the floor, made eye contact with Horst, and exchanged nods. "Done."

The Zeta hotel's black, segmented panels, pink and purple LEDs, and white pleather furniture dated the facility to the early 2000s. She sympathized with a DJ staring into space while a track list cycled through auto-play. *This hotel's like a child's vision of big city chic.* Eying scuffs on the baseboards and water stains on the ceiling tiles, she regretted the outing and thought of her apartment. She could find other ways to bring a smile to Johann's face. "This hotel is due for an upgrade."

He nodded. "We can leave."

She held up a hand. "Whoa. We're here, aren't we?"

Cupping her elbow, he pulled her toward the restaurant's velvet-roped entrance.

The bouncer took one look at Johann and lowered his tablet. "Drinks are in the back."

Johann jabbed the tablet. "They're paying you to check a list. Check it."

"Whatever, man. Name?"

"Frank zur Hausen."

The bouncer scrolled through the list. "Go ahead."

"*Ein Schwachkofp.*" Gripping her elbow, Johann stormed past the man.

Inside, a hoard of researchers and convention junkies made a meal of appetizers. Few people approached the private booth where Anna Claire sat and surveyed the crowd.

Hadley planted her feet and raised her voice above the music. "A whiskey, Johann. Whatever they have."

He found a corner booth. "Sit and don't move."

Why, you sweet, overbearing asshole. She smiled and nodded.

He went to the bar.

"I should have asked for something more exotic." She traced designs on the table.

"Exotics can be an acquired taste."

Looking up, she found Horst standing at her side. Without his suit jacket, his open collar matched the bar's vibe, and she could imagine him standing outside a German club while dignitaries partied within. She made small talk, but Horst frowned, and she followed his gaze.

Johann leaned over the bar and slapped the wood.

Nodding, the bartender stepped backward with his hands in the air.

What is he doing? Asking for the liquor's shipping manifesto? She sighed and looked at Horst. "Was today worth it?"

He jerked his head toward the VIP booth. "Let me introduce you to Anna Claire."

She shook her head. "I can't make a pitch above all this noise."

"What about a breath of fresh air?"

Nodding, she followed him through the crowd.

He waved off the catering staff, parted a sheer, gray curtain, and revealed an emergency exit. A narrow balcony led to a flight of stairs.

"Won't the alarm go off?" she asked.

He pointed to a wedge keeping open the door. "This is where the staff takes their phone calls and their smoke breaks."

She frowned. "Nobody smokes in San Francisco."

Laughing, he used his cane to hold back the curtain. "You spend too much time in your lab. Vaping doesn't satisfy everyone."

Looking over her shoulder, she spied Johann

heading toward them with a cocktail glass and a bottle of water. If he caught her on the balcony, he would lecture her until a flock of school children seemed like a mercy killing. "Maybe I would like to meet Anna Claire."

"Of course." Horst released the curtain. "Anything for Johann's friend."

Fuck being friends. Frowning, she followed Horst through the maze of tables.

Anna Claire looked up and smiled.

Her dark curls reflected the house lights, but Hadley wondered why her gaze looked more calculated than hospitable. *The richest woman in California doesn't waste her time on new friends.*

"Horst? Who have you brought me?" Anna Claire asked.

The crowds around the tech CEO shifted and accommodated their presence.

He urged her forward. "This is Hadley Heron. She's a Ph.D. candidate studying medicinal CBD. Her research focuses on synthetic production."

She nodded. *Let Horst make the introductions.*

Anna Claire tapped her chin.

Makeup and cosmetic injections prevented Hadley from gauging the woman's interest.

"Horst has a nose for opportunities," Anna Claire said. "Please, tell me more about your research."

She shifted on her aching feet. "What would you like to know?"

"Who funded it?"

The academic conference's lofty ambitions collapsed into dollars and cents. *Not what does it do or how did I do it? Just can you lock it down?* She cocked her head. "You're the second person tonight who's asked me that question."

Anna Claire flipped her hair over her shoulder. "Every research contract explicitly specifies the division of intellectual property rights. Did a large company pony-up the funds and grant liberal rights to build off your basic breakthroughs? Or did some boutique firm pin down your work to maintain a competitive advantage? If I can't own it, I don't care what you've done."

At least she's honest. Swallowing, Hadley reiterated the research contract's language. "A private donor funded my advisor's research group. The university retained IP rights, but it will automatically grant a non-exclusive license to the donor on demand."

Anna Claire looked at Hadley's mass-market suit and sighed. "Your dean already knows what you discovered, doesn't he?"

Not quite. She shrugged. "The university's Office of Technology Licensing requires me to disclose potentially patentable inventions. They have a checklist."

"How convenient." Anna Claire beckoned toward a hovering server.

She recognized the end of her opportunity. *I wouldn't trust this woman to make photocopies.* Widening her gaze, she channeled Buffy's enthusiasm for process and procedure. "The innovation program supports translational science and entrepreneurship. Without that program, I don't know what I would do. I follow their advice to the letter, lock, stock, and barrel."

Looking at Horst, Anna Claire raised her eyebrows. He smiled and turned to Hadley. "How about that drink?"

Stepping away from Anna Claire's enclave, she nodded. "Johann picked up one, but maybe I should go for a double."

He signaled a roving server and ordered a double whiskey. "What about food?"

"You're very solicitous."

He laughed. "I've known Johann for a long time. Helping him is the least I can do."

"What was he like?" She wondered if Johann's commanding presence and vigilant oversight started before or after he joined the BKA.

"Aloof at first."

"Yeah, I can see that, but he's loyal."

Horst smoothed a cocktail napkin on the table. "Is he?"

The question startled her. *The day I met Johann, I recognized his loyalty to Dr. Stefan.* She frowned and scanned the room. "Thank you for the introduction to Anna Claire, but I'm done."

He accepted their drinks from the server. "My pleasure. Why don't you grab some food?"

She shook her head. "I'm not hungry."

He rattled the drinks in his hand. "Drinking on an empty stomach is a bad idea. Don't worry. I'll hold them."

"She said she's not hungry, Horst."

Johann's comment sounded like the restrained menace of an idling sports car.

The men glared at each other.

At close range, their jawlines looked familiar, but Johann loomed, and his friend depended on a cane. *Who in the world would be stupid enough to challenge these two men's authority? Poor Lieutenant Jayne.* Smiling, she took the drink from Johann's hand, sipped the cold whiskey, and looped her arm around his back. Feeling his muscles shift, she remembered the feel of his skin and changed her opinion of the after-party. She begged for the drink she held, but the herbal aftertaste lacked something…bitters? "Thank you, Johann. These heels were a little too ambitious. Are you ready to leave?"

He nodded.

His curt response fell in line with his character, but their relationship omitted mention of who funded her research. *What do I know about the man? If I'm wrong, I might not have to choose the guest room. If I'm right?* She shuddered.

Horst stepped back. "I hope I see you soon, Hadley."

Taking Johann's arm, she smiled. "Same to you."

Chapter Eleven

Hadley made her way to the lobby with Johann at her side, and the crowd thinned.

"Will you wait with the concierge or the receptionist while I get the car?" he asked.

She shook her head. "I'll walk with you."

"You said your shoes hurt."

Tilting her foot, she revealed a modest, wedge heel. "The lie was an easy exit."

He smiled and linked hands. "Perhaps I should relax my standards."

His sure grip comforted her. Beyond the hotel's front doors, a crisp, cloudless night promised stars above the city lights. She took a deep breath. "Walk down to the water with me?"

He looked at her shoes and raised an eyebrow.

"I want to see the light sculpture on the Bay Bridge."

"And?"

She blinked. "And I want to tell you about what I discovered." The lie felt heavy and viscous in her throat.

He scanned the street and nodded, skipping Mission Street for the relative seclusion of Howard. An illuminated bridge connected the convention halls, but he headed toward the water where twenty-five thousand, individually programmed LED lights lined the Bay Bridge's suspension cables. When she called out his deception, she hoped the overhead lights illuminated every stunned nuance of his expression.

Walking to the railing near Pier 13, she gathered her courage and watched the installation of lights chasing darkness. The cables appeared to flutter and wave with a sophistication the hotel would never achieve. She sighed. The cool, salty air and the flashes of brilliance felt invigorating, but the city's residents would grow tired of the installation. *How long before the lights seem as dated as the hotel bar? How long before someone discovers what I've found?* She cleared her throat. "The artist intended the lights as a temporary installation."

He nodded and gripped the railing. "The city dismantled the artwork for bridge maintenance, but supporters brought it back to the public in 2016. Over seven hundred power and data boxes comprise the system."

"It's deceptively simple." *I have no leverage with him.*

He faced her. "I prefer the bridge's architectural engineering."

"A very German approach."

He shrugged. "My family builds things."

"Stefan used the same turn of phrase. Do holding companies build things, or do they keep them out of other people's hands?"

Releasing the handrail, he slipped a hand in his pocket. "Build, but you won't see our name on a building. We prefer anonymity."

She tapped his chest and ignored the way he stroked her back the previous night until she slept.

"Anonymous, my ass. I know you funded Dr. Stefan's research."

He narrowed his gaze and caught a hand. "The investment freed my uncle to pursue the research that interested him. My grandfather's decision to allocate his inheritance to one son created an imbalance. My investment equalized it." He released his grip. "The investment had nothing to do with you."

Shaking her hands near her head, she threw them toward the ground and grunted. "I don't care if the investment was an altruistic moonshot!" Her shout stopped a passing couple, and she lowered her voice. "Your investment means you have a license for my CBD research. It means a man with a majority stake in a pharmaceutical corporation controls something that could dismantle the company. Talk about a conflict of interest. You could bury me."

"My company has many assets, Hadley." He raised her hand and kissed it. "I will not stop you from publishing your work and building your foundation."

She tugged free her hand and let possibility fan her outrage. "But you could."

Wrapping an arm around her, he pulled her close.

The proximity stilled her restless energy.

"*Ja*, Hadley, I could."

His confirmation pushed the breath from her lungs. Breaking free of his embrace, she spun and faced the light sculpture adorning the bridge's cables. The installation rippled from Treasure Island toward a city shrouded in fog. In the distance, Oakland's cranes loomed like monsters from a science fiction film, and beyond the bay, her lab held a polymer capable of revolutionizing the treatment of pain. She rubbed her forehead. *The building also has a hole in it. What if Johann's behind the whole thing?* Turning, she saw him staring at the lights, his arms braced along the railing.

"My grandfather used money to shape his children. The code of conduct insulated our family, but it also created divisions. Because of their choices, my father and Uncle Stefan led different lives. Investing in Uncle Stefan's research evened his resource pool." He took a deep breath. "The commitment wasn't about you, Hadley. It was about atonement."

Feeling as selfish as a child, she nodded. "I'm sorry."

"I should have told you sooner."

Recalling her first impression, she shook her head. "I would have held the truth against you. I would have laughed at your misguided, old world gentility."

He straightened. "And now?"

A stiff wind blew across the bay and fluttered her hair against her face. Turning from the wind, she exhaled. "I understand you better."

He tucked her hair behind an ear.

The caress centered her attention, pulling her from the wild, windy bay.

"Come back to my house. I'll make it up to you," he said.

A pulse of need clenched her muscles. *Damn, I'm so easy.* Opening her purse, she searched for something to suck besides Johann's dick. The gaping, black hole she found left too much room for the simplicity of peppermints and credit cards. "My notebook's gone." She repeated the phrase, feeling her heartbeat accelerate and her breaths shorten. "Where is it?" She opened every zippered pocket, searching for her mistake. Each empty compartment swallowed her disbelief. Letting her mouth hang slack, she stared at the void where her dreams and research should dwell. At a loss for words, she let the bridge's lights mesmerize her, looked back at her purse, and dropped the satchel to the ground. Numb at the prospect of assault or stupidity, she screamed. "Johann, my notebook's gone!"

He rubbed her arms. "Shh. When did you last see it?"

The gesture failed to contain her rising panic. She twisted out of his embrace, absently rubbed her arms, and tried to get a hold of herself. "I don't know! Instead of sharing your bed, I should have been at the lab." She scanned the street. Couples milled, and a homeless man slept on a bench. The damp cold seeped across the bay, and she shivered. "Who could have taken my notes? Was Günter close enough to touch me? Why didn't you see him? Why didn't you stop him?" Her voice rose as fear bubbled through her logic. "How did you miss your brother?"

He rubbed a hand through his hair. "I would have seen him."

She bit her lip and pressed her eyes shut to stop the tears. *Tears don't solve problems; people do.* Opening her eyes, she stared.

Tucking his chin, he stared right back. "You don't think it was me?"

The city's sounds dimmed, and she saw one man. *He admitted funding Dr. Stefan's research group. He said he would never lie.* Her shoulders sagged. "Would you use me like that?"

He furrowed his forehead and pulled her close. "No."

Laying her head against his chest, she sighed. "I didn't think so." She looked up and cleared her throat. "Your time is up, Johann. I'm telling the police everything I know."

Frowning, he pulled back. "The week is *not* up."

She fought to stay warm against the wind. "Semantics don't interest me. You found your brother. Did he suffer a gunshot wound?"

He shook his head.

"I didn't think so."

He stroked her lower back. "What will the police do, Hadley? Ask you to lie low in your plywood palace?"

She raised her chin. "At least I would have my things."

"But not your notebook." He stared across the bay and looked down. "Come home with me."

She swallowed. "Silvia scares me."

He snorted.

Shaking her head, she pulled free of his arms. "I'm not going back to your house. Rolling around in bed with you hasn't solved my problems."

He raised an eyebrow. "You like the shower."

"Seriously? That's your argument?"

"I'll show you my argument." Grabbing her hand, he pulled her back up the hill.

Knowing she would enjoy the outcome, she followed.

Cars raced down the hills, depending on traffic lights to keep them safe. Pedestrians jaywalked through the traffic gaps, skirting disaster. *Have I jumped out of the pot and into the fire?*

"You can still go to your brother's side," she said.

He shook his head. "Günter made his bed."

On a street corner, she planted her feet. "Hospitals are cold and sterile. He needs you. I won't be the obligation that keeps you two apart."

Headlights illuminated his face. The walk signal changed, but he reclaimed her hand and lifted it to his lips. "You're the prize."

"Am I?" She looked toward the Bay Bridge. "I need space and time to recreate what I lost. Gary's family has a cabin near the Russian River. I'll go there."

"Mine's bigger."

She frowned. "Size is not a predetermination for success."

"Isn't it?"

Closing her eyes, she bit the inside of her cheek. "I don't need the notebook. I just"—she swallowed and looked at him—"don't want anyone else to have it, yet. I'm not ready. If I fail, I won't be able to pick up the pieces and try again."

He let the admission sink in, but he paused at the next intersection. "Come to Tahoe. You'll have everything you need, space to write, and time to decide what's next."

She nodded and stepped into the street. Silence accompanied her up the hill. Weighing her options, she considered her elusive dreams. In a few days, she would have her robes and her degree. The notebook held her discoveries, but few people could decipher the mix of German, chemical names, and technical references. From the corner of her eye, she looked at Johann. *I don't believe he took it, but who did?*

Stopping in front of his sedan, Johann tossed her

his key fob. "I have calls to make. Will you drive?"

Looking at the E-class, she tabled the question of her notebook and grinned. "On one condition."

He raised his eyebrow.

"We bring Gary."

Exhaling, Johann skewed his jaw and nodded. "As you wish."

****

The hour Hadley spent fighting Bay Area traffic reminded her how much she hated driving, but she punched the gas pedal and held onto the steering wheel. *Driving this car could be worth the headaches.*

Standing at the townhouse's front door, she felt Johann's hovering presence. By naming five senses, elementary teachers performed a disservice. People's sense organs collected data, but their brains defined the experiences. She could sense Johann's presence as clearly as she felt the ground. Struggling with the new lock, she fought the exhaustion weighing down her limbs. She finally opened the front door, and a dim light shone from Gary's bedroom. He loved the cold, but she shivered. Without the heater's dehumidifying blast, the carpeted rooms smelled damp and abandoned.

Knowing Johann's cameras recorded her movements, she tapped the admittance code into the security system. *Isn't he my best protection?* She wanted to lie down, but she trudged up the stairs and eased open Gary's bedroom door. His desk lamp illuminated a pile of papers and the soft blue glow of his laptop screen. "Come on, Gar-bear. We're getting out of here."

He rubbed the sleep from his eyes. "Hadley? I dreamed you left."

"Just for the night." She sat on the bed's edge and schooled her reaction to the crumbs littering Gary's stale sheets. "Come with me to Tahoe for a brief vacation."

"Tahoe?" He yawned. "Haddie, the snowpack melted weeks ago."

"We're not going there to ride boards, Goofball. Palo Alto isn't safe anymore."

Closing his eyes, he flopped back to his pillow. "I can't. I have to finish my lit review."

"You can do it there. I'll help you."

He turned his head toward the wall. "Distance won't help."

"It will," Johann said.

Turning, she saw him leaning against the doorframe. *I don't want to be distant from him.*

Gary sat. "Dude, nobody invited you."

Johann crossed his arms. "We're staying at my house."

"How convenient." Gary exhaled and scratched his scalp.

She reached for her friend's arm. "Gary, someone lifted my notebook. I feel like a target, and I don't want to leave you. You're too important." Pulling a duffle bag from the top of his closet, she tossed it on the bed. "Please, for me?"

Throwing back the bedding, he swung his legs over the bed's side and yawned. "I need more than a damn vacation."

She grinned. "Twenty minutes, Gar-bear. Twenty minutes and we're out."

He rubbed his face, dropped his hands in his lap, and jerked his thumb toward Johann. "Why is he here,

Hadley?"

Looking at the carpet, she rubbed the back of her neck and wished the claustrophobic bedroom had space for all their dreams. "Johann can keep us safe."

"Who's behind the threats and the theft?"

She met his gaze. "I'm attempting to find out."

"Then why the hell are you shacking up with autocratic hottie?" He rubbed his hands on his pants. "Go back to the lab, test more samples, and let the police do their work."

She smiled. Gary always called a spade a spade. He recognized patterns long before she finished constructing the problem statement. *So why can't he make progress on his research?* Shaking her head, she considered a range of responses to his question.

Gary stared.

"I trust him." Turning, she walked past Johann, looked over her shoulder, and smiled. "Plus, he's good in bed."

"Well, I'm glad you have your priorities straight." He shoved a pile of clothes into the duffle bag. "Fucking billion dollars on the line, and she wants to get laid."

Ignoring him, she walked down the hallway.

Johann followed. "Bring a pair of sensible shoes."

Pulling the wedges from her feet, she tossed them on the bed. "These are good shoes." Scanning her closet, she pulled out a pair of black sandals and a pair of leather Birkenstocks. "Which of these qualify as sensible shoes?"

He looked at the black sandals and scanned her body.

Smiling, she added both pairs to the pile on her

bed. "Only if you're good."

Clearing his throat, he straightened a statue of two little girls standing on her dresser. "I'm always good."

Not with me, you're not. Pulling a sundress from the closet, she gave thanks he knew enough of her backstory to skip asking questions about the statue's backstory.

"I'm not worried about a walk, Hadley. I'm worried you might have to run."

Oh. Swallowing, she added a sports bra. "I want you to invite your brother."

He dropped his hand to his side. "The doctors can give him the care he needs."

"Alcoholic neuropathy is painful, but so is isolation."

Sighing, he shook his head. "There won't be a happily ever after."

She reached for his arm. "You never know."

The townhouse's door opened. "Johann?"

Vivian's candied voice echoed from the textured walls.

"He must be upstairs," Silvia said.

Hadley turned to Johann. "Did you invite everyone on your staff?"

He smiled. "Team retreat."

She walked a few steps only to turn and stare. He summoned his staff for a *team retreat*, but she doubted an agenda and talking points would greet them in Tahoe. "Haven't you heard of traveling incognito?"

He glanced at Gary's room. "Haven't you heard of kenneling your emotional support animal?"

"Will you invite Günter?" she asked.

He nodded and pressed a kiss to her lips. "Only for

you."

Pulling him close, she claimed his lips until she heard the engine of a large vehicle. The engine quieted, and a door slammed. Peeking through the mini-blind, she saw Johann's SUV waiting by the curb. A ball cap shielded Damon's pockmarked skin, but she recognized his swagger. "You're ridiculous."

He glanced at the tchotchkes on her dresser. "I know."

Damon sauntered into the townhouse. "Vivi!"

Turning, Hadley released a smiled. *Vivi? I think Damon's my new favorite person.*

"Have you missed me?" Damon asked.

"Hardly. You're never gone long enough to miss," Vivian said.

He whistled. "I guess it's just me and you, Silvia."

The housekeeper laughed. "Unlikely."

Someone bounded up the stairs. Each footfall reverberated in the townhouse.

Damon stopped at the doorframe. "Hey, Boss. We're ready to roll. I love it when we take the wagon out for a spin."

She smiled and handed Damon her bag. "Are you driving?"

"I hope so. I've had enough sugar-laced caffeine to fuel a monster rave."

"Perfect," Johann said.

Gary cleared his throat from the hallway.

She made introductions and watched Damon offer the man a friendly fist bump.

Gary fumbled the dap and looked at his empty palm.

Damon whistled. "Where'd you grow up, man?"

He blinked. "Marin."

"Did your school have a blue ribbon of excellence?"

Gary scratched his head. "Yeah. What of it?"

"You want to get ahead in this world, you got to learn to roll with the punches." He bounced on the balls of his feet, jabbing at Gary's midsection.

Gary stepped back and yawned. "I just want to go to bed."

"No time for sleep. You gotta wake up and seize the day!"

Gary dropped his head, kicked the carpet, and walked down the hall. "Whatever."

Damon exhaled.

The narrow hall boxed in his caffeine-fueled energy, and she appreciated his restrained response. Stepping forward, ready to apologize for Gary's behavior, she reached for Damon.

He moved past her. "You think you're better than me, rich kid?"

Gary raised his middle finger and slammed his bedroom door.

"I was talking to you!" Damon clenched his fists.

"Damon?"

Vivian's voice drew closer, and Hadley worried the muted confrontation would outgrow the narrow hall.

She broached the stair landing, scanned the group, and blocked Damon's advance.

He jumped in place, his shoulders shaking.

She reached for his hand. "Help me rearrange the seats?"

Stilling, he looked at their hands.

"He's not worth it," she said.

Meeting Vivian's gaze, he dropped his shoulders and followed her downstairs, but before he departed, he flipped Gary the bird.

In their departure's wake, silence filled the hallway, and Hadley exhaled. *I've been in the lab too long. The only confrontations I experience are scheduling snafus and conference room doodles.* She looked to Johann.

"She's a handler," he said.

"Is that why you didn't intervene?"

He lifted her laptop case. "They're loyal people. I have confidence in them."

Her cheeks warmed. She had dismissed Johann's assistant as a discarded trophy, but Vivian's competency demolished her first impressions. "I'll try harder to like her."

Gary emerged from his bedroom carrying his laptop. Papers jutted from the side pocket. "Are these your new best friends?"

He helped her through the toughest time in her life, but tonight, he acted like an immature ass. Believing in his better qualities, she approached him. "Give Damon a chance. I think he means well."

He slung his duffle over his shoulder. "Doubt it."

Damon jogged up the steps. He looked at Johann and dangled the keys. "I'm ready to go when you give the word."

Gary glanced at Damon, and his gaze widened. "He's driving?"

Damon dropped his cheerful expression. "You got something to say? Say it to my face."

Gary rolled his eyes.

Damon looked at Johann. "We don't need

deadweight."

Johann shook his head. "He's coming."

"Gonna be tight."

Gary squeezed past the man.

Damon jutted his chin into Gary's personal space. "Boo!"

"What the fuck!" Gary swung a fist, but his punch missed, and his fingers grazed the textured wall. He shook them and cursed. "Shit. That hurts."

Damon laughed. "You're lucky you didn't hit my face."

Rubbing his fist, Gary made eye contact. "Let me try again."

She rolled her eyes and spread her arms to separate the men. Neither paid her much mind.

Damon tapped a fist on his open palm. "I was just playin', man. Maybe white boy can ride on the roof rack."

Gary pivoted.

Sighing, she chose the most familiar idiot, grabbed Gary's arm, and dragged him down the stairs. *So much for a vacation.* Ignoring Vivian and Silvia, she herded Gary toward the idling SUV and pointed toward the back seat. "Trust me, Gary. Johann's a decent man."

He climbed inside, leaned his head against the window, and glanced at the second-floor windows. "I hope decency runs in the family."

Thinking of Dr. Stefan, she smiled. "It does. Do you want ibuprofen for your fist?"

He closed his eyes. "I'm good. Just leave me alone and let me sleep."

"I can't leave you alone, Gar-bear. You're like the brother I never had."

He thumbed his nostril. "When will you grow up?"

Looking up, she saw the townhouse lights go off one by one. "I thought I did."

Johann waited until his staff exited the building and locked the front door. Her bag hung from his shoulder.

He takes care of people. She straightened. *I haven't needed a caretaker for a long time.*

Caressing her cheek, Johann raised an eyebrow. "What's wrong?"

"Whoever is behind these threats could come after Gary or one of your staff."

He dropped his hand. "I won't leave you unattended."

She nodded, claimed the seat next to Gary, and pushed her purse under the seat.

Johann walked around the vehicle.

Turning, she looked over the headrest and tracked his movements.

He loaded her duffle into the trunk and made eye contact. "Trust me."

She nodded, but she shivered. With the doors open, she wondered if the cold came from the bay or the steely resolve in his voice. She considered the dark townhouse. *That townhouse means more than playing adult. I signed the lease. I paid the rent. How could I be so naïve about the world?*

Damon slipped behind the steering wheel.

Silvia and Vivian claimed the middle captain seats.

"Johann, I find the vehicle quite cramped." Vivian pulled an inflatable pillow from her leather tote. "Maybe Silvia and I should stay behind or take a second car."

From the passenger seat, he looked over his shoulder. "We move as a unit. As far as anyone knows, we're still on the peninsula."

"Yes, of course." She snapped closed her tote and settled her arms on the bag.

He's protecting them, too. No longer concerned with the townhouse's overgrown shrubs and wood siding, Hadley leaned against Gary's shoulder and exhaled.

Damon put the vehicle in Drive, pulled out of the parking lot, and headed for the freeway. "C'mon, Vivian. You don't want to miss the party. What would you do without us?"

She stopped inflating the pillow. "Accomplish my to-do list."

He laughed and turned up the radio. "Overrated."

Turning, Johann made eye contact.

Hadley shrugged and left her head on Gary's shoulder. *I have everything I need in this car.*

****

A pink sunrise warmed the sky. Hadley peered between the front seats and admired the Lake Tahoe frontage and calm blue water in front of Johann's house. White firs and Jeffrey pines crowded the rocky beach. The trees parted for a swim platform and a boat lift before climbing a hill dotted with granite boulders and organic flowerbeds. The scenic retreat soothed her nerves.

Damon waited for the metal gate to slide open. "I'm ready for bed."

She focused on the home presiding over South Lake Tahoe like a bastion of strength. Streaks of wood and stone rippled through the house and supported expansive windows on every level. She considered what the house would look like to tourists motoring across the lake. "Nothing about this house is discreet."

Johann yawned. "Who said anything about discreet? It's secure."

She raised her eyebrows and wondered if he wore his gun.

The gate opened, and Damon put the car in gear.

At the sudden decline, Vivian, Silvia, and Gary shifted, coming awake in a tangle of seatbelts and mussed hair.

For the first time in hours, the wagon felt too full. She turned to Gary. "I want you to play nice."

He yawned. "How nice?"

"Nice enough that I don't have to call your mom and rat out your bad habits."

Brushing the hair from his eyes, he grinned. "Being an only child has its advantages."

"But I remember how to be a big sister." Jecca's sweet, trusting face summoned a pang of regret, but she had more immediate concerns.

Johann unlocked the house and revealed a beautiful, stone fireplace, open-beam ceilings, and large, recessed skylights. Over-scaled windows flooded the open-concept kitchen and expansive dining area with rosy light.

Silvia dropped her bag in a small, first-floor bedroom and bustled into the kitchen.

Standing in the entryway, Hadley shifted on the gray flagstone floor and wondered how to proceed.

Johann tapped a code into the security system and faced the group. "There is a second living room downstairs with a fireplace and a deck. The bedrooms have en suite bathrooms. Vivian prefers the blue room." He turned to her. "The other two bedrooms are available if you want them."

The other two bedrooms? She squinted. *Are we back to business associates?* His taste lingered in her memory, but she wondered if he had relegated her to a one-night stand.

Meeting her gaze head-on, he raised his eyebrows.

Warmth flooded her cheeks. *Oh, it's my choice.*

Damon shook his head. "Guess I'm sleeping next to the water toys."

Hefting her bag, she shrugged and descended the staircase to the second living room. If she bunked with Johann, Gary would tease her. If she skipped Johann's room, thoughts of him would keep her from ever sleeping again. *I'm too old to sneak around the house.* Gary's heavy footsteps echoed behind her.

He dropped his bag on the flagstone floor. "Damn, Haddie. This looks good."

"I thought you weren't interested in a vacation?" she asked.

He laughed and dropped to the soft leather couch. "I thought you weren't interested in chasing wealth?"

She sighed, curled into the couch's opposite corner, and clutched a throw pillow to her chest. "I'm not sure what I'm doing."

Standing, he wandered the room and stopped in front of a bookshelf holding DVDs. "*Robin Hood*? *Waterworld*? *Message in a Bottle*? Your man has a penchant for 1990s Costner."

She closed her eyes. *My man?* "It's a lake house, Gary. They probably stopped making DVDs in the 90s."

"At least they're not all rom-coms."

She opened one eye. "I love a good rom-com."

Gary closed the cabinet. "You would."

The steady tap of Vivian's heels announced her arrival. Hadley felt too tired to banter. She leaned her head against the couch back and feigned sleep.

"The blue room has exquisite views," Vivian said. "You're welcome to take it."

The peace offering roused her interest, and she sat up. "I'm sorry we're disrupting your life."

Vivian perched on an oversized ottoman and crossed her ankles. "Do you know how I met Johann?"

She reached for another pillow and held it close. "No."

"I shared an apartment in San Francisco with three other women. My MBA landed me a job as a management consultant, but I still worried about paying my rent." She wrinkled her nose. "Dreadful hours. Acres of research and bulleted computer slides. I hated it, but I grew up reading Bronte and Jane Austen. I thought if I was clever and pretty enough, someone would notice me. Someone would save me from a life of identity badges and formulaic paychecks."

"Johann saved you?"

"Not quite." She brushed lint from the ottoman. "I demonstrated how to reorganize his holding company and minimize his American tax liability. After the project closed, he took me to dinner, but the attraction faded. The day I dumped him, he offered me the job as his assistant."

She jerked back her head and reevaluated the woman. "After global consulting, isn't that a step down?"

Vivian smoothed her wrinkled skirt. "I run Hoat Analytics from a bungalow. The moment I feel confident enough to drop Johann's support, I'm gone, and he knows it."

She closed her eyes. "I get it. He's a businessman, not a knight in shining armor."

"He doesn't make allowance for pretty faces."

Gary snorted. "That won't be a problem. Haddie can go weeks without shaving her legs."

She rubbed her temples. "I have better things to do."

Vivian laughed. "Don't we all? But Johann's attention is a vote of confidence."

Dropping the pillows, she stood and stretched. "Gary, don't you have better things to do than wipe the dust off an old DVD collection?"

He wrinkled his nose. "Like what?"

"Exercise. Finish your literature review. Make nice with Damon."

He pouted. "Only one of those tasks sounds appealing."

She cocked her head, ready to tear into him.

"Gary, the red bedroom faces the road," Vivian said. "There are no views from that room to distract you from your work."

He wrinkled his nose.

Taking his silence as assent, Hadley looked at the remaining door. "Where does that leave me?"

Vivian carried her suitcase to the blue bedroom. "See for yourself."

Since Hadley's research breakthrough, nothing went according to plan, but she squared her shoulders and breezed past the blonde bombshell. Academia promised repeatable, predictable results, and she would burn her notebook before she let Vivian see her sweat. Patting the empty bag where her notes should rest, she swallowed and vowed she would find a way out of this mess.

Chapter Twelve

Hadley dropped her bag near the guest room closet and set her laptop on a smooth, quartzite desk. Running a hand along the polished surface, she looked out the window and smiled. *What a perfect place to work.* The bedroom wall's green paint highlighted the shoreline trees' recent growth. Looking at the soft white bed, she reminded herself work would be the only thing she did in this room.

At noon, Silvia appeared with a sandwich and a fruit salad. "You need to eat."

Hadley closed the laptop. "Thank you, Silvia. Maybe Gary and I can eat upstairs?"

"Mr. Gary is asleep."

Shaking her head, she looked at the closed door across the sitting room. "Then, I guess it's you and me."

The housekeeper nodded. "You can eat your lunch while I chop vegetables."

Frowning, Hadley wondered if the woman had always known how to boss around people. "Do you have a family?"

"Everybody has a family."

"Do you have a family in Palo Alto?"

Silvia crossed her arms. "No, but my sister and her children live on a legacy *ejido* in Guanajuato."

"What does that word mean?"

"The place is community property. We grew up there, but I left."

"Why?" she asked.

Silvia ran a hand along the desk. "I had no interest in group farming, government payments, and scraping out a living growing corn, wheat, or beans." Rubbing her fingers together, she frowned. "A foreigner tried to buy the land. Many people died."

Hadley took a deep breath. "I'm sorry."

Sighing, Silvia brushed clean her hands. "Take me as I am, Miss Heron. When I landed in Palo Alto, Mr. Johann gave me everything I wanted from him."

Shaking her head, Hadley followed Silvia up the stairs. She sat at the empty dining room table and ate her lunch while boats cruised the lake. The house felt empty, but six people moved within its walls.

Silvia obliterated a bowl of vegetables with a sharp knife.

The sharp chatter of metal meeting wood filled the room. *Maybe I should put on some music.* She rose to put her dishes in the sink. "What are you making?"

"Chicken with olives."

She eyed the ingredients and considered her research. She had finished responding to the editorial comments on her paper and needed Buffy to log-in to the network before she could begin processing assay results. "Will you let me help?"

Silvia raked onion slices across the cutting board. "You can do the dishes."

"That's not what I meant."

Putting down her knife, Silvia braced her hands on the counter. "What happened to your work?"

She opened pantry doors until she located an apron.

"I reached a stopping point."

"No more homework?"

"Nope." She adjusted the apron strings. "The rest of my work waits in the lab."

"Make yourself useful." Silvia gestured toward a second cutting board and a bottle of olives marinating in oil. Making a pile of fennel seeds and rosemary leaves, she diced the herbs into a coarse seasoning.

An hour later, Johann walked into the room holding an empty coffee cup.

Hadley paused at the stove, self-conscious in his kitchen.

He lifted the enameled pot's lid. *"Was machst du?"*

She slapped away his hand. The lid clattered into place. *What am I doing? I'm cooking a damn chicken.* "Silvia offered to teach me a recipe."

The housekeeper winked, filled a glass with Chardonnay, and offered it.

Using her hip, she edged out Johann, removed the pot lid, and poured in a liberal splash. "When in doubt, add more wine."

He cleared his throat. "I see."

Leaning on the counter, she sipped the remainder of the cold wine. His presence in the kitchen felt like a challenge. *"Ich weiß wie man Hähnchen kocht."* She smiled. *I can cook a chicken as long as "cooking chicken" means ordering takeout or eating in the dining halls.*

Settling on a chair, Silvia thumbed through a magazine.

"Did you run out of ideas?" he asked his housekeeper.

She looked up and blinked. "What? I thought we were only doing the German."

"Why is Hadley cooking dinner?" He enunciated the question.

She shrugged. "She wanted to cook."

"Silvia…"

Chuckling, Hadley tapped his arm with a wooden spoon. "*Ich kann ihr Deutsch beibringen.*"

He turned and crossed his arms. "Silvia speaks perfect English."

"Then I guess she doesn't want to answer you."

"That's not how this works," he said. "I'm the boss."

"I know." She put down her wine, reached for a cocktail napkin, and wiped her lips. *Everyone respects you, but Silvia has the most fun.* Taking Johann's hand, she pulled him toward the glass doors leading to the balcony. "It will be very good chicken."

He planted his feet and resisted, but he looked at their entwined hands and followed her outside. "You are mad about the separate bedrooms."

She shook her head and sat on a teak chair. "I know you didn't want to embarrass me."

He claimed a matching chair and sat. "Gary is important to you."

Nodding, she looked at the lake. *Gary has been important to me, but he's not my future.* She side-eyed Johann. *Once he gives his word, he never falters.* "I want you to know what I've been working on." Switching to German, she cleared her throat. "I finished my research paper on the production of synthetic CBD."

"Excellent."

She looked at the granite mountains exposed above the tree line. "I labeled the opioid replacement as T-83 in my research notes. The neural assays don't respond to increased polymer dosages. It's as if T-83 jams pain signals until the body metabolizes it. The compound could be the secret to addiction-free pain relief." Exhaling, she glanced at him.

He stared straight ahead. "Why are you telling me this?"

Worry scratched her throat. Clearing the obstruction, she forged ahead. "What if the threats are real?"

His jaw tightened, and he turned from the view. The chair scraped against the decking. "I will protect you."

"But who will protect you?"

His lips parted. Standing, he walked two steps, turned, and towered over her. "I don't need protection."

She looked up. "Johann, everyone has a vulnerability."

"That's not what I mean," he said.

Rolling her eyes, she grabbed his shirt and pulled him back to her level. "I'm developing a taste for you. Now sit before I lose my nerve."

He lowered his frame into the chair.

"I don't want to repeat this information. T-83 is a polymer of two CBD derivatives, HU308 and a secondary compound. It's the eighty-third polymer I asked Buffy to test."

"What's the secondary compound?"

That's it? No reaction? She repeated the chemical formula.

He recited the description. "That's a mouthful."

"I haven't given it an informal name."

"My uncle knew this information?"

"He knew the research sequence. He knew of my late nights." She exhaled. "He knew enough to get you involved."

Johann smiled. "Uncle Stefan said you were quixotic."

Choking on her wine, she slapped her chest and peered at him. "Quixotic?"

He raised an eyebrow. "Romantic."

The second description felt more flattering, but she focused on business. "Why did your brother call Dr. Stefan? How would he have known of my research?"

Johann steepled his fingers across his stomach. "My brother has few resources. I hired a car to bring him to the house. He'll be here by evening. Ask him yourself."

Throwing her arms around his shoulder and praising his breakthrough seemed like an appropriate response, but her muted reaction mirrored his nonchalance. Still, she smiled as she watched Gary and Damon walk toward a swim platform and a boat lift. Catching sight of her, Gary spoke to Damon and beckoned her to join them. She shook her head and waved him toward the water.

Leaning forward, Johann braced his elbows on his knees and watched Gary and Damon trade good-natured shoves. "How did you focus on the T-83 polymer?"

"The individual compounds reduced pain signals. I made an educated guess and discovered the polymer amplified the effect. What is science, but long hours and an educated guess?"

He tapped his foot against the decking and shifted in his chair. "Does Buffy know what you discovered?"

She watched the pair horse around on the boat deck. "Buffy's smart, but she thrives on procedure. If the results looked like an anomaly, she might have ignored the datum."

"My uncle noticed the results."

"My notebook is a mishmash of shorthand and German. Buffy wouldn't know how to replicate the source compounds."

He nodded and glanced away from the lake. "Your assay results might not play out in the actual world."

She bit her lip. Research promised highs and lows. Sometimes lab scale experiments failed in complex environments like the human brain. "Your uncle seemed confident they would."

"They could be a fluke."

Or they might change the world. Leaving him in the chair, she claimed a spot on the railing. "What if they're not a fluke?"

"Then you will be rich and famous."

She shook her head. "I don't want to be rich and famous. I want a foundation and social change."

Standing, he closed the space, cupped her arm, and compelled her to face him. "Is that the truth, Hadley? You don't want to splash your face on the cover of *Newsweek* and become the hero of modern medicine?"

Her gaze widened. "That thought never occurred to me."

"You don't want to prove you're the brilliant sister?"

Wincing, she tore free of his grasp. Some part of her did want to win a silly, sibling competition, but she wanted Jecca in her life more than she wanted to win. "Are you mocking me?"

He pulled back her shoulder and turned her to meet his gaze. "I'm not mocking you, but I've never met a person with pure motives."

"This discovery is mine." She raised her chin. "I organized Dr. Stefan's research. I ran the lab."

"You said your research was an educated guess."

She gripped his forearm. "Education is the only thing I have."

Raising his hand, he stroked her cheek. "That's not true."

His quiet statement deflated her indignation. She kept her gaze pinned to his chest. "When I understand the results, I'll publicize them. At that point, the person who stole my notebook can jump in the lake."

He laughed.

The sound should have cheered her, but the week's events exposed too many memories. She thought about Jecca's eyes glazing under palliative care and the loneliness of losing her parents. Looking up, she met his gaze. "I can't bear to lose anyone else I love."

He pulled her close, rested his head against hers, and rubbed her back. "I'll give you everything I have."

Shuddering, she took a deep breath and felt the tension draining from her muscles.

"You can mitigate the pain of your friends and enemies, Hadley, but you can't make it go away."

She pulled back and stared. "Why not?"

He traced her lip. "Pleasure is nothing without pain."

"Why can't pleasure be the absence of pain?"

He smiled. "Then we would spend our lives

chasing death." Leaning close, he kissed her lips.

His touch felt as soft and warm as a caress.

"Thank you for trusting me with your research," he said.

What about my heart?

A boat rumbled to life. Turning in his arms, she watched Gary and Damon motor away from the dock. Their bright-orange lifejackets shone against the clear blue waters.

Gary waved.

Damon revved the engine. The boat sputtered and choked.

Johann set her aside and cupped his hands around his mouth. "Cut the engine!"

His rough command echoed through the trees. She tensed.

Sprinting across the decking, he pounded down the stairs and raced toward the dock.

Damon slammed forward the throttle.

She braced both hands on the railing and held her breath.

Turning the craft in circles, he crossed the boat's wake. The vessel's engine roared, and the wake kicked up the prow.

"Stop!" Johann yelled.

She covered her mouth in horror. "They can't hear you."

Silvia ran outside. "What's going on?"

"Something's wrong with the boat."

The men on the boat laughed as the boat bucked. Then it stalled.

"Get off the boat!" Johann waved from the dock's edge.

Jecca's slow demise scarred her, but Damon and Gary spiraled toward disaster. Johann's terse commands and animated hand gestures confirmed her fears, but distance and splashing waves kept her from aiding Gary.

Gary slapped Damon's back.

Shrugging, Damon turned the key to restart the engine.

The boat's hull exploded, and the sound echoed in the granite bowl. Hadley covered her ears. Shards of wood flew through the air, and chunks of fiberglass splashed in the clear water, churned white with waves of destruction.

Each splash and piece of arching debris wounded her heart. She shied away from the explosion, but time seemed to slow. Keeping her gaze fixed on the water, she examined each piece of evidence and searched for Gary.

Thrown free of the wreckage, both men clawed their way to the surface. Sputtering and coughing, they waved their hands. "Help! Help!"

Her perception of time shot into motion. Releasing her breath, she blinked and confirmed they lived. Raising a hand, she confirmed receiving their distress signal.

Before anyone on shore reached the pair, a nearby captain cut his engines and coasted through the debris field. Pulling Gary aboard first, he reached for Damon.

Damon gripped the man's arm. His other hand capped a wicked gash above his left eye.

"Tsk-tsk," Silvia said.

Hadley turned. "Please call 911."

She held her palm against her chest. "Miss Heron.

Are you sure?"

Amid the chaos, the question's subtle censure registered in Hadley's mind. *How many times has Silvia looked the other way?* She gripped the tender pink skin on her arm. "An accident occurred. Damon and Gary need help. If you won't help them, I will." Without waiting for a response, she ran down the stairs.

The helpful captain motored Gary and Damon toward Johann's dock.

Vivian ran from the garage with a first aid kit and an armful of beach towels.

Hadley rushed to Johann's side and watched him support the two men as they made their transfer to the dock. She grabbed a beach towel from Vivian and wrapped it around Gary's shoulders. "Gar-Bear, look at me."

Vivian handed another towel to Damon.

He balled it up and pressed it against his head wound.

Hadley patted Gary's arms and frantically checked him for injuries. "Are you all right?"

He shook his head, his dull eyes blinking in the sunlight. Despite the lake's chill, he stood and slumped his shoulders. "Why would someone d-do that?"

Ignoring his stutter, she unbuckled his life vest. "Do what? The explosion was an accident."

He stilled her attempts to remove the orange plastic. "Hadley, it wasn't an accident."

"Of course it was." She looked at Johann, waiting for him to confirm the facts.

The two men made eye contact.

Gary looked away. "Someone's really after you."

Johann exhaled. "Go back to the house, Hadley."

They should have laughed or gone on about the estate's protections. Instead, the crease near Johann's eyes deepened.

Gary shook.

She itched to shake reason into their stubborn, male heads, but she stood her ground and focused on Gary's stunned response. "He's in shock. I need to get him inside."

A boat carrying first responders from El Dorado County tied up at the dock. Reflective lettering identified the craft as the Boating Safety Unit.

Johann waved them in and turned. "Go inside."

His hardened voice scared her. Stepping back, she looked at the debris floating on the water. Volunteer boaters used fishing nets to scoop up trash and keep the debris from sinking. Their slow, circling patrol looked like an act of solidarity beneath the cloudless summer sky. *What's going on?*

The first responders disembarked.

Damon swayed on his feet, but he pulled the towel away from his eye and tilted his head to give Vivian better access to inspect the wound. Blood dripped from his chin, staining the sun-bleached dock and Vivian's shoes.

Hadley watched the drops fall. She made a fist, and the tension sent vibrations up her arm. *It wasn't an accident.*

"Please," Johann said.

The soft request scared her more than his command. Fleeing, she ran up the hillside, shaking her head as she stumbled into the garage and searched a sheet of pegboard for the keys to Johann's SUV. *I have to get Gary and myself out of here.*

Silvia cleared her throat and walked across the concrete floor.

Her steps sounded slow and measured.

"You won't find the keys, Miss Heron."

Hadley gritted her teeth "This isn't your problem, Silvia."

"You're safer in the house."

Looking up, she found warmth in the woman's gaze. "Am I?"

Silvia nodded and reached toward her. "I trust him with my life." She patted Hadley's back.

Her touch felt warm and comforting.

"And yours."

Hadley closed her eyes. *Either Johann's never lied to me, or everything has been a lie.* The two extremes left her dizzy with confusion. His cold, blue eyes intimidated her, but they also shifted with desire. *Hasn't he accommodated everything I've asked?* She stopped searching the pegboard and prayed his gaze could penetrate the unknown.

****

An hour later, Hadley sat on the soft, leather couch's farthest corner. A throw pillow felt like a flimsy defense, but she clutched it to her chest and cursed her unworldliness. *If I had stayed in my lab like a good, little scientist, this wouldn't have happened.*

Silvia brought her hot tea and a guitar.

She ignored both offerings.

"The first responders left. Vivian took Damon to town for stitches. Mr. zur Hausen and Gary are sitting on the boat dock."

"Gary should be in bed."

The housekeeper toyed with the guitar's metal

string. "Mr. zur Hausen said you have a beautiful voice."

Frustrated at the woman's persistence, she shook her head. "I don't feel like singing."

"Perhaps you just want to play?" Silvia stroked the wood. "In the old movies with Pedro Infante and Jorge Negrete, music always helps." Smiling, she pushed the guitar toward her. "Either you sing or I will, Miss Heron."

Setting aside the pillow, she settled the guitar against her chest, tuned the strings, and worked her way through several old folk melodies. None fit, but familiarity soothed the tension from her shoulders.

Silvia remained at her side.

The woman was as comforting, serene, and unmovable as a damn mountain. Hadley smiled.

Gary and Johann came down the main stairs.

Looking up, she saw the set of Johann's jaw matched the intensity of his gaze. She paused her fingers. Gary still looked shell-shocked, but he glanced toward the exit. She left the guitar on the couch and rushed to his side. "Are you okay, Gar-Bear?"

His lower lip quivered.

She gripped his arm. "Oh, Gary. I'm so sorry I got you into this mess!"

Johann cleared his throat. "Tell her."

She looked at Johann and saw the pity in his expression. Fear strengthened her will. He could pity her, but pitying Gary portended far-reaching pain. "Tell me what?"

"I told you I would never lie," Johann replied. "I can't say the same for your friend."

Shying away from pain, she released Gary's arm.

He scratched his dirty-blond hair and averted his eyes. "I took your notebook."

In a louder room, she would have missed his faint, mumbling voice.

"I made a mistake." He scratched his nose. "A big one."

His words made no sense, yet she understood them immediately. Pulling him to the coach, she metered her response. "Where is it?"

He sank into the soft leather, closed his eyes, and hung his head. "In my laptop bag."

In the room's silence, she blinked. Academia had primed her competitive streak, but Gary loved her, and she had treated him like a thief. "Oh." Her relief felt anticlimactic. "Well, go get it."

Clearing his throat, he scratched his nose. "I didn't just take it. I sold it. If I don't deliver your research notes to the man who paid the price, I'm a dead man."

Standing, she paced the room and wanted to swipe the DVD collection from the shelf. Costner's haughty gaze mocked her, and she turned to face a real-life villain. "Why would you do this?"

"You talked about that damn foundation, and I thought, how much is this shit worth? What if I had the innovative research?" He rubbed his brows. "The idea festered, and the money was too easy to ignore."

She met Johann's gaze. "Did you put him up to this?"

Johann shook his head.

Anger held his jaw in tension. Faced with no other option, she loomed over Gary. Blood rushed through her body, and her legs shook. "Give back the money."

He cleared his throat. "I don't think the dark web

market has a return policy."

"How much?" She cradled her forearm. "How much am I worth to you?"

"It's not you. It's your research," he said.

Her heart beat faster, and blood pumped through her veins. "That's all I am!"

Johann stepped forward.

She drew a deep breath and held up a hand. "Gary, you can find a way out of this mess. Tell the buyer you were mistaken. Tell them you need more time." She scanned the room for substitutes. "Give them a piece of garbage."

"People don't pay ten thousand dollars for garbage."

She forced a laugh. "Ten thousand? You suck"—she struggled to catch her breath—"at bargaining. Do you know how much my discovery is worth?" Bracing both hands on her knees, she inhaled. "You don't even know what I found!"

"I know your strain gets me high as a kite." He smiled and toed the carpet. "I don't care what the buyer does with the work. I just needed the money."

She raised her head. "For what?"

"I lost a few rounds of poker."

"Ask your parents for the money."

He wrinkled his face.

The man looked like a dirty sock, but he had erased years of her life. She flared her nostrils and sympathized with the matador's bull.

"Eww, God, they'd kill me," Gary said. "I can't do that."

Pivoting, she clenched her hands over her face and struggled to come to grips with his weakness. "You can't even kill a bug! When I started collecting information on animal testing, you threatened to turn me in to PETA." Uncovering her face, she threw her hands toward the ground. "How is my life's work worth so little to you?"

He blinked.

"We've been friends since childhood."

Cocking his head, he stared. "We're not children anymore."

A laugh escaped her throat. "Do you know the difference between children and adults? Adults do their own fucking work. They take care of their business." Stalking to the couch, she kicked the soft leather. "Do you feel bad, Gar-Bear? Do you even care what you've done?"

Surging off the couch, he blew past her and turned. "I hate that fucking nickname."

She laughed, but tears pricked her eyes. "For twenty years, you cheated off my tests and looked over my shoulder. Now, you tell me you sold my research on a message board. You hate your nickname? Tough fucking luck."

Beneath her bravado, the enormity of Gary's betrayal broke her heart. Losing Jecca had haunted her, but time softened the memories, and her family's dissolution propelled her into research. She thought sweet, floppy Gary, who needed her as much as she needed him, was the one man on whom she could count. She sighed. "You were the only family I had." Her voice shook, but she held back her tears.

He dropped his shoulders, and he stared at the flagstone floor. "I get it. I made a mistake."

"You treated me like a sister, like someone you

loved."

"That's just it, Hadley." He looked up and smiled. "I love you, but I love myself more."

The admission made her laugh. Then she remembered the implications of his greed and rubbed a hand across her eyes. "You're so egotistical."

"And you're so naïve."

"You should have just smothered me in my sleep." Her throat burned at the visceral threat, and she swallowed to get out the words. "At least I would have never known you betrayed me."

"I didn't want to see you suffer."

Slack jawed, she looked at his flaccid posture and realized he had considered her death.

He walked to the window. "And I didn't want to get caught."

"Oh, they would have caught you, Gar-Bear." She dropped her voice. "You've never been clever enough to solve problems. Even word scrambles defeat you."

Turning, he raised a hand. "You're such a bitch."

She stood her ground. Gestures meant everything, but he stood on the room's far side. Even if he charged, Johann would intervene. Gary would never land the blow.

Dropping his hand, Gary cursed.

She tallied the number of times his aggression had surged and receded. "You're a coward, Gary. You've never believed in a cause or yourself."

His skin paled.

Turning her back on him, she walked toward Johann and claimed the hand he held out. She saw empathy in his gaze and readiness in his stance. His controlled response comforted her. "I'm surprised you didn't shoot him."

Johann's lip twitched. "I thought about it."

Standing by his side, she straightened her spine. *I don't need a code of conduct to understand the difference between right and wrong*—closing her eyes, she inhaled and released Johann's hand—*but I also don't need to depend on another man.*

Surveying their solidarity, Gary took a deep breath and backed away. "I guess I'll just, uh, catch a bus home."

Johann cleared his throat. "I don't think so."

Gary eyed the exit.

Silvia stood in front of the door, arms crossed.

"What?" Gary faced Johann and raised his chin. "Will you shoot me or something?"

"Don't tempt me. Hadley will decide what happens to you."

She sorted the problems into two columns. On one hand, her notebook waited in Gary's laptop bag. Retrieving it would be easy enough. The second problem felt like a rip current ready to drag her out to sea. "Who's the buyer?"

"I dunno. Someone who speaks German, I guess."

Johann crossed his arms. "Well, that leaves us with one hundred million possibilities. How does the buyer claim the notebook?"

Gary shrugged. "I mail it."

She stared. "You can't drop my notebook in the fucking mail. Give me back the book!"

He brushed his hair out of his eyes. "Um, no."

Laughing, she reached across Johann's chest and pulled his gun from his holster. Pointing the weapon at Gary, she steadied her arm and kept it true. "Go get it."

Swallowing, he backed up.

Placing her finger on the trigger, she raised her eyebrows. "Now."

Sweat beaded on his forehead, and he backed toward his guest room. "Haddie, you wouldn't…"

She tilted her head. "I would."

Bumping into the wall, he inched toward the doorway. "Haddie, just put down the gun."

His fear relaxed her stance. She straightened her arm. "Get. The. Notebook."

Turning, he fled into the room.

She lowered the gun and looked at Johann.

He exhaled and shook his head.

What? She mouthed the question.

Gary emerged from the guest room. His hands shook, but he held the notebook.

Raising the gun, she tilted her head. Years of thought and study resided in that book. She had bytes of data, but the notebook held her hypothesis, tricks, and unanswered questions. "Give it to me."

Tossing it at her feet, he shuddered. "Just drop the gun, okay?"

Keeping the firearm trained on him, she bent and lifted the notebook. The worn pages felt like a treasured blanket's soft comfort.

Drawing near, Johann removed the gun from her hands and leaned close. "You forgot to disengage the safety."

Hearing his whispered rebuke, she met his gaze and bit her lip to repress a smile. The notebook mattered far more than the armament. Walking toward the windows, she let the rippling lake soothe her nerves. The water looked deceptively calm, but the shimmering surface revealed every shifting wind. *Isolation isn't the answer. Even though Gary betrayed me, he was my friend when I needed one the most.* She closed her eyes. *I wish we had both grown stronger.* Opening her eyes, she turned and faced the room's occupants. "We still have the problem of the buyer."

"I have ten thousand problems," Gary said. "How the fuck can I give back the money?"

Recalling the sight of him flying off the boat, she wondered how often her heart could stop and beat again.

Gary sat on the couch and bit his nails.

We were never family, but I loved him. Aware of her audience, she exhaled. "Gar-Bear, did the explosion scare you into a confession? Did mortality make you fear for your life?"

Behind the fringe of blond hair hanging over his face, he sneered. "Well, that and your asshole boyfriend's intimidation techniques."

Hearing the derision in his voice, she cocked her head. "You should have just killed me."

Looking up, he mimicked her posture. "I told you, I thought about it."

Thinking doesn't yield results, does it? She considered the flagstone floor. "Someone's targeting the people I love."

Johann walked to her side and caressed her back.

The smooth pressure anchored her thoughts.

"Who are you worried about?" Johann asked.

She swallowed and wondered if she could put Silvia on guard duty and spend the remainder of the evening wrapped in his arms. "We'll discuss that question later."

He raised an eyebrow.

Gary sighed. "I should have photocopied your notebook. You would never have known I took the damn thing. Buffy would have helped me."

Laughing, she slapped her chest to still the reflexive response. "I doubt it."

Silvia hoisted the guitar, muttered about the stupidity of gringos, and left the room.

Watching her leave, Hadley thought about calling her back. She needed an ally, and her options had recently slimmed. Left with the two men, she looked at Johann. "What do we do now?"

He crossed his arms. "Double our defenses. Günter comes."

"Your brother called Dr. Stefan," she said. "He could have asked about the research."

Johann frowned. "He could have scrambled for ten thousand dollars, too."

"Are you sure?"

He exhaled. "No."

Gary flopped back on the couch. "Just shoot anyone who deserves it."

The insolent command snapped her last nerve. "Shut up, Gar-Bear!" Her shout echoed in the room. Clapping a hand to her mouth, she looked at Johann and wanted to apologize for the outburst.

Johann cracked a smile. "I doubt that will be necessary."

Chapter Thirteen

The dining room's bright lights clashed with Hadley's dark mood. *This meal's about as cheerful as a final exam.* Her purse sat on the kitchen island. The notebook peeked above the smooth leather. She kept glancing at the pages and wondering if the musings and results meant enough to destroy her family.

Johann, Gary, Damon, and Vivian sat around the table and silently ate.

Only Johann made eye contact like an admiral overseeing his fleet. *So much for our vacation.* Looking outside, she saw the clouded night's black opacity and thought about asking him to return her to the Bay Area. *Maybe I could sleep in the lab. That space might be the only place where I belong.*

"The chicken is good," Johann said.

She picked at the meat on her plate, lifted the soft morsels, and let them fall. "Silvia did most of the work."

From the kitchen, Silvia slammed a cabinet.

Vivian reached for the bottle of Chardonnay and refilled her glass. She offered the bottle to her neighbors.

Damon shook his head.

Gary kept his eyes on his plate. "The lemon is an interesting touch."

Hadley smiled. "Thanks."

Thunder rolled in the distance.

Damon scraped his fork against the plate.

Johann pulled out his phone and checked the radar. "A storm approaches."

She looked at the darkness. The lab isolated her from so many natural phenomena. More than once, she biked through the rain, but the peninsula's gentle showers lacked the rolling resonance shaking the mansion. "Is that bad?"

"I don't know."

"What time does your brother arrive?" she asked.

"Near midnight."

She no longer suspected him of orchestrating the threats, but she worried about how far he would go to protect her. She looked at Gary. "Anyone else who comes to the house means to hurt us. If I were you, I wouldn't leave the premises."

Lifting his fork, Gary pointed the metal tines toward Johann. "He's the biggest threat in the house."

"You can leave," Johann said.

Gary swallowed. "I need a ride home."

Sipping his water, Johann paused. "Ten thousand won't cover a cab ride?"

Gary paled.

"C'mon, man." Damon pushed back his chair. "Quit fucking with the loser. We shoulda just hauled him to the police station, ratted out his B-list plot, and left him."

Johann picked up his wineglass. "I thought about it."

She exhaled. Every time she let Gary copy an answer, she wondered if the cheat harmed him. The potential harm it caused her never registered, but his actions jeopardized her life's work. "Why didn't you?"

"Petty theft is hardly a felony." Johann stroked his chin. "Unless you're willing to explain what you discovered, they have no reason to hold him."

Vivian bridged her hands and rested her chin on them. "Hadley, what did you discover?"

She blinked. "A few interesting compounds."

Gary rolled his eyes. "This is bogus. I admit I made a mistake in my approach, but can we talk about the actual issue? Hadley's sitting on a gold mine, and she's too chicken to use it. Her synthetic production process makes CBD, but some components also produce an amazing high. I don't care what she does with her assay shit. If she sells the mind-altering product, she'll be rich."

I lost sleep over Gary's success, and he called my research shit. She narrowed her gaze. "And you'll ride my coattails."

Every person at the table watched her.

She ignored their attention and focused on Gary. "The high is a by-product, but I'm not chasing recreational drugs or a way to line my bank account. After I control the IP I need, someone else can market the mind-altering chemicals. If an entrepreneur beats me to the punch and files an IP claim, they can lock me out of my research."

Gary spread his hands on the table and leaned forward. "Just give me the rights. You won't have to lift a finger. I'll do everything."

He would sell the rights for peanuts, and she would have an unsavory character hawking her discovery on bus stop billboards. "Right now, I wouldn't trust you to load a roll of toilet paper."

He dropped his arms and leaned back. "You're so selfish, Hadley. Life has always been about you."

Looking at her childhood friend, she wondered when his playful affection had hardened into resentment. "I'm sorry you feel that way."

"Whatever." He pushed back his chair and stood.

Damon matched his stance but grabbed the table's edge.

Standing, Vivian cupped Damon's elbow and supported his weight while he regained his equilibrium.

Hadley exhaled. *Pain medication has so many side effects. One day I might have a better alternative, but I don't know what T-83 can achieve.*

Damon pressed the bandage above his eye and looked at Johann. "I won't be much use to you tonight."

"Go to bed, Damon. Let someone help you down the stairs," Johann said. "You can sleep in the green room."

Hadley nodded. *If all else fails, I'll sleep on the couch.*

"I'll get you settled." Vivian placed a hand on the small of Damon's back and guided him toward the stairs.

Hadley smiled at the familiar move. *Good luck, Buddy.*

Silvia removed two dinner plates. "Does anyone want coffee?"

Johann raised a finger.

"I'll have some, too." Hadley finished her water and surveyed the hostile dinner party's remnants.

Gary walked toward the exterior door. "I'm going outside to smoke."

Lightning split the night sky, and the flash of

brilliance illuminated the lake. A large branch dropped to the ground. Its impact made a heavy thud, and thunder rumbled along the shore.

"Is that a good idea?" Hadley asked. "You'll be safer inside the house"

"Are you sure?" Gary stared at Johann. "Do I need permission to leave?"

"Suit yourself," Johann said.

Mumbling about closing the borders, Gary opened the door to the deck.

Johann excused himself to the garage.

Left with the choice of sitting alone or helping with the dishes, Hadley followed Johann to the garage and wondered why he would abandon his guests for the machinery's oil-laden smells. Under fluorescent lights, she watched him open a drawer, withdraw a case of knives, and step into the cool, ozone-tinged air.

A security light illuminated the brush-free space surrounding the house.

More curious than afraid, she sat on the exterior concrete steps.

He turned toward the nearest pine tree. "Your friend's an idiot." Lifting a knife above his head, he shifted his weight and sent the steel projectile flying from his grasp.

The knife pierced the tree bark, and the sound echoed in the small clearing. "I agree."

He picked up a second knife.

She leaned back on her hands. "Were you a ninja for Halloween?"

He stared.

"I mean, some men have"—she swallowed and wondered how much latitude he would give her—"less violent hobbies."

Snorting, he turned and hefted the knife. "Some people have playmates they trust."

"So you're taking out your frustration on a tree?"

Lowering the knife, he nodded. "Give or take a few alternative realities, developers would turn this swath of land into a suburban development. The tree's lucky it's still here."

She smiled. "Before our next date, remind me to strip search you."

He pulled the first knife from the tree. "We've never been on a date."

Unless he picked her up and handed her a bouquet of roses, she would not recognize a date until she found herself halfway through it. Yet, his old school manners and classic good looks appealed to her romantic side. If he asked her to dinner, even after the Greek restaurant, she would have accepted. "You do date, don't you?"

Sending the first knife sailing, he added the second knife in quick succession. Its blade sank within inches of the first scar.

I'll take that as a 'no'. Straightening, she rubbed her arms in the cool air. "Come back to the house, Johann. We'll figure out what's going on together. You don't have to solve this problem yourself."

Pulling her to standing, he tipped up her chin. "What's your solution?"

She swallowed. *I trust him, but I can't depend on him to solve my problems.* Turning from the intensity of his blue eyes, she looked at the moon shining over the lake. "I don't have a solution, but tomorrow's another day, and I'll be happy to see the dawn."

The knives went back in the drawer, and he braced

his weight on the tool chest. "People call it 'the harsh light of day' for a reason, Hadley. Bright blue skies can't protect you from real-life horrors. That asshole you love"—he slammed his fist on the chest—"sold you out for scrap metal."

She thought of the hospital where her sister died and the times she walked to the neighborhood park and dragged her feet on the swings, wondering if anyone noticed. *He's right. Pain feels deeper under a blue sky.* "Are you telling me you can't protect me?"

"Is that all you want from me?" His voice cracked.

"I don't know what I want." His change of tone reminded her how little control either person had, and she softened her response. "I don't want to be an obligation."

He worked his jaw. "An obligation."

She clapped her hands and wiped off the step's grit. Gary had pushed her around, but she could learn from her mistakes. "Screw your family code of conduct!"

"This frustration has nothing to do with my family." He straightened and walked close. "I'll do everything I can to keep you safe. You're too"—the furrow between his brows deepened—"precious to lose."

She swallowed. "What happened to romantic?"

He rested his forehead against hers. "A work in progress."

Their breaths commingled, and she wondered if her touch eased his loneliness. "I won't lose you, either." Shifting, she traced his scar. "I'll never find another person like you."

Silvia opened the door at the top of the stairs.

"Your coffee is ready."

Kissing her forehead, he led her to the main floor. Two cups of coffee and a small pot of cream sat on the table.

Silvia glanced at Gary's patio silhouette and raised her eyebrows.

"Keep him downstairs, Silvia. Don't let him leave the green room."

She nodded.

Hadley swallowed. "Where did Silvia learn to cook?"

He smiled. "She had international references."

"You'll just pair them up? Vivian minds Damon, and Silvia keeps tabs on Gary?" She scanned the room and looked for inspiration.

"Do you have another idea? Teams work for a reason," he said.

Are we a team? She rubbed her ear and faced him. "Maybe we should sleep downstairs."

He raised his coffee. "You can sleep wherever you want to sleep."

"I can't." She added cream to her coffee and glanced at the door to the master bedroom. Her cheeks warmed with memories of their last encounter. "You gave away my bedroom."

"I'll sleep on the couch," he said.

"That's my line."

He raised an eyebrow. "Do you still trust me?"

She laughed. "I'm a poor judge of character. I trust parts of you."

"And the other parts?"

Picking up her cup, she took a sip of the bitter brew and acknowledged how much richer cream tasted than the university's powdered creamer. "I'm reserving judgment." *Will we ever have time for that date?* She eyed the long, leather couch and sat on one end. "Are you planning to stay up all night?"

He paced. "The security system at this house is less advanced than the one in Palo Alto. The windows and doors are secure, but the monitoring system is primitive."

Running her hands along the supple leather, she doubted a system existed that could remove her fears. "It's supposed to be a retreat."

He nodded.

Looking up from the couch, she buried her vulnerability and acknowledged the deeper lines near his mouth. Tangled in the sheets, he succumbed to sleep, but since arriving in Tahoe, he stayed by her side. "You've hardly slept."

"A few restless nights won't harm me."

She put down her cup. "You're waiting for Günter."

Stilling, he nodded.

I'd be excited to see my sister, too. "What did you hope to get out of Dr. Stefan's research? Instead of writing a blank check, you secured a license."

He closed his eyes and inhaled. "I'm not an idiot."

She laughed.

A smile tugged at his lips. He opened his eyes and offered her a smile.

She preferred to avoid idiocy, too, but in the face of danger, she wanted a kiss and the teasing tension that brought them together.

Sitting on the couch, he extended his legs and exhaled. "My uncle's interest in medical cannabis intrigued me. Stefan was a great fisher. I knew he"—he inclined his head—"and his research team would come up with something."

She looked for Silvia and found her tidying the kitchen. "Until my discovery, we came up with tweaks and improvements."

"Most people abandoned the bark of willow trees for pain relief. Now, they take aspirin."

She rested her head against a hand and leaned on the couch back. "Times change."

"But nature still inspires us. Penicillin originated in mold. Children with epilepsy take an oral solution containing prescription CBD. The medical world mines nature, and your research is a sign of progress."

"But the discovery won't benefit your company."

He nodded. "I'm also a selfish man. I won't live forever."

She tucked her legs beneath her. "I want to claim the credit for my discoveries, but I couldn't have done it without Dr. Stefan's guidance or your funding." She wrinkled her nose and thought of Buffy and the other graduate students. "I couldn't have done any of this work on my own. Even Gary's family paid half the rent on my townhouse."

Reaching for her hair, he rubbed a strand between his fingers. "You are a grownup."

She considered biting him but chose humor. "Saying that makes you sound old."

He pulled her into his lap and kissed the top of her hair. "I am older than you."

As his lips slid across her hair, she focused on his body's solid heat. Relaxing into his warmth, she thought of him in the shower, broad hands clutching her thighs as he held her against the wall. An echo of need flashed through her core, and she cleared her throat. "Age is just a number."

Laughter rumbled in his throat, and he kissed the soft skin behind her ear. "I'm glad you think so."

Gary stumbled back into the house, blinking in the bright light. "Um, it's raining."

Johann peered around her. "Go to bed, Gary."

Pursing his lips, Gary shook his head and walked toward the stairs. "Whatever."

She exhaled.

Pausing, he turned and sneered at Johann. "You know what? I don't need your permission to go to bed."

"Then stay out of my way." Johann cracked his knuckles.

The severity of his tone could have carved steel.

Gary rolled his eyes. "Asshole."

Johann shifted.

"Whatever." Gary clomped down the stairs.

"He always wants to have the last word." She stayed Johann with a hand to his chest and dropped her voice. "It's a coward's defense."

"That coward cares nothing for you."

Pulling back her hand, she sighed. "I know."

Silvia hung up her dishtowel, locked the deck door, and followed Gary downstairs.

The large room beckoned, but Johann's presence anchored Hadley to the couch. Scooting off his lap, she faced him and swallowed her nerves. "Before today, I would have risked my life for Gary."

Johann raised an eyebrow.

"When I needed him, I took comfort in his support." Frowning, she found the courage to continue her confession. "He held me while I cried, screamed, and raged at Jecca's death. When my parents forgot about me, I ate dinner with his family. His parents asked me to text them when I returned home. His family let me pretend I belonged. I didn't care that he cheated off my tests and copied my homework. He was the only thing I had."

"I understand the need for family." He stroked her cheek. "Do you believe he loves you?"

She closed her eyes and leaned into his touch. "He used me."

Johann dropped his hand. "Don't doubt yourself because Gary chose poorly."

Turning her head, she thought of the restrained man she met on the Greek restaurant's patio. Both severe and solicitous, he kept his humor and passion locked inside. She traced the shadow of a beard lining his jaw. "What about your choices? Will you continue to enforce the code of conduct?"

He turned her hand and kissed her palm. "I'll honor my commitment to my father."

The mixture of heat and abrasion threatened to steal her focus. She frowned. "But what about your children?"

Dropping her hand, he sighed. "Hearing you talk about your parents pains me. Knowing the wedge separating generations of my family causes me heartache. I don't want to inflict distress on the next generation."

The gap between their lives widened. She could adapt to his experience, wealth, and steely control, but foregoing kids was a nonstarter. "Why are you hoarding your wealth and your energy like a damned dragon?

What happens when this week ends?"

"I don't know, Hadley."

She pulled her hand into her lap and stood. "You'll untangle this mess and move on."

"Are you thinking about walking out on me?"

Looking down, she met his gaze. *I want it all, Johann. The kids, the noisy dinners, and the chaos. My research should make life better for the next generation. There has to* be *a next generation.* She sighed. "I don't know."

Standing, he ran a hand through his hair. "In some ways, my uncle was idiotic. 'Mitigate the pain of your friends and enemies' is a foolish motto." He shook his head. "The only way to accomplish that task is to choose death. Life brings pain."

Death would never be her preferred outcome. She blinked away her grief and turned her back. "Don't forget pleasure."

He pulled her back against his chest. "Ahh, the romantic."

His whisper teased the sensitive skin of her neck. No matter his ideology, he sat beside her and consumed her senses. Leaning into his touch, she dropped her head and wanted more.

"You deserve more than empty promises." He tightened his hold.

Turning, she braced her hands on his shoulders. "I believe your promises, if only you're willing to make them."

The resignation in his face softened. He framed her face, pressuring his lips against hers. Opening to accept the warmth of his touch, she wondered if this kiss would be the last time she tasted his lips. *He won't lie to me or lead me on. Pressed on the issue, he'll tell me the truth, even if it hurts.*

Pulling back, he held her gaze. "You're beautiful and brilliant, Hadley. You deserve everything you want."

She tilted her head. His words registered, but she struggled to place his affirmation among her life experiences. The people in her life—she frowned— hardly acknowledged her wants. "Right now, I want you."

Hitching her hips against his, he cleared his throat.

His erection pressed against her leg. "And you want me."

"I doubt you want to meet my brother riding my cock."

Choking back a laugh, she shook her head. "Well, he wouldn't doubt our connection."

Johann side-slapped her ass. "Tempting."

Looking at the shadows beyond the planes of glass, she swallowed.

"I'm listening for the car," he said, "but I can't hear past the storm."

She wiggled under the umbrella of his arm and mimicked his concentration. Wind and rain lashed the house. Doors opened and closed on the lower floor, and the dishwasher hummed in the kitchen. A heartbeat stole her focus, and she sighed. "I'm not sure if I hear my heartbeat or yours."

He ran a thumb along the ridge of her collarbone. "Yours."

She closed her eyes and focused on his touch. "Surely we have time for a quickie."

Sitting on the couch, he pulled her under an arm.

"Go to sleep, Hadley. I'll keep watch."

Like I can sleep with a puddle between my legs. Shifting, she matched her breath to his slow inhalations. The steady rhythm of his rising chest lulled her. Closing her eyes, she hoped her dreams satisfied her needs.

****

"Wake up, Hadley."

The urgency in Johann's command startled her into an upright position. She recognized the tension in his frame and looked at him, blinking. "What's wrong?"

Ear cocked toward the deck door, he stared at the darkness and drew deep, even breaths.

Following his gaze, she frowned. The dark trees shifted in the wind and kept her mind from finding a pattern. A bolt of lightning illuminated the sky, and she recognized a man's silhouette climbing the back stairs. Screaming, she scrambled to her feet, hands shaking with adrenaline.

Johann stood. "It's Günter."

She exhaled, smoothing her shirt. "Oh."

"Do you want to go downstairs?"

She kept her gaze trained on the door and waited for a bolt of lightning to illuminate Günter's face. When the storm clouds flashed, his hair whipped across his face, and his sinewy body leaned into the howling winds.

Looking at Johann, she saw tendons straining his neck. *So much for a family reunion.* "I'll stay."

Nodding, he walked to the door and unlocked it. Pulling it open, he stepped aside.

Günter stepped into the house.

His black hair hung in wet strands, and his pale-blue eyes looked clouded, but he raised his chin and met Johann's gaze. *He hurts.* She stepped forward.

"*Bruder.*"

His terse, German greeting halted her progress.

"Did you forget how to knock?" Johann asked.

Günter laughed.

The choked, rattling sound pained her ears, and the smell of cloves mingled with the rain.

"I saw the lights," Günter said. "Aren't we family?"

Looking at Johann, she saw the corner of his mouth tick up. Relaxing her shoulders, she examined the similarities between the men. Where she expected Johann's strength, she saw Günter's sinewy build. Where she expected neat lines and military precision, she saw layers of clothing and worn straps.

Günter wiped the rain from his face and faced his brother. "A new pet?"

"This is Hadley."

She waited for a qualifier. *This is Hadley, Uncle Stefan's student. This is Hadley, my girlfriend. My courtesy fuck.*

Extending a hand, Günter smiled. "Lovely to meet you."

His raspy voice matched the fluency of Johann's English. "*Guten Abend.*"

"Smart and lovely."

Johann cleared his throat. "As far as I can tell, her German is close to fluent."

Günter paled. "And by 'pet'…" he said in German.

She laughed. "Don't worry about it."

Gary stumbled into the light. "Enough with the damn German."

Johann shifted to her side. "Go back downstairs."

Rubbing his eyes, Gary yawned. "Dude, I am not one of your lackeys."

"And who is this?" Günter looked at Johann. "I didn't know your tastes were so…diverse."

"Fuck, no," Gary said. "I'm Gary Bezelle."

"Oh, the ambitious thief," Günter said.

His casual recognition stole her breath. She hoped for a final mistake to explain away Gary's duplicity, but Günter's acknowledgement shattered her final defense. She looked at Gary. "You used your own name? How stupid are you?"

"What?" He scratched his head. "I had to make sure he wired the money." Scanning Günter, he shrugged. "I should have known someone close to Dr. Stefan bought the notebook. Nobody else would believe what I said."

Günter stepped forward and stopped. "Where is it?"

"Hadley, leave us," Johann said.

Immobile, she felt caught between their stares. "Absolutely not."

Günter advanced. "Where is the notebook?"

Yawning, Gary flicked his wrist toward her. "Hadley took it back."

Günter glanced at her but cocked his head and advanced on Gary. "And my money?"

"Um, I'll give it back." Gary cleared his throat. "Mostly. I, uh, spent a little of it already."

"How much is a little?" Günter asked.

Swallowing, Gary looked away. "All of it."

Günter pulled a gun from his jacket and released the safety.

Scrambling to his feet, Gary backed away. "What

the fuck? What is it with this family and guns? My folks are rich! I've get you the money! Jeeze."

She wanted to run to his side, but the tension in the room anchored her to one spot.

"Drop your gun," Johann said.

His quiet command sliced through the tension like a note slid beneath the door of a hostage situation. Unable to resist the missive, every person in the room blinked.

Günter rubbed the water from his face. The hand holding the gun wavered, but he kept it pointed at the flagstone floor. "What the hell makes you think you're better than me?"

His question, posed in German, lingered in the silent house. Focusing on Johann's set jaw, she watched his chest rise with a deep, steadying breath. His confidence soothed her fears, but the corded muscles in his neck worried her.

"I've never thought that," Johann said.

"Oh, you're kidding yourself, big brother. You're always standing tall and carrying the mantle of family responsibility like a proud tradition. Did it ever occur to you to live a little?" He glanced at Gary and sneered. "You keep company with trash."

Gary eased toward the patio door.

Watching him creep toward the exit, she rooted for his escape.

Günter raised his gun and pointed it at Gary. "Stop moving."

Freezing, Gary pressed his body against the wall.

Johann's eye twitched.

She stepped forward, keeping all three men within her sight. "Günter, why did you call your uncle?"

He lowered his gun. "Do you know what it's like to be free from pain?"

She thought of Jecca's last days. "No," she whispered her response.

"Alcohol wrecked my body," Günter said. "The symptoms started slowly. I blamed age and my lifestyle." He shook his head. "Once, I was handsome."

"I bet you were." She swallowed.

Gary inched toward the door.

Günter rubbed his face. "The painful sensations didn't dissipate. Every brush and touch stung, like a brand's sear. I drowned the pain with more alcohol, but weakness weighed down my extremities. One day, I tripped, fell flat on my face, and figured I exhausted life's joys. Lying in the gutter, I waited for my body to give up."

"But you're here." She imagined him prone and knew she would have offered him a hand. "You lived."

He coughed. "Fucking Good Samaritans."

Does that make you the Prodigal Son?

"When I woke up in the hospital, I called Uncle Stefan and hoped he had a referral for a pain specialist. He offered me a dose of your miracle drug. It's good, Hadley. Congratulations. It's very, very good."

Longing laced his compliment. "Thanks." She choked out the acknowledgement and scrambled to organize her thoughts. *Dr. Stefan knew what we found. Why didn't he trust me? We could have managed the discovery together.* She swallowed. *Why didn't I trust him?* She wondered if keeping the discovery a secret caused undue pain. From the corner of her eyes, she saw Gary reach for the door handle, but she kept her face to Günter.

"Around the time the sample ran out, your shaggy friend offered to sell your lab notebook for a paltry sum."

She stepped closer.

Johann tracked her movement.

Feeling him at her side kept her voice strong. *I have to draw away his attention from Gary.* "We can figure out how to fast track the trials."

"Conduct your research on me," Günter said.

"I won't be responsible for unintended consequences." She tapped her chin. "Even if you improve, one subject doesn't prove a compound's worth."

The door's locking mechanism clicked.

Johann gripped her arm. "I cannot protect both of you."

His heavy, desperate warning stilled her impulses.

Frowning, Günter slowly turned and raised the gun. "You lied."

His sentence carried the weight of a deathblow. She heard generations of pride and consequences behind the statement.

"You took my money." He put his finger on the trigger.

Gary peed his pants. The bloom spread across his groin.

"You have no value." He fired the gun.

The bullet tore through Gary's chest without remorse, and the impact's force slammed him against the glass. His gaze and his mouth widened before he slumped and clutched his chest.

Gasping, she shifted her weight to run to his side.

A second gunshot ricocheted off the vaulted

beams.

Gritting her teeth, she waited for pain.

Günter's gun fell to the floor, and the heavy metal chattered against the flagstones. Clutching his shoulder, he dropped to his knees and watched blood seep through his fingers. "We are so alike, aren't we, brother?"

Johann held his stance. "I am nothing like you."

Lifting a hand, Günter looked at the bright red stain and choked out a laugh. Thunder crashed, and his laughter faded to a choking gasp. "Father taught us." He shifted his weight. "We must always be in control."

Johann cut off his path and pinned his brother to the ground. "Stay down, Günter."

She edged toward the stairwell, her hands shaking. Gary's injury might end his life, but if she could reach a phone and call for help, he might live.

Günter wheezed, struggling against Johann's strength. "Shoot me again, brother. Be the patriarch you've always wanted to be. Death would be such sweet relief."

Johann kicked his brother's gun across the floor and placed his gun out of Günter's reach. "I can't be there for you unless you let me help you. You are sick? Come to me for help. You are desperate? Come to me for relief. This is not the way our family acts."

Günter coughed up blood. "You're living in a fairy tale."

Günter's congested retort sounded as harsh and weak as a sigh.

Jaw set, Johann closed his eyes and shook his head. The moment of weakness ended as quickly as it began. Wiping the blood from Günter's chin, he stared at his hand and shook his head. "I'm not."

She looked at Gary and hoped first responders could save him.

Meeting her gaze, he closed his eyes.

Squeezing shut her eyes, she accepted the wound would kill him.

"Why do you gain by taking care of me?" Günter asked. "When I'm dead, you'll still be the favored son."

"You're not dead yet," Johann said.

Looking away from Gary, she met Johann's gaze. Sweat beaded on his temple.

He swallowed. "Go, Hadley. Say goodbye to your friend."

She fled across the room and cradled Gary's head in her lap. "I'm sorry."

He sighed. "You did nothing wrong."

His body shuddered, and she rejected her clinical understanding of death. As his body searched for a final breath, she knew his heart would stop, his extremities would turn blue, and his skin would grow cold, but he would still be her friend. Holding him in her arms, she struggled to equate the body with the animal-loving, floppy-haired friend she loved. A moment ago, he responded to her touch. Then his eyes closed, he went limp, and something bright and vital died. She closed her eyes and lowered his form to the ground. Helplessly reliving Jecca's loss, she wondered what she should have done differently.

Silvia wrapped an arm around her shoulders.

Breaking free, Hadley shook her head and sobbed.

Johann crouched over his brother.

Vivian and Damon stood at the top of the stairwell.

Accepting Silvia's comfort, Hadley collapsed into

her arms. "Did he feel it?"

"The good Lord settles our debts." She made the sign of the cross.

Closing her eyes, Hadley nodded and let the tears fall. "Call the police."

Damon cleared his throat. "We should wait until Johann…"

"Call the police!" She unleashed a scream, and the muscles in her throat constricted. Grabbing her neck, she swallowed. "I've seen enough death to last a lifetime."

Vivian engaged the dispatcher.

Hadley looked at Johann across the room.

He kept pressure on Günter's wound and tightened a tourniquet on his arm.

Slumped in a chair, Günter looked as threatening as a scarecrow.

Silvia sat on the couch. "I'm sorry, Miss Heron. Looking after Mr. Gary was my job. I shouldn't have fallen asleep."

Her muscles felt heavy and numb. "His death's not your fault."

"I will still say my penance," Silvia said.

The woman's quiet voice anchored her senses. *How lovely to believe in the ever after.* "Johann, I need you."

Standing, he came to her side. "I am here, Hadley."

She held her arms close. Falling into his arms seemed unreasonable, but shying away from his touch would hurt them both. "Vivian called the police."

"I heard."

Looking up, she swallowed.

He pulled her into his arms and tucked her head

against his shoulder.

She exhaled, buried her face in his neck, and searched for the calming notes beneath his aftershave. Wrapping her arms around his torso, she leaned into his strength.

He rubbed her back. "I'm sorry about your friend."

She hiccupped and clung to his shirt. Her body shook, and she anchored her thoughts where their bodies pressed together. "He didn't deserve death."

Sighing, Johann pulled back until their gazes met. "I'm sorry."

Seeing the question of forgiveness in his expression, she nodded. Despite Gary's abhorrent behavior, she believed Johann would have protected both of them if he could have done it.

"Thank you for staying still. Thank you for letting me handle him." He exhaled. "I never imagined how much this night would cost you."

The astonishment on Gary's face would always remain. Pulling back, she bit her lip and looked at the sodden mess of the man who had killed Gary. "Will your brother live?"

"I hope so."

"He must be in so much pain."

"We all have our illnesses," he said.

She met his gaze. "When you called, he came."

Johann's shoulders sagged. "He did."

Police sirens filled the silence.

" 'Mitigate the pain of your friends and enemies,' " she whispered Dr. Stefan's catchphrase.

Sighing, Johann rubbed his face. "Mottos fail. Protect, Salvage, and Evacuate only works when you can escape responsibility for the threat."

"What's the alternative?"

He sighed. "Consider whether you had a hand in creating the threat."

The strain of sleepless days left shadows below his eyes. She brushed his cheek and the stubble on his chin. "You didn't force Günter to shoot that gun."

Stepping away, he shook his head. "I gave him that gun. After Jonas von Becker's kidnapping, I insisted Günter learn to protect himself. You only see the best in people, Hadley. When will you learn to see the worst?"

She caught his hand and traced bloodstain beneath his nail. The lab, the cemetery, and the boat could have killed her, but none of the efforts succeeded. Johann had something to do with her survival. If the threat of violence bound them, she wondered what could keep them together. "Who was in the cemetery?"

"I don't know." He pulled free and crossed his arms. "Within minutes, first responders will fill the house. I don't have time to speculate. For now, you're safe."

Looking past the windows, she wondered who waited in the darkness and rubbed a chill from her arms. "Am I?"

"Yes."

His resolute response was as sturdy as the granite surrounding the house. "I believe you." Turning, she replayed her time with him and looked for a pattern. Vowing to find it, she exhaled. *I believe he'll protect me, but who will protect him?*

Chapter Fourteen

Hadley stood at the rear window and watched a parade of first responders come down the midnight drive. As they neared the house, the officers cut their sirens, but their headlights persisted, and the sounds of crunching gravel and heavy boot steps announced their presence. Turning her back to the window, she inhaled and schooled her expression.

Johann admitted the first responders and stood in the center of the room.

Pairs of officers split off and addressed the wounded man and the one lying beneath a sheet.

They moved with trained fastidiousness, their gazes scanning the room. She waited for a concerned glance, but Johann commanded their attention. *Don't they worry about more violence?* Walking to the kitchen island, she slipped her purse into a cabinet.

An officer holding a recorder approached Johann. "Tell me what happened."

"Günter shot Gary. To disarm Günter, I shot him in the shoulder," Johann said.

"The 911 caller said he's your brother?" The officer scratched the side of her nose.

Johann nodded.

The officer shook her head. "Your family has a penchant for guns."

He laced his fingers. "I have a right to defend my

houseguests."

"Was your brother a guest?"

Johann trained his gaze on the officer. "Yes, but family dynamics estranged us. I didn't know what he would do next."

Nodding, she scanned the room. "Did the shootings have anything to do with the boat explosion?"

He shook his head. "I don't know who was behind the boat explosion. Perhaps a mechanical failure occurred."

The officer clicked off the recorder. "The next time you host a family reunion, I'm taking a vacation day."

Hadley suppressed a grin, remembered her vow to protect Johann, and looked for patterns in the upheaval.

The paramedics exchanged radio communication with local staff. After assessing Günter's wound, they brought a gurney and lift board into the house. "Let's get him to the ER before he loses any more blood."

The remaining officers cordoned off Silvia, Vivian, and Damon in separate corners of the living room and took their statements.

Hadley knew the trio would corroborate Johann's account. *Do they have a choice?* A lean officer sporting a full mustache approached her. He looked like a cagey, Wild West movie extra or a lean, Seattle engineer. Wondering how Lieutenant Jayne would handle the situation, she decided to remain as truthful as possible without jeopardizing her freedom.

"What brought you to Tahoe, Ms. Heron?"

She swallowed. "Team retreat."

"You work for Johann zur Hausen?"

She shook her head. "His uncle guided my university research."

The officer scanned the room's occupants. "Is his uncle here?"

Shaking her head, she looked at the drops of blood surrounding the chair where Günter had fainted from blood loss. "No, officer. He's dead."

Shifting one foot forward, the officer nodded. "Has anyone else of your acquaintance recently died or received threats?"

She blinked. *I have no reason to burden Gary's family with their son's cowardice.*

"Is there a reason you have to think about your answer, Ms. Heron?"

She nodded. Someone would connect the sequence of events. "Threats to my life have occurred," she said. "I don't see a pattern." She swallowed. *Yet.*

"Then why do you look so pale?" the officer asked.

She chose honesty. "Your gun intimidates me."

He stepped back. "Does the Palo Alto police force know about the threats?"

Nodding, she exhaled and looked at Johann. As he weathered a storm of inquisition, his facial muscles barely moved. *I'm not quixotic, and he's not made of stone, but I can learn from him.* She straightened her shoulders. "Yes."

"Ms. Heron?"

"I'm sorry." She focused on the officer. "How do you stand the death?"

"Three hundred people a day suffer gunshot wounds in America, Ms. Heron. Homicides, assaults, suicides, accidental shootings, and police interventions. I've seen them all."

She swallowed. "What is this?"

The officer narrowed his gaze and looked at

Johann. "This was a deliberate act. The question is, why?"

She stepped forward. "Johann defended me."

"No offense, Ms. Heron, but when you defend a person, you shoot to kill."

"Not if the aggressor is your brother."

The officer smiled. "Don't worry about divided loyalties. His entire family might face indictments."

She thought of grabbing his arm and pleading, but she exhaled. "Officer, Johann could have killed that man as easily as you or I could kill a bug. I'm not saying he's right for what he did, but it could have been far, far worse." *Too theatrical.*

"Do you have something to add to your statement, Ms. Heron?"

She swallowed. "Johann is not a bad person."

"Life is full of dichotomies."

Nodding, she stared at the man's gun.

Johann accompanied a pair of police officers to the front door, paused, and walked from the room.

The pause gave her hope. She pushed away her worries, but she feared his action's consequences. Within the hour, the sun would come up over Lake Tahoe. If the police charged him with aggravated assault with a deadly weapon, he might not see the sight for a long time.

A field agent from the Medical Examiner's office arrived at the house and took notes and pictures. He contacted a contract ambulance and directed the ambulance driver to take Gary's body for an autopsy.

Listening to the exchange of information, she braced her hands on the counter and replayed her last days with her friend.

A lone officer remained and took pictures.

Each artificial click made her cringe. "He's dead. You have a multiple witnesses. Nobody can question the cause of death."

The officer lowered his camera. "The pictures are part of the routine crime scene investigation, Ms. Heron. Would you like to leave the room?"

She nodded, walked into the master bedroom, and dropped onto the smooth bed. The sheets smelled cold and sterile. They lacked Johann's herb-tinged, citrus scent. Tears swelled in her eyes. *Who am I kidding? I'm a lousy protector.* She covered her eyes and heard someone knock at the door, but she felt too tired to stand.

Vivian entered the room, sat on the bed, and offered her a glass of water and a sleeping pill.

She shook her head. "I'm not ready for sleep."

Putting her offerings on the bedside table, Vivian nodded and crossed her ankles. "The last officer is still here."

"He'll leave, eventually."

"And when he does?"

Hadley exhaled. "We'll be on our own."

"Trial and error build endurance," Vivian said. "You'll get through this experience."

Clutching a pillow to her chest, Hadley shook her head. "I don't want to get through anything like this ever again."

Vivian looked out the window at the sun coming up over the lake. "Then you should release Johann."

Hadley opened her eyes. "Release him?"

Nodding, she tucked a strand of blonde hair behind her ear. "He describes his father as an overbearing patriarch for a reason. Johann was a privileged boy who grew into a wealthy man. Beyond the holding company, he manages an army of interests, lobbyists, and loyal politicians. A house in Berlin, a sprawling compound on Hawai'i Island, and an expansive ranch in New Zealand round out his portfolio. Globalization opened a world of opportunities for his family, but it also opened a world of threats. Have you considered why he lives in compounds?"

"He needs places to relax. He's capable of handling the pressure." She rubbed her temples. "I'm not."

"I agree with that statement," Vivian said. "You're not equipped to handle his life. With your background, how could you keep up?"

She closed her eyes. *For a moment, I thought we were friends. Maybe protecting Johann means walking away. He survived this long without me. Why should I stay and get in the way?* She flung the pillow to her side. "He'll move on."

Vivian picked up a small statue of two embracing curves, considered it, and placed it back on the side table. "Why didn't he station Damon in your townhouse?"

"Damon's too busy hustling to support his emerging empire."

Vivian looked out the window. "Don't underestimate Damon. He has a poet's heart."

"Poets don't have a stockroom full of surplus military equipment and unlocked cell phones."

Vivian smiled. "I'm convincing him to diversify."

Hadley opened her eyes. "Is Hoat Analytics expanding?"

"I don't know. When I furnished my rented

bungalow, I picked airy white furniture and spotless floors. The decorator called the aesthetic 'rustic-tinged airspace'. Success might come, but it's lonely."

She has a heart. "I'm sorry for insinuating you were a prostitute."

Vivian's laughter filled the room. She stood and brushed the wrinkles from her lap. "Don't worry. People have called me far worse."

Hadley considered the beams in the ceiling. *I don't want to release him.* His physical presence and quick intelligence kept her on her toes, but she understood the difficult to observe and uncommon phenomenon of a cold flame. Beneath his controlled exterior, Johann burned. Acknowledging the reciprocal heat in her core, she refused to smother it with reason and logic. Smack in the middle of his bed, waiting for his return, she imagined their lives without the threat of violence.

How do I come home every night to a housekeeper and a network of sensors? I can't pursue my research and skip around the globe, worrying if I left my notes in Berlin or New Zealand. Smiling, she brushed aside the relative ease of international travel and secure data management. *But no kids?*

She put her head on the pillow and looked out the large windows. The lake glistened like Johann's eyes. *I'm not pursuing him based on his ability to keep me safe. His intensity and drive are the things I want. Who else has that split-second decision-making that allows him to weigh threats and decide on a course of action? Together, we'll figure out the subtleties of a shared life.* She swallowed. *If he wants one. In the meantime, I have to protect him.*

****

Hadley opened her eyes to Silvia rousing her from sleep. The housekeeper sported black shadows beneath her eyes and haggard lines near her mouth. "You look bad."

Straightening, Silvia raised an eyebrow. "Lunch is on the table, Miss Heron."

"It's Hadley." She released a yawn. "If you call me Miss Heron again, I'll pour a bottle of red wine on the bed."

Laughing, Silvia scanned the white sheets. "You wouldn't do that." She swallowed hard. "Would you?"

Hadley climbed from the enormous bed. "I might. Will you make coffee?"

Silvia nodded.

"The sheets are safe," Hadley said.

Laughing, the housekeeper retreated from the room.

Hadley splashed water on her face and found Silvia and Vivian clustered around a table set with grilled cheese sandwiches and chilled gazpacho.

Silvia unfurled a napkin and placed it on her lap. "We all need comfort food."

Yawning, Hadley dropped into a chair. "Where's Damon?"

"Sleeping off the hydrocodone," Vivian said.

"Have either of you slept?"

Silvia and Vivian looked at each other and shook their heads.

Hadley sighed. "I'll take the next shift."

"Is that a good idea?" Vivian raised her spoon and took a delicate sip.

Hadley leaned toward the window and tapped it. "Johann said it's secure." Eating in silence, she watched boaters troll the clear, blue waters of the lake. A curious squirrel ran along the exterior railing and paused in front of the back door. She avoided dropping her gaze and looking for a bloodstain.

Silvia whistled, and the animal ran off.

After lunch, Silvia poured the coffee. "Will you tell me the extent of your research?"

Hadley cleared her throat. "Dr. Stefan, my colleague Buffy, and I investigated the effects of CBD derivatives, though Buffy didn't know the extent of it. Johann's uncle and I wondered if combining chemicals could mimic opioids without the threat of addiction. We used neuronal cell health assays to test an array of CBD derivatives."

Vivian narrowed her gaze. "You found one."

She nodded. "The neurons responded to a polymer. The next major step would be clinical trials, but Günter said Dr. Stefan skipped the protocols and tested the compound on him."

Silvia sipped from her cup. "It must have worked."

"I guess so." Hadley sighed. "I can't publish results from an angry German analog."

Vivian choked on a sip of water.

"I've seen the effects of too many opioids," Silvia said. "When they're desperate, people turn to heroin."

"Heroin's an opioid without a branding team," Hadley said. "A man made it from morphine, a derivative of the opium poppy. Twenty years later, a chemist from Bayer re-synthesized the compound. The name 'heroin' allegedly comes from the German word meaning 'heroic and strong'. If you told patients you wanted to treat them with diamorphine, they probably wouldn't blink." Thinking of Johann's pep talk, she sighed. *Nature can be beautiful and cruel.*

"Pharmaceutical companies don't produce heroin," Silvia said.

Vivian raised her eyebrows. "As Hadley said, it's a matter of branding."

"Methadone, buprenorphine, and extended-release naltrexone are the three medicines physicians use to treat opioid use disorder." Hadley cleared her throat. "Nature gives us the strongest drugs we have, but I need to understand my research and compare it to those drugs before I release it into the public domain."

Vivian frowned. "Don't underestimate Johann's calculations."

She shook her head. "He understands what I'm doing."

Standing, Vivian rolled her head. "Some discoveries never hit the market."

Vivian had a point, but every researcher understood the possibility of failure. She crossed her arms. "Johann understands my vision."

"Of course. Johann is a gem." Vivian covered a yawn. "But he's not infallible. I prefer to work alone. The responsibility stops at my door."

"So does the innovation." She dropped her voice. "You said it's lonely."

Vivian inclined her head. "So it is."

Silvia tapped her fingers on the table. "If you two learned to get along, you would be formidable allies."

Vivian laughed. "Silvia, you've never liked me."

The housekeeper raised her eyebrows. "I never said I didn't like you."

"I'm surprised we're not having fish."

"I forgot my fishing pole." Smiling, Silvia turned

to Hadley. "What sent you down this twisty road?"

She exhaled. Feminine banter could smooth over rough edges, but her scars would never heal. "When we were teenagers, my sister Jecca battled cancer and died. After her death, my mother abused prescriptions. Pain destroyed our family."

Silvia looked out the window at the lake glittering in the sunlight. "Losing a child can shatter a life."

Intrigued by Silvia's contemplation, Hadley accepted old wounds could linger, but until Silvia offered more information, she would not probe. "My mother medicated her pain, but she pulled back before she spiraled out of control. Her restraint hurt as much as her neglect. Why couldn't she do more?"

Silvia exhaled. "Maybe memories of you and your sister kept her tethered to reality."

"After Jecca's death, reality hardly mattered. Good insurance and deep pockets kept her stable." Standing, she stretched. "She chose that life. If it's a disease, she refused to fight it. Breaking the cycle is my job."

****

Wandering through the quiet, afternoon house, Hadley lingered near the back door and tested her culpability against the bleach's harsh smell. *Did cleaning these walls help settle Silvia's nerves? What should I have done last night? How do you grieve a man who wanted you dead?* She replayed Gary's grousing entry and her fear Günter would shoot her just as he shot Gary. *Should I feel guilty for living?* Sitting outside, she called Gary's parents.

"Hadley! Hadley! Are you all right? We've been so worried about you," Mr. Bezelle said.

She closed her eyes. "I'm fine, but I'm so sorry."

The man exhaled. "Gary's mother hasn't come out of her room yet."

She recalled the folksy shadows of their redwood-shaded home. "I can't imagine her grief." *But I've seen the equivalent.* She pushed away memories of the days her mother retreated to her bedroom's dim sanctuary. *Please, let Gary's mother find strength.*

"The police told me the shooting was a domestic disturbance. Gary interrupted a dispute between two brothers? Who are these zur Hausen men? I can't understand how Gary knew them."

She leaned her head against the wall. "Dr. Stefan's family came to town for his funeral."

"Does this have anything to do with the explosion at the lab?"

"No, Mr. Bezelle, it doesn't."

"He was our only child. What possessed him to get mixed up with these people?"

She cleared her throat. Acknowledging Gary's greed and laziness would not help Mr. Bezelle mourn his son. "He was a talented scientist."

After a long silence, Mr. Bezelle sighed. "No, he wasn't. He loved animals, winning at sports, and eating his mother's cooking. Don't tell me about his days in the lab. Tell me about the times he beat you at tennis or the times you two lingered on the old porch swing. His mother and I always hoped you would fall for each other."

She closed her eyes. "Our relationship wasn't romantic."

"No, children never follow your plan." He sighed. "You need to take care of yourself, Hadley. You need to come home before another accident happens."

She considered what it would be like to take refuge in her childhood home. In the last ten years, the dark curtains and faded photographs in Tiburon had barely moved. "I don't think my parents would appreciate the disruption."

"You should call them."

Alone on the step, she smiled. "They haven't called me."

"Take the high road, Hadley. Life is too brief for regrets."

She thought of Johann and Günter squaring off. *What binds a family? Is it blood, or is it love? I can't fault the physical care my parents provided, but I only remember a shadow of feeling loved.* "I'm not ready to take the high road." *Hypocrite. I railroaded Johann into calling his brother.* The silence on the line stretched, as heavy as storm clouds.

Mr. Bezelle cleared his throat. "The grief counselors said we'll resume our normal lives. I can't understand how that will happen, but I want to believe them. I cherished the time we had with Gary."

"He loved the parent-child tennis tournaments. A framed photograph of the state tournament still hangs in his room."

"The win was easy, Hadley. The other dad only had one arm."

She smiled. "Either way, Gary just savored that day in the sun with you."

The old hippie laughed. "I hope his spirit feels nothing but the sun."

"I hope so, too, Mr. Bezelle."

"Will you sing at the funeral?" he asked.

His voice cracked, and she longed to hug him. "I'm

not sure that's a good idea."

"Gary always loved 'Blackbird'."

She smiled. The song's beauty and calming tones might be the salve everyone needed. *I hope Sir Paul McCartney never finds out I'm using his song to honor a traitor.* She hummed the major notes and hoped the melody eased the tension in her shoulders. "If it helps you, I'll sing for you."

"Thank you." He ended the call.

Checking her watch, she swallowed. *How long until Johann comes home, and how can I help him?*

Chapter Fifteen

Hadley's phone vibrated with a text message from Buffy.

—*Where are you? It's not like you to bail on lab time.*—

She tapped out a reply.

—*Busy. Be back in a few days.*—

Buffy responded.

—*Is this about Frank? Are you off drinking exotic German beers?*—

—*I'm very jealous.*—

—*Does he have a brother?*—

Hadley smiled and typed out her response before Buffy jumped to any more conclusions.

—*Yes, but you don't want him. I'm in Tahoe.*—

Before she could elaborate, Buffy's reply appeared.

—*And you didn't take me?*—

Looking out the window, Hadley spied Johann's SUV.

—*No room in the wagon.*—

As Buffy composed a response, three dots appeared on Hadley's screen. Worried about agitating her collaborator, she ignored the incoming text, took a deep breath, and placed a call.

Buffy answered on the first ring. "What's wrong?"

"A lot." She exhaled. "Dr. Stefan's death wasn't a gas explosion, and now another terrible thing has happened." The words came before she could overthink them.

"Is that why the good lieutenant and his partner were in the department chair's office?"

Buffy's casual tone undermined the severity of the situation. *I shouldn't lie to my friends. Buffy's strong enough to handle the truth.* She swallowed hard. "Gary's dead."

Buffy gasped. "Shit!"

She let the statement sink in before she tried the excuse meant to protect everyone's feelings. "He found himself caught in the middle of a family squabble."

"Fuck that," Buffy said. "My family doesn't shoot people. What happened?"

She closed her eyes and bit back a smile. "You need to be very careful with the research. If anyone asks, the first assay results were unreliable. We're still struggling to interpret our findings."

"But the results weren't unreliable. I've reproduced them. We can narrow the field and examine the anomalies."

The biggest anomaly is our winner. "I was so focused on proving myself that I didn't acknowledge how valuable you are, but two people are dead, Buffy. Imagining a third death isn't impossible."

Buffy sighed. "Well, thanks for the acknowledgment, but you need to come back to campus before you find out you're the next on the hit list. Who's behind this drama? I can name at least twenty biopharmaceutical companies with a global research focus. Was it Abbvey? Estrellas? Bison-Lisbon-Squid? Oh, please don't tell me it's…"

Hadley interrupted the woman before she could

recite a whole alphabet of drug companies. "I don't think those companies are to blame."

"Shindoh? Takeano? UGTBK?"

She cleared her throat and focused on protecting Johann. "I'm worried about the people who don't list their shares on the stock exchange. I'm worried about the people who use guns, instead of lawyers, to get ahead."

"Oh, shit, Hadley. You *are* in danger."

She thought of the women sleeping in the other bedrooms. Silvia and Vivian maintained a fierce loyalty to Johann. Damon's interests felt more divided, but he followed Johann's directive to look out for her. "I feel safe here." Buffy's silence felt like an acceptance.

The researcher cleared her throat. "But what if you aren't safe there?"

She looked at the glistening, blue lake. *Friends take care of each other.* "Play dumb, Buffy. If someone asks you what we're doing, tell him or her we're testing for contaminants. Tell the person we're looking for downers. Tell them anything you want until we can regroup and figure out how to protect the people we love."

"We're not looking for downers," Buffy said.

"I know, but the fewer people who know what we're truly doing, the better."

"Assays are one thing, but you need millions of dollars of investment to advance this research. You need an angel investor."

She swallowed. "The university has resources. We might find a partner foundation."

"Maybe, but you'll lose control of the final product."

She rolled her eyes. "Thanks for the vote of confidence."

Buffy laughed. "Gary got one thing right. Some synthetic production components produce an amazing high. Worst-case scenario, we run parallel businesses to continue our research."

"I'm not interested in getting people high."

Buffy sighed. "Good old Frank better be very good in bed."

She laughed. "He funded the initial research."

"Tell him we need a multi-million dollar fridge"— she snorted—"to store samples."

"We'll figure out this problem together. If the research pans out, you can fill a pool with beer."

"I don't have a swimsuit," Buffy said.

"Get one." She ended the call and heard a car on the drive. Standing, she took a deep breath. *Will the police arrest me for perjury? If I'm an accessory to murder, the university will strip my funding. How ironic that it's Johann's money.*

The footsteps climbing the exterior stairs paused for the entryway and continued through the foyer.

Only one person can move through this house with such precision and arrogance. Happiness and relief coursed through her system. "Johann."

He stopped at the edge of the great room.

His black hair stood on end, and the scar beneath his eye disappeared against the pallor of his skin. Fatigue had deepened the crow's feet near his eyes, and the nascent shadow of a soft, black beard crept along his face. He wore the same bloodstained clothes he had worn when he left the house.

"You're still here," he said.

His quiet observation heated her cheeks. She looked at the floor and prepared herself for rejection, then raised her eyes. "This is where I want to be."

Smiling, he held out a hand.

She rushed into his arms, inhaled, and lifted her face.

He claimed her lips, crushed her against his chest, and stroked her back. "Did you worry about me?"

Rolling her eyes, she pulled down his head for another kiss, bruising his lips as she fought to affirm his presence and her right to be part of it. When his hold tightened, she pulled back. "I thought they would arrest you."

He smiled and tucked her head beneath his chin. "They probably should." He smoothed her wavy brown hair from her face. "I'm so sorry about Gary."

She nodded and swallowed the lump in her throat. "I wouldn't have wished for his death."

"Even though he considered yours?"

"He made a coward's choice." She chewed her lip. "He must have been desperate."

Johann sighed. "Desperate men work on sanitation crews."

The practical observation irritated her. *Had Johann ever considered life without a fortune? When their back is against the wall, people make ridiculous choices.* She pulled free, walked into the kitchen, and turned. "Günter was desperate, too."

"My brother is in the local hospital." Johann rubbed his brow. "As soon as he is stable, I will arrange for his transfer."

"So he'll be okay?"

He nodded. "The gunshot wound won't kill him,

but physicians said the side effects of alcoholic polyneuropathy might be permanent."

"The research drug could have exacerbated his problems." She exhaled, relieved to voice her fear. "I could be responsible for his psychosis."

"Günter willingly took the drug." He ran a hand through his hair. "He declined to press charges."

"You look relieved," she said.

He walked into the kitchen and tipped up her chin. "I'm sorry I couldn't save Gary."

She pulled back. "Have you ever killed someone, Johann?"

He stroked her cheek with the back of his hand. "Is there a right answer?"

"Yes." She shivered.

"I won't lie, but think long and hard before you ask me again."

"I need to know the answer."

He dropped his hand and stepped back.

She felt the freedom to flee.

"Seven people," he said. "I've never shot a person unless I feared for my life or for those under my protection. I only shoot to kill."

She closed her eyes. "You didn't kill the shooter in the park or your brother."

"*Ja.*" He gathered her close. "Though I thought they were the same."

"You still hoped for a non-lethal resolution. The next time you're looking down the barrel of a gun, remember you're aiming at someone's loved one."

"Indecision will slow me down," he said. "It will put people at risk."

"You told me you're fast. Get faster."

He rested his head on top of her hair. "What if I'm not fast enough?"

"What if you're too fast?"

"Then I would have killed my brother." He sighed. "The man has plenty of atonement to do before we're on equal terms."

"I'd do anything to have Jecca back by my side. I don't want to be your problem."

He took her hand and traced her palm. "I told you to grow up, but I don't want you to be as cynical as I am. Hold on to the romanticism. It gives me hope for the future."

His lips brushed hers, as light as a moth's wing. Instead of rejecting him, she leaned into his embrace and pulled his lip between her teeth, goading him to open.

Cupping the back of her head, he trailed kisses down her neck. "*Du gefällst mir.*"

Come to my bed. She smiled at the note of desperation in his voice. "I've already been there." He raised his eyebrows and looked toward the master suite where the wrinkled bed beckoned for a repeat of their last engagement. "Will you return?"

Looking at the hunger in his gaze, she nodded and offered him a mischievous smile. "After you shower." His laughter promised brighter days.

Nodding, he pulled her toward the bedroom, kissed her soundly, and retreated to the bathroom with a promise to return.

She sat in the middle of the rumpled bed and watched the late afternoon sun dip below the mountains surrounding the lake. Hearing Johann moving behind the closed bathroom door, she flopped on the blankets and counted the beams in the ceiling. *Seven. Can I keep the number of bodies from rising to eight? Can I make him smile? He's not a bad boy billionaire. Life hardened him into a disciplined and controlled man.*

The door to the bathroom opened, and Johann emerged, wearing a towel.

Droplets of water glistened on his shoulders.

He approached her and ran his hand from her nape to the swell of her ass.

The heat of his touch blazed a path of desire along her spine, and she abandoned her concerns for the pleasure of living in the moment. Turning toward him, she cupped his face and felt his skin, slick from a recent shave.

He turned his head and kissed her hand.

"Have you thought about me?" she asked.

"Since the moment you left my bed in Palo Alto."

"And how long will it go on?"

He grabbed her wrist and raised her hand, suckling her thumb.

The heat and tension of his mouth made her want to drag him to the bed and give him other things to tease and lick. She pulled free her hand and leaned on an elbow. "How long?"

"So many questions." He pulled back. "What are you asking me?"

"Now that you've quarantined your brother, will you drop me back on campus and walk away?"

He pulled her to the edge of the bed and spread her arms. "Hardly."

"Trauma amplifies emotions."

He repeated the line and spread a hand across her collarbone. "So clinical."

Sweeping his palm down her midline, his touch sensitized every inch of skin between her neck and her crotch. She hated how her body rose to meet his touch without waiting for his answer.

He cupped her heat, thumbed her clit, and smiled at her gasp. "You're dealing with desire. Admiration. Respect. I have enough contracts in my life. Can't emotions be enough for us?"

Her body's response overrode her rational thoughts. Closing her eyes, she sighed. "I want emotions to be enough." She might be lying through her teeth, but the results never felt so good. "I want you to please me. I want to please you."

He raised his head. "You deserve to have everything you want."

His hard voice belied his intimate touch. He kept stroking her, putting pressure where she needed it most. Narrowing her gaze, she decided to test his limits. "Get on your knees."

He complied and cocked his head.

Stripping off her clothes, she turned on her side and hooked her leg around his waist, their bodies pressed together, perpendicular and waiting for action. She maneuvered her body and felt him probing her entrance, then he grasped her hips, hot and impatient against the shift in dynamics. She stilled and looked at him, raising her eyebrows. *Who's in control?*

His grip on her hips tightened.

The challenge spurred her on. She smiled, flexed her hips to guide his first thrust, and set the rhythm. Pleasure flooded his features.

He closed his eyes, and his hand palmed her ass before he swore and held her hips, struggling to catch his breath.

Smiling, she flexed and enjoyed her ability to influence his reaction. He had the upper hand in so many ways, but linked together, she had as much power as he did. She flexed again.

He hissed. "*Ja*, Hadley."

Shifting to ride his thigh, she arched her back and changed the angle of penetration. Moving against him, pressure built in her body. She reveled in his hair rubbing against her skin and the way his muscles tensed.

He braced his body. "You humble me."

Satisfied with his response, she shifted her hips, squeezed his thigh, and lost herself in the action. Each stroke pulled her higher, and the friction promised to overload her system. She shifted, searching for her release. "This is more than desire." *I care about you.*

He managed a guttural response and slapped her ass.

The bright shock of pain left her gasping for breath, but it anchored her senses.

"Now, Hadley, stop holding yourself back," he said.

His command sent a thrill through her body and chased off the pleasure of retaining control. She closed her eyes and followed his rhythm, working with him as he grabbed her hips and let her pivot off his strength. His other hand slipped between her legs, intensifying the pleasures of heat and muscled friction. Caught by his strength, and her designs, she rocked against his touch.

He slapped her ass again.

Blood rushed to the site, her focus narrowed, and

her control shattered into pieces. His shout followed hers, and her body softened.

After several minutes, she pulled away.

He held her fast.

She tested his hold. "We can't stay like this forever."

He released his grip. "Anything can happen."

Instead of rolling away, she leaned into his warmth and steady breaths.

His breathing slowed.

While he slept, she rested in his arms, content to feel his weight anchoring her to the bed. She thought about the photograph in Dr. Stefan's office. Two little boys had shared an inner tube. Life's coincidences bound people together, without care for compatibility or outcome, but social norms kept them afloat. *Don't kick, don't bite, and don't drown your friend. Jecca got it, but Gary and Günter did not. Do genes compel us to swim in the same direction, or do circumstances train us to reach for a common goal?*

The luxury of the Tahoe house and her upbringing made her think about her next steps. *Thriving in Johann's circles will require a fight. I won't release him, but I won't sit back and let him make all the calls on what we do next.* She focused on the next steps for her research. *A utility patent would last for twenty years from the filing date. Unless we defend it, when the patent expires, T-83 would become part of the public domain. Is it better to control that patent directly and ensure accessibility or let global outlets manufacture it like any other generic? Which pathway would lead to the greatest public health benefit?*

Johann stirred. "I can hear you thinking."

She smiled. "I'm not thinking about myself."

"Are you thinking about me?"

"No."

He grunted and draped an arm around her waist. "Then your thoughts can wait until we get up."

She closed her eyes and focused on her breathing. *We're a long way from production, but Johann's resources would be assets.* She exhaled. *I have to separate the business and pleasure between us.*

He tightened his grip.

His arousal pushed against her leg, and she smiled. "You have many fine assets, and I plan to protect every single one of them."

Growling, he turned her until she lay on her back, wide-eyed and laughing. He braced his hands on either side of her head and smiled. "Now I'm up."

Chapter Sixteen

Toying with a pencil and a crossword puzzle, Hadley whiled away the next morning in the cavernous, lakeside living room. Johann and his guests occupied themselves with books and electronics, but she itched to find a bicycle and move. "Can't we get out of here?"

"The police officer asked us to remain in Tahoe for forty-eight hours," Johann said.

Vivian huffed. "What will we do for forty-eight hours?"

He kept his gaze fixed on his laptop. "The same things we would do before Günter showed up. Maintain our defenses. Work on dismantling the threat to Hadley's life."

"Perhaps you're the target," Hadley said.

Johann rolled his eyes.

"Hadley's right." Vivian frowned. "Anyone could be a threat."

He closed the laptop and looked at his assistant. "Do you have a better plan?"

Hadley imagined the two of them dissecting a business plan, tearing off each other's clothes, and having cold, dispassionate sex. She cleared her throat. *To find a pattern, I have to keep myself from baiting Vivian, and we need to leave the house.* "Maybe we could go to the casinos."

Vivian snorted and grabbed her nose, stifling the

sound.

Damon laughed and slapped her back. "Vivi, I love when you lose control."

She glared.

Silvia turned the pages of her magazine. "Would you rather play board games? Mr. zur Hausen has a garage of water toys like kayaks, paddleboards, and jet skis."

Damon shook his head. "No more motorized watercraft."

"He's right." Vivian glanced at the gash on his forehead. "We need to get out of this house. What do you feel up to?"

"Sitting in a hot tub and going back to bed." Damon traced the bandage over his eye. "My face didn't need this kind of abuse. I was already ugly."

Vivian frowned. "You're not ugly."

"Mama Clarke disagrees."

Hadley suppressed a laugh.

Vivian tilted her head. "You might pass out in the hot tub."

"Great. Let's do it." Damon grinned. "Maybe you'll take advantage of me."

She rolled her eyes. "Hardly."

His cocky smile faltered.

Hadley tilted her head. *They would make an interesting couple.* She pulled out her phone and searched the map near their location. "We could go hiking. Seraphic Ski Resort keeps its gondola open during the summer. We could ride up to the top of the mountain and take in the view."

Vivian pulled out her phone. "How sweet."

Hadley looked up. "What's wrong with sweet?"

The woman picked at her nails. "Nothing. Maybe when we're done, we can bake cupcakes and cook s'mores around the campfire."

"Oh!" Hadley overplayed her response and attempted to catch Vivian off guard. "That's a great idea. Then we can linger around expensive houses and pretend we live there. We can probably get a group rate for that Scandinavian Castle at the edge of the lake."

Johann cleared his throat. "I vote for the gondola. It will help everyone clear their head."

I have other methods to clear your head. Hadley looked at Vivian and smiled as if they sat at a local coffee shop. *So much for friendship.*

"But a gondola's so exposed," Damon said. "You're asking for trouble."

"The police report on my brother will give away our location," Johann said. "Staying inside the house is relatively pointless."

"Man, I hope you know what you're doing."

Johann rolled his neck. "Sometimes I do."

Silvia flipped through a section of glossy advertisements. "I think I'll stay at the house."

Looking back and forth between the pair, Hadley recognized their survival instincts but wondered who would come out ahead.

****

Riding in the gondola, Hadley stared at the stippled, granite mountains. A clear sky let sunlight reflect off the mountains' quartz, lending the range a shimmer like the windswept lake. She glanced at Johann's profile and smiled at the juxtaposition of his outward persona and the immovable granite mountains. *How many times had he made an exception for her?*

Sitting next to his strength and discipline, she felt safe enough to let her gaze drift and to admire the beauty of the blue-green water circling the shore. The emerald hue fell away until the center of the lake looked like a hole swallowing the sky. Drawn to the combination of clarity and power, she leaned forward. "I feel like I can see the bottom of the lake."

Vivian lowered her sunglasses and fanned herself with a brochure. "Hardly. It's the second deepest lake in the country."

"Water near freezing is very clear," Johann said.

Damon shuddered. "I'll vouch for that fact."

Johann cleared his throat. "In the 1960s, you could see down to a depth of about one hundred feet, but population growth led to nutrient runoff and algae growth. Current visibility is about seventy feet."

Hadley smiled. "Seventy feet? No wonder the water looks so clear."

Vivian rolled her eyes and looked out the window.

The gondola station came into view, and the pod swung in the slight wind.

"Here's Larch Lodge." Johann cleared his throat and nodded at the attendant opening the gondola's door. "Let's get a drink."

Hadley climbed out of the gondola and made her way off the platform before the next group of people disembarked. Signs for *Epoch Discovery* covered every surface of the gondola station. The photographs showed happy models hanging from colorful ropes and grinning at each other. The advertisements near the information kiosk showed kids grasping the edges of a mountain coaster like they built the contraption themselves.

"White people," Damon said. "I'll see you at the

lodge."

She considered the advertisements. *To flush out the threat, we need visibility.* The longer she considered the images, the more appeal they held. Plummeting through the trees with juvenile delight seemed like the perfect antidote to the tension of the last few days. *I'm stepping out of my comfort zone, but when Vivian breaks a nail, I wouldn't mind hearing her scream.* "What's wrong with climbing walls and zip lines? I want to do it."

Johann looked at the advertisements. "Even a novice marksman could take a shot while you're hanging from a wire like a trussed pheasant."

She widened her gaze. "Did you bring a gun to the ski resort?"

He cocked his head. "Have you learned nothing about me?"

Looking at the jacket he wore in the summer heat, she felt like she left her common sense at the bottom of the mountain. *Of course he did.*

He jerked his head toward the lodge. "Let's go."

Smiling, Vivian fell in line behind Johann.

Hadley joined the procession like a dutiful caboose. *I don't care if you're cool and jaded. I'm alive, and after I get a drink, I'm going on every single one of those damn zip lines.*

The sloped roof of the lodge covered a two-story wall of windows. In the winter, snow might slide right off the structure, but the roof overhang provided summer shade. The building's fashionable, high-alpine interior normalized antler chandeliers, but the families chowing down on smoked meats and pepperoni pizzas gave the room warmth.

Damon chose a table in the bar area and gestured to

the server.

The menu ran the gauntlet from a Bloody Mary to a rich, Mexican hot chocolate. Hadley considered her options and put down the menu. She smiled at the college kid holding a pen and notepad. "I'll have the Bloody Mary."

"Good call," Damon said.

The server nodded. "Can I see your ID?"

Shrugging, she fished it from her purse.

Johann chose iced tea and a sandwich.

Vivian pored over the wine list.

The server tapped a foot.

"Ridge," Vivian said.

"Feeling thematic?" Hadley asked.

"No, but I recognize quality."

Hadley turned to the server. Given a choice between quality and innovation, she would choose the excitement of a new discovery. "I'll have extra banana peppers in my Bloody Mary."

"Cute," Vivian said.

Doubling her smile's wattage, Hadley beamed at the server.

"Do you want to come back to the kitchen and garnish it yourself?" he asked. "We usually make it table-side, but this number of kids makes moving the bar cart near impossible."

"Are you guys always this busy?"

He ran a hand through his hair. "This is nowhere near busy. During winter, we have live DJs, half-priced drinks, and food specials for après-ski. Last February, one of the table-top dancers tripped on a French fry and landed in a VIP's lap." He lowered his voice. "The man's name rhymes with Edison."

Standing, she wondered who deserved her sympathy for the fry incident. "Sure. I'll stuff my drink with so many garnishes you'll barely have room for the mix." She glanced at Vivian. "It's like a salad, right?"

The server laughed. "Follow me."

Johann reached for her arm. "I don't think that's a good idea. You need to stay within sight of me."

"Like a child?"

"Like a woman with a bandage on her arm."

She sighed and looked at the families plotting their afternoons. "I want to go on the zip line. I need some space from this…level of protection."

He stepped back.

"Not from you," she added.

"Please?" he asked.

Exhaling, she reclaimed her chair.

The server looked back.

Waving him off, she rested her chin in her hand. "I liked my life better when my biggest worry was catching HPV from Gary."

Johann's jaw tightened. "You said your relationship wasn't passionate."

She toyed with the sugar packets on the table. "It wasn't." Looking up, she grinned. "Just one time, in college. Trust me, the event was nothing to write home about."

"You should have told me," Johann said. "Affairs can complicate emotions. I would have spent more resources vetting him."

Vivian laughed. "Isn't this the pot calling the kettle black?"

Damon shook his head. "Doesn't matter what they did in the past, Vivi. That man had no loyalty. Hadley could have cited him as a co-author, and he still would have screwed her."

"Again?" Vivian raised her eyebrows.

Jonathan frowned

"Sorry." She toyed with a sugar packet.

Hadley cleared her throat and avoided thoughts of her friend occupying a morgue. "Gary didn't blow up the lab, shoot me, or rig the boat. I've had on blinders. This group"—she met every gaze and settled on Johann—"needs to consider other explanations."

Leaning back in his chair, he nodded. "I've reviewed the security tapes from the house for the last few weeks. No unauthorized people approached the boat."

"Fire your mechanic," Damon said.

Drumming her fingers on the table, Hadley rested a hand on her chin. "Or someone planned the boat a while ago." She toyed with her silverware. "I think I prefer crimes of passion. The premeditation"—she straightened—"who plans out that far?"

"Someone with a grudge," Johann said.

"Who have you wronged?"

He raised an eyebrow.

"Inadvertently?" she asked.

"I'm capable of mistakes."

She sighed. "Thank goodness."

Vivian smiled.

The server returned with drinks and food. He presented a plate of garnishes and winked.

Hadley forced a smile. "Oh, you'll get a big tip."

The server laughed. "Flag me if you need anything else."

"Maybe the two of you could exchange numbers,"

Vivian said. "You're about the same age."

Hadley sipped her drink and smiled above the rim. The banana peppers were a good call. "Good idea, Vivi."

She stroked the wineglass stem. "I don't like that nickname."

Damon shoved a nacho in his mouth. "What about Bibi?"

Handing him a napkin, she sighed. "Vivian. And talking with food in your mouth is rude. How on earth do you manage to be so charming and so incorrigible?"

He wiped his mouth and laughed. "It's a skill, Miss Vivian."

Hadley drummed her fingers on the tabletop. "I'm replaying who visited the lab in the weeks leading up to the explosion."

Johann reached across the table and stilled the repetitive motion.

The pressure of his touch captured her attention, and she smiled.

Damon swallowed a nacho. "Can we do the touchy-feely detective shit after lunch?"

She laughed. "Sure." Sipping her Bloody Mary, she listened to the chatter of families and compared it to the nuanced silence at her table. *If I wanted to have this much fun, I could have stayed home with Silvia.*

After the break, Hadley led the group to the ticket station, but the wait for the zip line dashed her hopes for an adventure. She surveyed the resort map and considered her options. "What about the shorter course? Forty miles per hour is still fast, and the wait is half as long."

Vivian wrinkled her nose. "It's five zip lines and

an aerial bridge. It'll be midnight before we get back to Johann's house."

Johann checked his watch. "I doubt it. The base closes at five o'clock." He shrugged his shoulders. "Hitting a target moving that fast is difficult. Let Hadley have her fun."

Twenty minutes later, purses sat in lockers, and Hadley wore a ground school harness while another college-aged kid demonstrated how to navigate ten feet of mocked-up cable.

Vivian brushed her hands on her pants. "This is ridiculous."

Hadley smiled. *That's what makes it so much fun.*

The guide continued issuing instructions on the chairlift ride to the course. He checked Hadley's harness and moved to the next member of their group.

Johann claimed the vacated space and checked her harness again.

"You don't think it's safe?" she asked.

"I don't enjoy taking chances."

"You said we could leave the house."

He tightened a rope. "You're not a prisoner."

She looked at the tree line and imagined the moment of freedom when she would fly. Johann saw threats in the shadows, but she knew the pleasure of letting go. "What could go wrong?"

He followed her gaze, "If the group gets separated, do your best to stay with me."

"What about Vivian?"

He checked the rope above her head. "Damon can protect her."

Nodding, she took a deep breath and climbed the ladder to the first zip line. Views of Carson Valley and

Lake Tahoe beckoned her to savor the moment. *Johann's here. It's a professional course. I'll land safe and sound.*

The guide gave her the signal to proceed. "Just hold on tight and watch your landing."

She grasped the overhead system and flung herself from the platform. A moment of weightlessness sent her stomach into her throat, but the slack caught her weight, and she flew down the mountain on the engineered line. The wind stung her eyes, but she smiled against the speed until her cheeks ached.

The receiving guide caught her and directed her to the second landing.

"It's amazing." She laughed, embarrassed by her enthusiasm.

Johann landed next, followed by Vivian and Damon.

By the time the group crossed the aerial bridge and the remaining lines, rain clouds hovered above the ridgeline.

Vivian brushed a pine needle from her hair. "That was better than I expected."

"So, you had fun?" Hadley asked.

Shrugging, Vivian rolled her shoulders. "Don't push it."

Two side-by-sides waited at the base of the final platform. The guide gestured to the vehicles. "You're the last group of the day. My partner, Mike, has to secure the ropes. We can wait, or I can lead you back to the gondola station and circle back."

"It'll pour," Vivian said.

The guide tossed the second set of keys to Johann. "You look like you can handle yourself."

Johann caught the keys and looked at the vehicles. "We should wait."

"That's fine by me," the guide said.

A low rumble of thunder bounced off the mountains, and the silhouette of Günther's rain-soaked form flashed through Hadley's mind. She shivered. *If two explanations account for the facts, the simpler explanation is probably correct. Occam's razor is the right principle, but Günther's in jail.*

Vivian claimed a seat in the first vehicle. "We can wait, but I'm sitting."

Damon took the spot beside her, but he lost his footing. Grabbing the steering wheel, he regained his balance and shook his head. "I forgot to take my pain medication."

Johann looked at the dark clouds. "All right. Let's go."

The guide revved the engine on the first side-by-side and took the lead.

Johann kept his foot on the pedal, but the distance between the two vehicles grew.

She shifted closer to him and strained her eyes for a glimpse of the base camp. "Shouldn't we try to keep up?"

He gestured toward the black exhaust. "Seraphic needs to hire a new technician. There's something wrong with the fuel injection system."

The first raindrops fell cold and wet. Fearing a repeat of the boat explosion, she shivered. Flying through the warm sunlit air felt exhilarating, but the afternoon shadows menaced. *The assailant chose distance. They've never gotten close.* Lightning flashed, and the air smelled of ozone. She hoped the first vehicle doubled back.

Johann glanced over. "Are you okay?"

She bit her lip and nodded.

"At this speed, we can limp along to base camp, or we can stop and check the air filter."

"Why do I get to choose?" she asked.

"Why not?"

The wind shifted and blew black smoke in her face. She crossed her arms and scanned the pine trees. "While we're moving, the trees make us a difficult target. If we stop, we'll be sitting ducks."

He nodded. "We should continue."

The side-by-side bucked.

Swearing, he eased off the accelerator and cut the engine.

She shivered, scanning the landscape for cover. Enormous boulders peppered one side of the trail. Left behind by melting glaciers, the smooth erratics had weathered many storms, but she trusted Johann's instincts.

He pulled his gun from his holster and handed it to her.

His instincts! I trust his instincts! Her hand shook.

Opening the engine cover, he retrieved a paper filter caked with dirt, dust, and mud. He knocked the filter against his boot, dislodging layers of grime, and slid the filter back into the compartment. "That should help bring down our fuel ratio."

She looked at the trees. They shifted with the approaching storm, their top branches swaying in the wind. The force pulled long, wooden groans from their trunks. "Hurry, Johann."

The gunshot came from nowhere, chased by a bolt

of lightning, and her blood-curdling scream. She focused on the side-by-side's tire, punctured like an overripe plum, and wondered if she might be next.

Johann pulled the gun from her grasp and pivoted. Dropping to one knee, he faced the tree line. "Show yourself!"

His command echoed in the granite amphitheater, but it died without a response.

"Coward." He hurled the German insult and waited.

A second shot punctured the back tire.

Crouching on the far side of the vehicle, she locked her arms around her knees and quelled her shaking limbs. *Why did I think I could protect him?* She peeked over her shoulder and the protective edge of the vehicle. Trees never looked so ominous.

Johann walked toward the trees. "Keep down your head."

"Stop!" she yelled. "I'm not your problem."

He paused. "I want you to be my problem."

The implications of his words washed over her. "Not at the expense of your life." His vulnerability felt more important than her cowering fear. "Johann! Come back."

He shook his head, breached the edge of the trees, and disappeared between the shadows.

She looked to the sky, wondering if the wind stole her words or he ignored them. Her stomach clenched, and she thought she might be sick. *Please let him come back unscathed.*

The second side-by-side rounded the curve in the road.

Exhaling, she waved both her hands to signal

danger but knew the sound of the gunshot had carried. *Would Damon and Vivian force the guide to stay back or charge to Johann's rescue?*

The guide cupped his hands and slowed the side-by-side. "What happened to you guys?"

Damon leaned toward him and spoke.

The guide navigated the vehicle next to her and frowned at the blown tires.

Jumping down, Damon made eye contact.

She jerked her head toward the spot where Johann disappeared between the trees.

Breaking into a run, Damon followed.

The guide scratched his beard. "Where's he going?"

Climbing down from the vehicle, Vivian toed a piece of rubber on the packed, dirt road. "Perhaps Damon's gone to relieve himself." She walked to Hadley, pulled her to standing, and draped an arm around her shoulders.

Is she using me as a shield? Trying to relax, she accepted the woman's gesture.

Vivian approached the intact vehicle. "Try not to worry about him."

She shook. "I can't help myself."

Pulling a bottle of water out of the front console, Vivian offered it. "Try harder."

Her whispered command lingered, but she watched Vivian return to the guide and the abandoned vehicle.

The guide looked at the shredded tires and scratched his jaw.

Vivian yawned and covered her mouth. "They must have hit a rock."

Hadley almost smiled, but she gripped her shaking

elbows and feared a third, life-ending gunshot.

The guide scanned the ground. "Where's the rock?"

Looking up the mountain, Vivian pointed toward an outcropping. "Johann's a terrible driver. You never should have given him the keys."

Hadley rubbed her eyebrows and let a hand cover her nervous grin.

The guide shook his head and exhaled. "I hope they didn't mess up the alignment."

Damon and Johann emerged from the trees without injury. They exchanged glances and walked toward the two vehicles.

The guide squared his shoulders and faced Johann. "I'm afraid you'll—"

Shaking his head, Johann sat in the passenger's seat and pulled her into his arms. "You okay?"

She threw her arms around his neck, buried her face in his warmth, and felt his heartbeat, vibrant and alive beneath her skin. His crisp, citrus smell enveloped her, and she pressed a kiss against his skin, tasting the subtle salt of sweat. Pulling back, she cleared her throat. "I'm sorry."

He rubbed her back. "Shh. I have you."

"But who has you?" she asked.

He tightened his hold.

Damon and Vivian claimed the back seat.

The guide counted heads.

"We'd better go before the rain kicks in," Vivian said.

The guide turned the ignition. "My supervisor will be so mad."

"Don't worry." She yawned. "We'll sort it out

while you get Mike."

The guide slammed on the brakes. "I forgot about Mike."

"Drive," Johann said.

Explaining the situation to management took nothing more than a confident explanation and Johann's credit card. Hadley stood at the back of the room, wondering if she should help. *Why did I think I could connect the dots Johann missed?*

By the time their party climbed into the last gondola car, a steady rain coated the windows. Clouds and droplets gathered on the glass and blocked her view. The humidity in the pod felt thick, but Johann sat by her side. Leaning against the wall, she sighed. "I want to go home."

He nodded. "I'll take you back to Marin."

"No. I want to go back to my townhouse."

Vivian turned her gaze from the gray-blue scenery. "Won't that place bother you?"

She pressed together her lips and replayed the helplessness of watching him fall to the floor. "No."

Vivian frowned. "But Gary's death…"

She held up a hand and cut off Vivian. "I'm still alive, aren't I?"

Damon whistled. "The second we showed up, the marksman must have bolted. We found footprints, but nothing worth following." He crossed his ankles and exhaled. "Catching the bastard would have been easier in the snow."

Hadley focused on the outcome. "You sound disappointed."

He looked up. "And you sound relieved."

"How do you know it's a man?" She looked at

Vivian. "Maybe an old girlfriend's out for revenge."

"You into chicks, too?" Damon asked.

"I'm talking about Johann! Correlation doesn't lead to causation. Just because I've been present every time something bad happened doesn't mean the killer's after me." She shifted and elbowed Johann. "He's been there, too."

"Who are my enemies?" he asked. "I keep a low profile. The contract…"

She slapped her knee. "Screw the contract."

Damon whistled.

Turning, she stared out the window and felt the gondola sway. *I want to go back to my lab and hoping I can change the world. I want to go back to the innocence of thinking people are binary.* Peeking at Johann's set face, she imagined him balancing on the fulcrum between good and evil. *Seven people? Damned if he shoots and damned if he doesn't. Living on the edge must exhaust him.*

"Hadley, you're a target," Damon said. "Stay with the group."

The suggestion would have meant more coming from Johann, but he sat as resolute as stone. Channeling Vivian's confidence, she waved a hand in the air. "I'm going home and letting the police continue their investigation." She inhaled, afraid to tip her hand. "At least I'll be able to sleep at night."

"I thought we were a team," Damon said.

She swallowed. "Divide and conquer. If something else happens to Johann, he'll figure out who's targeting him." *Without having to mind me, he'll probably kill the person.*

Johann closed his eyes for a heartbeat. "And if I

can't?"

In the quiet gondola car, shadowed by twilight and the rippling shadows of the evergreen trees, his blue eyes flattened to gray. She looked out the window and wondered which mission had become a fool's errand, alleviating pain or protecting a man too stubborn to defend himself. "Then somebody else will win."

Chapter Seventeen

The ride back to Johann's Tahoe house upset Hadley's stomach. Unsure if the mountain switchbacks or the thought of leaving Johann brought on her queasiness, she stayed quiet and steeled her nerves.

Silvia scanned the silent group and set four wine glasses on the counter.

"Thanks, but I'm not feeling great." Hadley retreated to the green bedroom, folded her clothes, and placed them in her bag. Her laptop joined the pile, its muffled slide as solemn as dirt on a grave. She slid her notebook on top and slung the bag over her shoulder. Closing the bedroom door, she stood in the common room where Gary had admitted his theft. "Goodbye, Gar-Bear. I hope you're the last man I mourn." Climbing the stairs, she prepared to face the crowd and the tension of a quiet ride home.

Johann came out of his room and set his bag on the table.

She lingered near the stairs, feeling like a shadow of the bold woman he needed at his side.

He looked at Silvia. "Vivian arranged for a rental agency to deliver a car in the morning. The police asked us to remain in Tahoe for forty-eight hours, but I'm taking Hadley back to Palo Alto."

Silvia reached a hand across the table. "Are you okay, Miss Heron?"

She summoned a smile, unsure how much the housekeeper knew. "The events were too much. I'll be okay when I've had some down time."

Shaking her head, Silvia put two glasses back in the cabinet. "You need friends."

Hadley glanced at the rear wall and imagined Johann slumped in a pool of blood. *Losing Gary hurt, but losing Johann would hurt more.* "Thanks, Silvia."

Johann opened the garage door and climbed into the driver's seat of the wagon.

Approaching the passenger side, Hadley placed her items on the backseat and climbed into the passenger seat. She gripped the door panel, her fingers white. "Johann, I want you to know…"

He hit the accelerator.

The car lurched forward, slamming her against the cool leather. "I realize you're mad."

Shaking his head, he slammed the console between the seats. "This stupid, half-assed imitation of a proper transmission is about as effective as a"—swearing, he gripped the wheel—"altered and individualized, my ass."

Feeling the car's speed level out, she loosened her grip. "You're not mad at me."

He sighed and glanced over. "I'm not sure I could ever be mad at you."

She tilted her head. "Really?"

"Don't test me."

Suppressing a smile, she bit her lip. "Then why were you driving like a Bond villain?"

"You don't think I can protect you." His voice hitched, and he cleared his throat.

She pivoted and pulled up her knee. "That's not

true! I just don't"—she chose her words—"know if the person targeting us wants to hurt you or me. If it's you, I thought I could see a trend and help you."

"Hadley." He sighed. "Stick to what you're good at doing."

Jerking back her chin, she gaped. "What?"

"You spent your nights in the lab chasing a dream. That romanticism is beautiful…"

"Wait!" So much of her lived experienced taught her to reject aesthetics and focus on achievements, but in his arms, she felt capable. For a relationship to work, romanticism and beauty could never be insults. "I'm a scientist, not a philosopher."

He smiled. "I know. After a few hours, I would have thrown the glassware at the wall and walked out of the lab." He shifted the wagon into a higher gear. "You persisted. You had a hunch, and you worked through the experimental design until you confirmed your hypothesis."

"Right, so somebody wants you or me dead, and I…"

He shook his head. "You have nothing."

"How do you know?" she asked.

"I have nothing."

You have me. She settled a hand along his thigh, waiting for a knee-jerk rejection.

His shoulders relaxed.

Content to maintain contact, she closed her eyes.

Four hours later, Johann slowed the car for the traffic and congestion of Palo Alto.

Blinking, she straightened in the passenger seat and yawned.

"Are you hungry?" he asked.

She shook her head. Her dreams of a maze leading to a dead end felt ominous. No matter how many times she had retraced her steps, the path had brought her back to the same bleak wall. *I have so many things left to experience.* The campus bell tower shone over the campus like a nightlight. "Have you been to the observation deck?"

"Not in a long time," Johann said.

"The carillon of bells rings for special events like graduation."

"A charming sound."

She smiled. "The largest of the original bells has an inscription. *Uno Pro Pace Sono.* I ring for peace." Turning to face him, she watched the play of headlights illuminate his features. "What makes you ring, Johann?"

He looked over but kept his gaze on the road. "I can think of several things."

"If you didn't worry about me, what would you do?"

"Work."

"Surely you have hobbies," she said. "What's on your bucket list?"

Slowing for a red light, he stopped the car and faced her. "Germans don't have bucket lists. We live the lives we have."

She tapped her fingers against the center console. "Of course you do."

He stilled her hand.

The intimate gesture almost undid her reserves. How quickly had they fallen together and let each other's quirks and idiosyncrasies become part of their lives? He hated her nervous twitch. She accepted the correction, and neither of them said a word. Given time, she would find something in his manner to hate, but she felt the luxury of time slipping from her grasp.

He gripped the steering wheel.

Without the heat of his touch, she fought a shiver.

He nodded toward the bell tower. "Hanover's principal Lutheran church has one of the highest bell towers in Germany. My family and I went to church every week. During the services, I memorized the images of Saint George and Saint James and wondered when my turn would come to defend the castle and fight the dragons. When I grew older, my attention shifted, and the bas-reliefs depicting World War II haunted my conscience." He shook his head. "The church is cold, Hadley. The red bricks and wooden chairs absorb the winter chill. No matter how high the furnace blows, the solemnity of the church seeps into your bones and centers your life on goals, not hobbies and dreams."

"Everyone needs a dream." She wanted to comfort the boy who carried the weight of the world on his shoulders, but the man sitting in the driver's seat needed nothing from her.

He cleared his throat. "Then the clapper fell off."

She frowned. "Excuse me?"

He smiled.

The web of laugh lines softened his features.

"After a funeral, the church leaders rang the biggest bell. Metal fatigue sent an old clapper crashing through the bell tower's dusty, wooden floor."

"That's terrible. Was anyone injured?"

"No, but the accident felt like a warning. I didn't want to spend my life in that old, brick tomb." He reached for her hand. "Sometimes you only notice the bells when the silence goes on too long."

She shook her head. "Bells always ring. People are the ones who must keep listening."

Squeezing her hand, he nodded. "Hadley, nobody asks me about hobbies, but you did. You helped your friend scrape his way into a Ph.D. program. Researching pain relievers to keep together families is your calling. You're just like the bells, cheerful and sharp. Stay that way. Don't worry about the realities the rest of us face."

Pulling free, she ignored the tears brimming in her eyes. "I'm supposed to say goodbye."

The light changed to green. He pressed the accelerator, two hands clutching the steering wheel. "I didn't put you in this situation, but I'm doing my best to free you."

She shook her head and clenched the side of the seat "Let the police department handle the cases. Isn't that what your uncle wanted? You're supposed to commercialize my findings, not forfeit your life."

"My uncle had a guilty conscience," he said. "He couldn't help Günter."

"But you can help me."

"Maybe I'm not the right person." He changed lanes and exhaled. "The last week complicated things between us. Günter acted out, but he's my blood. What happens if I make a mistake with you?"

She wanted to comfort him. "You're not your brother."

He shook his head. "I'm a selfish man. My family's code of conduct isn't charming; it's a legal agreement to preserve wealth. That's how I grew up,

Hadley. No hobbies. No bells. Protect, Salvage, and Evacuate fits me like a second skin."

"You're more than a motto." She shifted in the seat. *I wanted to give him space to focus, but I thought I could come back.* "You've put yourself in danger for me time and time again. Don't I mean something to you?"

"You're more valuable to me than any asset." He made eye contact.

She smiled, but she hoped he saw his life as more than a series of assets with serial numbers, catalog descriptions, and valuations. She had a heart, and every time he said her name, it beat faster.

Turning his face to the road, he adjusted his grip on the steering wheel. "But I don't want you to stay because you're worried about danger. I will protect you under any circumstances, but I don't need a friend."

She closed her eyes. Finding everything she needed in his arms satisfied her, but she might fail to satisfy him. "What do you need?"

"You, without reservations." Parking the sedan in front of her brown townhouse, he turned and pulled a hand to his lips. " 'Love alters not with his brief hours and weeks, but bears it out even to the edge of doom.' I don't need a contract. I need a commitment."

The warmth of his lips left her resolve teetering on the edge of a precipice. "Johann, I'm attempting to protect…" She sighed and pulled free her hand. "I can't ignore the threats."

He narrowed his gaze. "Hadley, the threats will end."

"And if you get caught in the crossfire?"

"Then my life will have been worthwhile." He

exhaled. "Life always ends."

"No." Reaching across the seat, she gripped his shirt. "I should have been the sick sister. I should have known Gary was desperate. Don't make me carry another death on my shoulders."

He covered her hand. "You don't trust my ability to protect you."

His fixed gaze waited for her answer, as patient as a glacier, but she pulled free her hand. *Even ice shatters and breaks.* Shaking her head, she reached for the door handle. "Read your family code of conduct again, Johann. Even the BAK knows when to move on."

His fingers grazed her back. "Hadley?"

She stilled.

"Why can't you trust me?"

Closing her eyes against the warmth of his touch, she climbed from the wagon. "I don't remember how to lean on someone. Every time I try, it ends in disaster."

Pulling her duffle from the second row of seats, he walked around the car and presented the bag. "Will you feel better with police protection?"

"I grew up in the Bay Area. Nature's my church. Earthquakes and wildfires are my catechism. From an early age, I learned evacuation is the safest option." Turning her back on him, she walked toward the townhouse. *If I'm the target, at least the body count will remain at one.*

Johann climbed back in the car, but he remained in the parking lot.

Refusing to turn on the lights and face memories of Gary, she let a streaming movie overwrite her concerns. When the credits rolled, she opened the mini blinds and expected to see an empty parking space. Johann's profile glowed from the light of his phone.

She showered and climbed into bed, trusting him to leave after he arranged alternate security. The townhouse creaked, and the musty carpet smelled two decades past its prime. Reaching for her bedside table, she lit an incense stick and threw a hand over her eyes. *I didn't think coming back here would bother me, but I was wrong.*

The sun woke her, and she looked out the window, relieved and saddened to see a police car. Swapping her pajamas for a simple dress, she padded downstairs and listened for strange sounds. The townhouse looked no different from the day she left. Dishes waited in the sink, and Gary's sweatshirt draped the old futon's arm. She accepted the repercussions of his betrayal, but the dirty windows and the constraints on her life felt too much like a tomb. Searching for fresh air, she opened the front door.

Lieutenant Jayne stepped out of a blue cruiser wearing casual attire. "I'm sorry about your friend." He scratched his head. "I never took him for a thief."

She swallowed. "Why are you here?"

"Your boyfriend's paying me to keep watch over you."

Dating implied casual affection and easy romance. Dr. Stefan's death jump-started her relationship with Johann, but the spark burned too bright for easy labels. "He's not my boyfriend."

The man scratched his cheek. "Are you sure about that? You trust him?"

She crossed her arms. *I value the lieutenant's life as much as I value Johann's life, but Lieutenant Jayne would protect anyone in his jurisdiction. If everything goes to hell, I won't be the person who put him in harm's way.* Scanning the parking lot, she dropped her arms and exhaled. "Implicitly."

"I'll figure out what's happening. What did you cook up in that lab?"

She thought of the large, black tarp covering the hole in the lab's side. *My research's isn't responsible.* "Nothing but plant sex and synthetic CBD."

"A common thread must exist."

She ran her tongue over her teeth. "Greed?"

He shoved his hands in his pockets. "I should have done more to help you. I don't understand your research, but I understand fear. You look scared."

"Is that your professional opinion?"

He nodded.

She forced a smile. "Nobody has a reason to hurt me."

Pulling free a hand, he tapped the cruiser's roof. "Let me give you a lift to campus."

"No, thanks. I'd rather walk."

****

Unwilling to expose her coworkers to danger, Hadley headed for the arboretum and sat on the white marble steps below a statue of a robed woman draped over a funeral altar. The statue's wilting wings and hidden face epitomized grief and utter abandonment, but she thought the statue looked as cold and lifeless as quarried stone. *You have to love a person to grieve their loss.*

Buffy strolled up the gravel path. "I've always hated this statue." Toying with her sandy-blonde ponytail, she offered her a piece of bubble gum. "Her grief should move you to tears, but you look fine. I get it. Who has time roll around and wail?"

She laughed.

Sitting beside her, Buffy rested her chin on her hand, toyed with a handful of mulch, and tossed pieces in the air. "What are you, like the sacrificial virgin?"

"Hardly." She tossed a pebble into the bushes and sighed. "I'm admiring the arts."

"The arts." Buffy snorted. "When I arrived on campus, lichen covered the whole statue, and the angel's left arm was gone. The ground crew left her with a rusting piece of metal sticking out of her side. Hell, even some of her wingtips and fingers went missing."

She looked at the lamenting statue. "Poor thing."

Buffy waved a hand in front of her face. "Hello! Don't get hung up on the statue. She's a reproduction of a reproduction. Who wants a third-tier knockoff memorial?"

"At least somebody remembered her." She faced Buffy. "Do you still hate the statue?"

Buffy shrugged. "When I arrived on campus, I was eighteen years old. I thought I knew everything about the world."

She smiled. "And you're what, like, twenty-three now?"

"I piped a twenty-eight on your fucking birthday cake."

She laughed. "A world of difference."

Grinning, Buffy tossed a handful of mulch in the air. "I found out the statue marks the university's founders. The current administration tries to uphold its academic mission, but they have too many balls in the air. When I arrived, the statue's condition wasn't a priority. Look at her now."

She stared at the gleaming white marble and thought of the advanced lab space that enabled her research. "Progress comes first."

"Yeah." Buffy wrinkled her nose, "but statues don't give a shit about their legacy. They could have saved their cash and paid me a bigger stipend. We're the ones who have to get on with life."

"Gary wouldn't see it that way."

Buffy snorted. "Gary probably stole the arm."

She laughed. "I keep thinking I should miss him."

"The two of you grew up together."

"But?" Adjusting her seat, she studied Buffy's expression.

Buffy sighed. "I never liked that douche bag."

She frowned. "I thought everyone liked Gary."

"Sure, if we needed someone to go on a beer run."

"Fair enough. He called you 'Speed Bump'."

Buffy laughed. "Somebody has to stick to procedures."

Looking at the repaired statue, she inhaled and focused on the air inflating her lungs. "I don't care if the statue's a knockoff. The University fixed it because it means something to someone."

Buffy nodded. "You'll die, too, but unless you finish your research, you won't get a statue."

"Thanks." Hadley laughed. "But I'm not dead, yet."

"Your life only matters if you move on from this crap with Dr. Stefan and Gary."

Hadley sighed. "My parents never moved on."

"Until they test their limits, some people don't know how strong they are. Your parents failed the test.

You don't have to fail."

She thought of Johann waiting outside her door. *Even after I spurned him, he stuck by me. Maybe he'll come back.* Standing, she offered a hand to Buffy. "Good pep talk. How did you know where to find me?"

Buffy smiled. "A Black man wearing a baseball hat showed up and asked if you'd arrived for work."

Damon might hate sentry duty, but if Johann asked him to follow her, he would trail her across campus and watch for threats. "What did you say?"

"I said 'yes,' but when he asked to see you, I stalled."

"Is he still waiting at the lab?" Hadley asked.

Buffy shook her head. "I sent him toward the tennis courts and told him you were taking your frustration out on the practice wall. Then I came here."

Hadley frowned. "But I could have been anywhere."

Buffy looked at the statue. "Most people don't even know about this shit statue, but you've always kind of liked it. I figured you might be here beating up yourself or some such shit. Can we acknowledge we're all human and move on?"

She laughed. "Thanks for the pep talk."

"Glad it helped, but I'm tired of stalling on the research." Standing, Buffy dusted off her jeans and made eye contact. "I didn't think the assay work would play out, but repetitive data is no longer anomalous. T-83 is special, but you knew that fact, didn't you?"

Squaring her shoulders, she nodded.

"Hadley, what *is* T-83?"

She took a deep breath and hoped her intuition and experience with Buffy held more water than her relationship with Gary. She never treated him like an equal, but she met Buffy's gaze and saw a true collaborator. "A polymer of two CBD derivatives, HU308 and a secondary compound." Whispering the details, she removed the knowledge barrier so Buffy could participate as a peer. *Plus, if I die tomorrow, she won't need to decipher my notebook.*

Staring into the distance, Buffy worked her jaw. Her eye twitched. Drawing a deep breath, she nodded and looked back. "You'll take this all the way?"

"I am," she said.

Buffy looked at the mausoleum. "I would make a very good pharmaceutical executive."

"How about President and Chief Executive Officer of a foundation?"

Buffy rubbed together her hands. "Do I get staff?"

"If we're successful," she said.

"Yeah. I'm all in."

Walking back to the lab, she glimpsed Damon's unobtrusive profile. Every loud noise made her flinch, and she closed her eyes for the briefest second while she waited for the pain.

****

Late that afternoon, Vivian arrived at Hadley's lab.

Hadley watched the woman pass two researchers sitting in the break room. She knew the researchers and guessed they swapped weekend tales over their bowls of steaming curry. When Vivian walked past them, they both looked up.

Pausing near the break room door, Vivian wrinkled her nose and continued walking.

Hadley shook her head. She had to escort Vivian to the lab, but she did not have to enjoy the visit. The woman's heels clicked on the polished floors, and her curled blonde hair and immaculate lipstick gave everyone she passed a reason to look up from their work. Opening the door to the lab, she gestured toward an empty, plastic chair. "Why are you here?"

Vivian glanced at Buffy's workstation and raised her eyebrows. "Is there somewhere we can go that's private?"

"Dr. Stefan's office? Wait. That won't work. Gary's office? Bad idea." She gestured toward the room filled with humming machines. "I guess this space will have to work."

Vivian jerked her chin toward Buffy. "Out, please."

Buffy crossed her arms.

Hadley considered letting them go head-to-head, but the battle could have unintended repercussions. "Don't worry about it, Buffy. I can handle her."

Her friend grabbed her phone. "I liked the Black guy better."

Vivian narrowed her gaze.

Buffy held up her hands. "Peace. I'm out."

Clearing her throat, Hadley wondered why Vivian had deigned to visit the glass-lined room. "What are you doing here?"

The woman laid two sets of documents on the table. "I need your signatures."

"On what?"

"The first document is an amendment to the funding contract between Johann and the university. Barring the rights of the university, you own fundamental IP and the eventual proceeds associated with your research outcomes. The university retains their IP rights, but Johann assigned his non-exclusive license to you."

Hadley swallowed. "That was generous."

Vivian flipped the page. "Independent of the person appointed to fill Dr. Stefan's vacant faculty position, this document names you as the primary investigator for the duration of the grant Johann funded. Sign it."

She paused, her pen hovering over the signature line on the second paper. Every Ph.D. student in the country would cheer to receive such a gift. "Tell me the catch."

"No catch," Vivian said.

She considered the page. "The university won't kick me out."

"Correct."

Exhaling, she scratched her signature across the line. "I'll find a way to thank him."

"I hope you're creative." Vivian flipped over the signed page. The third page bore the foil-pressed seal of a German bank. "Johann also established provisions to fund your work in perpetuity."

She dropped the pen. "No."

"What do you mean, no?" Looking up from the paperwork, Vivian frowned. "Drug discovery programs and clinical trials aren't cheap. Without cash, you're vulnerable."

She swallowed. "I won't be beholden to Johann."

Vivian laughed. "If you spend your life fearing debt and doubting your abilities, you'll never get ahead. The credit line comes with a stipulation. Proceeds from drug sales pay back the investment. Whatever you spend, Johann recoups."

"And if I don't?" Hadley asked.

Vivian scratched her lip. "You're an expensive failure."

"Oh, is that all?" She rubbed her temples. "Why is he doing this? There has to be a caveat."

"Oh, trust me. I searched for the caveat. The man writes contracts as if they're his native language. If he wanted to trick you, he would have done it."

"I don't want his money," she said.

"Hadley, don't be an idealistic idiot." Vivian pointed to the signature line. "If you don't need the money, you don't have to use it. Sign here."

Picking up a pen, she yearned to sign the paper, but she shook her head. "I have to read the document."

"Smart woman." Vivian toyed with her cuticles. "While you read it, I'll wait, but you might want to engage a lawyer."

"Great, I keep a spare one in the broom closet." Setting aside the pen, she reached for the paper and hoped the legalese made sense. "What's the fourth document?"

"Citing lack of proof, the forum administrator deleted Gary's boasts about your notebook." Vivian yawned. "Gary wasn't terribly creative. He used a decentralized site on a network of peer-to-peer users. Instead of IP addresses, a public key cryptography and communication protocol identifies the sites. It's all open source. As far as dark goes, he didn't go deep."

"What?" she asked.

"Nobody has proof of your experiments," Vivian said. "Take your time and get them right." She smiled. "That advice is on me."

Sinking into her chair, she closed her eyes. "Why

are you being nice?"

"You're ambitious."

She exhaled. "Plenty of women are ambitious."

Vivian nodded. "But Johann doesn't care for them. He cares for you."

Organizing her thoughts, she searched for euphoria but found loneliness in the rigid, legal text she held. *I need more than a blank check and a gold-plated lab. I need hardened discipline and a wry, indulgent man. Why didn't Johann come himself?*

Vivian perched a hip on the edge of the table. "I've never seen Johann lie. If he says he'll fund your research, he'll do it. Honesty might be his biggest flaw. It was certainly the most painful part of our relationship."

"I'm sorry he hurt you." Vivian's expression softened.

Touching up her lipstick, Vivian shrugged and met Hadley's gaze. "I wanted the house in Berlin and the ranch in New Zealand. I didn't see Johann as a partner, and he knew it."

Hadley exhaled. "I'm not sure I'm capable of living in his world."

"Few people have the strength to walk away from a gilded cage."

But life with Johann isn't a gilded cage. Every compound has an open door, and he's courageous enough to walk through them. She opened her mouth to defend Johann.

Slipping her mirror in her purse, Vivian stood. "In the past few days, I've learned a lot about you." She walked toward the glass door and fixed her hair in the reflection. Looking at Hadley, she turned and smiled.

"You're more than capable of rising to the challenge."

"What does that mean?" she asked.

"You don't have to handle the man, Hadley. Accept him."

Lifting the pen, she signed Johann's documents. He gave her the freedom to pursue her research, but his absence left her with so many unanswered questions. If she never saw him again, she would move on, but her memories would be impossible to forget.

****

Standing in front of her townhouse later that afternoon, Hadley considered giving up her lease on the carpeted rooms and fenced-in regrets. *I'm paying market rate, and I can swap one set of rotten boards for another.* She looked beyond the bushwhacked landscaping and focused on the dingy windows. Layers of dirt coated the glass, and mold grew in the corners. *I can't take Johann's money. The offer is a test. If I take the money, he'll hate me. If I refuse the money, I'm an idiot.*

Lieutenant Jayne picked his teeth with a toothpick. "You planning to wash those windows?"

I'll apply for grants. I'll be patient. She chewed the inside of her lip. *I'll spend ten years nickel and diming my research toward success when the drugs could already be on the market.* She rubbed a finger along the gritty glass. Black residue coated her skin, but the glimpse of transparency promised a flood of light. Cleaning the windows seemed more manageable than taking the bus to Johann's compound and demanding an explanation. *I doubt the bus even runs there.* She exhaled. "Don't you have something better to do?"

"Nope."

She considered a garden hose, but apartment life limited her choices. Going inside the townhouse, she grabbed the mop bucket, an old dishrag, a roll of paper towels, and a bottle of vinegar. The only thing she had to keep the interior sill dry was a faded beach towel. *Like the landlord will ever give me back my deposit.* Walking outside, she dropped her cleaning supplies on the ground, faced the windows, and put her hands on her hips. "I can do this."

"I'm not helping you wash your windows," Lieutenant Jayne said.

She sighed. "Just look mean and scare off the bogeymen."

"Your boyfriend's worried, isn't he?"

She slammed a palm against the window, and the glass shook. For a moment, she feared the pane would break, but it held fast. Exhaling, she looked at Lieutenant Jayne. "He's not my boyfriend."

"Right, well, he's still paying me to be here or sending his lackey to watch over you. The sooner you tell me what's going on, the better I can protect you."

I don't know what's going on. She rubbed her arms. "He's overprotective."

"He's worried about you."

He said he would take care of me. The credit line and the protection officer help, but I don't want them. I want him. Picking up the dishrag, she wet it and slapped it against the glass. *Making due with memories isn't enough.*

Black water oozed down the siding.

Shaking her head, she rubbed circles through the filth, considered the gunk in the corners, and organized her demands. She spent hours in the lab deciphering results, but she missed the normal laughter and affection everyone deserved. Dropping the rag in the bucket, she turned to Lieutenant Jayne. "I need a ride."

"Where are we going?" he asked.

"Johann's house." She moved toward the car, but she stopped and looked at her dirty hands. "Right after I grab a shower."

Chapter Eighteen

"Do I get to ride in the front or the back?" Hadley asked.

"Up to you," Lieutenant Jayne said. "Do you want to show up like a criminal or like the police?"

Neither. What do I need to do to show up like a peer? She remembered the black car that carried Vivian for lunch. *If I asked Johann to send a car, would he do it?* She exhaled and pulled open the passenger door. The heavy metal resisted her effort, and she yanked. "Just bring me to the gate and drop me off."

Lieutenant Jayne buckled his seatbelt. "Embarrassed?"

She ran her hands through her shower-wet hair. "Nervous as hell."

He nodded. "I'll take you to the front door and wait."

"He'd never harm me." She flipped down the visor and smoothed her damp hair out of her eyes. "I'm nervous I'll be the one to cave."

"I doubt it."

She smiled.

The lieutenant rounded a curve and approached Johann's thick, metal gate. He closed the cruiser.

Remembering the gate swinging open for Johann, she looked for a call box. Manicured olive trees lined the drive, but no protruding console offered an intercom. Thinking of her antiquated alarm panel, she sighed. *I can do this.* Shifting her jaw, she considered her options. "Just honk," she said. "He has enough cameras to guard Fort Knox."

Lieutenant Jayne laid on the horn.

She grabbed his hand. "Geeze."

He pulled free. "What?"

"You'll wake the entire neighborhood."

"People don't sleep at five o'clock."

Shaking her head, she pointed to the open gates. "Drive."

He wound the car through the tunnel of Italian Cypress trees. "Don't you think the grapes are over the top? He could have slapped down an acre of drought tolerant, xeriscape lawn alternatives and still impressed his neighbors."

Or let the grounds run wild. Thinking of the first windswept kiss she claimed, she imagined letting Johann's solicitous, legal offers cap the relationship, and she shuddered. *Neither of us would be happy.*

The tunnel gave way to Johann's sleek, gray estate. He stood outside the panoramic glass walls, like a shadow of the man who gripped her arms and seared her soul with his vivid, blue gaze. A fire blazed on the patio, and a single glass of wine waited on a side table beside an open bottle. She swallowed. *He wasn't expecting me.*

Lieutenant Jayne slowed the cruiser. "You want me to wait?"

Shaking her head, she gripped the door handle. "I can handle him." She climbed from the car. The warm, evening wind lifted her skirt. Walking toward Johann, she paused on the firepit's opposite side. "You didn't have to send the paperwork."

He looked over the rows of vines. "The paperwork was nothing."

Rounding the firepit, she downed his wine. *Sobriety might be an advantage, but alcohol works.* Wiping the back of a hand across her mouth, she smiled.

"Excellent vintage?" he asked.

"It'll do."

He smiled and crossed his arms. "Are you here to thank me? A text would have been fine."

Rounding the firepit, she grabbed his hand and yanked it. When he turned, she claimed his lips, pressed into his heat, and unleashed the pleasure and frustration of reunification. Finding an opening, she fought for the rhythm and heady possession she craved.

He snaked an arm around her waist.

Her body tingled, the feel of his muscled frame as forbidden and as alluring as the pleasure of letting him lead.

Tightening his grip, he shifted his mouth and changed the kiss.

His hungry, intense pursuit weakened her knees. Tearing away her lips before she let him carry her inside the house, she braced her hands against his chest and fought to catch her breath. "I'm not here to thank you." She inhaled and met his gaze. "I don't need your money."

His gaze widened. "Don't be ridiculous."

A slap seemed out of line, but she considered the gesture. "I'm attempting to save your damn life! What happens when your shadow pulls a gun? Will you waste a second checking my whereabouts?"

He dropped his chin. "I always know where you are."

"That's not creepy!" Spinning away and wondering how he monitored her, she drew a deep breath. "Wait, is it?"

He pulled her back against his chest. "When I wake up, you're the first person I think about. Why can't you trust me to protect you?"

Because I love you, you asshole, and losing you would shatter me. I would never recover. She sighed and leaned against his chest, closing her eyes against the last, golden rays of the sun. "I trust you, Johann, but you don't have to buy my love."

Shifting his embrace, he tipped up her chin. "I find the thought of losing you unbearable. Take the money, Hadley. Continue your research, but stay with me."

She nodded, knowing the real bargaining had begun. "I can't spend my life second-guessing myself." She swallowed and scanned the hillside. "Taking your money would feel amazing, but the invisible strings would tug at my conscience. Every decision I made would hinge on your implicit approval."

He shook his head. "I support your work. I acknowledge the circumstances that brought us together, but they don't have to define us."

"We could have met in other ways." She wet her lips. "A café."

He smiled. "Or a courtroom."

She exhaled. "And who would have won?"

"I always win."

She stepped back and tucked her hair behind her ear. "Thank you for surrendering your license."

"It was nothing," he said.

She took a deep breath. "Am I nothing to you?"

He pulled her close. "Hadley, you're everything you want to be."

She inhaled against his chest. "What if I want more?"

The tension in his frame relaxed. "Then you'll have it."

"I'm not talking about money." Looking up, she met his gaze. "When I walked away, offending you wasn't my goal."

"What was your goal?" he asked.

Keeping you safe. She swallowed. "Taking responsibility for my life. You mean too much. The way I feel in your arms?" She closed her eyes. "You can't put a price on it."

He stoked her back. "I don't want any barriers to exist between us."

Good thing I'm going commando. She grinned but let him continue and listened for what she needed to hear.

"If money is an issue, it's yours," he said.

She exhaled. If every conversation with him involved a transaction, she needed a currency chart. "Money doesn't solve every problem."

He gripped her hair, pulling it downward until she raised her chin. "How much is your life worth?"

The hint of pain centered her focus. Staring into his eyes, she swallowed. He stared like a man focused on one goal. "The price depends on who you ask."

He released her hair. "To me, your life is priceless."

She looked at the pale scar marring his right cheek and understood the damage his upbringing caused.

People can't manage relationships as strictly as they manage assets. Günter railed against his restraints, but Johann embraced them. Every time she saw Johann's scar, she would remember the man who held himself together, as well. A lifetime of loneliness had cracked his heart, but he saved the pieces, and she would bind them.

She replayed Johann's lessons in her head. *Never leave your escape vehicle in a parking lot. Don't make threats unless you can follow through with them. People don't shoot me; I shoot them.* "Do you remember your lessons from the night of Dr. Stefan's funeral?"

He nodded.

"I have lessons for you. This week changed my life. I thought I could use science to overcome everything that went wrong in my life, but I don't have control over other people's actions."

"Does this mean you'll let me hire security to protect you?"

She stepped back and crossed her arms. "No, and I would rather you didn't carry a gun."

He shook his head and pulled her back into place. "I will use all the tools at my disposal."

His warmth soothed her, but she couldn't spend her days trapped in a cocoon. "I understand that, Johann, but do you recognize the outcomes?"

Nodding, he turned toward his home. "What's your second lesson?"

"The enormity of a person's grief doesn't matter. Their life only matters if they move on from their pain. I have to focus on the people who live. I need to mend my relationship with my parents."

He furrowed his brow. "Even if it means accepting their emotional neglect?"

She heard the self-reflection in his voice and nodded. "Otherwise, they're already gone."

Linking his fingers with hers, he raised them to his lips. "No regrets."

"I guess that's the third lesson. Death doesn't dismantle life, but it's part of the process. The people left behind are the ones who do all the work. We all need unwavering loyalties and second chances. If we choose to be together, you and I are taking a risk." She shifted, rolling her hips against his muscled thigh. "As soon as we iron out the details, I'll do everything I can to enjoy the outcomes."

He raised an eyebrow. "Maybe I should write more contracts. Releasing your financial constraints seems to put you in an excellent mood."

She laughed. The sunset's last rays reflected off the walls of the estate, and the wind teased her skirt against her legs. "Being close to you puts me in an excellent mood."

He stroked her cheek. "We can spend our lives behind these walls."

Leaning into his touch, she shook her head.

"I value discretion."

Turning, she kissed his palm. "Discretion does not ensure success or happiness. You and I will find our happiness."

"You'll take the money?"

She exhaled and nodded. "I'll take you."

He grinned.

Looking at the house, she rocked her hips. "Is Silvia home?" He grew hard against her touch, and she smiled. "I'll take that as a no." His laughter lightened her mood.

Gripping her ass, he leaned close. "I wouldn't care if she sat on the front steps and watched."

Laughing, she grazed the hard contours of his chest. "We'd shock her, and then who would feed us?"

He smiled. "I thought you were an excellent cook."

She swallowed. "Excellent was an exaggeration."

Taking her hand, he nodded. "If all else fails, I will grill."

A soft, yellow glow surrounded the estate, but in proximity to him, every location felt safer. "It won't fail."

He walked toward the house.

Despite her comfort, butterflies fluttered in her stomach, and she braced for his intensity. Every passion-tinged encounter had satisfied her, but she had sensed him holding back. Now, she hoped he would let go.

The moment she stepped inside, he spun her and pushed her against the glass door.

His lips claimed hers, and she grasped his hair, fighting to match the fervor of his kiss. Pinned between the cold glass and his warm strength, her resistance melted. "Johann?"

He lifted his head, his breathing heavy and strained. "I didn't think I'd see you again."

Feeling his teeth graze her neck, she shifted her hips and closed her eyes. "I'm here."

He unbuttoned the front of her dress.

Arching her back, she enjoyed the tension-soaked revelation.

He yanked apart the panels.

The brush of cold air sensitized her skin, and she watched the small, cloth-covered buttons scatter across the floor. "Impatient man."

He pushed aside her bra, cupped the weight of her breasts, and made a low, guttural sound of appreciation. "You have no idea. I thought I'd lost you."

Tilting her head, she leaned on his strength and savored his mesmerized appreciation. "Is that why you sent Vivian with the paperwork? You didn't think I would see you?"

Shaking his head, he pulled her close and kissed her until she gasped for breath. Breaking free, he traced her swollen lips. "If you said 'no', I wasn't sure what I would do. My schoolboy sonnet slid right past you."

"Some things are worth saying in person." She tugged his shirt from his pants. "In your own words."

He raised his head. *"Ich bin in dich verliebt."*

His hesitant phrasing charmed her, but she vowed not to let him off easy. " 'I am falling in love with you' is not enough."

Running a hand through his hair, he sighed. "What does falling in love mean? I'd do everything in my power to help you? I'd give my life for you? Those words sound foreign."

Some men use actions instead of words. Life conditioned both of us to expect shadows, but darkness doesn't have to guide our lives. Shaking her head, she took his hand. "Johann, I'll never hurt you on purpose."

Raising her hand, he brought it to his lips. "I believe you."

She tugged free her hand before the warm caress unnerved her. "Then say it."

Grazing his hand along the side of her breast, he

exhaled. *"Ich habe mich in dich verliebt."*

'I've fallen in love with you.' Can such a soft evasion be enough? Exhaling, she recognized the cost of his words, pulled his shirt over his head, and traced the ridges between his muscles. His unique scent wrapped around her, and the bright allure of his desire quickened her breath. *Give him time; he's only had a week.*

Stilling her hand, he claimed a kiss and gripped a hip.

Her pulse raced, and her chest heaved. *I can still leave.* Recognizing the lie, she shuddered.

He pulled her close and lowered his head.

The steady rise and fall of his chest matched the rhythm of her breathing. He kissed the tender spot on the side of her neck.

"I love watching you get lost in facts and details," he said. "My sweet, romantic Hadley. You're a scientist, but your heart pulls you back to the warmth of my touch."

Closing her eyes, she nodded and leaned into his enticing whisper.

"You accept my life, and yet, you still argue about the differences between right and wrong, even when you're wrong."

Pulling back, she swatted his chest. "Stalling is a crime."

He caught her hand and raised it to his lips. "So is stubborn pride. I've been guilty of both."

She stroked his back. "From the start, you intrigued me, but your arrogance and loneliness frightened me. Now, I know the depths of your emotions. I know you," she said. *"Ich kenne dich."*

He stroked her cheek. "Is that all you have to say?"

She smiled. "I won't be the first one to cave."

The sound of his laughter echoed through the house. Shaking his head, he claimed her lips and tugged her dress over her hips. "Stubborn woman."

Naked, she grinned.

Widening his gaze, he admired her smooth skin. "What is this?"

She winked. "My backup plan."

He crushed his lips against hers.

His touch stole her rational thoughts and left her gasping for breath.

He pulled back. "You don't need a backup plan."

Cradling his face, she feared losing the moment. "I love the way you weigh the consequence of your decisions. I love the way you fight for your brother and boss me around."

He rubbed his hand across over his face. "No, you don't."

She dropped her hands to his shoulders. "I love how you let me do whatever I want and still help me pick up the pieces."

Sighing, he fitted her against his chest. "I love the way you take on enormous challenges"—picking her up, he waited until she wrapped her legs around his waist—"like me."

Cantilevering against his strength, she pressed into his chest and felt free. If he wanted to admire her breasts, she would give him an outstanding view. Arms wide, she felt free, but she snaked one arm over his shoulder. "You are a challenge."

He tightened his hold, his thumb stroking the bare skin of her ass. "Yet, you're willing to give away your research to save strangers from pain. If you had the resources, you would help every person you meet."

"You have the resources"—she took a deep breath, knowing she could advance her research without depending on his wealth—"but you don't have to subsidize my life to earn my love." Grabbing his silky, black hair, she surrendered and let happiness chase the acceptance in his gaze. "I won't keep T-83 from the people who need it, but everything else I have is yours."

"That's my line."

Lowering her head, she grazed his lips. "I know."

Chapter Nineteen

Johann's phone rang.

Hadley frowned. Unwilling to surrender the warmth of sleeping by his side, she kept her eyes closed to block out the light.

"I have a problem."

Damon's voice came from the speaker. His frenzied whisper chased away the remnants of her sleep. Propping herself on one arm, she played with Johann's chest hair and listened.

Johann stilled her hand. "What kind of problem?"

"A problem like an SUV full of cops with a warrant. Mama Clarke can hold off their search, but they'll tear the store to bits until they find my side gig."

The sound of loud, authoritative banging came through the phone speaker. She thought of the shelves of merchandise and the bins of cell phones grouped by make and model. Trying not to imagine Damon crouched in the small, airless room, she sat and let the sheets pool around her waist.

Johann sighed. "Damon, I can't help you with that problem."

"C'mon, Boss. Why won't you help me out of this jam?"

"How can I make an SUV full of federal agents disappear?"

"Cash?"

"Adding bribery to their list of charges against you would thrill the authorities," Johann said. "They'll trace the cell phones."

"The phones are clean."

"And your customer lists?"

Something heavier than a fist shook the locked door.

"The lists are in my head," Damon said.

Johann leaned against the pillow.

"Can't you help him?" She stroked his arm.

He shook his head. "He knew what he was doing."

"But he's your friend."

Nodding, Johann closed his eyes and exhaled. "Damon, I'll send Vivian to post your bail. You're looking at multiple felony counts. Cooperating is the smartest thing."

"I'm hustling. You make me sound like an extortionist."

She rolled her eyes and flopped on the pillow. "He's making excuses."

"If anyone asks, this phone call was a courtesy notification. I understand you won't be reporting for work tomorrow," Johann said.

"You can't do anything else to help me?" Damon asked.

She heard the desperation in the quick, whispered question.

"I'm posting your bail. When they call you for an arraignment, enter the plea your lawyer recommends. You have to work your way out of this mess."

The battering intensified, and Damon's phone clattered to the floor.

"Don't shoot!" Damon said.

She covered her face, but she wanted to help.

Johann ended the call.

Exhaling, she gripped his thigh. "Will he be all right?"

He exhaled and shook his head. "I don't know. How do you give someone the freedom to decide without feeling responsible for the consequences? We all knew what he was doing. I'll post his bail, but if he runs, he'll have to hide for the rest of his life."

She moved to climb from the bed. "I don't think he'll run. The money went to the neighborhood kids, didn't it? His intentions were good."

Johann reached for a hand and stilled her progress. "Legal would have been better."

Recognizing the truth, she nodded, but people made allowances for friends and family. "What Dr. Stefan did was far from legal. He could have killed Günter."

He released his hold and rubbed his face. "I should have made more of an effort to know my uncle. Politeness kept our connection far too superficial."

"He knew you well enough to call you the good nephew."

Johann smiled. "Was he right?"

"I hope so," she said, "but I think he loved you both."

He stroked her thigh. "My romantic."

She nodded and crawled across the bed. "I judged you too soon, Johann. You're not stoic, you're disciplined, but you're also a sucker for damaged goods." Pushing him to the bed, she straddled his chest. "I'll help you cope with the fallout."

Grabbing her hips, he watched her massage her

breasts. After a moment of heavy-lidded enjoyment, he eased aside her hands. "Please, let me."

She positioned his hand and squeezed to demonstrate the pressure she preferred. "Today we're working on self-control."

"I have plenty of self-control."

Smiling, she rose on her knees and brought her assets to his eye level. "We'll see about that control."

****

Johann lounged on the single bed in Hadley's townhouse.

She ignored his hedonistic gaze. For the past few weeks, it kept her in bed and made her late to work. Fixing her dress, she savored the graduation ceremony that would crown her achievements. "The diploma ceremony is on the Green. I confirmed my attendance. You won't need physical tickets. The school provides plenty of seating and refreshments."

He looked at the informational flyer lying on her duvet. "I can't believe the university uses an open tent for your college ceremony."

"Were you expecting a pavilion with columns?"

He shook his head. "No, but the main event happens in a secure, ticketed stadium."

"Nobody wants to hurt me." She scratched her cheek. "Everything's been quiet."

He put down the flyer. "You're safe at my house."

She shook her head and reached for her earrings. "We can't live behind bulletproof walls."

He jimmied the window trim. "Bulletproof walls have numerous benefits."

Laughing at his dour expression, she toyed with her doctoral regalia. The cardinal red hood, edged with golden yellow, smelled like cellophane packaging and fresh fabric. It matched the red-and-black doctoral robe hanging from the edge of her bedroom door. She waited years to wear the marks of distinction but resisted the finality of donning them. Johann wanted her to move her things to his home, but ending her Ph.D. career in the same humble place where she began it felt right.

Glancing at Gary's bedroom door, she sighed. At his funeral, she played the guitar to comfort his family during the service. The funeral company offered burial sites amid heritage oaks and bay laurels, but his parents chose a sun-filled meadow with views of Mount Tamalpais. Shaking her head, she reached for the robe. *This is not a day for regrets.*

The bells rang to celebrate the graduates and the conclusion of the main convocation. She heard the distant sound and smiled, straightening her robe over her simple, black dress. "We can't be late for Anna Claire's speech. Even though this is like the fifth time she's done it."

Standing, Johann held out the black wedges waiting on the floor. "I'm very proud of you."

Grinning, she reached for her purse. "Thanks. I'm pretty fucking proud of myself, too."

He laughed, pulled her close, and bit her earlobe. "So humble."

She yelped and shook her head. "That bite will leave a mark."

"Nobody else will see it." He withdrew a rectangular box from his coat pocket and offered it. "I wanted to give this to you earlier, but you have a way of distracting me."

She accepted the box. "You love it."

"I do."

Grinning, she opened the box and revealed an elegant pendant made of interlocking gold bands. Small diamonds traced the bands, adding flash to the links that would move against her body. "You didn't have to buy me anything."

He lifted the necklace from her hands and released the clasp. "What else can I give you?"

The metal felt cool against her skin. Feeling his thumb trace the tender mark his teeth left, she smiled. "Just you."

Pressing a kiss against her shoulder, he cupped her breast.

She shifted, enjoying the pressure, but she checked the time. "I have to go."

He dropped his hand. "I'll drive you."

She smiled. "I hoped you would."

She climbed into his sedan and leaned back, leaving him to navigate campus traffic. Admiring the necklace, she watched the play of sun and shadows across her fingers. *Two joined rings, but they both move.*

"Are you nervous?" he asked.

"I'm sure by the time two o'clock rolls around, the whole thing will feel anticlimactic." She swallowed. "I called my parents and asked them to attend."

He checked his watch. "I can ask Silvia to put together a celebration at the house."

She frowned. "I don't know if I'm ready to spend that much time with them. Baby steps?"

He kept his gaze on the road. "Ask anyone you want to attend."

Dropping the necklace, she sighed. "I can't ask

Silvia to go to that much trouble."

"I can." He shifted the sedan.

She smiled and imagined her parents emptying bottles of wine, Buffy skinnydipping in the fountain, and Vivian yawning at such a pedestrian spectacle. *Maybe a party's not such a bad idea.* She thought of Damon in the county jail and wished he could have joined them. "I appreciate what you did for Damon."

"I did little."

"Um, you interrogated his public defender."

He smiled. "Knowing someone pays attention improves outcomes." He stopped the car at the edge of the Green, but he lowered the window and left it idling.

Climbing out, she prepared to join the line of graduates at the sign-in table.

"I'll see you in thirty minutes," he said.

"Wait, you're parking?"

Laughing, he drove off.

She inhaled and turned to embrace the celebrations. The flag of the School of Humanities and Sciences fluttered over the white pavilion tent erected on the lawn. The degree candidates who had already signed in milled with their families and nibbled on hors d'oeuvres. They clutched glasses of water and iced tea, but she assumed their robes also concealed flasks.

Lieutenant Jayne approached. "Congratulations, Miss Heron."

She blinked at the glare of the sunlight reflecting off his hair. "What are you doing here?"

He scanned the crowd. "Augmenting the university's resources."

"The university has plenty of security." Johann's overbearing approach to her safety endeared and frustrated her, but she was determined to play nice. "But thank you for coming."

He shrugged and raised his hand to a uniformed officer stationed at the other end of the tent. "Your boyfriend's the one footing the bill."

No wonder Johann felt comfortable enough to park.

The officer receiving the hand gesture stared at Hadley.

She blinked.

"How come I never heard of Johann before this month?" Lieutenant Jayne asked.

She swallowed. "I think he prefers to keep a low profile."

"Most criminals do."

Tilting her head, she raised her eyebrows. The lieutenant's company should have comforted her, but his presence affirmed why she felt vulnerable, and she had little bandwidth for the suspicion in his stare.

He looked away.

Scanning the road, she searched for Johann amid the crowd.

"I don't believe in coincidences," Lieutenant Jayne said.

Placing a hand against her chest, she felt the necklace beneath her robe and took a deep breath. "Neither do I."

"Hadley, honey! We're over here."

She froze. Turning at the sound of her mother's voice, she watched her parents wind through the crowd. Her mother held a bouquet, and her father beamed. His wavy, brown hair sported more gray than the last time she had seen him, but his tan skin looked like he still spent Wednesday mornings on the tennis courts. *A long time has passed since I wanted to stand by his side, but he and Mother came, and the effort has to count for something.* "You're early."

Dad beamed. "I had to get the best seats in the house."

Thrusting forward the bouquet, Mom nodded. "Hi."

She smiled, but she refused to take the blooms "Save it for the end."

"Right." Mom let the flowers hang.

Feeling like a jerk, she forced a smile.

Dad slapped a program against his hand. "Fancy titles around your name. You'll have to tell your old man what you've been doing."

She swallowed the anger roiling her stomach. When the lab exploded, neither parent called, and neither attended Gary's funeral. She stood on the hillside, strumming her guitar, while Johann had waited in the car.

"Hadley Marie," said Mom. "Tell him about your research."

Her reprimand removed the pretense of politeness that could have carried her through the day. She straightened her spine. "I grew up, Mom. Didn't you notice?"

"He's just interested in your research."

"Then he should have come to my thesis defense."

"You didn't invite him."

Mom tilted her head and squinted like a far-sighted, old woman who ate too many bonbons. She looked at Dad. "I did."

He held her stare for a moment but looked away.

She cleared her throat. "I didn't expect you to come, but thanks for making the effort. I'll tell you about the research later tonight. Maybe we can have dinner."

Dad cupped Mom's shoulder and nodded. "We claimed seats near the front. Your friends Buffy and Vivian are already there. They're quite the pair."

An announcer cleared his throat at the podium. "All degree candidates should report to the reserved seating in front of the stage."

She swallowed. "I have to go."

"We'll be waiting for you." Mom smiled. "I know we've had our differences, but your father and I are proud. We never dreamed you could take your studies this far."

She translated the phrase into "we never dreamed you were this smart and capable" and swallowed a tart response. *So much for common ground.* "Thanks, Mom." Watching her parents make their way toward the front rows, she exhaled.

"Seem like friendly people," Lieutenant Jayne said.

She met his gaze. "My mother's a recovering drug addict."

He rocked back on his heels. "Like I said."

Nodding, she made her way toward the registration table and replayed the conversation with her parents. *Why couldn't they just show up for pictures? I need baby steps.*

"Hadley!"

Startled, she spun.

Horst walked toward the line of degree candidates. His cane pressed into the soft, green grass.

"Anna Claire's the speaker," she said.

He nodded. "I didn't realize this was your graduation ceremony. Is Johann here, too?"

She scanned the crowd, searching for his comforting presence. "I hope so."

"You two are a thing, huh? I wasn't sure at the convention, but he rarely shows his face in public. You must be important to him."

She fingered the necklace beneath her robe. "He's important."

"After you sign in, come to the speaker's tent and cool off."

Glancing at her parents, she nodded, half-considering his offer.

"I'll tell you a few stories about my time with him in the BKA. He was quite the rule-follower."

She smiled. "I bet." The line shifted, and she inched forward. "How long did you two serve together?"

"Couldn't have been more than a year. He climbed the ranks so fast. I guess in hindsight, his family had connections."

She swallowed. "You injured your leg in the BKA."

He slapped his cane against his leg. "Ahh, this old thing? Could have been anybody." He smiled. "Could have been Johann."

She frowned. "What?"

"The injury happened during our last assignment as partners." Horst shook his head and stared into the crowd. "Johann was a stickler for protocol. We came up against live fire, and I wanted to run. He stayed to fight, and foolishly, I remained by his side to avoid looking weak. Pressed by a sharpshooter, we took shelter behind a car, but a nearby car bomb ripped the vehicle sheltering us to shreds."

"A bomb?" Apprehension roiled her stomach.

"Lorry bombs often kill people near the blast site and damage buildings." He skewed his jaw. "Johann acted like he was invincible. Maybe when you're as rich as he is, you think you are invincible."

The thought of Johann bloodied on the street corner stole her breath. She stepped back.

"Hadley?"

At the sound of the voice, she turned.

A fellow degree candidate stood ten feet away and beckoned her to advance.

"Horst, I'm sorry about your leg," she said.

He laughed. "I didn't lose my leg. I lost my life."

The hollow sound scared her, but she frowned. "Now's not the time, but can you tell me about it? Maybe later?"

He smiled. "Of course."

The cold expression died on his lips, and she scanned the crowd for Johann's comforting presence.

Turning, Horst walked toward the speaker's tent.

She watched his limp and wondered how much the old injury still hurt.

"Hadley!"

"Shit. Sorry!" Turning, she jogged toward the registration desk and gave her credentials. A stern woman asked how to pronounce her name. Receiving her copy of the program, she walked toward the candidate seats and searched for her people in the shifting crowd.

"Hadley."

Johann's deep bass calmed her nerves. Pivoting in

the bright light, she turned toward his voice.

He removed his sunglasses and squinted.

Worry deepened his laugh lines, but she appreciated his presence in the crowd. "You're almost late."

He frowned. "I'm never late."

"No, of course not." Smiling, she took his hand. "I have to warn you, my parents are front and center."

Nodding, he looked down. "Will you introduce me?"

"Do you want me to?"

He slapped her ass. "Brat."

Laughing, she hoped nobody noticed or cared. "The only people who get to see me shine are the ones who bother to look. You've always looked."

"Hadley—"

Holding up her hand, she kissed his cheek. "Not now."

He exhaled.

Leaving him, she turned and threaded her way through the chairs. Staff had marked the seats with alphabetical labels and symbols related to degree plans. She lifted the label bearing her name and tucked it in her robe's pocket for posterity. *I'm only walking across this stage once.*

When commencement started, the invocation and the National Anthem commanded the crowd's attention and brought the audience members to their feet. Anna Claire offered her remarks on her Haitian ancestry and her mother's lifelong encouragement. "My mother, Tallulah, built a business at the top of a mountain, and if she could do it, I could, too. In my case, the mountain was ideological…"

Hadley sighed and scratched the back of her neck where sweat gathered at the edge of her robes. *Anna Claire's a lucky woman, but brevity would have been a nice lesson, too.*

The department chair climbed the steps to the podium. "Like Anna Claire, our department also explores frontiers, but we limit ourselves to basic science and molecular medicine."

Members of the audience clapped.

Hadley covered a yawn.

"Life allows us to choose our paths," the chair said. "At this university, we seize opportunities! Our students find themselves at the crossroads of cellular, chemical, and computational biology, but they don't know their ultimate destination. Each of the candidates seated before you took a step on their journey. The undergraduates followed established trails, but they picked electives that will guide the rest of their lives."

Looking over her shoulder, Hadley saw Johann and Vivian next to her parents.

Buffy grinned and held up an air horn.

"Our master's students explored the possibilities of new ideas and found their footing on uncertain terrain. Our Ph.D. students applied their expertise to decipher the complex regulatory systems associated with physiology and disease states.

"Because of these achievements, the National Research Council named our department the top pharmacology-related training program in the United States. I'm proud of our students' GRE scores, faculty publications, and research resources, but I'm prouder of the men and women who earned the rating." The man waved an open palm in front of the crowd of candidates.

Students shifted in their chairs. A few clapped.

"Yet, nobody is infallible."

Hadley swallowed. Despite the tent, she felt the heat of the day and the weight of her academic robes.

"Let us remember our colleague, Dr. Stefan zur Hausen. His death reminds us of incomplete tasks. Every day on this earth is an opportunity, and nobody knows when their allotment of opportunities will end. I trust every graduate to make the most of their gifts and determine what they have yet to give."

His rousing remarks pulled parents and observers to their feet. Clapping, a few shouted encouragements and whistled.

Towing the line, Hadley stood and clapped along with the crowd.

A master's candidate leaned close. "What a canned speech. Did you even know the late Dr. zur Hausen?"

She swallowed. "He was my advisor."

The student blushed. "Oh, right. I'm so sorry."

Dropping her gaze, she looked at the grass clinging to her wedges and thought of the errant strands she left in Johann's car. *I should have stayed home.* Looking up, she faced her future.

The department chair stepped away from the microphone and smiled at the department manager.

Clearing her throat, the woman opened the roster of matriculating students. "Abdullah Almasi, Bachelor of Science."

Instrumental music filled the spaces between subsequent names. The candidates walked across the stage, received their red portfolios, and shook hands with the chair. Trophies in hand, they turned toward the photography area at the right of the stage and smiled for anyone who cared to take their picture.

"This is taking forever," the master's candidate said.

Hadley nodded. "The ceremony's almost over."

Twenty minutes later, the master's candidate stood and made her way to the stage. At the top of the steps, she claimed her diploma cover and her moment of fame, then beamed at the crowd.

"Hadley Heron, Doctor of Philosophy," the announcer said.

She stood and swallowed.

"Dr. Stefan was Dr. Heron's advisor. In his absence, when she receives her honors, the department chair will hood Dr. Heron."

To steady her nerves, she turned and looked at Johann. Amid the chaos and heat of the day, she needed his cool discipline. Hundreds of people fanned themselves with programs, but she focused on his smile. He sat close enough to soothe the erratic beating of her heat, but too far away to calm her nerves with a reassuring touch. She tried focusing on his clear, blue eyes, but the crowd beneath the tent pressed too close. Cradling her arm, she swallowed. "Cotton Candy." Her whisper died beneath the applause.

Johann stood.

Vivian turned toward him and grabbed an arm.

He shrugged off her touch and made his way toward the end of the row.

"Hadley Heron," the announcer said.

Taking a deep breath, she considered fleeing the orchestrated grandeur of the ceremony, but her parents sat in the audience, and Johann neared. Years spent fighting yeast strains and neural assays should mean something. *Johann's here, and I deserve this moment of recognition.* Facing the stage, she scanned the perimeter of the crowd for Lieutenant Jayne.

The man and his partner stood at the back of the tent.

He cocked his head and stared.

She took a death breath and processed. Climbing the steps to the stage, she smiled to prove she had earned the crowd's patience. At the other end of the stage, she saw a cluster of people standing around the exit stairs and congratulating the impatient master's candidate. Ignoring the bevy of people jostling for pictures, she turned to face the department chair.

The man took the hood from her right arm, placed it over her robe, and handed her a diploma cover.

The crowd clapped.

Buffy sounded the air horn. Twice.

Savoring the moment of accomplishment, she shook the chair's hand and pivoted toward the photography area.

Pushing through the crowd, Dad found space to raise his camera.

The chair patted her shoulder. "You deserve everything you've earned."

"Thank you so much." She swallowed and watched Johann approach. *I want to be close to him, feel his strength, and know one person cares about me above all else. I could search the world and never find the combination of excitement and security I feel when I'm in his arms.*

Dropping his shoulder, Johann made his way through the supporters. He pushed aside a pair of uncles and shrugged off their objections.

The impatient master's candidate turned and put her hands on her hips. "What the hell?"

Hadley smiled, ready to reach for his hand and apologize for overreacting. A flash of metal caught her eye, and she turned.

From the rear of the stage, Horst used his cane to take down a well-wisher. He raised a gun and fired it into the air.

The master's student screamed.

Attendees dropped to the ground, covered their heads, and shuddered on the Green.

She considered her choices and followed suit, desperately dodging Horst's attention, but knowing he came for her or the man she loved.

Johann sprinted up the steps and looked over his shoulder.

Struggling to navigate the crowd, Horst met his gaze. "*Man kann nicht alles haben.*"

You cannot have everything. She scrambled to her feet, knowing he spoke the truth. "Horst!" The name ripped from her throat, searing her vocal cords with the frustration of missed opportunities.

Johann slammed into her and knocked the breath from her lungs. Each time Horst's bullets pierced his back, his body jerked. Hitting the ground, she closed her eyes, waiting for pain. *Let my death be quick.*

He released his hold and rolled away.

Opening her eyes, she saw the blood staining his shirt and reached for him. Pain etched his laugh lines into heavy grooves.

Bracing himself on one arm, he gritted his teeth and aimed his gun at Horst.

His arm trembled, and she knew his body fought to preserve blood flow. "Johann, stay down." She choked on the words.

He grunted and steadied his gun with two hands.

Horst climbed the steps.

His face, skewed with hatred, terrified her. She wanted to stanch Johann's blood flow and comfort him, but she feared his iron reserve and his gun. Stripped of niceties, his determination left her feeling utterly exposed. Horst terrified her.

Horst pointed his gun at Johann. "You always thought you were better. Faster. Stronger. Smarter."

The guttural, German adjectives sounded cruel.

Horst swung his gun toward her.

She looked at Johann and said goodbye. Her bravery cracked, and she mourned the possibilities slipping through her fingers.

Johann's gaze remained fixed on Horst. "I am." Pulling the trigger, he collapsed.

She screamed.

Lieutenant Jayne's bullet went straight through Horst's skull. An exit wound bloomed below his right eye. Sinking to his knees, he fell down the steps.

The master's student fainted.

Body splayed across the stage, Johann glared at Horst and clutched his gun.

Heavy boots clattered across the wooden stage, and Lieutenant Jayne checked Horst's pulse. "Put down the gun, zur Hausen. You and your lawyers better pray you have a concealed carry permit."

Scrambling to her knees, she put herself between the men. "Call an ambulance."

Lieutenant Jayne dropped to his knees. "I said, put

down the gun."

Gritting his teeth, Johann complied and gritted his teeth. "Hadley, are you okay?"

"I'm fine, Johann"—she stroked his face—"I should have listened."

He sighed. "I was too close."

Beneath the bright blue sky, his black eyelashes scored his ashen face. Unsure where to touch him, she cupped his cheek and refused to lose another person she loved. "Stay with me, Johann."

He exhaled. "You were worth it."

"No!" She screamed, held a shaking hand against his chest, and desperately searched for a heartbeat.

Chapter Twenty

With nothing to do but wait, Hadley paced the hospital waiting room. Harsh cleaning chemicals and disposable plastic packaging conjured a familiar smell, but Johann lingered on an operating table, and she needed more than the scientific method to save him. Internet searches and trips to the nurses' station yielded few clues. Bartering for his life seemed like the best option, but she wondered who would hear her case.

"He's strong, Hadley. Stronger than both of us put together." Vivian straightened her skirt in the waiting room.

Tears threatened to spill down her cheeks, and she sniffled. "I don't need him to be strong; I need him to live."

"Can you imagine the weight of his responsibilities?"

She tilted her head. "Are you bringing up the ranch?"

Vivian smiled. "No, but all that wealth comes with a heavy burden. Since the day he was born, his family has trained him in responsibility. Endurance training strengthens people, Hadley. If anyone can pull through this ordeal, Johann can."

Sighing, she closed her eyes. "Wealth and endurance training don't make people bulletproof."

"No, but they make people stubborn," Vivian said.

She nodded and scanned the waiting room. Two lines of chairs met in a neat enclave and offered full views of the television. Her parents sat in the corner, watching a made-for-TV movie, their faces tilted up to the screen. As Mom followed the captions, her lips moved, but no sound emerged.

Hadley appreciated their presence in the stark waiting room. *They don't know Johann. They're here for me.* She exhaled. *Reconciliation has its own timeline.*

Standing, Dad poured the dregs of his coffee into the black plastic liner of a short trashcan.

She winced, imagining the janitorial staff dealing with the soupy mess. The arrogance of the gesture chafed, and she closed her eyes, channeling her frustration away from her family.

"Does anyone want anything from the cafeteria? Coffee? Snacks?" he asked.

She shook her head and dropped her head to her hands.

Mom adjusted her seat in the corner chair. "Oh, honey, eat. Keep up your strength."

"I'm not hungry."

"You've always been so stubborn, Hadley Marie. Even as a child, you wouldn't let me help you. Your spelling and handwriting were atrocious."

She rubbed her temples and accepted her mother's point of view froze the day Jecca died. "Well, that's why they invented computers."

"It's just a cup of coffee, Hadley. Let your father help you."

Looking up, she saw Dad's worry and realized he spent the last two decades triaging his family's needs.

"A cup of coffee would be fine."

Nodding, he patted her mother's back, left the corner, and walked down the hall.

Mom returned her gaze to the movie.

Vivian glanced at the clock and frowned.

"How long has he been in surgery?" she asked.

"Three hours."

She checked the clock again. "Something's gone wrong. I buried myself in research so I could skip the pain of relationships. I'm not ready to lose someone again."

Vivian patted her shoulder. "The nurse warned us that cardiac trauma could complicate the surgery. They're doing the best they can."

Looking at their entwined hands, Hadley acknowledged she and Vivian rooted for the same outcome. *She still cares for him, too.* She frowned. *How does she keep her skin so soft?*

"Johann used to do some foolish things," Vivian said. "When I first met him, he rented out the best restaurant in town. We ate dinner in the middle of the atrium, and an army of staff waited to whisk away our forks. I've never been so on edge."

The ivy-covered restaurant closed almost a decade ago, but she knew the spot. Taking a deep breath, she smiled. "He tried."

"I think he saw it in a movie," Vivian said. "He had no clue how to date."

She smiled. "I stumbled into his life over Greek food."

Vivian folded her hands in her lap. "You offered him warmth and hope. I didn't realize he needed it, but you did. He sprinted up to the stage because he loves you. Don't throw away that gift."

She shuddered and buried her hands in her armpits. "What if he doesn't pull through this surgery? What if I lose him, just like I lost Jecca?"

Vivian toyed with her cuticles. "He'll pull through the surgery, and you can spend your free time pampering him. I suggest starting with a mountain of throw pillows." Looking up, she winked.

She stared. "Are you messing with me?"

"Just a little. I'm not always a cold-hearted bitch," Vivian said.

She forced a smile. "Thank you for staying."

Nodding, Vivian looked out the hospital window. An array of low-slung office buildings transitioned to the technology centers and arrogant compounds of local business magnates. "Weathering tough times on your own is much harder, but I think I'll consider a new position. CEO sounds nice."

"Full speed ahead on Hoat Analytics?" Hadley asked.

Vivian smoothed her skirt. "That's the plan."

An older man in a dark suit strode toward the waiting room. Despite the gray in his hair, he moved with the confidence of a man who could pull the strings of a market economy. Hadley didn't need to see the man's eyes to recognize him as Johann's father. *Behold, the overbearing patriarch.*

Rudolf zur Hausen strode across the floor.

She smelled aged herbs and citrus. The scent brought a fresh tear to her eye.

He stopped and appraised her. "Are you the woman who cost me two sons?"

Knowing how his code eroded his sons' abilities to

love, she stood and cleared her throat. "My name is Hadley Heron."

"Miss Heron, I flew to California to retrieve my youngest son. I wasn't in his hospital room for an hour before my secretary informed me of Johann's condition. I have two injured sons, and you seem to be the common denominator."

Vivian rose. "Good evening, Mr. zur Hausen."

He nodded.

Hadley stayed her with a glance.

Vivian sat.

Focusing on Johann's father, Hadley summoned her courage. "I didn't injure your sons, Mr. zur Hausen. Günter shot a man, and Johann defended me. Twice. Dr. Stefan was my research advisor. You lost him, too."

Rudolf's shoulders drooped. "I grieve the loss of my brother. I hated the press when he won that international prize, but I hated his absence even more."

She chose her words carefully. "Perhaps you shouldn't have made him choose between two outcomes."

He raised his eyebrows.

The arrogant glint looked achingly familiar, and her heart lurched. Taking a deep breath, she chose words to mollify Johann's father and treat him with the same respect she showed her advisor. "Johann told me your family prefers to escape notice."

He scanned the occupants of the room. "What else has he told you?"

"That he comes from a long line of stubborn men." She smiled. "Stubborn, determined, handsome men."

Rudolf cleared his throat. "Stubborn and determined are the same character traits. They lead to results."

If the man wanted to play hardball, she would go to bat for the man she loved. "How about obstinate? Blinded? Have you considered the downsides of pushing your sons along a pre-determined path?" She clapped a hand over her mouth.

"Yes, I have." He cocked his head. "Have you considered the downsides of leaving them defenseless?"

"Your family's code of conduct drove apart your sons, Mr. zur Hausen." She softened her tone. "I'm sure you had good intentions."

He ran a hand through his gray-streaked hair. "You don't know me, and your relationship with my son has no bearing on my life."

"When I was a teenager, I lost my sister, and I'd do anything to have her back in my life. I think Johann has the same need for connection. He gave Günter as many chances as he could."

Rudolf shook his head. "Günter did not send Johann to the operating room."

She glanced at Mom and accepted the weakness that came from accepting events beyond your control. "No, Horst Sakmann shot him, but greed put the ball in motion. I put my peer, Gary, in an untenable situation. Instead of doing something he loved, he followed me to graduate school and found he couldn't swim."

"Most people would give up and go back to shore."

She nodded. "Desperate people clamor for purchase on whatever they can find."

He cocked his head. "What are you saying, Miss Heron?"

She exhaled. "Your son doesn't want children, Mr. zur Hausen. He doesn't want responsibility for the next generation. You've piled all these expectations on his shoulders, but they've given him no joy. He doesn't know why he's treading water."

Squaring his shoulders, he crossed his arms. "He is very successful."

"His success is a testament to his strength. Instead of protecting wealth, what would happen if you protected the bonds between two brothers, collaboration, and open communication?"

"I'd be poor." Rudolf swallowed. "But I'd still have my brother."

She nodded. "I believe in second chances. Be thankful you still have both your sons."

He sighed. "Ridiculous, left-coast hippies."

Laughing, she met Vivian's gaze.

The woman shrugged.

Dad rounded the corner carrying two cups of coffee and a bag of potato chips.

"Mr. zur Hausen, this is my father, Jim Heron," she said.

Handing her a cup of coffee, Dad shook Rudolf's hand. "I can't thank you enough for what your son did today. My wife and I owe him a great deal."

Rudolf looked at the assembly and swallowed. "I am very proud."

"Why don't you have a seat and join us? Potato chip?"

Mr. zur Hausen eyed the proffered chips and swallowed. "No, thank you." He took a seat next to Dad, checked his watch, and crossed his arms.

Vivian leaned close. "Anxiety is making you a little crazy and reckless."

She cleared her throat. "Did I go too far?"

Shaking her head, Vivian reclined in her seat. "He challenged you first."

Hadley considered Rudolf's profile and watched him absentmindedly stroke his chin. "I could have settled for praising his son."

"You've given him something to think about," Vivian said.

The nurse appeared and smiled. "Johann's out of surgery."

Hadley scrambled to her feet.

"The surgeon will be here shortly to give you an update."

A second later, the surgeon came through the doorway.

She saw the sweat rings staining his scrubs and felt her stomach clench.

Hair black as night, the surgeon looked at each of them and focused on Rudolf. "Your son will be okay."

Relief flooded her system, and she sank to the cold plastic chair.

"He required several blood transfusions. That's how close you came to losing him." The surgeon cracked his knuckles. "He'll be weak for some time and require rehabilitation, but he'll live."

"How weak?" Rudolf leaned forward.

The surgeon took a deep breath. "The CT showed a bullet in the pericardial sac. Pericardial effusion compressed the heart, and hemorrhagic shock caused prolonged surgical intervention. To alleviate pericardial tamponade, we retrieved the projectile and used volumes of blood and colloid solutions. The second bullet punctured his lung, but we re-inflated it." He cleared his throat. "Should I go on?"

Rudolf paled. "He'll have everything he needs. Thank you, sir."

The surgeon nodded and faced the group. "At the moment, Johann remains sedated. As soon as he's awake and comes out of ICU, family can see him one-on-one."

Hadley nodded and looked at Rudolf. "I'm sure we all want to see him."

The older man crossed his arms. "We do."

Her parents got to their feet and collected their belongings. Looking at the suspended television, she saw credits rolling across the screen.

"I'm taking your mother home. When we left Marin, we didn't expect this level of excitement," her father said.

I'm surprised you crossed the Richmond Bridge. Taking a deep breath, she extended an olive branch. "Thank you for coming to the graduation ceremony. I'm sorry it didn't end well. We'll find another way to celebrate."

Dad smiled and led Mom toward the elevator. Turning, he winked. "You did good, kid."

Their approval felt like an old Hollywood sendoff, but she appreciated the gesture and smiled.

Two hours later, Rudolf followed the nurse through the swinging doors.

Ignoring her jealousy of their familial relationship, she closed her eyes and rested her head against the wall. *What if this shooting changed his mind about me?*

Half an hour later, Rudolf emerged from the double doors and exchanged words with the nurses behind the desk. He returned to the group and stopped before her. "Johann asks for you. Room nine."

Swallowing, she left him and Vivian to battle. Avoiding looking at the other patients, she moved through the hallways. Tubes and monitors meant nothing, but she understood the fragility of anatomy, and every beep validated the hospital's importance. *We're all doing the best we can with the tools on hand.*

At the doorway to Johann's room, an officer stood guard.

She stopped. "Can I go inside?"

He nodded.

White hospital blankets draped Johann's bandaged chest. His skin looked too pallid to belong to the robust man she knew, but she walked forward. *I came so close to losing him.*

He turned his head.

His bright blue gaze softened, and she would never forget her relief.

"Hadley." A cough stole his breath, and he winced.

She rushed to his bedside. "Can I get you anything?"

"Just you. Sit with me, please."

She looked at his right arm, anchored to the bedrail by an IV and a set of handcuffs. Picking up his left hand, she cradled the warm weight between her hands.

"I'm sorry for letting you down." He closed his eyes. "I should have kept you out of the limelight."

"No." She shook her head. Dr. Stefan brought him into her life, but he stayed of his accord. She understood his commitment, and she loved him. "You did everything you could and more. I didn't need to walk across that stage. I didn't need to put you in that position, but I wanted to celebrate everything I accomplished. Thank you for supporting me"—she

401

swallowed—"and saving me."

He smiled and took a deep breath. "You looked so confident on stage. I'm sure your parents were proud."

"Their attendance means something, but I'm not sure how hard I want to fight to rebuild that relationship."

"Relationships are everything, Hadley. *Ich liebe dich*," he whispered. "I love you, Hadley Heron."

"Shh." His recovery mattered more than his declaration. "The drugs are talking."

He gripped her hand. "Say it, Hadley, or I swear I'll die on your watch."

She swallowed past a lump in her throat. "*Ich liebe dich.*"

Releasing her hand, he closed his eyes. "Finally, we are equals."

Goose bumps appeared on his chest as his body fought the remnants of the anesthesia. She pulled the white hospital blanket from his waist to his chest. "What do you need?"

He sighed. "You. I need to know you're safe."

She kissed the hand she held. "I'm here. Let me watch over you."

****

The next day, an attending physician waltzed into Johann's room with an entourage of nurses and attendants.

Hadley rubbed the sleep from her eyes.

The physician examined Johann. "I'm Jack, and you're a lucky bastard."

A resident laughed.

Jack turned to the student. "Report."

The first year nodded and spoke, but her voice

cracked. She cleared her throat and tried again. "The bullet missed the patient's arteries and stopped in his pericardium." She looked at Johann and shook her head. "The textbooks don't cover this shit."

Hadley yawned.

"The narrow space between your heart and the surrounding membrane is no place for a projectile. The pericardium is not that thick, and the likelihood of a bullet stopping there before damaging cardiac tissue seems very unlikely." She checked her notes. "You *are* a lucky bastard."

The attending coughed. "Enough sucking up, Ellie. I haven't had my coffee yet."

Another resident raised his hand. "I'll go get it."

The physician nodded and waited until the man left the room. "He won't last." He tossed a plastic bag on the rotating tray.

The unmistakable metallic thuds drew every person's gaze.

The physician focused on Johan. "We removed these bullets from your chest, but I suggest you keep them in a safe place. Palo Alto's finest tells me a rash of violent encounters have plagued you. I'm sure the police will demand these bullets as evidence, but medicine keeps me too busy to worry about municipal details."

Johann raised his shackled hand. "Like I could forget them."

Hadley raised the bag and examined the brass bullets. "I'll take care of him."

"Hadley has a secret painkiller." Johann coughed and grimaced. "But she's holding out."

The surgeon laughed. "Women."

She rubbed her temples. "Not that kind of painkiller."

Johann closed his eyes. "The drug's impressive. Low cost of production and no addictive quantities. The problem is, she's not ready to share it with the world."

She kept her mouth shut and blamed his loquaciousness and endearments on the pain medication.

Checking Johann's temperature, Jack shrugged and led the medical team from the room.

Johann faced her and grinned. "What?"

"You're ridiculous." She shook her head and brushed his hair off his face. "When did you develop a sense of humor?"

He sighed and closed his eyes. "When I could stop worrying about your life."

"Smooth sailing from here on out?" she asked.

He coughed and winced. "I doubt it."

She laughed and wondered if she and Johann could enjoy a worry-free lifestyle.

Captain Wilson knocked on the door. "Is this a good time?"

Johann raised his handcuffed arm. "My time is yours."

"The Police Department placed Lieutenant Jayne on administrative leave. The department is conducting an internal investigation into the shooting." She pulled out her notepad. "You might be familiar with this drill." She raised her eyebrows. "Start at the beginning."

Hadley cleared her throat. "Can you be more specific? Johann recently came out of surgery."

"How did you know Mr. Sakmann?" Captain Wilson raised her pen.

"We served together in the *Bundeskriminalamt*."

The woman frowned. "Can you spell that word?"

Johann smiled. "The acronym is BKA. After injuring his leg, Horst retired from the BKA. I didn't expect to see him in the Bay Area, but he seemed to have reinvented himself as a security expert for a tech CEO."

Captain Wilson leaned forward. "Which one?"

Hadley thought of the hotel's purple-hued lights. "Anna Claire. She spoke at the graduation. Horst had every reason to be there."

"When did the leg injury occur?" Captain Wilson asked.

Johann frowned. "Ten years ago."

Captain Wilson frowned. "He had a fresh wound on his leg."

Knowing how close she came to losing her life in the cemetery, Hadley swallowed. She believed Horst aimed for her to harm Johann, but at the time of Dr. Stefan's funeral, she meant nothing. She rubbed her arm and thought of the bomb. *He aimed for Johann all along.*

"What reason would Mr. Sakmann have for shooting you, Mr. zur Hausen?" Captain Wilson asked.

Johann shook his head. "I can't speculate on his motives."

"Witnesses reported hearing a foreign language. What did he say before he shot you?"

"*Man kann nicht alles haben.*"

"Can you translate?"

"You can't have everything," he said.

Hadley stroked his leg and reveled in the warmth seeping through the blanket. "He was wrong."

Captain Wilson frowned. "You can't come up with a single explanation? Did you bully him when he was a kid? Steal his girlfriend? Spit in his food?"

"No, Captain Wilson. I did none of those things," Johann said.

She turned and tilted her head. "What about you?"

Hadley could sum up her interactions with Horst in three sentences, but she wanted Captain Wilson to leave sooner rather than later. "I definitely didn't spit in his food."

The captain closed her notebook. "This isn't a joke. Lieutenant Jayne killed that man." She sighed. "I should have been there to help."

Johann rattled his handcuff and grimaced. "No, it isn't a joke. I hired off-duty police officers to patrol the diploma ceremony, and you two let an armed man get within five feet of the stage. If I hadn't had been there, Miss Heron would have perished, and you two would pray administrative leave was the worst thing that could happen."

Captain Wilson swallowed. "We can't be everywhere at one time."

Johann coughed. "Neither can I. That's why I trusted you and your partner to do your job."

"I've never shot a man with live fire." Captain Wilson swallowed. "In all my years wearing a badge, I've never shot a person."

Empathy softened Johann's face. "When necessity called for it, Lieutenant Jayne saved my life. Now he needs your support."

The officer stared. "How many people have you killed?"

Johann let the question hang in the room. "Too

many. Hadley pushes me to look at life as a series of second chances and alternative possibilities."

Bathing in his recognition, she reached for his hand.

Captain Wilson walked toward the hospital bed and unlocked the handcuff restraining him. "I would advise you to go back to Germany until this story dies down."

He frowned. "I hear your suggestion, but my home is with Hadley."

Captain Wilson crossed her arms. "Will I be seeing you again?"

"I've never shot a person unless I feared for my life or those under my protection."

Hadley smiled at the evasion.

"Do you know of any additional threats?" Captain Wilson asked.

He shook his head.

Taking the handcuffs, Captain Wilson hooked them on her belt. "I hope we can explain your history with Horst." Sighing, she left the room.

Hadley waited until she and Johann were alone and exhaled. "Would you have killed Horst?"

He closed his eyes. "Every part of me wanted to shoot him, but if I missed, I had no guarantee what he would do next." He turned his head and made eye contact. "Your safety is non-negotiable. You're more important to me than my life."

Fussing with the blankets surrounding his body, she tested his priorities against her needs. "I don't want you to make that choice again, Johann. I don't want the burden of worrying you'll lay down your life."

His thumb skimmed her face. "I love you, Hadley. Let me carry the burden."

Leaning into his touch, she smiled. "You need to rest. A swipe of antiseptic gel won't make you better."

He smiled. "No, but you will. I heard you said quite a few things to my father."

She cleared her throat. "Nice man."

Grinning, he pressed a hand to his chest. "So you questioned the foundations of his principles?"

"I don't want to see you and Günter at odds for the next fifty years." She smiled. "One day, he'll leave prison and want to rebuild his life."

"And?" he asked.

"You'll be there. Your father will be there. A lot of untapped potential exists in this world. Take advantage of it."

He smiled. "I told you to grow up, but I hope you never abandon your romanticism."

"Remember that sentiment when I'm at the lab at ten o'clock." She winked.

He closed his eyes. "I'll build you a lab at the house."

"Buffy runs the assays."

"Great." He sighed. "She can move in."

She smiled. "I'll find a grant to run the foundation."

Turning, he narrowed his gaze. "What's wrong with my funding?"

"Vivian said your offer might complicate the accounting."

He looked at the ceiling. "I'm surrounded by scheming women."

She nodded and stroked his cheek. "You'll get used to it."

****

A week later, Hadley held up a printed shirt she found buried in Johann's closet.

Silvia stood in the doorway of Johann's bedroom. "Is there anything I can do to help you, Mr. zur Hausen?"

He opened and shut closet drawers. "Don't I have a pair of thongs?"

"I already packed your leather sandals." Silvia hefted the suitcase, checked its weight, and nodded.

He emerged from his closet holding a second pair of shoes. "What about swim trunks?"

Hadley smiled and handed him a pair of cargo shorts. "I think he has everything he needs. Thank you, Silvia."

Silvia nodded. "I called the airport. The plane is waiting."

Johann dropped the shoes and shorts in his bag. "Excellent."

Hadley walked toward the bathroom, checked her hair in the mirror, and watched Johann for signs of exhaustion. His nurses cleared him for physical activity, but she liked to stay close. Looking at the shower, she smiled. *Not that kind of physical activity yet.*

He walked up behind her and wrapped an arm around her middle.

She hesitated to lean on his chest.

He pulled her close. "You are so beautiful. I can't wait to get you alone on an island."

The world had many islands, and the summer wear suggested a tropical locale, but she itched to know the destination. "I've never been to Fiji."

"Who said anything about Fiji?" he asked.

"Tahiti?"

He stroked her side. "Maybe I'll take you back to Tahoe."

Smiling, she felt the heat of his arousal against her back. A subtle shift brought him into alignment, and she met his gaze in the mirror. "You wouldn't bring flip-flops to Tahoe. Or anywhere else you had a home."

He smiled. "Who told you about the other homes?"

Wondering if she made a mistake, she paused. "Vivian?"

He laughed and shook his head. "She needs to keep her mouth shut more often."

"Johann, I don't care about the other homes." His gaze softened, and she exhaled.

"I know."

Turning, she braced her hands on his shoulders. "I am curious why I need to bring my passport."

He pressed a kiss against her neck. "We're going somewhere warm. Somewhere where you won't mind spending every minute in my bed."

"Every minute?"

He nodded and dropped his lips to her shoulder. "Every minute you'll have me."

"That's the most romantic thing you've ever said." She stroked his freshly shaven cheek.

"Better than I love you?"

Biting her lip, she wondered why he kept the words to himself outside the hospital room. *Maybe he was thankful to be alive, and reality set in.*

He tipped up her chin.

Focusing on his steady, blue gaze, she leaned into his touch.

"Marry me, Hadley Heron."

The whispered command brought a smile to her

face. Raising a hand, she traced his facial scar. Waking up next to him and seeing his skin flushed with sleep brought her peace. The thought of spending a lifetime of nights with him brought her everything but peace. "Aren't you jumping the gun, Johann? We've only known each other a few weeks. Your family probably needs"—she gestured toward the luxury of the house—"pre-nups and stuff."

He caught her hand. "Everything I have is yours."

Recognizing the vow, she bit her lip. His assets impressed her, but she wanted an optimistic future. "What if I want more?"

"How much more?"

She looked at the floor, wondering if his love and his devotion could be enough. Looking up, she met his gaze and swallowed. "Kids, Johann. Tiny little terrors who wake us at six in the morning and tell us everything we're doing wrong."

He smiled. "Our family's agreement should have protected us, but it tore us apart. I never thought I wanted kids, but I believe you can make the world a better place. Maybe we won't mess up the next generation."

"And if we do?"

Raising a hand to his lips, he kissed her knuckles and nodded. "If we're building a new life together, let's choose happiness. Fate will fill in the gaps and remind us of our limitations. I'd much rather risk the responsibility of children than lose you. You're my dream."

She savored his words. "I'm not talking about tomorrow. I just want the possibility to exist. A couple of little girls to chase you around the house."

"One?"

"Two." Pulling back, she crossed her arms and held firm against the counter.

He laughed. "Two kids aren't off the table."

Relieved at the prospect of family laughter and good-natured squabbles, she closed her eyes and smiled. "Yes."

"Yes?"

Placing a hand flat against his scar, she opened her eyes and exhaled. "Yes, Johann. I want us to marry. I want us to make this love between us a permanent contract."

A champagne cork popped in the kitchen.

The sound startled her, and she pulled away. "Can Silvia see us on the camera system?"

He laughed. "No, but I told her you'd say 'yes'."

She dropped her arms. He cared for Silvia, and her invaluable presence eased his life, but she was a force of nature. "You told her you would propose?"

"I needed her to confirm arrangements and pick up a few things. You and the therapists teamed up and kept me in the house."

She put her hands on her hips. "What arrangements?"

He pulled a velvet box from his pocket and revealed an engagement ring.

She clutched the matching necklace she wore.

"I wanted to wait until we arrived on the island. Then I convinced myself to wait for the plane."

She tore her gaze away from the ring. "You planned to propose on a plane?"

He grinned. "It's a very nice plane."

Laughing, she reached for the ring.

He snapped close the box.

"Johann!"

Taking her hand, he slipped the diamond-studded band onto her finger.

A perfect fit. She twisted the ring, loving his thoughtfulness. *He's learning to be romantic.* She looked up and grinned, vowing to savor every moment of his proposal. "Then what happened to your plans?"

Cupping her cheek, he lowered his lips until they hovered above hers. "I'm impatient."

His kiss tasted of loyalty and dedication, but her body answered with a growing need. She let him lead the kiss, content to give his recovery precedence, but impatience might be contagious. She gripped his T-shirt. "Johann, how long will the plane wait?"

"As long as we want it to," he said.

"And Silvia?"

"I think she's enjoying her new executive position."

She glanced toward the door and thought about closing it.

Silvia walked into the room carrying two glasses of champagne. "The car is here."

Hadley wrinkled her nose, but his health had to take precedence.

"Try not to look so disappointed." He leaned close. "I told you. It's a very nice plane."

Nodding, she took the offered glass and downed its sweet, bubbly contents. "Silvia, what will you do while we're gone?"

The woman smiled and pulled a pair of sunglasses from her pocket. "I'll do what I always do: hold down the fort." Picking up his duffle, she brought the luggage to the waiting driver.

Hadley trailed.

Silvia let her hips sway. "When Johann's away, I'm queen."

"I heard that," he said.

She followed Silvia to the kitchen and saw a third glass of bubbly waiting next to her favorite magazine. She glanced at Johann and gestured toward the setup. "Your new executive assistant takes liberties."

"I can't reprimand her." He put his glass on the countertop. "The bottle would go to waste, and she knows too much."

Smiling, Hadley raised her eyebrows. "What about me?"

He approached the panoramic wall of glass. The vines and the oak trees swayed in an early morning breeze. "You already do whatever you want to do."

She focused on the jut of land piercing the bay. Sometime soon, she and Buffy would share a small office on the peninsula. Together, they would coordinate the Outcomes Foundation and advance the drug trials. *As long as Johann doesn't masquerade as a grant funder, he's welcome to visit.* She considered cancelling the flight and spending the coming weeks ensconced in his bed. *Tahiti can wait.*

"Do you like the ring?" he asked.

She nodded and extended her hand. The metal felt cool against her skin, but her body heat would warm the ring until it felt like an extension of her love. She rolled her shoulders, and the necklace she wore shifted in response. *Marriage is a contract, but I'm already committed.* "I love it."

"Good." He triggered the home automation system.

"I am taking a trip," he said in German.

"Have a pleasant flight," the computer said.

"Monitor Silvia."

"Yes, Mr. zur Hausen."

Silvia entered the room and eyed the control board. "How do I turn off that thing?"

Johann held Hadley's hand and pulled her toward the door. "Ask Vivian to show you."

Frowning, Silvia tapped her fingers on the countertop. "I don't need Miss Vivian. Hadley turns off the system every evening."

Thinking of Johann's lessons on self-control, she blushed. *The therapist said no intercourse, but he can still watch me pleasure myself.*

He shrugged and ushered her toward the door. "What can I do? She has a mind of her own."

A word about the author…

Amy Craig lives in Baton Rouge, Louisiana with her family and a small menagerie of pets. She writes contemporary romances and women's fiction with intelligent and empathetic heroines. She can't always vouch for the men. She worked as an engineer, project manager, and incompetent waitress. In her spare time, she plays tennis and expands her husband's honey-do list.

https://www.amy-craig.com/
https://www.instagram.com/author_amy_craig/
https://www.facebook.com/AuthorAmyCraig/
https://twitter.com/AuthorAmyCraig

Another title by this author
A Winter Rose